**Julia James** lives in England and adores the peaceful verdant countryside and the wild shores of Cornwall. She also loves the Mediterranean—so rich in myth and history, with its sunbaked landscapes and olive groves, ancient ruins and azure seas. 'The perfect setting for romance!' she says. 'Rivalled only by the lush tropical heat of the Caribbean—palms swaying by a silver sand beach lapped by turquoise water... What more could lovers want?'

**Chantelle Shaw** lives on the Kent coast and thinks up her stories while walking on the beach. She has been married for over thirty years and has six children. Her love affair with reading and writing Mills & Boon stories began as a teenager, and her first book was published in 2006. She likes strong-willed, slightly unusual characters. Chantelle also loves gardening, walking and wine!

### Also by Julia James

*The Greek's Secret Son*
*Tycoon's Ring of Convenience*
*Heiress's Pregnancy Scandal*
*Billionaire's Mediterranean Proposal*
*Irresistible Bargain with the Greek*
*The Greek's Duty-Bound Royal Bride*
*The Greek's Penniless Cinderella*

### Also by Chantelle Shaw

*Wed for His Secret Heir*
*The Virgin's Sicilian Protector*
*Reunited by a Shock Pregnancy*
*Wed for the Spaniard's Redemption*
*Proof of Their Forbidden Night*
*Her Wedding Night Negotiation*
*Housekeeper in the Headlines*

Discover more at millsandboon.co.uk.

# CINDERELLA IN THE BOSS'S PALAZZO

JULIA JAMES

# THE GREEK WEDDING SHE NEVER HAD

CHANTELLE SHAW

MILLS & BOON

First Published in Great Britain 2021
by Mills & Boon, an imprint of HarperCollins*Publishers*
1 London Bridge Street, London, SE1 9GF

Cinderella in the Boss's Palazzo © 2021 Julia James

The Greek Wedding She Never Had © 2021 Chantelle Shaw

ISBN: 978-0-263-28238-2

Printed and bound in Spain
by CPI, Barcelona

# CINDERELLA IN THE BOSS'S PALAZZO

JULIA JAMES

For CB—for her immortal original.

# CHAPTER ONE

JENNA STARED AGAIN at the letter she was holding in her hand. Typed on thick, expensive paper, it was signed by someone calling themselves the Executive Assistant to Signor Evandro Rocceforte at Rocceforte Industriale SpA in Turin. She reread it, feeling a mixture of trepidation and gratification at the offer within.

She'd felt the same conflicting emotions the day she'd received her confirmed offer of a university place to read Modern Languages eight years ago—the offer that had dispelled all the dismissive disparagement and indifference she'd grown up with. Her degree had been proof that she was right to believe in herself, as had the teaching certificate she'd achieved after that. There was also the fact that she had survived the last four relentless years at an overlarge, understaffed primary school in one of the most deprived parts of London.

She was ready for a change, and this post, if she took it, could not be more different: tutor to a seven-year-old girl—her sole charge—working and living in a *palazzo* in Italy.

Anticipation unfurled inside her, along with a desire to accept this next challenge in her life, this complete change of scene. She wasn't outgoing or charismatic, and certainly no great beauty. She knew and had accepted that she was the kind of person who could walk into a room and no one would notice. But that wouldn't matter in her new post any more than it had mattered at the school she'd taught at.

Resolutely, she sat down at her keyboard and began to type her letter of acceptance.

Evandro Rocceforte stared darkly at his computer screen, his strong, commanding features stark, his formidably astute business mind not on the impressive company accounts displayed in front of him, but on the most recent conversation he'd had with his lawyer, who was deploring the punitive settlement he'd agreed to make his ex-wife.

In the bitter, gruellingly protracted divorce proceedings Berenice had played ruthless hardball for one purpose only. To punish him. Not just for daring to divorce her, but for a crime even greater.

For seeing through her.

For seeing through the glamour, beauty and glittering charisma she presented to the world—had once presented to him, until, disillusioned and hardened, not least by her constant infidelities, he'd seen her for the woman she truly was. Self-obsessed, manipulative, and narcissistic. A woman who lived by the motto Me, Me, Me.

She wanted every man in the world to adore her, pander to her, do what she wanted. Once, he had been such a man. Such a fool.

But no longer—regardless of Berenice's attempts to use her seductive charms to lure him back. He knew she would eventually turn on him with a savage fury when he refused to be beguiled. The way she had turned every weapon she could on him when he had finally pressed for divorce.

Including the most powerful of all.

The bleak expression that Evandro knew marred his slate-dark eyes hardened. Ever since Berenice had given birth to Amelie she'd used the child as a weapon against him, and now she had forced Evandro into a hellish, no-holds-barred custody battle.

But Evandro had fought back hard—for this was a battle he must win. He *must* protect Amelie from her toxic mother, who could no more love her own daughter than she could love any human being who was not herself. It had cost him a fortune, on top of the divorce settlement, but Berenice had eventually agreed to relinquish Amelie to him, with one further condition...

He slewed his mind away, refusing to think about the final condition Berenice had imposed on him in exchange for custody of Amelie—the vengeful threat she'd made in order to gratify her monstrous ego and assuage her fury at his rejection. But her threat would never find meat to feed on. He would make sure of it.

Since his divorce had finally come through he had celebrated his hard-won freedom up to the hilt—his torrid affair last winter with the voluptuously sultry Bianca Ingrani was proof of that. Bianca—or any of her equally attentive sisterhood—would have been only too happy to become the next Signora Rocceforte. And why not? He'd just become one of Italy's most eligible single men—mega-rich, midthirties, and with the kind of striking, powerful looks that had always drawn female eyes to him.

But affairs were all that Bianca would get—or any woman he might take into his life now.

His lawyer's objection to the final price Berenice had extracted from him sounded in his head again, but he pushed it ruthlessly aside. It would never matter—he would not permit it.

He shifted position, flexing his broad shoulders. All he'd sought with Bianca was celebration, diversion, hedonistic indulgence—only that. He took an incisive breath. He had another focus to his life now. Something far more important. Some*one* far more important.

Amelie. The child he'd fought for so relentlessly, so determinedly.

His mood grew dark again. What did he really know about fatherhood? Berenice had deliberately kept Amelie abroad with her, minimising his contact with his daughter, right up to the moment of finally conceding custody.

Well, he would do his best by Amelie, however much of a stranger he was to her. His daughter was safely here in Italy, installed in the tranquil *palazzo* that would now be her home, and her future looked good.

That was all that mattered.

'Finish all the sums, and then it will be time for lunch,' Jenna said, brightly but firmly, to her pupil.

She spoke in English for lessons, as she'd been asked to do at her appointment, but in French or Italian otherwise. Her charge, thanks to her parentage and upbringing, was trilingual, and Jenna knew it was her own ability in all three languages, as well as her experience as a primary school teacher, that had landed her this job.

Not that her young pupil was very keen on schoolwork. Getting Amelie to focus on anything, least of all maths, was a challenge. But that was not surprising.

Only very recently brought to Italy, to live with a newly divorced father she'd seen very little of up until now, the poor mite had been dragged around Europe and America all her life by her jet-setting socialite mother, living in luxury hotel suites or staying as fleeting house guests in mansions and villas from Beverly Hills to the

Hamptons and back to the South of France, constantly on the move, never knowing stability or a traditional home life.

Jenna had gathered that the young girl was treated, at best, as some kind of dressed-up doll, to be shown off to cooing friends. When not useful, she had been indifferently handed back to an endless succession of nannies and maids, often for days and weeks at a time, while her mother swanned off elsewhere. Inevitably, Amelie's education had suffered, and Jenna had been tasked with trying to bring her up to speed, preparing her to start school in the autumn.

Jenna's eyes went to the sash windows of the spacious room that had been set aside as a schoolroom, glancing out over the gardens beyond, verdant in the early summer sunshine. It must surely help that the little girl now finally had a chance of a stable home life here at this beautiful *palazzo*, set deep in the Italian countryside amongst rolling hills, farmland and vineyards, with wonderful gardens and extensive grounds to play in, an outdoor swimming pool to enjoy, and woods beyond to explore.

Jenna had been enchanted by the eighteenth-century *palazzo* from the moment of her arrival three weeks ago. A miniature masterpiece, built as a rural retreat for a now extinct aristocratic family, it was beautifully decorated, with painted ceilings and walls stencilled with classical-style murals. The wide sash windows were draped in light-coloured, delicately patterned silk curtains, and the elegant fireplaces were all gleaming white marble, like the floors. It couldn't have been more different from the ugly concrete-block urban school she'd taught at in London.

*How incredibly lucky I was to get this job*, she thought

appreciatively. *And as it's only till the autumn, I'll make sure to make the very most of it.*

Her thoughts were recalled to her charge, whose fair head was now bent—brow furrowed in novel concentration—over her work. Jenna found herself wondering just who the little girl took after. She had seen a photograph of Amelie's mother, set on the little girl's dressing table—looking glamorous, as any self-respecting jet-setting socialite should—but apart from the shape of her face and her brown eyes, there seemed little resemblance. Amelie's mother was dark-haired—so had the little girl's blond locks come from her father's side?

From what Jenna had learned from the housekeeper, Signora Farrafacci, an English woman who had married an Italian, Amelie's father was from a prestigious Northern Italian family which had come to wealth and prominence in the nineteenth century, when Italy had started to industrialise.

'Will Amelie's father be living here too?' Jenna had asked, as there had been no sign of him when she'd arrived, nor since. Other than her young charge she had only seen the staff who looked after the *palazzo*, and she found herself hoping that Amelie had not simply been shuffled from one absent parent to another.

She knew from experience that it was all too easy for the children of divorced parents to slip between the cracks—to be important to no one, and parked wherever might be the least inconvenient for the parents. Made invisible.

*As I was...*

She did not want that to be Amelie's fate.

'Signor Rocceforte likes to visit whenever he can, but he is a very busy man—one of Italy's top industrialists!' the housekeeper had answered Jenna proudly. 'So his arrival is never predictable. I keep everything in good order, and it would be prudent for you—' she'd cast an eye at Jenna '—to bear in mind that he may arrive at any point. He is a good employer,' she went on meaningfully, 'but he does not suffer fools gladly. He'll want to see what progress the little *signorina* is making.'

As she checked Amelie's work now, Jenna hoped he would appreciate that maths was not proving to be his daughter's best subject...

'The more you do, the easier they'll be,' she said encouragingly.

'But I don't *like* it!' Amelie retorted. 'Maman never does *anything* she doesn't like. She gets angry if someone tries to make her. She throws things! She threw a shoe at a maid once, because she brought her the wrong colour scarf. The heel was sharp and it made the maid's cheek bleed. She ran out and that made Maman angrier, yelling at her to come back. Then she sent me out of her bedroom, because she said I made things worse...'

The speech, which had started with an air of defiance, ended with a quiet trailing off. There was a pinched, unhappy look on the girl's face, and Jenna found her heart squeezing with both pity...and memory. Memory of her father's wife snapping at her to get out of the way, to stop making a nuisance of herself...

To divert Amelie from her distressing thoughts, Jenna chose her words carefully. 'Do you know, there's a saying in England that goes, *Keep your temper; nobody wants it*?' she said lightly.

For a moment, the unhappy, pinched look was still on the little girl's face, and then, to Jenna's relief, she broke into a smile.

'That's funny!' she exclaimed. *'Keep your temper; nobody wants it!'* she repeated in a sing-song voice. Then her expression changed again. 'Do you think my *papà* will lose his temper with me?' she asked, and the fearful, unhappy look was back on her face.

'I'm sure he won't,' Jenna said.

After an ill-tempered and capricious mother, the last thing Amelie needed was a critical father finding fault with her.

*She needs love, and warmth, and open affection—and to know above all that she is wanted and valued. Something I didn't ever know...*

Setting aside Amelie's schoolwork, they went down to lunch and did what they always did when the weather was fine—took their food outside to eat on the wide, paved terrace overlooking the spacious gardens.

Jenna looked with growing fondness at her charge as the little girl tucked into an appetising chicken salad.

*I see so much of myself in her—uprooted, anxious and unsure. Wanted by no one. Doomed to a lonely childhood... I don't want that for Amelie.*

But that depended on the little girl's still absent father. Would he come home soon? No one seemed to know.

Evandro glanced out of the window, impatient to land and deplane. His non-stop schedule had taken him across Europe and up and down Italy, checking on various multimillion-euro projects and assessing and clinching potential new ventures first-hand.

He had crammed three months of business travel into three weeks for one purpose only—to clear his diary and enable him to get to the *palazzo*. To see the little girl he had finally extracted from the unloving arms of her vengeful mother. To give her a better life.

*I'll build a good relationship with her—even though*

*I'll have to learn from scratch. I'll protect her from the ills of her mother—protect her always...whatever it takes.*

Like a sudden shadow over the bright sun, his lawyer's warning sounded in his head.

'Do you realise the implications?' his lawyer had asked forebodingly.

Evandro had looked the man in the eye. 'They won't apply,' he'd answered tersely. Then, with a twist of his mouth, he'd added, 'Not after finally escaping ten years of a hellish marriage. No, it's Amelie who is the focus of my attention now—she's my only priority.'

A priority he would be making real from this very day onward.

The plane's wheels touched down with the merest bump, and minutes later he was on his way to his office. He had a few essential debriefings to get through before he could go to his apartment and pack for the *palazzo*. Then he would take the autostrada south. To Amelie.

Jenna glanced up at the sky, still overcast from the rain earlier that day. Dusk was gathering, but this was her first chance of fresh air today and she wasn't going to miss it. Amelie had opted for staying indoors with the housekeeper, playing noisy card games with her and the two maids, Maria and Loretta.

Jenna would be back in time for the little girl's supper, but for now she was enjoying her walk along the woodland path that emerged at the top of the private road to the *palazzo*, which wound steeply uphill from the public highway a kilometre below. Lower down, another path would allow her to cut back up to the grand front entrance of the *palazzo*.

On her way down, the narrow road kinked around a rocky outcrop, and she gave a little gasp to see there had been a rockfall; heavy scree and large boulders littered the road's surface. She surmised that it had been caused by the heavy rain they'd had, loosening the soil on the side of the hill.

The spread was extensive, and as she stared she saw it was potentially dangerous. Any vehicle approaching from the highway, slewing as it must around the outcrop, would not see the rockfall until it was upon it. This would put it at risk of hitting it full on, or swerving towards the sheer drop to the valley on the other side.

As she hovered, wondering what she should do, knowing she needed to get back to the *palazzo* to alert the staff of what had happened, she froze. She could distinctly hear the noise of a car, turning off the public highway and roaring uphill with a throaty growl of acceleration. In moments it would reach the outcrop, swerve around it…and hit the littered boulders.

She ran forward, scrambling over the fallen boulders and rounding the outcrop. The daylight was fast fading and the oncoming vehicle had its headlights blazing, piniioning her in their glare in the middle of the road, right in the car's speeding path. For a second terror seized her, and then, with a screech of tyres, the car—some low-slung, flashy-looking monster of a car—ground to a halt.

The engine cut out but Jenna couldn't move, fear pinning her in place. Then someone was getting out, slamming the driver's door angrily.

As angrily as he snarled words in a burst of furious Italian. '*Idiota!* What the hell do you think you're doing, running into the middle of the road? I could have killed you!'

He stood, silhouetted in the glare of his car's headlights, towering over her, his strongly planed face cast into stark relief by the glaring headlights. His charcoal business suit sheathed broad shoulders and long legs, its superb cut—along with the grey silk tie and gold tie pin—telling her just as clearly as the obviously expensive car that there was only one person this scathingly irate man could possibly be.

This was Evandro Rocceforte.

# CHAPTER TWO

JENNA FELT HER heart sink—then she rallied again. Her chin went up.

*'Mi dispiace.'* Her voice was breathless and shaky, but she ploughed on. 'I had to stop you!' She reverted to English, not knowing the Italian translation for what she had to explain. 'There's been a rockfall just around the outcrop.'

She gestured sweepingly with her hand and saw her employer frown. Without a word he strode past her, to see for himself. Then he turned.

The furious look had gone from his face, but it remained dark.

Impressions tumbled through Jenna's mind—irrelevant to the moment but pushing into her consciousness all the same. Her overpowering initial impression of a man with formidable presence had lessened not one iota. Nor had the visceral impact of his height and powerful body.

'That's a hell of a mess,' he said, his face tightening in angry displeasure.

He frowned, looking back at his car and then striding to it to turn off the headlights. Then he got out his phone, speaking into it rapidly in curt Italian, too fast for Jenna to follow. Hanging up, he slid the phone back in his inner jacket pocket and looked across at her again.

He frowned, as if seeing her for the first time. 'So, just

who are you?' he demanded. Realisation clearly sinking in, he answered his own question. 'Ah, of course—the English teacher.' He gave a short, sardonic laugh. 'You look more like some kind of woodland sprite, melding into the landscape at dusk. Well—' his voice became brisk '—get yourself back to the *palazzo*. Take care as you go. They're coming down to collect me, and to block the entrance to the drive so no one else risks their lives here. They'll clear the rockfall in the morning.'

He turned away, striding back to his car, and Jenna watched him yank open the boot, extracting some luggage. Then, mindful of his order—for an order it certainly had been—she retraced her steps around the outcrop, picking her way carefully through the rockfall to gain the path back up through the woods.

Her thoughts were hectic.

*So, that's Amelie's father.*

She lifted aside the drooping branch of a tree, quickening her pace. He'd yelled at her and given orders, and he looked every inch a rich, powerful captain of industry and the owner of a historic *palazzo*. But there had been something else in his tone... She heard it in her mind again—the short, sardonic humour in his voice as he'd likened her to a woodland sprite.

That, surely, was out of character?

But it was not her ponderings over his character that dominated her thoughts as she emerged into the extensive rear gardens at the *palazzo*. It was that formidable impression of height, a powerful physique, strong, arresting features and a deep, mesmerising voice that burned in her consciousness.

She felt her heart rate quicken with her pace, and hurried on.

When she got inside, it was to find the *palazzo* hum-

ming like a disturbed beehive, thanks to the unsched-
uled arrival of its owner. The staff were bustling about
and Signora Farrafacci only briefly paused to inform her
that Amelie was to dine with her father, and that Jenna's
own dinner would be brought up to her quarters later.

Jenna retreated gratefully, taking refuge in the large,
generously appointed bedroom and adjoining sitting
room she had been allocated on one of the upper floors
of the *palazzo*. A connecting door linked her sitting room
to a mirror room on the other side, set up as Amelie's
playroom, which the little girl's own bedroom opened off.

She crossed now to the window in her sitting room,
sliding it up and leaning on the sill with her elbows,
breathing in the soft mild air, scented with the honey-
suckle growing far below. Night had gathered completely
now, and she could hear owls hooting mournfully in the
woods beyond the gardens.

Her abrupt, adrenaline-fuelled encounter with her
charge's father replayed in her mind with vivid impact—
and not just because of the danger she had both invited
and averted by impulsively running forward to warn
him of the hidden rockfall. His tall, powerful, broad-
chested physique and frowning brows were also vivid
in her mind's eye. As was the way he had yelled at her
angrily for running into the path of his car.

Her chin lifted defiantly.

*Well, if I hadn't, both he and his horribly expensive car
might now be at the foot of the valley, smashed to pieces!*

She walked through into her bedroom, and on impulse
decided to have a leisurely bath while waiting for her
dinner to arrive. Baths were a rare and luxurious indulgence for her; showers were quicker and more efficient.

As she sank into the deep waters she found herself
replaying, yet again, that encounter with her employer.

But not, this time, his initial harsh words to her. Rather, that throwaway likening of her to a woodland sprite...

It was a description of her that was as fanciful as it was unlikely. Sprites were elfin and beautiful—they were always described as beautiful. She was nothing like that.

She was of medium height, with medium-length hair—always neatly confined in a French plait. Slightly built, she wore clothes chosen for practicality and comfort. Her unremarkable looks were the opposite of eye-catching, and she did not bother with make-up—it was not needed in the classroom, and her limited social life was mostly confined to school functions with her colleagues.

So, no—nothing like a woodland dryad. Nothing at all. What on earth had made him say such a thing?

As she slid deeper into the warm water she felt it lapping her body like a caress. Around her shoulders her loosened hair floated freely, and the water buoyed her whole body, almost to make her float. It felt warm and sensuous, playing at the sensitive points of her wrists as her hands hovered in the water.

A strangely dreamy mood started to overcome her, induced by the heat of the water, the steamy atmosphere of the thickened air she was breathing and the feeling of absolute relaxation as she gave herself to the moment. The single soft light above the vanity unit added to her languor, bestowing upon her an awareness of her physical body, the weightlessness of it in the shimmering water.

She let her eyes fall shut, lids lowering into drowsy somnolence, yet she was still conscious of the contours of her half-floating naked body... In the darkness behind her closed eyelids an image of her employer sprang to life, strong and vivid—as if he were beholding her vulnerable nakedness as she lay there, his dark gaze sweeping over her, enjoying what he saw...

She surfaced with a start, her eyes flying open as she levered herself upward, her soaking wet hair instantly heavy and soggy on her shoulders and back. Her cheeks heated suddenly—and not from the heat of the bathwater. She shook her head, as if to shake that thought, wherever it had come from—however it had come to her—right out of her brain, where it had no business to be.

She took a breath, staring at the tiled wall at the foot of the capacious bathtub, blinking to dissipate the vivid—and unbidden—image. Then, resolutely, she reached for the bar of soap and the bottle of shampoo to get on with the actual point of bathing—to get herself clean.

And not—*not*—to indulge in thoughts that were as inexplicable as they were outrageous.

With vigorous movements she soaped herself briskly, shampooed her hair, then set the bath to drain and turned the shower head on as cold as she could bear it to rinse off not just the soap and shampoo but her outrageous thoughts as well.

Ten minutes later, wrapped in her sensible dressing gown and wearing her sensible cotton pyjamas, she was sitting on the sofa in front of the TV, switching on the English news channel. After dinner she'd check her lesson plans for the next morning and jot down a brief report on Amelie's progress so far, in case her employer enquired about it.

Her *employer*.

She repeated the word firmly to herself.

The tap on her door announcing the arrival of her dinner was timely.

Evandro stood out on the terrace overlooking the gardens, hands thrust into his trouser pockets, looking out into the night. High in the sky, the moon appeared to be moving through the scudding clouds. An illusion, just like so much in life was.

Like his bride had been.

He frowned. Why the hell was he thinking of his wedding day, ten long, damnable years ago? A day that, for all the vast sums of money spent on it, had been a sham. Their lavish, no-expenses-spared wedding had been like Evandro's bride—as gaudy as a carnival float and just as shoddy...fake and cheating.

Berenice—seductively sensual, dripping in diamonds, her wedding dress having cost as much as a house—had revelled in being the glittering star of the whole over-the-top show, and it had been splashed all over the gushing celebrity magazines with himself cast as the adoring bridegroom, dazzled by her brilliance and beauty.

His frown deepened. How, just *how* had he come to be so incomprehensibly stupid?

His jaw tensed. He knew exactly how he'd become that stupid, that gullible.

He had been led by the nose by the woman he'd married...and urged on by his father.

He could hear the older man's eager words even now.

*'She's got everything...absolutely everything. Ravishingly beautiful, and with her father dead now she inherits all the voting stock in Trans-Montane that we need.'*

It had seemed a combination made in heaven.

It had turned out to have originated in hell instead.

But out of it had come Amelie.

His expression changed. The meeting between them this evening had been strained—she'd been shy and subdued, the same way she had been when he'd collected her at the airport on her arrival from Paris, bringing her here to the *palazzo* three weeks ago. But that would change, given time. Time he would devote to her.

As for the woman he'd hired to be Amelie's teacher… He frowned now, as he tried to remember her unremarkable features… She would simply have to work around the time he spent with her pupil.

He frowned again, shifting position once more. The woman had rushed headlong into the path of his speeding car, as if discounting the possibility of her own destruction in order to warn him of the possibility of his. His expression flickered. Had her behaviour been recklessness…or courage?

Or both?

Jenna walked down the wide marble staircase to the grand entrance hall, carrying Amelie's schoolbooks and artwork. The expected summons to report on her pupil's progress had come, and now she knocked lightly on the door of the library before entering.

She'd left Amelie up in the schoolroom with a spelling worksheet to get on with. The little girl's mood this morning, following her father's arrival the evening before, was… Jenna sought for the right word before settling on *unsure*.

She could understand it well enough. She, too, felt a flutter of trepidation now, as she walked into the large, book-lined room, with its imposing fireplace flanked by deep leather armchairs.

Illuminated by large French doors—open to the terrace today, to admit fresh air—was a desk of considerable size and grandeur, bearing a PC and some paperwork. Seated behind it was her employer.

Jenna deliberately used the word inside her head, to counter the sudden tightening of her stomach muscles as he looked up. The impact he made on her was just as instant, just as powerful, as it had been last night.

That impression of toughness and power was every bit as overwhelming.

But she must not let herself be overwhelmed. She was being summoned to give an account of her progress—or not—with Amelie, and the man she was approaching would likely make an impact on anyone approaching for any reason at all.

He had a presence about him, Jenna found herself thinking. A look of formidable gravitas which presumably went with being the head of an international company with global reach, turning over huge revenues and employing vast numbers. There was no doubt he was a man of power and responsibility.

Currently, he was observing her approach with an unreadable expression, deep lines carved around his mouth.

*What's caused those deep lines? What has he had to endure?*

The questions flitted across the surface of Jenna's mind, unbidden.

She pressed her mouth tightly. It was irrelevant—absolutely irrelevant—what he looked like, or what experiences in life he'd been through. Just as the impact of his powerful physique, strongly saturnine looks and air of wealth and gravitas was nothing to her.

She stopped in front of the desk as he gave her a curt nod and bade her to sit on the chair set for her.

'So, Miss Ayrton...' he addressed her in English, his deep voice brisk and only slightly accented. 'How have things been with Amelie these first few weeks? Please make your account as brief as possible.'

Jenna placed the bundle of paperwork she had brought down with her carefully on the desk, away from his own papers, and calmly and concisely ran through her assessment of Amelie's current educational level, before moving on to where she was focusing her efforts—on building key skills in reading, comprehension and maths, plus providing a general syllabus of geography, history and basic science.

She was in mid flow, pointing out the developmental impact of Amelie being multilingual, when her employer raised a hand to silence her.

'Enough,' he said curtly. 'Show me her exercise books.'

He held out a hand in a peremptory fashion, and Jenna docilely handed him the required items. He flicked through them, then handed them back, making no comment.

'Amelie *is* making progress.' Jenna wanted him to know that. 'Having lacked formal schooling, her biggest educational challenge is application,' she went on. 'Of course, that is true for children generally—play is nearly always preferred to work!'

A sardonic expression formed on her employer's face. 'And not only by children, Miss Ayrton,' he observed caustically.

Jenna looked at him, uncertain as to whether to smile. He might have intended that as a humorous remark, but it was impossible to discern. So she simply nodded, and then continued, picking her words with care.

'Routine and stability,' she said, 'are essential for children—especially to develop focus, concentration and attention span. I acknowledge the fact that has been largely absent up till now.'

She saw her employer's face darken sharply.

'She's been dragged from pillar to post across Europe and the USA all her life. It's a wonder the child can read, let alone anything else.'

The harshness in his voice echoed the tone he'd used

the night before, when he'd excoriated her for running into the path of his car.

Jenna said nothing. It was not her place to comment on the friction that she knew, after many all-too-often fraught parent-teacher evenings, could erupt between warring divorced parents.

Then, abruptly, the anger was gone. And in a voice that was not harsh, merely brisk, he addressed her again.

'Is there anything she *is* good at?' he demanded.

Jenna did not trouble to hide the shocked look on her face. 'Yes, of course!' she retorted roundly. 'Maths may never prove to be Amelie's strong suit,' she allowed, 'but art and creativity definitely will be.'

She extracted several sheets of art paper, showing the top one to Evandro.

'Look how good this is! Oh, not necessarily in terms of technical execution—that will come in time—but in imagination and use of colour. And this one too.' She slid out the next one to hold it up. 'And this—'

She let her employer's dark-eyed gaze peruse—impassively—the fruits of his daughter's artistic labour, which depicted a mix of multitowered fairy-tale castles, populated by fantastical animals and opulently dressed princesses.

'Any and all ability and enthusiasm should always be encouraged and fostered,' she went on resolutely, suddenly urgently wanting to defend Amelie from her father's potential criticism. Wanting him not to be critical at all.

Jenna's chin went up, and she looked straight at him. She refused to be cowed by his forbidding expression, and was determined to have her say...to make him see. This was for Amelie, a little girl whose father should praise her and value her.

*As mine never did.*

Remembered pain bit at her. She did not want that for Amelie.

'It's vital—*essential*—for children to be encouraged, to know there is something they have a flair for. No child should *ever* be made to feel worthless or useless.'

There was a passion and a vehemence in her voice she could not hide as memories scythed through her mind. Bad memories—of her father's dismissive criticism, his impatient indifference…

She became aware that she was under perusal. Not the employer-employee kind of perusal, to discover whether she was adequately performing the job for which she had been hired; there was something different in his assessment of her.

Then it was gone.

He sat back in his chair—a large, modern, leather, executive-style chair, at odds with the antique desk and leather-bound gold trimmed books lining all the walls. Making no comment on what she'd urged, he simply said, with a brief nod, 'Very well—thank you for your report. Continue with what you are doing. That said…' his gaze flicked over her '…you must be prepared to re-arrange lessons on the fly and without notice. They are not a priority while I am here. My time with Amelie is the priority. Now, have you any questions of me? If not, then go back to your pupil.'

Jenna got to her feet, gathering up Amelie's school-work. She wanted to get one more vital message across, to fight Amelie's corner for her.

'Though it isn't my place to say so, Signor Rocce-forte, I completely agree that lessons aren't a priority for Amelie right now. It's far better, with your having been away for so long, that she has extensive quality time with you—'

'You are quite right, Miss Ayrton,' he cut across her, his voice brusque, his expression closed. 'It isn't your place to say so.'

For a second she froze, feeling the force of his displeasure at her intrusive comment just as she'd felt the force of his fury last night. But just as she had last night, she rallied. What she'd said had been for her charge's sake—for the sake of a little girl who reminded her so much of herself, wrenched from all she knew to be abruptly taken to live with her father, a stranger to her.

*Please let it be better for Amelie than it was for me. Let her father want to bond with her, spend time with her, become a good, loving father to her.*

The silent plea was strong and heartfelt.

She looked across at Evandro. His expression was forbidding, but for Amelie's sake she had to get through to him—make him see how vital it was for his daughter that, however much of a stranger he was to her, he must reach out to her. She would not shy away from telling him so.

She stood in front of him, her shoulders squared. 'My place, Signor Rocceforte, as Amelie's teacher, is to look out for the best interests of my pupil,' she said, quietly but unflinchingly, unapologetically, her eyes steadily on him.

He was a man of power and wealth, but to her, right now, he was merely her charge's father—the man who had a responsibility for his daughter's emotional well-being, a responsibility not to blight her childhood any more than it already had been.

'My responsibility,' she went on, never taking her eyes from him, 'is only and always to Amelie. She is a fractured child, a child from a broken home and, however affluent her upbringing has been, it has lacked what she needs most—stability, constancy and security. The security not just of routine and predictability, but also, far more essentially, the security of knowing she is valued, wanted…and loved.' A low, compelling insistence filled her voice now, and her gaze was resolute on Evandro. 'That last above all.'

She turned away, not caring what his reaction might be, and walked to the door and opened it, leaving the room and the formidable Italian behind.

As the door closed, shutting her away from sight, Evandro looked at the place where she had been. His expression flickered. If he'd had to go into a witness box to give evidence of the clothes she'd been wearing, what height she was, what her eye colour was, he'd have no idea at all.

Yet he could have repeated, word for word, what she'd just said to him in her quiet, pointed address.

'Valued, wanted…and loved.'

The triad echoed in his mind. Well, the first, surely, he could testify to—the grim face of his lawyer as he'd perused the sum his client had been prepared to hand over to Amelie's mother was proof of that. And the second he could also testify to—as evidenced by the bitter year-long custody war.

But the third…?

He felt himself shying away from the word, remembering instead the deliberately cruel words hurled at him by his jibing wife.

Abruptly, he pushed back his chair, getting to his feet, walking to the French doors and pushing them open. He suddenly needed fresh air.

# CHAPTER THREE

JENNA AND AMELIE were left to lunch on their own, but it was served in the schoolroom, not out on the terrace where, presumably, they might have disturbed her father at work in the library.

Amelie's mood was still unsettled, and Jenna decided diversion was needed. She could do with diversion herself, as her final words to Evandro that morning were still echoing in her mind. Had he taken offence, been angered by them? She did not care if he had—only if he chose to ignore them. For she stood by every single word she'd said to him.

'We'll go on a nature walk!' she announced, and Amelie's little face brightened.

They went out to the terrace, ready to set off across the extensive gardens.

'Where I taught in London,' Jenna said, 'there were no fields, no woods—so think how lucky you are to have all this beautiful countryside and these beautiful gardens,' she said, gesturing expansively with her arms at their surroundings as they headed off.

A voice behind her spoke. 'I'm glad you think so.'

She turned, surprised and taken aback. Evandro was approaching them, rapidly closing in on them with his long strides.

'I saw you through the library window. Where are you off to?' he asked.

Aware of Amelie slipping her little hand into hers, as if for reassurance, Jenna said, as composedly as she could, 'A nature walk through the gardens.'

'May I come with you?'

Jenna looked at him in surprise. Not just because of what he'd asked. But because his tone of voice was so different from the brusqueness of her interview with him that morning. Then she realised why. It was for his daughter—not for her.

And she was glad of it. Glad to see him—the first time she'd seen him with Amelie—being so different from the forbidding way he'd been with her that morning. He was addressing his daughter directly now, still with the same genial tone of voice.

'What do you think, Amelie? I'm sure there are things about nature that Miss Jenna could teach me, as well as you. I know very little, for example, about the domestic habits of slugs.'

Was there some deadpan humour in his declaration? Jenna could not decide—just as she couldn't know whether he'd intended humour in his remark to her that morning about adults, too, preferring play to work.

She could still feel the little hand in hers, and knew that it meant Amelie felt, as she did herself, unsure about Evandro's sudden presence. A little ache formed in her. Every child needed to be wanted by their father—not to be ignored by them. Invisible to them.

Amelie was looking wary. 'I don't like slugs,' she said.

'Fortunately,' her father observed, his voice dry, 'slugs like each other. So there will be lots of baby slugs in the spring.'

'Slugs are hermaphrodites. So are snails,' Jenna heard herself saying.

The new word had caught Amelie's curiosity. 'What's that mean?' she asked.

'Every slug is both a girl and a boy,' Jenna explained. 'So they make babies with each other. It can sound odd to us, but it's natural to them.'

'I wouldn't want to be a boy as well,' Amelie declared. 'I wouldn't want to be a boy at all!'

'You're exactly right just as you are,' Evandro said decisively. 'And I'm very glad,' he went on, 'that you've come here to live with me.'

Jenna heard the warmth in his voice as he spoke to Amelie, and felt her own uncertainty ease a fraction. He was saying the right things—making his daughter feel welcome, making it clear that she belonged here in the *palazzo* with him—and that had to be good.

He gestured towards the gardens, speaking in the same good-humoured tones. 'Now, what about this nature walk—where are we off to?'

'I thought we might go into the rose garden and watch the bees collect nectar, and find out how that helps the roses and the other flowers,' replied Jenna.

She found herself noticing what a difference it made when Evandro unbent. A welcome difference, definitely. But it was not, she reminded herself, on her account. She knew why he'd joined their little expedition, and knew her role now was to act as bridge between father and daughter. The nature walk would be an occasion for the two of them to spend time together that need not be focused entirely on each other, but on a shared activity, so they could get used to being around each other.

She led the way onwards, deliberately letting Amelie's fingers casually slip from hers as they went into the circular rose garden. The afternoon sun beat down, and Jenna hoped it would not be too hot. She and Amelie were in summery clothes, but her employer was in a business suit. Although, it was lightweight, in a superbly cut dark grey material—that matched, she thought irrelevantly, his dark, slate-grey eyes.

She led them to a beautiful dark red rose, carefully folded back its velvet petals, and started to explain pollination. 'Now let's see if we can spot any bees visiting the roses,' she ended.

'There's one,' she heard Evandro observe, pointing to another rose that a fat bee was investigating.

'So it is! And look, Amelie, you can see the yellow pollen from a previous flower on its legs.'

They watched the bee at work for a while, then it buzzed away, and Jenna led the way out of the rose garden. She was pleased to see that Amelie was beside her father now, as they took the path to the ornamental pond in the centre of the gardens. He was talking to her, still in that good-humoured, reassuring fashion, describing how these gardens had been laid out over two hundred years ago, when the *palazzo* had been built.

'One day this week,' Evandro was saying, 'we'll get the fountain in the middle of the pond working. The water comes from a spring higher up the hill, beyond the woods.'

He kept talking, explaining the rudiments of the fountain's mechanism. Just how much of the science Amelie was taking in, Jenna wasn't sure. But the important thing was that she was paying attention—and that she was with her father.

Her eyes went to the tall figure perched, like Amelie, on the stone rim of the pond. She'd avoided looking directly at him since he'd emerged to join them, but now,

as he and Amelie talked together, she found her gaze
stealing to him. It was extraordinary, she thought, how
different he was being now that he was with his daughter. Oh, the gravitas was still there, but it was leavened...
lightened. She found her gaze wanting to linger...

Then, thankfully, he was standing up. 'Shall we head
back?' he suggested.

Jenna nodded, letting them take the lead, walking behind. She tried to focus on how good it was that Amelie
and her father were together like this rather than on how
broad his shoulders were, how sable his dark hair, how
deep his voice...

As they regained the terrace, she made to lead Amelie
back to the classroom, but she was halted.

'Amelie, please go and ask Signora Farrafacci for refreshments to be brought out here. You must be thirsty—I
know I am. And Miss Jenna, too, no doubt.' He turned to
her and raised an eyebrow in a quizzical, sardonic manner. 'Being an Englishwoman, you must surely think it's
time for afternoon tea?'

Amelie skipped off, glad to postpone any resump-
tion of lessons, and Jenna suddenly felt awkward, self-
conscious at being left on her own with her employer
like this.

*But why am I being like this about him?* she wondered.
*He's just the father of my pupil.*

And that, surely, was no reason to feel awkward and
self-conscious...

'Come and sit down,' he said, pulling out one of the
chairs at a table under a wide parasol.

The shade was distinctly welcome to Jenna and she
did as she was bade, hoping Amelie would return quickly.

Evandro settled himself down at the table, too, opposite her, pausing only to shrug off his jacket and hook it

around the back of a spare chair, loosening his tie thereafter. The casual way in which he did it made the atmosphere informal in a way that contrasted starkly with his brusque, businesslike formality from the library that morning.

'So,' Evandro said, easing back into the padded chair, 'am I making progress, do you think? Being a good father?'

He let his eyes rest on the woman who had stood up to him without hesitation or diffidence to make it clear what fatherhood was all about.

She held her ground now, too, as she answered him.

'Yes,' she said plainly. 'Amelie became noticeably more at ease with you as our walk progressed.'

He saw her pause for a moment, and take a breath.

'She is bound to be a little shy at first, but if you draw her out, praise her, encourage her, she will blossom, I know she will.'

He heard the warmth in her voice—and something more than warmth. He frowned inwardly. It had almost been a plea.

*Now, why should that be?*

The musing question hung in his head for a moment, and then she was speaking again.

'I hope,' she said, more hesitantly now, 'that you don't object to the idea of my teaching Amelie outside of the schoolroom sometimes?'

He waved a hand—not to silence her, but in an expansive gesture. 'If today is an example of your approach, I'm fine with that.' He paused, then continued, 'Overall I'm fine, Miss Ayrton, with what you are doing and achieving with Amelie.'

He paused again, conscious that there was something he must say. Something he owed her.

'I apologise if I was…brusque…this morning. You must understand…' He felt a frown form on his face. 'I am new to all this.' He fastened his eyes on hers, intent on getting his next point clearly across to her. 'My absence from Amelie's life so far has not been with my consent. She has finally come here to live, however, and I shall be doing my best to give her the safe and happy childhood she deserves—the kind of childhood you so eloquently urged me to provide.'

He saw her colour slightly, noticing almost absently that it brought a discernible improvement to her pale cheeks. Out of nowhere, he found himself wishing she was wearing something less nondescript than the beige knee-length skirt and indifferently styled matching blouse which did nothing for her.

*No one should be allowed to look so dowdy*, he thought with passing disapproval.

Then she was speaking, and his thoughts went from her lacklustre appearance to what she was saying.

'I'm sorry if I was stating the obvious,' she replied, in a quiet, but far from diffident way, 'but you see the children of divorced parents can often become—'

She stopped abruptly, and Evandro frowned. 'Become what?' he prompted.

'Invisible,' she answered flatly.

She dropped her eyes, looking down at her hands, folded in her lap, the knuckles suddenly white.

His frown deepened. Clearly this was not just about Amelie…

'You say that,' he said slowly, his eyes not leaving her, 'as if you have experience of it yourself?'

Hazel eyes lifted suddenly to his.

*No, not hazel alone. Hazel with a flash of forest green in the depths.*

'Yes,' she said, in that plain way she had. But only that one word.

'Tell me more,' he commanded.

It was important, he told himself, that he understood what might be affecting Amelie.

Then he gave a quick shake of his head. 'I apologise—I do not mean to speak so brusquely. But I am used to giving orders.' His face twisted. 'I am not a man of airs and graces—I speak as I find. But for all that...' he drew breath '...please explain, if you will. For Amelie's sake.'

He saw her expression flicker, but whether it was at his words or memories of her own he could not tell. Then she was speaking again, and he could see her fingers tighten in her lap.

'Children know when they are not wanted,' she said, her voice low. 'And they learnt to...to adapt their behaviour accordingly. So—'

She broke off, and for a moment Evandro assumed she was reluctant to say more. Then he realised she had seen Amelie, as he now had, emerging from the *palazzo*, followed by one of the maids carrying a tray of refreshments.

He felt a stab of frustration that their arrival had silenced Miss Ayrton. Then, mindful of the moment, he thanked the maid as she placed the tray on the table and bade Amelie to take her seat.

There was a pot of tea for Miss Ayrton, strong coffee for himself, and a jug of fresh orange juice for Amelie, together with another of iced water for them all, and a plate of biscotti.

He watched as Miss Ayrton poured some orange juice for her pupil, diluting it heavily with water. 'Very healthy,' he observed, reaching for his coffee.

'Signorina Jenna says too many fizzy drinks make

your teeth fall out,' Amelie informed him with an air of virtue as she took a gulp of her juice.

Evandro nodded. 'Quite true,' he said, straight-faced. 'I knew of someone whose teeth fell out—all of them, all at once—right in the middle of his making a speech at a grand dinner. The audience was very glad, as his speech was very boring. He's had to wear false teeth ever since— and because they don't fit properly they click when he speaks. Like this...'

He made the appropriate noise, and Amelie giggled. It felt good to hear. Of their own accord, his eyes went past the little girl to her teacher, as if seeking her approval, and he caught the slight smile on her face as she poured herself a cup of tea. He noticed how some colour had tinged her pale cheeks, and how a smile, however slight, seemed to improve her nondescript appearance.

He found himself wanting to see her smile again. And then wondered why. Jenna Ayrton was here to teach Amelie. That was all.

He turned back to her pupil. 'I am pleased to hear that you are making progress so you can be ready for school in the autumn. How much are you learning about your new home country of Italy?' He smiled at Amelie, wanting to draw her out. Wanting to show her teacher he was making the effort to do so.

'We are doing lots of history and learning about the mountains and rivers. And where the cities are,' Amelie answered, and then reeled off the names, in English and Italian, of half a dozen.

'Very good.' Evandro nodded approvingly. 'What about the city I work in?'

'Turin,' Amelie supplied. 'Torino in Italian.'

*'Esattamente!'*

He went on to ask her about Italy's mountains, telling

her he liked to go skiing on them in winter, and saying she might like to come too next time, after Christmas.

'Would you like that?' he asked. 'You could try skiing, or snowboarding, or just stick to tobogganing.' His gaze flicked to Miss Ayrton, sipping her tea quietly, and suddenly he wanted to draw her out as well. 'Do you enjoy winter sports, Miss Ayrton?' he asked.

She looked startled at his suddenly addressing her, but then replied in the quiet way he was becoming used to.

'I've never done any,' she answered.

Amelie turned to her teacher, her expression animated. 'You could come with us!' she said.

She shook her head. 'I'll be gone by winter, Amelie,' she replied. 'As soon as you've started school I'll be going back to England.'

Evandro saw Amelie's face fall. Unease welled in him.

*Amelie must never grow close to any woman—it's too dangerous.*

In his head, his lawyer's warning echoed yet again, carrying with it Berenice's final venom. He, too, must never grow close to any woman in his life...

He shook away his uneasy thoughts. That warning might be true in general, but it was utterly irrelevant to the current situation. Jenna Ayrton—a woman no man would even notice was in the room—was Amelie's temporary teacher, nothing more.

And once Amelie was settled into school she'd soon forget all about her.

And so, obviously, would he.

# CHAPTER FOUR

JENNA CHECKED HER appearance in the elegant cheval glass in her bedroom. Somewhat to her surprise, she had been summoned to accompany Amelie to dinner with Signor Rocceforte. Amelie was here, now, dubiously looking her teacher over.

'Have you not got any cocktail frocks?' Amelie asked her, eyeing the plain navy-blue long-sleeved dress critically.

Jenna shook her head. 'No—and even if I had, I wouldn't dream of wearing one. I'm your teacher, Amelie—an employee—not your father's guest.'

Her eyes went to the little girl, and she tried to keep her expression more neutral than her opinion. It was obvious to Jenna that the child had been treated like a fashion doll by her socialite mother, and tonight Amelie had gone to town. And not in a good way.

Out of her huge designer wardrobe she had chosen a miniature version of an adult cocktail dress, in a vivid fuchsia satin, patterned with gold and black swirls making the initials of the designer—who was known, even to Jenna, for his gaudy, overblown designs. It was completely unsuitable for a child her age, but as Amelie twirled happily about Jenna did not have the heart to say so.

Amelie's father, however, clearly had no such compunction. As his eyes lit upon his daughter when they entered the dining room Jenna saw his dark brows snap together in instant condemnation of her oversophisticated dress.

'Amelie wanted to wear a party dress to look particularly nice for you tonight,' she interjected swiftly, and was relieved that he said nothing, switching his glance to her instead.

'Unlike yourself, I see, Miss Ayrton,' he replied, his tone sardonic, his slate-dark eyes flicking over her modest attire.

She made no answer, for none was required, but Amelie spoke up instead.

'If I were taller I would lend you one of *my* frocks!' she said, rising to her defence, and Jenna was touched by it.

'She may thank the good Lord you are not, then,' Evandro observed mordantly.

Then, apparently done with the controversial subject, he bade them both to sit down at the table, its polished mahogany surface now graced with silver cutlery and crystal glasses.

Despite the formality of the setting in the grandly appointed dining room, her employer's manner and appearance were more casual. He'd changed into elegantly cut dark trousers and a grey cashmere sweater. Even casually dressed, however, he'd lost none of his imposing presence, nor his disturbing ability to draw her eyes to him— which was *irrelevant*, Jenna reminded herself trenchantly.

He reached to put a strong, square-palmed hand around the bottle of wine that was breathing in a silver holder.

'Do you drink wine, Miss Ayrton, or is that against your principles when in the company of your students?'

he enquired, with a lift of one dark brow. There seemed to be a quizzical, almost challenging note to his voice, and a mordant glint in his dark eyes.

'If you have no objection, then nor do I,' she returned equably, not rising to his taunt.

He filled a wine glass, passed it to her, then filled a glass with juice for his daughter. Once done, he lifted his own glass, bidding Jenna and Amelie to do likewise.

'*Saluti!*' he announced, then glanced at his daughter. 'That is what we say here in Italy, instead of *Santé*, as they do in France, or *Cheers*, as they do in England. Isn't that right, Miss Ayrton?'

His dark glance came Jenna's way, and she nodded.

'Good,' he pronounced. 'Then drink up!'

He took a draught from his glass, and Jenna took a more modest sip from hers. The wine was rich and heady, and out of nowhere Jenna felt herself relax, realising only as she did so that there had been a tension in her that was a combination of concern for Amelie and—yet again—a sense of self-consciousness about being in the company of her employer.

*I can't make him out, with that mix of acerbic wit and good humour*, she thought, lowering her wine glass, flicking her eyes towards him as he greeted the arrival of their dinner, served by the two maids. He thanked them, and Jenna suspected that the two young women were as conscious of his brooding, powerful masculinity as she was. As probably all females were.

It was a disquieting thought. She had no business being aware of her employer in any terms other than just that—her employer. Nothing more.

Then a familiar, if bleak, reassurance came to her. It didn't matter a jot what she thought about Evandro

Rocceforte—or any other man. Men never really saw her and she was used to that. It was safer that way.

She'd tried, long ago, to be noticed, to be regarded as someone worth noticing, worth paying attention to—and had failed miserably. So it was safer never to try.

Her eyes went to Amelie, the little girl she felt so drawn to. Amelie was glancing at her father, and Jenna could tell she was not entirely at ease. Her father was still such an unknown quantity to her, and it was understandable that she should be uncertain in his company.

*I don't want her ever to hunger for her father's attention. To know the hurt of rejection, the kind of loneliness it once condemned me to.*

The loneliness she was still condemned to...

She gave herself a mental shake. Self-pity was both objectionable and pointless. She had accepted long ago that she had no appeal to men—and if that made for loneliness, then it was, in its way, protective.

*'Buon appetito!'*

The deep voice from the head of the table banished her introspective thoughts and she made a start on the beautifully cooked first course—a layered terrine of salmon and seafood bathed in a lobster bisque, garnished with radicchio and rocket, and served with curling melba toast. She glanced towards Amelie, in case the sophisticated dish was more than she could cope with—she had much plainer fare for her meals with Jenna, her teacher. But the little girl seemed undaunted, daintily using the correct fork, neatly demolishing the terrine without question or objection.

'You must bear in mind, Miss Ayrton,' Evandro informed her, as if he'd noticed Jenna's covert observation of his daughter, 'that in Italy—as in France—children are not packed off to bed early, but spend the evenings with their parents, including going out to restaurants.'

'Sometimes Maman let me go out with her and her friends,' Amelie put in. 'I had to wear my best dresses and not chatter, and not make a mess when I ate, or she would get cross with me...'

Her little voice, which had started out brightly, trailed off unhappily, as it so often did when she was recalling her life with her capricious and demanding mother, and Jenna's heart squeezed for her. Automatically she began to say something reassuring, but Evandro was there before her.

'Well, I can see, *mignonne*, that your table manners...' he swapped to Amelie's mother tongue, French, his voice warming approvingly, '...*sont par excellence!*'

Amelie beamed in pleasure at the praise, and Jenna smiled, too, glad for the little girl's sake, and yet feeling a strange pang inside her as well. She could remember no instances of her own father ever praising her for anything at all, however much she'd longed for a kindly word from him.

Knowing such memories were as useless as they were painful, she refocused, becoming aware that the slate-grey gaze from the head of the table was once more directed at her.

'You approve?' he asked pointedly.

'I approve of your approval,' Jenna answered, less pointedly.

If he was asking if she approved of his praising his daughter, in the way he just had, then of course she did. Though why he should seek *her* approval she did not know.

'I shall take that as a singular compliment,' came the reply.

Then he moved the conversation on, speaking to Amelie again, his tone encouraging.

'Miss Jenna tells me you enjoy art, *mignonne*. She showed me some of your pieces this morning. I would like to see more of them. Will you do a painting for me, hmm?'

Amelie's face lit up, all trace of uncertainty gone. 'Oh, yes! I'll do my favourite kind. Signorina Jenna likes me to paint things like flowers, and things that I imagine, but what I like doing best,' she announced boldly, 'is making fashion pictures. Because fashion is *so* important,' she finished portentously. 'Maman says it's essential to be *toujours à la mode*!'

Jenna saw her employer's face tighten, and poised herself to intervene with a mediatory comment. She did not want Amelie to be slapped down for her remark, or for the child's father to undo the good work he'd done in praising her.

But, despite his tightened expression, she was relieved when all her employer said was, 'Well, in fashion-conscious places like Paris and Milan, yes…'

Jenna could tell he was trying to modulate the tone of his voice so it would have the best effect on Amelie.

'But only when you're grown up. Or at least a teenager,' he finished repressively.

A confused look crossed Amelie's face, as if what he'd said went against everything her mother had taught her. This time, Jenna found herself interjecting. Yes, Amelie had a precociously unhealthy obsession with designer fashion, thanks to her mother's influence, but that could easily be channelled into something far more harmless and far more appropriate for a little girl.

'But what *is* fun at your age,' she said decisively, 'is dressing up! At the school I taught at in London,' she went on, 'every year there was a World Book Day, and all the children dressed up as someone out of a book or story they'd read. Who would you dress up as, Amelie?' she asked, wanting the little girl diverted from the subject of *haute couture*.

'A medieval princess!' she said immediately, not surprising Jenna in the least. 'Like Sleeping Beauty—but after she's woken up!'

*'Perfetto!'* her father pronounced, and Amelie looked pleased.

Then his dark gaze went to Jenna, and that caustic expression, increasingly familiar to her now, was back on his face as he addressed her, reaching for his wine glass. But there was humour in his expression too. Dark, but definitely there.

'So, tell me, if you will, Miss Ayrton, as the strict teacher that you are, what character would you recommend for me? Should I expect the worst? Or hope for the best?'

There was a decided glint in his eyes that told Jenna this was one of his ironically voiced remarks she was beginning to get the measure of. Calmly she replied, 'Well, I think any ogre would be far too harsh, so perhaps one of the stern kings in a fairy tale, despatching knights in armour on perilous quests?'

He gave a bark of laughter, his mouth twisting. 'And there I was, hoping you might cast me as Prince Charming!'

Jenna frowned slightly as the twist of his mouth increased, becoming almost bitter... She watched as he took yet another drink from his wine glass.

'Perhaps you are,' she heard herself saying quietly, the words seeming to form themselves, 'but in the story you are under a malign spell.'

Something moved in his slate eyes, and the lines around his mouth deepened.

'Cast by an evil enchantress?' he supplied.

Jenna felt in his gaze a weight that was suddenly crushing.

'Can such a spell ever be broken, do you think?' he asked.

'All such spells can be broken,' she answered.

For a moment—nothing more than a moment—her eyes held his. 'But how?' he asked, his voice low, and there was something in it that chilled her, for all this fanciful talk of fairy tales.

Then a new voice spoke up. Amelie's. 'The good fairy always breaks the spell, Papà!'

The dark gaze that had pressed upon her suddenly switched to the little girl, and Jenna felt herself breathe again.

'So, where do I find this good fairy, hmm?' he quizzed, addressing his daughter.

'She floats down in a silver bubble,' Amelie informed him. 'With silver hair and silver wings and a silver wand and a silver dress.'

Jenna saw her charge's face become animated as she described the vision. 'Why don't you paint a picture of her for your *papà*?' she suggested.

'An excellent idea!' Evandro agreed. His voice was jocular once more. 'I shall look forward to seeing it. Now,' he went on, 'if we are all finished with our *primo*, we shall proceed to the *secondo*.'

He pressed a discreet buzzer by his place setting, and within moments the maids had arrived to clear their plates and replace them with lamb fillet in a rich sauce.

Again, Amelie seemed undaunted by the gourmet fare. And also increasingly undaunted, Jenna was glad to obscrvc, by hcr father's presence. She could see the little girl relaxing, being assiduously drawn out by her father, who was now asking her what she knew of Italy's long history.

Jenna herself said very little, only prompting Amelie from time to time if she sounded unsure, and listening with interest as Evandro elaborated on what his daughter knew, telling tales from history in a calculatedly dramatic fashion to hold Amelie's interest.

The subject lasted through their final course, a delicate pear parfait—which, although delicious, Jenna could see Amelie was struggling to finish.

Her father saw it too. '*Piccolina*, you are falling asleep!' he pronounced. 'Time for your bed!'

Jenna made to rise, but hc staycd her.

'No—Loretta or Maria can see to Amelie. I would like adult company with my *formaggio*,' he declared.

When Loretta appeared at his summons, and led a sleepy Amelie away, he bade her goodnight in a gentler voice than Jenna had yet heard him usc, speaking in Italian.

'*Dormi bene, piccolina...*' He smiled. 'And dream of silver fairies.'

Then, with Amelie gone, and an extensive cheese platter placed on the table by one of the maids, he turned back to Jenna. For a moment his eyes rested on her, their expression unreadable, and Jenna felt a spurt of awkwardness. It was one thing to dine with her employer in order to keep his daughter company, but to sit here at the table with only him seemed quite different.

His next words made her realise why he'd sent Amelie upstairs with Loretta.

'So,' he said, pushing the cheese board towards her and indicating that she should help herself, 'your judgement, if you please, Miss Ayrton. How have I done so

far? Am I anywhere close to meeting your stipulations
as regards Amelie?'

Did he actually want to know her thoughts, or was this
another of his ironic challenges? It was hard to tell. Hard
to know just how to read this darkly enigmatic man, the
likes of whom she had never encountered in all her life.

But he was putting her on the spot, and she must answer as required.

'If my opinion holds any validity, Signor Rocceforte,
then I would say, very readily, that you are well on the
way to building a good relationship with your daughter,'
Jenna replied. Her voice warmed. 'I could see Amelie relaxing more and more—especially when you praised her.'

'There is much to praise,' came the reply. Then his expression tightened. 'Except her choice of dress.'

Carefully, Jenna made her selection from the array
of *formaggi*, and even more carefully gave her answer.

'I do realise that the majority of Amelie's wardrobe
is…unsuitable, but…' she eyed him cautiously '…if
fashion is what Amelie's mother was most interested in,
then it is only to be expected that her daughter will have
sought to gain her mother's favour and approval by copy-
ing that interest. It would be unfair to condemn Amelie for—'

'For her mother's sins.'

The voice cutting across hers was harsh, silencing
Jenna. She saw him move restlessly in his chair, refilling
his wine glass and swirling it moodily. His eyes dropped
from Jenna, as if his thoughts were many miles away.
Then, abruptly, his gaze lifted to her again, darker than
ever.

'My ex-wife's predilection for squandering obscene
amounts of money on couture clothes was the least of
her sins,' he bit out.

He moved restlessly again, taking another draught from his wine. Jenna got the impression he was exerting a formidable control over himself now, to curb his outburst. Deep emotions were playing beneath that carapace of control. Just how bitter had his divorce been? Jenna found herself wondering.

Then, as if banishing thoughts that brought him displeasure, he said, 'Well, one thing is obvious—a new wardrobe must be purchased for Amelie.' He looked directly at Jenna. 'You must help in the selection—I know nothing about children's clothes.'

'If you wish,' she answered.

'I do wish,' he said imperiously, helping himself to several wedges from the cheese board, and crackers to go with them. A frown creased his brow. 'You were telling me something this afternoon on the terrace,' he said in his abrupt way. 'About the children of divorced parents. Continue, if you please.'

Slowly, she buttered a cracker, not in the least sure that she wanted to do as he bade. But he was clearly waiting for her answer. An answer that might help Amelie if she could make the little girl's father understand it.

Tentatively, she began, feeling her way as she spoke. 'Children can get…lost…in the divide between warring parents. They can become, as I said, invisible. And sometimes…' her voice changed, she could not stop it '…that becomes exactly what the child begins to want—'

She broke off, conscious that she had veered into territory she did not want to give voice to. But Evandro, it seemed, was not a man to permit evasion.

'You speak of yourself, I assume?' he said. His gaze narrowed, arrowing down the table at her. 'But why should you want to be invisible?' His expression hardened.

Jenna shook her head. An air of unreality was swirling

about her. Perhaps it was the late hour, or the quietness around them, and the fact that no one else was present. Perhaps that was what made it easier to say what she said now, her voice low, but unflinching.

'When my mother was killed in a car crash I was sent to live with my father and the woman he'd left my mother for. My presence was…not welcomed. Neither by my stepmother and her children—nor by my father.'

His dark, unreadable gaze rested on her. 'How old were you?'

'Younger than Amelie—just six years old.'

She saw his mouth twist.

'I held on, continuing to hope that one day…' she swallowed '…one day my father would…would *see* me. That one day I would stop being invisible to him. But it never happened. And after a while it seemed better to accept that. Safer.'

His dark brows drew together. 'Safer?'

She felt her grip tighten on the cheese knife in her hand. 'Safer not to want what could not be. Safer to stay invisible.'

He nodded, but slowly, his heavy gaze never leaving her. 'And you are still invisible,' he said softly.

She felt it like a blow, which was odd, because she knew very well that she was invisible. Knew she could walk into any room and no one would notice. It was the way she'd come to want it, because it was safer than the alternative. Being condemned for her very existence, as she had when a child.

She sought to clear her head—clear the emotion that had risen up within her at remembering the unhappy childhood she had endured.

As if surfacing from beneath a deep sea, she realised

he was speaking again. His voice had changed, become decisive.

'Well, if that is your concern for Amelie, you may set your anxiety at rest. Amelie is very, very visible to me, I assure you. And I will be doing all in my power, as you admonished me to do this morning, to make her feel wanted and valued. Because, Miss Ayrton, I promise you that nothing will take her from me. *Nothing.*'

There was a vehemence in his voice and a grim determination in his face that made her look at him, setting aside her own troubling recollections.

His avowal should surely be welcome to her, dissipating her fears for Amelie, the little girl uprooted to a new home, a new parent. Yet for a moment, nothing more than a moment, his vehemence and determination seemed to chill her.

Then, in the abrupt fashion she was beginning to get used to, his mood changed.

'But enough of grim topics,' he said. 'Tell me, if you please—for you doubtless know better than I does Amelie like swimming? The weather is getting warm enough to start enjoying the pool. And what else have you discovered that she enjoys—or does not?'

Grateful for the return to easier topics, Jenna provided what answers she could to his questions, continuing until the maid returned, saying Amelie was tucked up in bed, and asking for the *signorina* to come and say goodnight to her.

Jenna took it as an excuse to withdraw. And as she bade her employer goodnight she saw his dark gaze flicker over her as he nodded his reply, as enigmatic as it was brief.

Only later, back in her sitting room after Amelie was asleep, did she find herself wondering how on earth she had come to say what she had to him about her childhood, about what ran so very deep within her. Things she had never spoken about before—let alone to a man like him.

A man whose softly spoken words echoed anew in her head...

*Still invisible.*

She gave a dismissive shake of her head—as dismissive as his words—and reminded herself of the home truths she should not forget.

Of course she was invisible to him. A man not only of wealth and power, but of formidable dark good looks, who surely would expect—and receive—the eager attentions of the most beautiful and beguiling of women. Women to whom she was the very antithesis.

To such a man as that, what else could she be but invisible?

What else could she want to be...?

Memory rose in her head of how she'd lain in that sensuous, too-relaxing bath last night, entertaining fantasies she'd had no business entertaining. Fantasies of slate-dark eyes resting on her...

She pushed the memory forcibly from her head. It was as inappropriate as it was pointless to think like that about a man who was like none she had ever encountered before.

In the elegant dining room, Evandro sat back in his chair, poured himself a cognac and, his eyelids half closed, rested his gaze on the foot of the table, where Miss Ayrton had been sitting.

Invisible, she'd called herself.

He pondered the word. It was the very opposite of what Berenice was. She was no more capable of being invisible than a peacock. But then, of course, a preening peacock was exactly what she was. A self-obsessed narcissist who required everyone to indulge her, to desire her, to fall under her malign spell.

A malevolent enchantress, indeed. She had destroyed whatever he'd been of a youthful Prince Charming.

He reached for his glass, stretching out his long legs and recalling that exchange over dinner about fairy-tale characters, hearing his own voice asking how evil spells could be broken.

Amelie's piping voice played in his head. *'The good fairy always breaks the spell, Papà.'*

His expression changed. Did such a being exist?

More memories flickered in the tawny cognac, fuelling his senses, playing out myths and legends, fairy tales and folklore. Then into his head came the throwaway remark he'd made to the woman who had appeared out of nowhere in front of his speeding car.

*'You look more like some kind of woodland sprite...'*

He frowned. She had been foolhardy indeed to risk her life like that—but she seemed to have thought nothing of it.

*Just as she thought nothing of standing up to me and telling me my responsibilities to Amelie—not with bombast or vehemence, but with quietly spoken, intent determination that I should hear what she was telling me.*

And now he knew why. He could understand now, after the sorry tale of her own childhood, why she felt so strongly about what she had urged him to do.

His meandering thoughts came full circle.

*Invisible—is that what she is?*

It was hard not to concur. There was nothing about her to draw his eye, his interest. He ran a catalogue of items through his head, recalling her nondescript appearance.

*Mid-brown hair, drawn back into a plait, no make-*

*up to enhance her face, and nor did that plain dress and
those low-heeled shoes enhance her figure.*

She purposely did nothing to draw any attention to
herself. Wanting, indeed, to be invisible.

As he took a slow mouthful of the rich cognac he
thought again that there was something about her—not
just the self-effacing way she looked, but something in
the way she spoke to him, answered him, and looked at
him with those clear hazel eyes of hers. Something that—

*That what?*

The question hung in the air, unanswered.

# CHAPTER FIVE

JUST AS HE had told Jenna he would, Evandro took time every day to be with Amelie.

He did so unapologetically, interrupting lessons to whisk Amelie off with him—sometimes down to the pool for swimming, sometimes off in his monster of a car to see the latest children's movie in the nearby town, or to go sightseeing, or to a store to add to the growing toy collection in the little girl's playroom. One expedition had seen them return with a pink bicycle, upon which Amelie had proceeded to hurtle along the terrace and the garden paths, much to her delight.

Jenna could only be glad for her, however disrupted her lessons were. Before her eyes she could see Amelie gaining in confidence with her father—and he with her. It warmed her to see it, and to see the efforts he was making to build a loving relationship with his daughter.

A little catch formed in her throat. She must not be envious of Amelie… And yet when she watched the little girl run happily to her father and be caught up by him in a hug, then set off with him for another outing, she was aware that envy was, indeed, what she was feeling.

And something else too. Something she had not expected. Could not explain. Had never felt the force of before.

All her life she had made herself content with her own company—yet now, as she waved Amelie off on another excursion with her father, she could feel the pluck of loneliness inside her.

She should not be feeling it, she knew—had no business to feel this way. Amelie was her pupil and Evandro was her employer. This beautiful *palazzo* was only her temporary place of work. And yet for all her reminders of how she was only passing through, she was aware that, however occupied she kept herself—swimming lengths in the pool when Amelie and Evandro were away, going for walks in the woods and planning her pupil's next set of lessons—her customary solitude was not welcome any more.

It was a strange, unsettling feeling to be unsatisfied with her own company. To wonder what Amelie and her father were doing together. To miss the little girl's constant company. To realise—and this was most unsettling of all—that the highlight of her day was coming to be the brief exchanges she had with Evandro on the evenings when she accompanied her pupil to dine with him.

She found herself looking forward to those times. Looking forward to that mix of outspoken directness and sometimes caustic, sometimes straight-faced humour that he could bring to any exchange. Found that as the days passed she was becoming more and more at ease in his company.

She wondered at it, trying to find an explanation. After all, a man like Evandro Rocceforte was utterly removed from her own world—wealthy, cosmopolitan, a man of high corporate affairs. A man who surely could find little to interest him in a woman like herself.

And yet after they had dined, and Amelie had been despatched upstairs to be put to bed, Evandro would lean back in his chair, extend his long legs under the dining table, refill their glasses and start a conversation with Jenna that had nothing to do with his daughter. It might be about current affairs, or Italian art, or works of literature—or any other topic of his choosing.

'Speak plainly, if you please, Miss Ayrton,' he would say, reaching for his wine glass and levelling his mordant gaze at her. 'I would have your honest opinion. Come, I know that you have one—and very likely a trenchant one at that. However quietly you speak, you will skewer the subject. I have come to expect nothing less.'

It was curious, Jenna thought. As perpetually aware as she was of the formidable presence of Evandro, when it came to conversing with him she was finding it a heady experience. One she was not used to at all.

Evandro, when his unnerving slate-dark gaze settled on her and his deep-timbred voice addressed her, required her to respond to him. He would not let her be reticent, and she—and this was the most unsettling thing of all—was becoming increasingly and disquietingly aware that perhaps she did not wish to be reticent. She found it mentally stimulating—invigorating, even—to have her opinions sought and listened to.

The days passed, and although Jenna was no longer needed to act as any kind of bridge between Amelie and her father, Evandro repeatedly invited her to join them for lunch, as well as dinner, or on another nature walk, or a ramble through the woods, or—much to Amelie's excitement—to help when he set the ornamental fountain working.

Another realisation slowly built up in her a realisation that changed all her boundaries, all her expectations, and created, in their place, a hunger to behave differently from the way she had always lived her life. To reject all that she was familiar with, comfortable with, safe with.

She was wishing, for the first time in her life, something she had never wished before.

*I don't want to be invisible any more.*

Not to Evandro Rocceforte.


'*Piccola*, Signora Farrafacci says she is going to teach you to make cookies this afternoon,' Evandro announced at lunchtime. He turned to Miss Ayrton. 'So you and I,' he said, 'shall go for an energetic walk through the woods. You dawdle, *mignonne*,' he threw at Amelie with a smile. 'Enjoy your cookie-making instead.'

Jenna started to make some protest about the proposed walk, but he overrode her.

'No—no retreating to your sitting room, if you please. I require both exercise and good conversation, and only you will do for both.'

Just why only she would do he was not prepared, at this juncture, to waste time examining. Jenna Ayrton might be badly dressed, determined to downplay her appearance, and altogether devoid of any obvious sex appeal, but that had nothing to do with why he wanted to spend time with her. However much he was prioritising time with Amelie, he was also deriving a surprising degree of enjoyment from the company of her teacher— company he was increasingly seeking.

He found he was looking forward to such times— to conversing with a woman the likes of whom he had never encountered before. A woman who, self-effacing as her nature was, he could see was becoming more easy in his company day by day. And he was glad to see it— glad to see her reticence ebbing away under his refusal to let her retreat behind it, glad to see her manner relaxing more and more when she was with him, glad that her smile was readier.

Not everyone found him easy company. His years with Berenice had scarred him, he knew, with a stab of bitterness. Prince Charming had been lost long ago. Now he knew he could be brusque and impatient, peremptory and cynical. But somehow—and he did not really know why, only that it was so—with Jenna Ayrton he seemed to be lifted and lightened.

Perhaps it was because she'd shown she was unfazed by it—perfectly prepared to stand up to him for what she thought was right when it came to Amelie, wanting to guard her against the misery she'd endured in her own sad childhood. Perhaps, too, it was because she seemed to instinctively understand his sardonic sense of humour, responding to it with limpid ripostes of her own that always drew a satisfied smile of acknowledgement from him.

And perhaps most of all, he was coming to realise with a growing awareness, it was because she never answered him without honesty, sincerity or candour. He knew he could trust that what she said, she meant. She never trimmed her answers to fit his views, nor sought to alter his, just accepted the differences between them with untroubled tranquillity.

*She holds her own—stands her ground. She answers me rationally, yet with a quiet conviction that can silence me. Just as she silenced me that first morning with her impassioned plea for Amelie. She says what she feels, what to her is right. She puts nothing on—there isn't a shred of artifice about her. With her, what I see is what she is.*

His expression darkened, his mouth tightening.

*The very opposite of the woman I married...*

His eyes shadowed. Was that the reason for Jenna Ayrton's appeal to him? And if it was, then—

For a moment…just a moment…he felt unease furrow his brow—then discarded it. Why recall his lawyer's warnings? How could they possibly apply? Jenna Ayrton was Amelie's teacher, here for the summer only, and if he found enjoyment in her company it was for the sake of her conversation, because of her natural interest in the little girl she was here to teach—the child who was now safe from the malign machinations of her mother. To give the slightest heed to his lawyer's warning would be absurd.

Now, as he set a vigorous pace through the steep wooded hillside, he glanced back at the woman who was so unlike his toxic ex-wife—unlike, come to that, any of the woman he'd celebrated his freedom from Berenice with. She was a good few steps behind him, but not lagging.

'When I was younger,' he remarked, 'I used to run through the trails here, and as a boy I had a treehouse, where I would hide out. I might get it rebuilt for Amelie. Would she like that, do you think?'

'I'm sure she'd love it,' Jenna replied. 'Any child would.'

'And you? Would you have loved a treehouse?' he enquired, throwing another glance at her.

'Oh, yes,' was her answer.

It did not satisfy him. He paused in his stride, letting her catch up. 'Is that all? You know I am not content with monosyllables.'

She looked away, through the cathedral of trees. 'It would have been a good place to hide,' she said. 'My step-siblings resented my presence in their home, so I learnt to keep out of their way. A treehouse would have been ideal for that. As it was, I had to make do with cowering behind the garden shed, where it was full of brambles and nettles, hiding there for hours sometimes, frightened they would find me and delight in taunting and tormenting me.'

There was a bleakness in her face as she looked back into her miserable childhood—the kind of childhood she had feared Amelie might be similarly doomed to had he himself turned out to be cut from the same cloth her callous father obviously had been.

His mouth set. Well, Amelie's childhood was safe now. There was no question—*none*—of anything else. But as for her teacher...

He had probed into her wretched childhood, confronted the misery she'd endured—the misery that had reaffirmed for him how absolutely essential it had been for him not to condemn Amelie to the custody of an unloving parent. But the misery still cast a pall over her. Haunting her. Blighting her.

Evandro rapidly marshalled the thoughts in his head, rearranging them in a way he had not seen, had not expected, shaping them into a new, fast-strengthening resolve.

His eyes went to her. The dappled sunlight played on her light brown hair, loosened from its plait by the hard-paced walking and forming tendrils that softened her features. Her cheeks had become flushed by exertion, her hazel eyes were made green by the canopy of leaves overhead, and her slight breasts were lifted by her faster breathing after their hike. Into his head came, once again, the description he'd given her during that first dramatic encounter by the deadly rockfall.

*A woodland sprite... A sylph of the forest...who might vanish away into the forest's depths, unseen.*

Invisible.

As invisible as her callous father had made her feel.

As invisible as she still thought herself.

Evandro's eyes flashed with sudden intensity. Sudden decision.

*I don't want her to be invisible. Not any longer. Not to herself.*

*Nor to me.*

The added thought came into his head unbidden, but he quickly banished it.

# CHAPTER SIX

EVANDRO RESTED HIS elbow in relaxed fashion on the rim of the open driver's window of the sleek, silver-grey saloon car which carried the three of them far more comfortably than the low-slung supercar he'd arrived in. He was waiting for his passengers to emerge from the *palazzo* and he was looking forward to the day ahead.

Ostensibly the outing was to buy new, far more suitable clothes for Amelie, but there was something else he had every intention of achieving today.

His eyes glinted, satisfaction filling him.

His glance went to the front door, and he was rewarded by its opening and two figures coming out. Amelie—wearing a sequinned pink top and a yellow puffball skirt, thereby demonstrating to him the absolute necessity of a new wardrobe—ran forward as he got out to open the rear passenger door for her with a deliberate flourish, restricting his comments on her dire appearance to say only that she looked so dazzling he would need sunglasses.

She clambered in, settling herself on the booster seat, and he checked her safety belt was secure before turning back to Jenna.

She was looking, he noticed immediately, somehow less plain this morning. Perhaps because they were going out for the day.

The light blue shirt dress she was wearing looked surprisingly neat on her, with its narrow belt emphasising her small waist and its lapels—whether she was aware of it or not, and he suspected she was not—drawing attention to the discreet swell of her breasts beneath the prosaic cotton of her bodice.

And although, as usual, she had not a scrap of make-up on, there was a glow in her eyes, and in her complexion, that was also perhaps due to the prospect of the day out ahead.

Whatever the cause, he welcomed it.

Firmly, he closed the rear passenger door of the car. He had no intention of letting her sit beside Amelie in the back.

'I want you here, beside me,' he declared, gesturing to the front passenger seat, 'so that I may point out the sights. You've been cooped up far too long, so we shall be combining shopping with sightseeing.' He threw a glance at her as she complied with his wishes and settled herself in the front. 'It's time you saw something of the region.'

'There really is no necessity to take me sightseeing—' Jenna began, making a predictable objection to his plans, but he overrode it briskly.

'We'll also be including a visit to a nearby Roman villa—a notable archaeological site, which I'm sure will be sufficiently educational for Amelie, in case you have any reservations about her taking a day off.' He gunned the engine. 'And now...*avanti*!'

He swept off in a spray of gravel towards the narrow drive that dropped steeply down to the highway below. The memory of Jenna running into the path of his car to stop him hitting the rockfall sprang vivid in his head and he turned towards her.

His tone as he spoke was different from his earlier

light-hearted pronouncement. Serious now…sombre. 'I never thanked you for what you did back then—only yelled at you. You most likely saved my life.'

A sudden cold filled him.

*If I'd died then—smashed myself to pieces—Amelie would have been returned to Berenice, doomed to grow up twisted and distorted like her mother, either to become as selfish and as narcissistic as she is, or else hurt and damaged beyond measure, forever craving a love the woman is incapable of.*

It was a thought beyond bearing.

'So, belatedly, I thank you now,' he said.

Jenna's eyes met his, and in that moment there was a sudden intensity, even if it lasted only a fraction of a second.

And as he pulled his focus back to the narrow road, the moment reverberated in his head.

'Pasta for *pranzo*!' Evandro declared as they settled themselves down at one of the outside tables of a trattoria in the *piazza* of the ancient medieval hilltop town where they'd stopped to eat lunch.

The day so far had been wonderful—Jenna had enjoyed it all. First, they'd gone to see the excavated Roman villa, where Amelie had admired the mosaics and her father had explained the hypocaust heating system to them both, and then they'd driven on through the rolling countryside, past cornfields and vineyards, and stately cedars marching along the roads, with Evandro pointing out sights of historic and geographical interest, telling them about wine production and how people had lived in the past, and tales of famous and heroic figures.

Whether or not Amelie had taken it all in, Jenna wasn't sure, but it was all part of her learning curve, and it brought to vivid life the lessons she'd had in the schoolroom.

As for herself, she couldn't deny how enjoyable it was to see the wider countryside of this part of Italy— which she had never previously visited—and nor could she deny how enjoyable it was be included. Or how enjoyable it was to feel so comfortable as she did now with Evandro.

She replayed in her head the way he'd thanked her for stopping his car from crashing into the rockfall, his voice so sombre. The way he'd looked at her as he'd spoken had had something about it that had stilled her with its intensity. But then it had gone, and his attention had been on his driving again.

Her eyes went to him now, as he discussed the pasta options with Amelie, their heads bent together over a menu, one so dark and one so fair. A memory plucked at her of how she'd wondered from which side of her parentage Amelie had got her blond hair and fair colouring. But what did it matter? Her expression softened as she watched the two of them, so natural together now, so completely at ease with each other.

Her fears for Amelie had been completely eliminated.

*She will never be the lonely outcast with no place to belong that I was.*

She felt her throat tighten. Was that not still true for her? However lovely it was to be taken out like this, to be on such easy terms with the man who employed her, to be so fond of the little girl who was her pupil, to be so glad that the child and the father were building a close, mutually affectionate relationship, she herself was only an outsider—an observer.

*I'll be gone by the autumn and I'll likely never see them again.*

The thought was like a needle, piercing her, and the sharpness of it shocked her.

She seized a menu, making herself focus on the contents. Yes, her time in Italy would end—her time with Amelie at the beautiful *palazzo* and her time with Evandro.

But till then... Till then she would enjoy all that she had here.

'Are we going shopping now?'

Amelie's hopeful voice piped up as they got back into the car. After a leisurely lunch, they'd gone to look inside the church in the *piazza*—famed locally, Evandro had informed Jenna, for its *quattrocento* murals. Though Amelie had enjoyed lighting a candle to the Madonna and the Infant Jesus, she was keener on heading off to the shops for the promised shopping expedition.

'Yes, you little magpie, we are!' her father confirmed, and they set off, leaving the picturesque hilltop town and heading towards the largest town of the region, which had a sizeable shopping district, including a department store, where they parked.

Once in the children's clothes section, Amelie ran gleefully forward.

'And now,' Evandro informed Jenna ruthlessly, 'I shall leave you to it. Get her everything she needs. And make sure you include a couple of dressier pieces that are preferable alternatives to her current appalling collection,' he finished grimly. 'I'll be back in an hour to pay.'

Then he was gone.

The hour, naturally enough, flashed by, and by dint of steering Amelie's pleasurable indecision with her gently firm guidance, Jenna helped her select a sufficient number of suitable garments.

On the dot, her father reappeared.

'Much better,' he said approvingly of Amelie's simple gingham sundress, promptly paying for it and all the other purchases with the flick of a very exclusive-looking credit card.

Then he hunkered down beside Amelie and spoke to her in a low, conspiratorial tone. Amelie's eyes lit up, and she nodded vigorously.

Evandro straightened, hefting up the plentiful carrier bags. 'Now it's your turn,' he said to Jenna.

She stared. 'I don't understand.'

'Amelie wants you to have a new dress,' he informed her, his voice as smooth as butter. 'To say thank you for all the maths lessons.'

Amelie tugged at Jenna's hand. 'It isn't really for the maths lessons,' she told her. 'Because I don't like maths and I would rather not have maths lessons, so Papà is only teasing. But it *is* to say thank you.' She was gazing up at Jenna. 'It's a present from me,' she said. Uncertainty hovered in her face suddenly. 'If...if you *want* a present from me...' Her little voice trailed off, her eyes anxious.

It was impossible to refuse—unthinkable.

Jenna caught Amelie's other hand and squeezed both tightly. 'I'd *adore* a present from you,' she said warmly. 'And a new dress would be absolutely *lovely*.'

How could she possibly reject the little girl? Even though she'd been ruthlessly—shamelessly—manoeuvred into this by Evandro, for whatever amusement that it might afford him. Though for the life of her she could not imagine why, unless it was an act of casual lordly benevolence... Or maybe—and more likely, she thought with her customary painful honesty—it was masculine revulsion at being seen out with a female who was so utterly unlike any kind of female he'd have chosen for companionship.

Amelie's face had lit up at her fulsome reply and, consigning herself to her fate, Jenna let herself be led towards the womenswear department.

She'd fully expected her employer to disappear again, but he deposited himself in one of the large leather armchairs positioned for the convenience of those males haplessly corralled into clothes shopping, and availed himself of the several sporting magazines provided to lessen the grim ordeal.

Amelie, happily in her element again, marched Jenna up and down the racks of clothing until she found one that displayed what she was after.

'These are like my dresses, but in your size,' she told Jenna, starting to rifle through the display.

A shop assistant glided up and joined in enthusiastically.

Jenna gave in, defeated.

Evandro logged off his computer, all the work he'd intended to do today satisfactorily completed. His senior executive team was happy, his shareholders were happy, his clients were happy, his project managers were happy—and he was happy.

He sat for a moment, wondering at that. Wondering that he should be happy at all. It wasn't an emotion he was used to. Not for years. Then, getting to his feet, he stopped wondering, and simply enjoyed the sensation.

He glanced at his watch—four o'clock. Time for afternoon tea. A very special afternoon tea—a tea *party*, in fact. With everyone looking the part.

Including Jenna Ayrton, who would be wearing the new dress he'd shamelessly manoeuvred her into accepting.

He'd done so quite deliberately.

As they'd walked through the woods that day he'd resolved not to let her be invisible any more. Not to let her be haunted by her miserable childhood. He didn't want her endlessly hiding from the world, tucking herself away, out of sight, thinking so harshly of herself...

And now he would see what his scheming had achieved. He'd given Amelie strict instructions that morning—instructions that had made her eyes light up gleefully and enthusiastically—and now, as he strolled out of the library, his eyes went to the wide marble stairway descending into the hall.

And there they were. Amelie and Jenna. Coming down the stairs.

Amelie looked as pretty as a picture in one of the new dresses purchased the previous day, with her long golden hair held back by a floral Alice band that had a bow on it to match the yellow sash of her full-skirted dress with its delicate pattern of little yellow roses. She was beaming widely, sedately holding Jenna's hand, and Evandro felt something clutch at him to see her smiling so trustingly at him, filling him with an emotion that gripped him with an intensity he had never felt so fiercely.

She was safe here, with him to look after her as best he could. And he would keep her safe—for her sake and for his own. The child who had been deliberately kept from him, deliberately used as a weapon against him, was a stranger no longer.

He felt his heart clench with protectiveness...with love.

*I may have no qualifications to be a father, and I may have had to feel my way, day by day, to win her confidence, her trust, but now...*

In his head he heard the words that Jenna had spoken to him.

*Every child should be valued, wanted...loved.*

Emotion welled in him as Amelie, letting go of her teacher's hand, ran up to him.

*And she is all of those—all of them. Valued, wanted... and loved.*

He stooped to hug her, feeling her little arms wind about his neck, feeling again that welling of emotion inside him. Then he stood up, his eyes going to Jenna.

*Por Dio!*

She was not invisible at all.

*Like a woodland sprite...*

The words popped into his head of their own accord as his gaze rested on her, unable to tear itself away. Her slender figure was as graceful as a dryad's in the soft green of her ballerina-length, fifties-style dress, with its gathered skirt and the sweetheart neckline that ruched over her shoulders, left her arms bare, emphasised her tiny waist.

For the first time she was wearing her hair loose, in the same style as Amelie, held back softly from her face with a green velvet ribbon. As for her face... His eyes glinted. She was wearing make-up. Not much—a little mascara, some smoky eyeshadow to deepen her eyes, turned now to a forest-green like her dress, and a touch of lip gloss to bring a sheen to her curving mouth—but it was enough for him to see that her delicate features would draw the male eye as they had never drawn it before...making it want only to appreciate...to linger...

Then Amelie was speaking to him, her voice eager. 'Do we look nice, Papà, Miss Jenna and me?'

'You look enchanting!' he said promptly. 'Both of you!'

He worked his eyes over Jenna once more, knowing it made her colour heighten, and glad of it.

'At last,' he said softly, stepping forward. 'You have

come out of hiding. Made yourself visible.' He took her hand, which seemed to quiver in his, and raised it to his lips in a formal, stately fashion. 'Never hide again,' he said quietly, for her alone.

For a moment he held her gaze, and something—he did not know what—seemed to change in the world around him. Inside him. Something that he had not known could change...

In his head, like a poisoned dart shot at him from far away, he heard his lawyer's words of foreboding. He shook them out, refusing to acknowledge them or let them penetrate the strange emotion filling him now, which seemed to permeate him with a warming glow.

Jenna's slender hand was still in his, cool beneath his fingers. He tucked it into his arm, did the same with Amelie's hand, and led them both forward with a smile.

'And now that I have a *bella donna* on either arm—what a lucky dog I am—it is time,' he announced, with satisfaction and triumph in his voice, 'for our tea party.'

'Party' was certainly the word for it, Jenna conceded. Just as she'd had to concede there had been no way out of Amelie's excited, gleeful insistence that she must wear her lovely new dress today and put on make-up for the occasion.

Just as she had in the department store, Jenna had given in. She had not been able to disappoint Amelie, who had been visibly thrilled to be dressing up, and thrilled at the thought of her teacher dressing up too. So she'd left her hair loose, borrowed a ribbon from Amelie's vast collection, and then, with trepidation and Amelie's enthusiastic guidance, made up her face. Not too much, but just enough.

*Enough to make my eyes look larger, smokier, my lashes longer, and to give a soft sheen to my lips.*

And somehow, though she didn't really understand how, wearing her hair loose seemed to set off her cheekbones and reveal the delicate contours of her jaw that she'd never noticed. The beautifully cut fifties-style dress also seemed to enhance her slight figure, giving her a shapeliness she had not thought she possessed.

She'd stared at her reflection wonderingly. The experience was very different from her feelings when she had examined her unexciting workaday appearance that first night she had been summoned to dine with Amelie and her father.

How different she looked now!

She gazed, trying to take it all in. Trying to remember when she'd last worn make-up, last made any attempt to style her hair attractively, last worn something that might pass for fashionable. At uni, probably, some freshers' bash. Useless, though, because no one took notice of quiet, dull females whom even their own fathers had no interest in, and who were focused only on their studies, not on their social lives. And, as a teacher, all that was needed was for her to look neat and sensible, capable of keeping order in an overcrowded class with more than its fair share of children from disturbed backgrounds and impoverished families.

It was a life a world away from this beautiful, elegant Italian *palazzo*—a world away from the likes of Evandro Rocceforte.

She gave a little tremble now, as she felt her hand hooked around his strong forearm and walked into the rose garden with him and Amelie, where a pretty ironwork table had been set out under a shady parasol.

Had Evandro really swept his slate-dark eyes over

her, taken her hand and kissed it as if he were Prince
Charming himself?

*And I Cinderella...*

A Cinderella who had buried herself in her work. Hidden. Invisible.

*'Never hide again.'*

She heard his voice, low-pitched, intense, and a sense
of wonder filled her at how she had found herself wishing, for the first time in her life, for something she had
never wished before.

Not to be invisible any longer.

Not to Evandro Rocceforte.

# CHAPTER SEVEN

'WELL,' ANNOUNCED EVANDRO's housekeeper, 'this is a treat!'

Evandro gallantly ushered her to her seat as she sailed into the rose garden, resplendent in a sky-blue skirt and jacket with a jabot blouse, her hair freshly styled.

'Signora Farrafacci has created our repast...' Evandro smiled at Jenna '...so I think it only fair that she should enjoy it with us.'

'Well, I'm a dab hand at a Victoria sponge, if I say so myself,' his housekeeper agreed comfortably.

She beckoned Loretta and Maria forward, each carrying laden trays, which they deposited on the table, adding to what had already been set out.

It was a full English afternoon tea, with gold-rimmed porcelain plates bearing wafer-thin finger sandwiches—Jenna spotted egg, smoked salmon and cucumber—and a display of cakes that made her dizzy with indecision. The icing-sugar-dusted Victoria sponge, oozing raspberry jam from between the layers, looked as resplendent as its creator, and was flanked by rainbow-hued fairy cakes thick with colourful buttercream icing, and there was a far more sophisticated gateau St Honoré, made of choux pastry and golden spun sugar.

And as for what to wash it all down with—tea itself was the very least of it...

* * *

'What tea party would be complete without champagne, hmm?' quizzed Evandro, lifting the bottle nestling in its ice bucket by the table and opening it with a practised easing of the cork.

Champagne was ideal for the occasion. An occasion he'd created and orchestrated to perfection. His mood was excellent—beyond excellent. Everything had worked out just as he'd planned.

His eyes went to Jenna, revelling again in the transformation he had wrought in her. Goodbye, sad, haunted ghost of her miserable childhood, and welcome—oh, very, *very* much welcome—to the woman he had made reveal herself.

His gaze softened again in satisfaction and a wry, appreciative bemusement. Who would have thought a dress would make such a difference? A hairstyle? A touch of make-up? But there was more to it than that, he knew. It was a new glow that was about her, a light in her eyes, a smile on her lips that came from within.

*She knows she is no longer invisible. It is* that *that makes the difference. That which draws my eye to her—*

He cut off his wandering thoughts. The transformation he had wrought in Jenna was for herself, not for him. It was essential to remember that.

Swiftly, he reached for the champagne flutes, filling three of them to the brim and handing one each to Signora Farrafacci and to Jenna, keeping one for himself. Then he reached for another flute and poured in a quarter of a glass, topping it up generously with fresh orange juice and bestowing it upon Amelie.

'This, *mignonne*,' he informed her solemnly, 'is the only fizzy drink it is civilised to consume!' He glanced at Jenna. 'Do not be alarmed—as I said to you earlier, here in Italy, as in France, as well as becoming accustomed to dining out, children are exposed to wine from an early age, but in very small quantities.' He looked back at Amelie. 'Well, what do you think of it?'

The little girl took a cautious sip and wrinkled her nose. 'It tickles!' she said. 'But it's lovely and orangey.'

'It's called a Buck's Fizz,' Signora Farrafacci informed her. 'But I prefer mine straight, thank you very much,' she said, raising her glass to her employer.

He watched as Jenna hastily did likewise.

*'Saluti!'* he exclaimed, and clinked his glass against theirs and Amelie's. 'And now,' he pronounced, entirely and completely satisfied with what he had achieved, 'the feast may begin!'

His gaze washed one more time over the woman he had released from invisibility, who could now finally, belatedly, take her due place in the world, no longer barring herself from what she was entitled.

Signora Farrafacci did the honours, pouring cups of tea for everyone, though Amelie stuck with her Buck's Fizz.

Evandro sat back, a smile on his face. 'How exceptionally pleasant this is,' he announced expansively. 'We should do this more often—all through the summer, even. And we shall all—what is that strange expression?—wear our best bib and tucker when we do so.' He frowned. 'What in heaven is a tucker?'

'I've no idea,' Jenna confessed with a laugh. 'I shall look it up!'

'Well, all I know,' quipped Signora Farrafacci, 'is that I can't wait to *tuck* in!' Which brought a giggle from Amelie.

So they did, and as Jenna sipped at her champagne it was as if the bubbles were seeping into her bloodstream,

lifting her into a state of light-heartedness and enjoyment
that brought a constant smile to her face.

The convivial atmosphere was led by Evandro, reinforced by Signora Farrafacci's good-hearted joviality,
and most of all buoyed by Amelie's stream of giggles
and beaming smiles.

Moved, Jenna swept her eyes over the scene, wonderingly.

*This is the very definition of happiness.*

Her eyes went to the man sitting opposite her, genially
teasing his daughter and praising his housekeeper for the
excellence of her magnificent Victoria sponge. She could
not stop them and had no wish to, she realised, and the
welling of happiness within her became radiant.

She could not take her eyes from him. His strong,
powerful body relaxed back in the ironwork chair, and
the open neck of his pristine white shirt and the turned-
back cuffs acknowledged the warmth of the afternoon,
all emphasising the masculine strength of his body.

This was the man who had wrought this transformation in her, brought her out of her lifelong hiding from
the world—from men. The one man in all the world to
whom she was no longer invisible.

Rich, warm, wonderful happiness filled her to the
brim—like the sparkling, effervescent champagne in
her glass.


'Well, I've eaten my fill and no mistake!' Signora Farrafacci announced. She got to her feet. 'And now I must be
off—I'm visiting my son tonight.' She nodded at Evandro as he started to stand up as she did. 'No, no, don't
get up. Thank you for this first-class tea party. And,'
she finished, 'for requesting a cold dinner tonight so I
can go out.'

She lifted the remains of her magnificent Victoria sponge, and Evandro encouraged Amelie to take the left-over fairy cakes to the kitchen. Jenna moved to start clearing the table, but Evandro stopped her.

'No, stay awhile. There is still the champagne to finish,' he said lazily. *'Carina,'* he addressed Amelie, 'if you want to play, either choose something that will not risk your new dress or change.'

Amelie nodded, going after Signora Farrafacci and happily helping herself to the icing on one of the remaining fairy cakes as she did so.

Evandro leisurely reached for the champagne bottle and refilled their glasses. 'So...' he looked at Jenna, stretching out his long legs and lounging back in the iron-work chair '...did you enjoy our tea party?'

His quizzical glance got the reaction he'd expected.

'It was a triumph!' Jenna confirmed.

He laughed. 'As is your new dress.' His eyes drifted over her lazily, appreciatively. 'You cannot imagine the difference it makes.'

He saw her lashes drop over her eyes, more forest green than hazel today, reflecting the colour of the dress that was doing so much for her.

'Thank you,' she said, in a low tone.

There was a quiet intensity in her voice that told him the depth of her feelings. Told him what she was thanking him for.

He reached for her hand. Raised it to his mouth, grazed it lightly, then set it back on the table. It seemed to him the right kind of gesture to make. Anything more might—

He pulled his thoughts away. He'd done what he had for Jenna's sake, he reminded himself. *She* was to be the beneficiary—not himself.

He shifted, suddenly restless. 'And I thank you in return,' he said, his voice half-serious, half-caustic. 'The dress you chose for Amelie, the one that she wore today, is an infinite improvement on what her mother dressed her in.'

A smile lit Jenna's face. 'She looked enchanting—just as you told her,' she said warmly. 'She wants to please you.'

A frown pulled Evandro's brow. 'I don't need her to want to please me.' His voice was harsh suddenly. 'And if that is the impression I am giving her—and you...' he drew a razor-sharp breath '...then my inexperienced attempts at...at fatherhood—' he spoke the word flatly, almost bleakly '—are failing,' he finished tersely.

He saw her expression change—at first to dismay, at his harsh response, and then to its opposite. Warmth and encouragement.

'You are *not* failing!' she exclaimed feelingly. 'You are making a wonderful father. Wonderful!'

Her face worked, and he could see she was searching for words—the right words.

'It is natural for a child to want to please their parents,' she told him, her voice persuasive, 'and if it's mutual, and you want to please her too—as I can see you do, in so many ways when you are together—then it is entirely justified. It is only if it is one-sided that it becomes dangerous. Unhealthy,' she finished, and now it was her voice that sounded bleak.

'And it is unhealthy between adults too,' he bit out. 'Trying to win the love of someone who is incapable of returning it. Falling under their spell.'

'Cast by an evil enchantress...'

The words dropped from Jenna's lips and hung in the space between them. The same words he'd spoken at that first dinner together.

His shadowed eyes rested on her. She was unreadable—and yet all too readable. He did not need to spell out to her just who the evil enchantress in his life had been. She'd had enough malignity in her own life to know the damage that could be done when love of any kind—whether between parent and child or husband and wife—could not be returned because the other person lacked all capability for that most vital of emotions.

'Just so,' he said, and his gaze held hers. Then, abruptly, he reached for his glass, gesturing that she should do the same. 'Come,' he said, lightening his voice determinedly, to banish all shadows and darkness, 'let us not waste champagne on morbid memories. My ex-wife is in the past—as is your father. The only power they have over us now is the power we allow them. Nothing more than that.'

He raised his glass, touching it to hers. Knowing that what he had said was a lie for him. Berenice still had the power to poison.

But he would not think of that—not now, not here.

He let his eyes go to Jenna again, still finding her transformation wondrous. There was no danger, surely, in letting his gaze drink her in.

Peaceably, they sipped their champagne, with the heat of the day softening to a gentle warmth. Above them, from the open window of Amelie's playroom, he could faintly hear her talking to her dolls, discussing their fashion choices with them. He gave a resigned half-smile. Perhaps Amelie would end up making a career in fashion.

He said as much to Jenna. She smiled. 'Well, whatever she chooses, it won't require maths, I suspect.'

He laughed. 'What made you study languages?' he asked, curious.

She made a face. 'I had a facility for them, but mostly,

I think—with hindsight—I chose them because they opened my horizons to lives other than the one I had.'

'An escape route?' he said, understanding why she'd wanted that.

She nodded. 'Though then I became keen on teaching—and again,' she said with a rueful half-smile, 'that was to encourage children in their abilities as I was never encouraged in mine.' She looked at him, curiosity in her eyes. 'Did you ever have any choice but to take over Rocceforte Industriale?'

'I wanted to,' he replied. 'Perhaps because it's in my blood. But also because—' He stopped for a moment, took a slow mouthful of his champagne. 'Because it pleased my father. Oh, it's not that I sought his love and regard—I had that plentifully. But for the same reason that I—'

He broke off again. The shadow of Berenice was threatening. He set his mouth. Perhaps it would help to say it. After all, if there were anyone he could say it to, it was this woman here, scarred as she was by the cruelty of others.

'For the same reason that I was so glad to marry Berenice. I was all too willing—but it made my father happy too.' He paused again, his mouth twisting. '"The road to hell is paved with good intentions..."'

Restlessly, he drained his champagne, getting to his feet. Damn the woman he'd married so blindly—damn her to the hell she'd put him in!

*The hell she still seeks for me.*

Determinedly, he shut down his morbid thoughts, refusing to let them spoil this special day.

'Come,' he said, drawing Jenna to her feet. 'If your glass is empty, too, let us take a stroll to work off all these cakes.'

Good mood restored, he led her off.

Leaving Berenice far, far behind. If he could.

Jenna stood out on the terrace. The sun was near to setting, filling the gardens with rich gold light. The tea things had long been cleared away, and they had all spent the last hour or two on the sofa in Amelie's playroom, first watching one of her favourite movies with her, then playing her favourite computer game—both of which had involved medieval princesses, heroic quests and assorted mythical beasts.

It had been fun and relaxed and convivial.

Now Amelie had been handed over to Maria for her bath time, and Evandro had disappeared into the library to check his emails. Loretta had just brought out an *aperitivo* for them both, after Jenna had helped her set the table in the dining room and fetched the cold collation of salads and *antipasti* that would suffice as dinner after their lavish afternoon tea.

Bidding Loretta goodnight as she went off duty, Jenna stood gazing out over the vista beyond, feeling still that rich, warm glow of happiness that had filled her all afternoon.

She turned as she heard Evandro's distinctive step emerging onto the terrace. Her face lit—she could not help it.

Was there an answering light in his as he strolled up to her? In the fading light she could not tell.

He paused by the table and she watched him, knowing she could not look away. And nor did she want to, as he casually picked up their cocktails, then came across to her.

'See what you make of this,' he said genially, handing her a martini glass. 'It should refresh the palette after our afternoon champagne.'

She took a cautious sip—it was tart and citrusy—and, she suspected, more potent than was probably wise after two glasses of champagne earlier. But today was a special day and surely, on a day like this, caution could be set aside. And wisdom too...

'Well?' Evandro enquired with a lift of his brow.

She gave her judgement and he nodded, satisfied.

'We'll toast the setting sun,' he said. His eyes went to her. 'And more than the setting sun...'

The sunlight was in her eyes and she could not make out his expression as he spoke—knew only that there was something in his voice that had never been there before. Something that, just as his show of gallantry when he'd kissed her hand as she descended the staircase in her new dress revealing her new self had done, made her tremble slightly.

She turned to watch the sun pool on the horizon and then slip slowly beneath it in a final glory of gold as they sipped their cocktails. Dusk started to gather, and cicadas were giving soft voice in the air all around them. It was a strangely intimate moment.

Thoughts flickered in Jenna's head, then quietened. This was not a time for thinking, or for wondering, least of all for questioning. Only for standing quietly, as the day turned into night. Standing side by side... Evandro and herself...

A sound behind her made her turn. Amelie was at the open French doors of the dining room, wrapped in her dressing gown, her feet in fluffy slippers. Jenna held out her hand to her, smiling, and the little girl ran up, taking it in her warm, small clasp.

Her father smiled down at her. 'We're looking for the first star, *carina*. Can you see it yet?'

Amelie's eyes strained upward, then her little face lit. 'There! There—I see it, Papà! Up there!'

She pointed to where, almost invisible to the naked eye, the first faint star gleamed in a sky that was leaching slowly of its colour.

'So it is!' exclaimed Jenna.

'Clever girl,' said Evandro, taking his daughter's other hand. He caught Jenna's eye and smiled. A warm smile of companionship and closeness. A smile that seemed to linger...

She felt the glow that had filled her all afternoon well up in her again. Happiness. Just...happiness.

So simple. So precious. So good to feel.

So unknown in her life—till now.

For a moment longer they stood together, watching the star steadily brighten and the sky darken, Amelie between them, holding hands with each of them.

*As if we were a family*, Jenna thought. *With Amelie my daughter and Evandro my—*

Abruptly, as if Amelie's hand had suddenly become red-hot, she dropped it, stepped away. Appalled at what she'd just thought.

What she'd dared to want...

Softly, Jenna dropped a kiss on the sleeping child's forehead before turning to head back downstairs. The *palazzo* was in silence, its staff all off duty. She slipped noiselessly into the dining room, where Evandro still sat, long legs extended, his empty wine glass in his hand. His expression was shuttered.

He must have sensed her presence because his head turned and he saw her. Did something change in his eyes? She couldn't tell as the light from the wall sconces was so low.

He got to his feet. 'The moon has risen,' he said. 'Come and see.'

Though she was used to his direct manner, there seemed to be a staccato note to his voice now that was different. But then, she thought, frowning slightly, he had been different over dinner as well. As had she, she knew.

The meal had been an informal affair, and although Evandro had been his usual genial self with Amelie, Jenna had felt his glance often flickering towards herself. Was he still taking in how different she looked—how he had wrought such a transformation in her? Making her visible to his eyes. As she had longed to be.

She had been confused, conflicted. Dismayed by what she had allowed herself to think as they'd stood stargazing after sunset. She had found it hard to look at him, to meet his eyes, and yet she'd been burningly aware of his flickering glances. They'd both focused their attention on Amelie, until her reluctant yawns had drawn Jenna to her feet and she'd taken her up to bed.

She followed Evandro out onto the darkened terrace. Her mood was strange, still conflicted. Perhaps she should not have come back downstairs again. Perhaps she should have bidden him goodnight when she'd taken Amelie up to bed. It would have been better...safer...to wait until tomorrow to see him again, when she would be in her workaday clothes, her hair pinned back, her face plain of make-up.

The dangerous thought that had come to her as she had stood hand in hand with Amelie, the child between them—linking them, uniting them—still assailed her. She knew she must not think it. Knew it was only the result of the moment...an after-effect of the day.

A day that had been made for her, created for her, given to her like a wonderful, precious gift—one she would forever be grateful for. A day like no other in her life.

But she must not read into it her own longings. The longings of someone who had never belonged to a warm and loving family—never belonged at all. Someone who had never had anyone to love her—who had had loneliness imposed upon her and who had had to accept it because it was all she had known…all she had expected from life.

But just because she no longer wanted to choose loneliness it did not mean she could have any place here. Or any claim on anyone here.

Not Amelie—*and not Evandro.*

No claim at all—however much her eyes went to him, however burningly aware she was of him as a man with an overpowering physical impact on her that had been there right from the very first moment, that she had never experienced before.

None of that mattered.

*I am Amelie's teacher—that is all. And if her father choses to treat me kindly and decently, that does not mean…does not mean…*

She felt her throat catch, as if a barb had lodged there suddenly.

*That does not mean anything at all.*

And yet…

And yet she felt herself longing for it to mean something. Wishing that it was for *himself* that he had turned her from plain to pretty, from drab to desirable, turned her into the kind of woman who could light up the eyes of a man like Evandro Rocceforte. A man who had given her a gift she had never before received.

She heard again the words he had spoken to her as he had kissed her hand, paid homage to the woman he had revealed.

*'Never hide again.'*

And she did not want to. Not from him. She wanted him to go on seeing her—now, tonight. Seeing her made lovely by him. *For* him.

*I don't want this day to end—not yet.*

The longing sang in her head and her eyes went to him—as they always seemed to want to. He had paused on the terrace and was now turning back to her. She felt her throat catch again, but for a different reason now— because her breath seemed to have vanished on the cool night air.

All around them the chorus of the cicadas filled the air, the scent of fragrant flowers perfumed it. He was looking at her, holding out his hand to her. Saying nothing, only waiting for her to accept. She lifted her face, looked up at him. His strong features were shadowed in the night, and she caught the faint scent of his aftershave.

His outstretched hand touched her hair. 'Always wear it long and loose and lovely. It's a crime to hide it with pins.'

There was a smile in his voice as he spoke, but also something more than a smile. Something that seemed to reach into her, touching her deep within.

With the lightest touch his hand smoothed down the length of her hair. The sensation was so light it was scarcely there, yet it made her tremble. She could not move—not a muscle. Could only stand gazing up at him, eyes wide...so wide...drinking him in...wanting nothing more in all the world but to be here like this. Looking as she did now for him, for this man.

*For this man who is like none other in all the world. The man who, alone of all the men in all the world, has the power to make me feel as I feel now.*

She tried to remember—hopelessly, uselessly—what

she had just told herself. She was his daughter's teacher—
only that...

But how could she think that? How could she think
that as she stood there, so very close to him, feeling the
fall of her hair flowing down her back like a silken river,
feeling the soft folds of the skirts of her beautiful dress
brushing her bare legs, feeling the night air drift over
her shoulders, feeling the smooth material of her bodice
shape her rounded breasts?

She felt the silvered moonlight play upon her face,
knowing it enhanced the long-lashed smokiness of her
eyes and etched the contours of her delicate features,
highlighting the softness of her lips as she gazed up at
him, eyes wide, filled with all she felt.

Never before had she been so conscious of her body.
Never before had she felt she could do as she did now—
gaze upon a man whose strong, powerful physique and
whose shadowed face were always and for ever imprinted
on her consciousness.

In her breast she could feel her heart beating, and the
pulse at her throat was alive. She felt her lips parting as
if...as if...

'Oh, Jenna...' he breathed, and there was something
in his voice that was like a warning.

But was it a warning to her—or to himself?

'Jenna. Don't—'

There was a break in his voice, a sudden starkness in
his shadowed face as he seemed to draw back from her.
Her eyes distended, filling with dismay at his withdrawal.

She heard her voice, faint and faraway, whispering
his name. 'Evandro...'

All her yearning was in the sound of his name—all
that she could no longer deny, no longer withhold. From
the very first it had been so. And now... Now...

A rasp broke from him, and the flashing of his dark eyes was caught in the silvered moonlight. Something changed in his face... The lines around his mouth lessened, softened...

For one endless moment time stopped and the universe stopped—her heart stopped. He stood immobile, as if riven by the tension that was racking his strong body, keeping it imprisoned. Then, as though breaking free of bonds, he let his long lashes dip over his dark eyes and lowered his mouth to hers.

His kiss was cool and slow.

Her eyelids fluttered shut and she gave herself to him entirely, with all her being, as his mouth moved across hers softly, sensuously. She felt her heart turn over and over...

His hand closed about her waist, drawing her to him, and of their own accord her own hands lifted, pressing against the broad wall of his chest, feeling its muscled strength beneath her fingertips, her palms, delighting in it, glorying in it.

His kiss deepened and instinctively, willingly—oh, so willingly—her mouth opened to his, returning his deepening kiss, feeling the pleasure of his arousing touch lighting a spark within her. His free hand shaped her face, his thumb curving into the tender hollow behind her ear, fingers spearing gently into the fall of her hair as softly and as sensuously as his kiss...and just as wondrously arousing.

She leant into him, felt the hand at her waist splaying broadly, holding her to him as he kissed her, not cool now, but with a building sensuality that made her breathless, helpless... Wanting this...only this...

Nothing else existed in the world—only this moment now, in his arms, his embrace, with his mouth on hers.

He was taking her where she had never been—where she longed to go. Where she longed to be always and for ever.

And then, like a sudden blow, he pulled away from her, lifting his hand from her waist, lifting her hands away from him. Stepping back. Moving away.

She reeled, bereft, her eyes flying open, wild and strained. Her heart was beating wildly, hectically.

He towered over her, blocking the moon. 'Go to bed,' he said. His voice was harsh and rough. His expression was closed. 'Go to bed,' he said again. 'This never happened.'

She did not move. Could not. The solid stone of the paved terrace beneath her feet was cold and hard. As cold and hard as his voice. She felt her nails press into the palms of her hands, as if her nails were the tail of a scorpion, stinging her skin, wounding her flesh.

'This never happened—do you understand?'

His voice was a blade now, and something flashed across his face, flaring in his veiled eyes.

'I take full responsibility—it was my doing, not yours, so the blame is mine and the moon's and the stars'. It's the wine I've drunk and anything and everything else you can throw at me. Throw whatever you want—but go.'

She did not cry out or make a noise, nor any sound at all. Only turned and fled. Invisible once again.

# CHAPTER EIGHT

EVANDRO PRESSED THE accelerator, urgently wanting to be back in Turin, at his desk, as fast as the powerful car could take him there. A glance in the rear-view mirror showed him that his face was grim and bleak, as if an iron mask were over it.

*Dio*—how could he have done what he had? Been so reckless?

Although he had, he acknowledged, courted exactly this kind of danger right from the start.

*But I never thought it was a danger. Never thought that a woman I didn't look twice at could ever...*

Could ever what? Get under his skin little by little, slowly but surely, day after day?

He'd thought he was safe. But he had come to want more than their walks and their smiles and shared laughter. Had come to want her to stop concealing herself behind the protective cloak of invisibility.

*But it wasn't just protecting her—it was protecting me as well.*

That was the mocking irony of it. He had told himself he was doing it for *her* sake, not for his—his gift to her, to make her see herself as she could be, not as she thought she must be, blighted by what she had endured as a child.

He had shown her how beautiful she could be—and shown himself in the process.

And that fatal realisation had been his downfall.

*I should never have let her come back down after taking Amelie to bed. Never have been insane enough to take her out onto the moonlit terrace—never let her gaze at me with such longing in her eyes...*

He had sought to resist—but how could he have found the strength to do so? From the moment she had come down the staircase in that dress, revealed to him as she truly was, no longer hiding from the callous cruelty that had condemned her, he had felt danger pluck at him.

Oh, he had denied it, blanked it out, been a convivial, benevolent host at the tea party—the same relaxed, good-humoured conversationalist he'd come to be in their times together, enjoying her company as he always had. But underneath, a tide had been turning, an awareness had been pulsing, making him want to look at her, take her in, notice every part of how hauntingly lovely she now looked.

*A woodland sprite. Lifting her lovely eyes to the stars, to the moon... To me.*

And he had kissed her. And been lost.

Lost to all warnings...all danger.

Lost to the danger that he had only truly recognised when she was close, in his arms. The danger that had made him wrest himself from her, set her aside, say such harsh words to her. Send her fleeing.

Leaving him standing there, cursing the moon and the stars and the night, and above all himself.

And cursing the cruel chains Berenice still bound him with...

* * *

'Papà has gone!' Amelie's voice was mournful and unhappy, and she was unwilling to settle back into the routine of daily lessons. 'Back to Turin.'

'He has to work, Amelie—he cannot be here all the time,' Jenna answered steadily, though it was an effort to do so.

Misery filled her. And self-recrimination—bitter and galling—at her own folly. Clinging to him when he'd kissed her, kissing him back with such ardency—only for him to push her away from him, reject what had happened.

She had to reject it too. For his sake—and for hers—she had to consign it to nothing more than a tormenting memory and then starve that memory.

But how? Oh, dear God, how? How could she ever forget? Forget being in his arms...forget his kiss? Forget everything that she had felt and longed for? Forget the touch of the man she had fallen in love with—

She froze, horror washing over her. No—no, that could not be. It couldn't!

That was a folly that was unendurable.

And yet it was as undeniable as the sun in the sky.

She turned her face to the window as the truth hammered into her, not wanting Amelie to see her expression, knowing her face was likely drained and whitened in shock.

*I love him. I love him and I can't stop it, or turn it off, or make it unhappen. I love him and it is unbearable that I do. Unbearable to love a man who pushed me from him—sent me away.*

Yet bear it she must—what else could she do?

One thing only.

She set her face, still likely white as bone, knowing

that all she could do now was endure and return again to being the person she had been all along. She would retreat into her safe place, where she would keep herself safe from more rejection—retreat into her familiar, self-effacing invisibility.

Evandro stood, his eyes half-lidded, before the unlit fire in the gilded salon that was seldom opened except when there was company.

As there was now.

The dozen or so guests he'd brought back with him from Turin filled the room, chattering and loud, knocking back his champagne with music blaring. The French doors were open wide to the terrace beyond, which was lit up like a stage. Several couples were out there now, dancing to the throbbing music that pulsed throughout the house and across the gardens.

'*Tesoro—mio caro!* Don't stand there like a grand *seigneur* of old. Come and dance!'

The woman gliding up to him, champagne glass in hand, her tight dress emphasising every lush curve, was well-known to him—if physical intimacy counted as knowing someone well.

*Sometimes one can know a person well when a harmony exists between them that has nothing to do with how long one has known them...*

He pushed the thought from his mind. It served no purpose except to reinforce why he was doing what he was doing now—filling the *palazzo* with people he didn't like and didn't care about in order to set a distance—a vital, essential distance—between himself and the person he did care about.

*To protect her from me—and me from her.*

As it had when he'd raced back to Turin, a sense

of mocking irony assailed him at the thought that he should need such protection. The kind of protection that the woman currently inviting him into her arms could provide.

Bianca Ingrani was safe specifically because he didn't desire her. Unlike...

His eyes searched the room and found their target.

She was sitting on a chair, right at the back of the room, knees pressed together, hands folded in her lap. Her eyes were on Amelie who, overexcited by all the partying going on, was whirling around to the music, applauded by some of the guests who were making a fuss of her.

He frowned with displeasure at the outfit his daughter was wearing—another of her mother's dire choices. How had the child been allowed to don such execrable clothes tonight?

His condemning gaze went to the person who had permitted it. Her face was still—as still as the rest of her.

*Invisible. She's gone invisible again.*

His mouth twisted.

*And can I blame her?*

The question was as rhetorical as it was mocking—and the target was still himself. Always himself.

The woman he had once passed his nights with during his celebratory indulgences post-divorce followed the direction of his glance. Her expression changed.

'Who on earth is that?' Bianca exclaimed. Then her eyes went to Amelie. 'Oh, some kind of nanny... I see,' she said dismissively. Her voice turned saccharine, like sticky honey. 'How adorable your little daughter is, Evandro. I so want to meet her. Just in case...' she threw a heavily flirtatious look at her former lover '... I ever get to be her step-*mamma*.'

He watched with cynical eyes as Bianca went up to

Amelie, cooing over her. While she did so, his eyes went to Jenna.

He said her name. Low, inaudible to all. Yet her eyes, which had been fixed on Amelie, then on Bianca, turned to his. But though they were open, they were closed.

Closed to him.

Closed to him for ever.

*As they must be. I can allow nothing else.*

He went on looking at her, his face as closed as her gaze. She sat only a handful of metres away from him, and yet she was on the other side of the world.

A cry pierced the noise around him and he turned. It had not been a cry of pain, or distress—only one of anger.

'You clumsy thing! My dress! You knocked right into me with your idiotic whirling.'

His eyes shot round to see a champagne glass rolling on the floor, its contents splashed across Bianca's tight ivory silk dress. Amelie was standing stricken, her face as white as Bianca's dress and puckering with tears. He started to move, but someone else was there before him, swooping down on Amelie, taking her hand, holding it fast.

'It's way past bedtime, poppet. You're so tired you're wobbly!'

He saw Jenna look at Bianca, whose over-made-up face still flashed with fury, all coy pretence of Amelie being 'adorable' gone.

'I do apologise,' he heard Jenna tell the other woman, her voice low and tight. 'I should have been keeping an eye on Amelie. I hope your dress can be cleaned. Amelie—come along.'

He watched her take the little girl off, out of the room. Though he had stood so close, she had not looked at him.

As if she could not bear to.

* * *

Jenna lay staring at the ceiling in her bedroom. Midnight had come and gone, and she could still hear the clash of laughter and conversation, the bass throb of the music. It was coming through the floorboards, throbbing into her head, into her misery.

The misery of seeing him again—the man she had so stupidly fallen in love with.

She had watched him roar up to the *palazzo* that afternoon in that gleaming monster car of his, followed by a cavalcade of cars and limos that had disgorged guests like birds of paradise, gorgeous in their couture clothes, their designer sunglasses, their glamour and their glitz. Talking and laughing with abandon, like noisy parakeets, they had streamed into the *palazzo*, taking it over.

And Evandro, the *seigneur*, the millionaire...billionaire? Who knew what he was, besides a member of an elite world that she was not part of and never could be?

She screwed her face up, flinching at the way she had thought herself lovely in his eyes when she'd worn that green dress, how she had glowed, thinking about his likening her to a woodland sprite...

When all along she had still been invisible. As invisible as she had been this evening, sitting there in her corner, unnoticed and ignored.

*How could I possibly compare to that stunningly beautiful woman who was all over him?*

She felt her heart harden. However stunningly beautiful she was, she'd upset Amelie horribly with her sudden anger. Amelie had been tearful as Jenna had hurried her upstairs, as she'd got her out of that frightful outfit she'd so wanted to wear. And Jenna had had to listen to her anguished whispers as she'd got the overtired, upset little girl into her nightgown.

'I spilt Maman's wine, once…and it was red wine… and it stained her dress…and she was so angry with me…just like that lady.' The little face had puckered again, tears welling. 'I don't like that lady—I don't! *I don't!*'

Jenna had hugged her, aching for her—and for herself. 'No one likes that lady, poppet,' she'd said. 'She's a horrid lady.'

She'd pulled Amelie's nightie over her head, guiding her towards her bed.

'Papà likes her,' Amelie had said, climbing in and looking up at Jenna, her face still anxious.

Jenna had smoothed back her hair, tucked her in, turned down her bedside light so that it only gave a glow, and stayed until sleep had taken the overwrought child. Then she'd gone back to her own room on leaden feet, hearing Amelie's parting words tolling in her brain.

*'Papà likes her.'*

She heard those words again, and then heard, like a bleak counterpoint against it, her own word—the single word that repeated over and over again in her head.

*Fool.*

Because what other word could describe her but that? She who had never been good enough for anyone at all…

Least of all the man she had fallen in love with.

Evandro slid open the sash window of his bedroom. At last, the blessed hush of the night lapped all around him, that infernal music silenced. There was only the soft, incessant murmur of the cicadas—the eternal chorus of the Mediterranean night, lifted to the heavens. The same silver moon that had lit the night when he had taken the woman he must not desire into his arms hung over the deserted, darkened terrace and gardens, but it was waning now.

He knew he must not take Jenna in his arms again. However much he ached to do so.

In his head tolled the ever-present warning his lawyer had given him.

He sliced the window shut, knowing that what he should do now was go to Bianca—all too willing and waiting for him.

*If I spend the night with her—resume my affair with her—that will put what I cannot have, dare not have, behind me for ever.*

But revulsion filled him at the thought of Bianca's lush embrace. She was not the woman he wanted.

Bleak-faced he retreated to his solitary bed to stare at the ceiling, knowing sleep would elude him, wanting what he could not have and must not want.

Seeking the strength to stop. Failing.

For two long, endless days Jenna watched and endured. Doors opened and closed ceaselessly, and voices— overloud and piercing—filled the *palazzo*. She heard cars come and go, engines roaring, gravel scattering under tyres, music playing inside and out, heels clattering on the marble stairs and floors.

The staff were being kept on their toes, bringing food and wine and champagne, fetching and carrying. And over all the noise, cutting through it like a scimitar, were the deep tones of the man she had been such a fool over.

She tried to ignore it all—to focus only on keeping Amelie undistracted by the house parties going on all around them. After all, she reminded herself with bitter self-recrimination, Amelie was her pupil and the sole reason for her presence here. She must never forget that.

*As I did so fatally that night.*

Mortification burned in her. How had she thought that a man like Evandro Rocceforte might look twice at her when he had sultry beauties like Bianca Ingrani to bewitch him?

*But surely he would never think of marrying her? Not when he saw how harsh she was to Amelie?*

That was her sole comfort. After the incident with Bianca, Amelie did not want to join in any more with all that was going on downstairs, so Jenna did not have to witness Evandro and Bianca together.

Except in her tormented imagination.

There, it was impossible, in her misery, to banish images of them together…

Evandro stood out on the gravelled carriage sweep, watching the last of the motorcade heading off. Relief filled him. They were gone, the whole damn crowd of them. Taking Bianca with them and leaving him with one resolve. A resolve that had formed and then hardened with every moment since their arrival.

*I brought them here—brought Bianca here—with one purpose only: to sever myself from the woman I must not desire.*

But the attempt had been useless, instead serving only to have the opposite effect.

In his mind's eye he saw Jenna again, sitting there in the salon like a ghost…lost to him.

*But I will not lose her. I will not. I refuse to turn away from her.*

His benighted marriage had ruined enough of his life. For this, for what was happening now, he wished Berenice and all her lawyers to hell, despite her threats.

*I'll seize what happiness I can while I can. Cost me what it may—I'll pay the price.*

Resolve strengthening, he strode indoors with only one destination in mind.

He vaulted the stairs as if the devil himself were goading him on—and laughing as he did so.

But he did not care for devils—nor their mocking laughter.

# CHAPTER NINE

'AMELIE, YOU STILL have another page of sums. They won't go away until you've done them.'

Jenna's voice was sympathetic, but firm. Like Amelie, she'd heard the noise of the departing house party—the loud goodbyes and the cars disappearing into the distance—but now it had gone quiet.

'Can I not go and find my *papà* now?' Amelie asked plaintively. 'Now that all the people have gone?'

'He'll ask for you or come and see you when he's ready,' Jenna replied, and her reluctant pupil sighed.

Then suddenly she sat up straight, turning her head towards the schoolroom door. Footsteps, rapid and distinctive, sounded outside on the landing.

'Papà!' cried Amelie, ecstatic.

Jenna had only a second to prepare. To steel herself. Then the door was flying open and Evandro was striding in.

Amelie launched herself at him and he caught her up, swinging her around in a bear hug, then put her back on her feet.

'Time for a swim,' he said. 'Be off and get your things.'

Amelie needed no urging, and hurtled happily out of the room.

Evandro straightened, heading straight for Jenna with

purpose in his stride, gold glinting in his slate eyes. Catching her face in his hands, he turned it up to him. And then he crushed her mouth with his.

'Who's for ice cream?' Evandro's question rang out over the swimming pool.

'Me! Me!'

Amelie scrambled out of the water, running up to him where he stood, three towering cornets clustered in his hand, freshly scooped from the freezer in the kitchens. Happily seizing the one he offered her, she settled down on a sun lounger to consume it.

'That just leaves us,' he said, lowering himself down on the lounger beside Jenna and handing her one of the two cones he still held.

She took it, knowing her eyes were glowing. She had felt as if she were glowing—as if the sun itself was radiating from inside her—since Evandro had swept her up into that crushing, possessing kiss.

Dear God, could it really be true? Had it really happened? Had she gone, in a single moment, from misery and anguish and hopelessness to radiant happiness?

But it had happened, and it was true—entirely true!

His kiss had been everything she could have dreamt of. And as he'd released her he'd cupped her cheek with his hand. Pooled his gold-shot gaze with hers.

'Forgive me,' he'd said.

And in that instant, in that moment, it had been all that needed to be said. The rest of his apology had been in his eyes, in the clasp of her hand in his, in the smile playing at his mouth, as it did now, as he watched her catch at the fast-melting ice-cream.

She asked for no more. No more than this. This happiness so profound that it was in every pore of her being, every cell in her body. She did not question it or examine it—only accepted it. With all her heart.

Evandro leant back against the trunk of the ancient chestnut tree that edged the woods above the *palazzo* gardens. The afternoon had become close and sultry, so they had brought a picnic high tea up here to the woods, where there was more shade from the oppressive heat. A little way away Amelie was playing teddy bears' picnic, with leaves for plates and acorns for cups, absorbed in her game.

He was glad of it—it allowed him to give more attention to Jenna.

He drew her back against him, leaving the remains of their picnic on the rug.

'She's happy,' Jenna said, looking across to Amelie.

There was a warmth in her voice, a fondness, that made it sweet for him.

'And so am I,' he said, nestling her under his shoulder. 'Totally and entirely happy.'

Because happiness was what he was going to claim. The happiness he had never thought would come his way. The happiness that had been bestowed upon him by this special woman—his very own woodland sprite...as he had called her from the first.

He smiled to think of it, their first encounter that had started him on this path and led him here, to this. This happiness he was claiming now. A summer's happiness... that nothing, surely, could blight...

From far away, through the too-still haze, across the heat-pooled valley where the hot gold sunshine was slowly turning to molten bronze, came a low, scarcely audible tremor on the windless air.

Amelie's fair head lifted from where she was playing. 'What was that, Papà?' A thread of anxiety was in her voice.

'Thunder,' he said. 'This heat must break, so a storm is coming.' His eyes went upward, beyond the leafy bower under which they sat. Clouds were massing, and he could feel the static building in the atmosphere.

'Are you sure it's going to be a storm?' Jenna sat up, looking out over the vista.

Amelie clambered to her feet. 'I don't like storms,' she said fearfully.

Jenna got up as well. 'Evandro, perhaps we'd better go back. Woods are not the safest places in a thunderstorm.'

She started to close up the picnic basket, and Evandro levered himself to his feet.

'It may pass by,' he said. 'The storm may never break—'

But Amelie was already setting off, teddy bears clutched to her chest, and Jenna was following with rug and cushions, leaving him the picnic basket. The sky was darkening overhead now, the static mounting, and the bronze sun had disappeared behind heavy clouds.

He hurried them all back to the *palazzo*, welcoming the failing daylight, whatever the cause. After all, when night came it would, he knew, bring him his heart's desire...

Night meshed them in, and the airless stillness of the dark embraced them as they embraced each other. Evandro's strong body arched over hers and it was wonderful to her...wondrous that he desired her, was claiming her as he was now.

Joy filled her and she pulled his mouth to hers, feeling the arousing pleasure of his deepening kiss. And it was a pleasure that was only beginning, that grew more and yet more as his hand gently but insistently slid between her thighs, which slackened to his caressing touch. His other hand moved between her breasts, his skilled fingers ministering to them so that wave after wave of a pleasure she had never tasted before brought little sighs and catches from her throat.

His mouth lifted from hers, descending to one breast and then the other in turn, engendering yet more catches in her throat and then, quite distinctly, a moan of pleasure so exquisite her eyes could only flutter shut with it as his hand, parting her thighs, found what it was seeking with infinite skill and slow, sure movements.

She knew, with an uplifting of her heart, that he was making her ready for him. Her moans came again, her spine arching now, hands spearing into the nape of his strong neck as his dark head lowered to her ripened breasts.

And then, as her pleasure mounted and mounted more, and a restlessness started to fill her, making her legs strain outwards, it was as if her body, driven by an instinct older than time itself, was readying itself to receive him.

He was lifting his head from her breasts, kissing her mouth once more, before easing his long, powerful body so that with a movement so smooth she did not realise it was about to happen he sought his way within her. His control was absolute—she knew that—and she knew it was for her sake that he was bending every fibre of his will to make this moment the way it should be…a wondrous union of flesh with flesh.

And she took him into her, holding him, cradling him within her body, within the circle of her arms.

He lay still for a little while, as her body accommodated itself to his, before slowly, infinitely slowly, and infinitely arousingly, he started to move within her. He stroked her hair and his hand, she realised, was trembling very slightly as he took his weight on his arm, not wanting, she knew, to crush her.

Then, his eyes holding hers in the dim light of the night, he lowered his mouth to kiss her softly, exquisitely. Once more she felt as if a glow were starting up inside her—a warmth, a heat, a pleasure so extraordinary, so intense, welling up and melting through her. It was a pleasure she had never known nor imagined, consuming her whole body, her whole being. Wonder filled her, lifted her spine, parted her lips...

And it went on and on, flowing through her to every extremity of her body, this molten fusion of her being combined with his.

With the dimmest part of her consciousness she realised that he was moving faster within her, that his torso was lifting from her, his muscled thighs straining now against hers, his body rearing up, head thrown back. She felt their bodies meld into each other, fusing in the heat that was making them one single, searing flesh.

Did she cry out? She didn't know—knew only that it was the most glorious moment of her life, and that she was giving, and had been given, a gift whose worth was infinite.

Love poured from her—and if it was a love he'd never asked for, never sought, it did not matter. Because it was her gift, freely given, in return for this burning moment of union, of ecstatic joy.

His arms enfolded her and she felt the sheen of his exhaustion on his cooling skin. She knew it was the same for her as he drew her close into his encircling embrace. She felt his breath, warm and ragged, at her shoulder.

'Did I hurt you? For all the world I would not have—'

She heard the tremor in his low voice and caught his hand, curving it into hers, turning and lifting her head so it was resting against his broad chest, allowing her to brush his lips with reassurance.

'You will never hurt me,' she said.

And in her eyes, though it was too dark for him to see, was all the love she had for him and always would.

It was in the early hours of the morning that the storm rolled in, with thunderous clouds unleashing a torrent of rain upon the *palazzo* and lightning jagging the night. The tempest was silent at first, felt only through the charged static of the atmosphere, then it was ripping through the sky with a belligerent crackling roar of deafening thunder and noise.

Evandro levered himself up from the bed and strode to the window to lower the sash, shutting it against the driving rain exploding out of the heavens, pounding down upon the stone paving of the terrace below like bullets as another fork of lightning sliced across the sky and another thunderclap crashed overhead.

*'Amelie!'*

Jenna's anxious voice made him turn. 'I'll go to her.'

He seized his bathrobe, belting it swiftly around him, and left the room, returning moments later.

'Sound asleep,' he announced.

He discarded his robe, getting back into bed and wrapping Jenna in his arms. It was all that he wanted.

Certainty filled him. And defiance too.

He had made his declaration—claimed Jenna for his own. This woman who was everything that Berenice was not, nor ever could be with her cankered soul. Jenna—whose clear-seeing eyes, kindness and compassion, honesty and sincerity, quiet ways and subtle beauty, could wash away the taint of his accursed marriage and draw from him all its poison.

He would not turn away from her again.

He did not care—*would* not care.

If there was danger, so be it.

If there was risk, he would face it.

But until they came—*if* they came—he would have all the happiness that surely life owed him after so many bitter, wasted years.

All the happiness that the woman in his arms could gift him.

Jenna—his sweet Jenna—his own, his blessing and his bounty.

He folded her to him, feeling her soft, warm body moulding to his, hearing her gentle breathing easing into sleep once more.

The storm started to die away as swiftly as it had broken, thunder descending to a mere rumbling, lightning to mere flickers. His arms tightened around her, holding her close, so close.

It was the only place he wanted her to be.

With him.

His breathing slowed, his limbs becoming heavy, and sleep washed over him...with Jenna safe in his arms.

Outside, jagging down from the fleeing storm clouds, a fork of lightning more vivid than anything before illuminated the woodland above the gardens in lurid, livid light.

But the crack of thunder that came an instant later was not the only deafening sound to be heard.

At the edge of the woods the chestnut tree Evandro and Jenna had sat under only a few hours ago split violently in two, severed by the final vicious knifing of the storm.

# CHAPTER TEN

'WELL, IT WILL save on the watering,' Evandro said cheerfully, surveying the rain-battered gardens.

His eyes went to Jenna, bathing her in a visual caress, and the sight of her standing next to Amelie out on the still-damp terrace, where the bright, clear morning air was sparkling and fresh, lifted his heart.

*I have them both—Jenna and Amelie. All that I could ever want.*

'The world new-made,' he heard her say now, a smile at her lips.

*The world new-made.*

Her words echoed inside him, resonating with a clarity and an intensity that crystallised all that he felt.

*I have made it new—made the world new for myself...*

Clean and clear and untainted by the world he had lived in with Berenice.

But he would not remember her or think of her. The long shadow she had cast over his life, blighting it, must never reach here...not now.

He shook his head free of the thought, placing his arm around Jenna's slender shoulders, drawing her against him and dropping a kiss upon her head. Then, taking Amelie's hand in his, he held it tight in a silent vow never to let it go.

They were his. The woman he had claimed as his and the child he would always protect and cherish.

For an instant, as the vow formed so vehemently in his head, he saw a shadow pass across the face of the bright sun. Heard—as if in an ugly echo, summoned by his unwelcome thought of Berenice—her mocking, vengeful laugh...

He banished it.

He squeezed Jenna's shoulder, and Amelie's hand.

'So, what shall we do this wonderful day?' he asked genially, his heart glowing within him. 'Shall we have another pool day, or drive off somewhere? And, if so, where? And if we stay here, shall we have another tea party and dress up in our best again? Or have a dinner party, and even more dressing up?'

Amelie caught on the last option he'd suggested. 'Dressing up!' she cried enthusiastically. 'Oh, Papà, can we dress up like Miss Jenna said? Like the children at her school did?'

He smiled down at her. 'Why not?' He nodded. 'Will you be the silver fairy you described?' Then his eyes went to Jenna, softening. 'Though that should be you— *you* are the good fairy in my life.' His eyes held hers. 'Breaking the evil spell...'

Her hand lifted to his face, her eyes full of warmth. 'And you, Evandro, are my Prince Charming,' she said.

He gave a crack of laughter, dropping a light kiss upon her mouth, then ushered them all to the breakfast table. As they settled down around it he reached for the coffee pot and another brilliant idea struck him.

'You know what I think?' he asked. 'How about taking a holiday? At the seaside? We'll go next week.'

Amelie's eyes brightened at the magic word. 'Yes... *yes*! Seaside! Seaside!' she exclaimed excitedly.

'You've done it now,' Jenna murmured, smiling. 'No going back on it now that you've said it.'

He grinned. 'I have no intention of going back on it—on anything.'

No, there would be no going back now. And nothing that might yet come would threaten his new-found, wondrous happiness.

*But it might not come.*

That was what he must cling to.

The same reckless defiance that had filled him as he'd sent Bianca and her friends packing—the defiance that had steeled him with ruthless resolve and sent him racing up the stairs to stride into Amelie's schoolroom and claim the woman he wanted, despite all his own warnings to himself, now filled him again.

His gaze swept between them, Jenna and Amelie. Then moved out beyond them, across the sunlit gardens to where, at the edge of the wood, the burnt and stricken chestnut, severed by that final lightning bolt, lurched brokenly, blackened and crippled.

Victim of the storm that had broken overhead, destroying all that defied it.

'This is bliss!'

Jenna leant back, legs outstretched, on the warm, soft sand, her arms straight behind her, her palms supporting her weight. Her hair was held back by a colourful bandeau and she lifted her face to the sun.

But then, all of life was bliss these days. How could it be anything else?

Her eyes went to Evandro, lounging on the sand beside her, and her insides gave a little flip. Evandro in a business suit was powerful and formidable. Evandro in chinos, an open-necked shirt and deck shoes was darkly, magnetically attractive. But Evandro lying as he was now, on his side, a hand supporting his head, his magnificent body completely on show apart from the bathing shorts he was wearing, was simply…breathtaking.

'You look like a fifties film star,' he was saying now, his eyes lazily appreciative. 'But twice as glamorous.'

His eyes held hers, and in them was a look that made Jenna wish they were not on the private beach at this extremely swish family resort in the Cinque Terre, but in their own bedroom.

To deflect her thoughts, she looked towards the sea's edge, where Amelie was playing with another little girl she'd palled up with. They were busy building a sandcastle together.

'It's so wonderful to see Amelie so happy,' she said warmly. Her eyes went back to Evandro and that warmth was still in them. Her gaze softened even more. 'You are a *wonderful* father, Evandro—you would do anything for her.'

There was a catch in her voice as she spoke. She was remembering her own father, who had done nothing for her—never loved or wanted her, only ignored and resented her. She dropped her eyes, not wanting to remember.

And then Amelie was running up to them, asking if she and Luisa could go and get ice creams from the beach bistro.

'If Luisa is allowed by her parents,' said Evandro, and the two children hared off to where Luisa's parents, with a smaller toddler in tow, were sitting on sun loungers in the shade of a parasol.

The mother nodded at her daughter's request, smiling across at Jenna and Evandro as the girls ran off to the bistro.

'You two have a lovely little daughter,' the woman called across to them. 'With excellent manners!'

'I return the compliment entirely,' Evandro assured her.

Jenna saw the other woman's eyes linger a moment on Evandro and could not begrudge her—because his physique *was* perfect. Powerful and smoothly muscled, long-legged and...

She ran out of adjectives, but knew she did not need them. She had the real thing, so words just weren't important.

There were other words that lingered in her head instead.

*'You two have a lovely little daughter.'*

They echoed again now, and with them came the memory of how she'd stood out on the terrace at the *palazzo*, watching the sun set with Amelie and Evandro.

*Like a family...*

Emotion welled in her. It had not been true then, and she'd berated herself for the thought.

*But are we now...a family?*

If wishing could make it so, then it would be true. But though she might love Evandro, and though he might desire her—wonderful as it was that he did—was that enough to make her dream come true?

*And is it his dream?*

The question lingered in her head like a crab pincering its claws on her flesh. And for all the happiness and joy that flooded her day after golden day, night after passionate night, it lingered still.

Unanswered.

Unanswerable.

After their fortnight at the seaside—leisurely days on the beach interspersed with days exploring the charm and delights of the famed Cinque Terre, visiting the impossibly pretty harbour villages with their painted houses climbing up steep cliffs, lunching at open-air trattorias, taking boat trips out to sea to spot dolphins and flying fish—Evandro announced that he could no longer postpone looking in at his office.

So they drove north, inland to Turin, after Amelie and Luisa had vowed faithfully to message each other daily, as proof of their enduring friendship.

In Turin, Jenna settled down with Amelie in Evandro's ferociously modernistic apartment, using the time he was at work to resume her pupil's studies. Evandro pitched in as well, helping his daughter with maths every evening upon his return from the office.

'Imagine if I couldn't do my sums correctly,' he quizzed Amelie. 'I wouldn't be able to tell if I was making any money at all—or, far worse, if the bridges and dams Rocceforte Industriale builds would fall down!'

'You're so good with her,' Jenna said to him fondly, when the maths book had finally been put away and Amelie had been released to play her favourite computer game online with Luisa before dinner. 'A natural-born father. It's clearly in the genes.'

She kissed him lightly on the cheek, wanting him to be free of the doubts he'd once had that he could be a good father after so much separation from his daughter.

But he did not reply—only got to his feet, his expression suddenly shuttered.

A moment later it was gone, replaced with a smile.

'So, what gastronomical delights are in store for tonight?' he asked, and there was only good-humoured enquiry in his face.

'I thought I might do something completely different,' Jenna answered solemnly and straight-faced, knowing the limit of her culinary skills. 'Pasta in a totally different shape from last night's.'

He laughed, strolling into the kitchen to the huge fridge to fetch himself a beer and settling down at the breakfast bar to oversee the preparation of the sauce she would painstakingly assemble from vegetables freshly purchased that morning.

It was a pleasure to venture out with Amelie—not just to explore the busy, bustling city together, with its mix of architectural styles, boulevards and covered arcades, but for the fun of feeling like an Italian housewife doing the daily shop—confirming to her, if she needed confirmation, that all her joy stemmed from being with Evandro and his daughter, enjoying these ordinary, domestic days.

*Like a family.*

As she added freshly chopped beef tomatoes to the sauce and stirred them in, the ache for it to be so for ever rose piercingly within her. Perhaps one day he would love her as she loved him...

*And one day he will see a future that has me in it—a happy future for him and Amelie, after all the misery his marriage put him through.*

But would it come, that day? *Could* it come?

The sound of Evandro's phone ringing was an interruption she welcomed to thoughts that were as fruitless as they were aching.

Evandro lifted his phone from the breakfast bar, expecting it to be the project manager he'd asked to report in that evening. But the call was from someone quite different.

'Evandro, *cara*, my spies tell me you are back in town!'

The sultry tones were breathed across the ether, and

he gave a silent curse that he had not checked the caller before answering.

'Bianca,' he replied evenly, keeping his voice neutral. He was aware that Jenna had stopped stirring the fragrant contents of the saucepan and had half turned, before freezing.

'You must have been bored out of your mind in the country once we'd all gone,' Bianca was purring now. 'Come over for drinks—and anything else you might feel like…' She trailed off seductively.

'That isn't going to be possible,' he said.

He kept his tone somewhere between even and repressive. He'd prefer, if he could, to get out of this gracefully. He caught at the one thing he could say to put Bianca off—other than the truth. Which was none of her damn business.

*No one's business except mine and Jenna's.*

The defiance with which he'd claimed the happiness he was now enjoying with Jenna filled him again. As for Bianca Ingrani—she was swiftly dismissible.

'I've got Amelie with me,' he told her.

Bianca's annoyance was obvious. 'What a shame,' she said. 'Of course, there are always agency nannies who can be summoned to babysit,' she said hopefully.

'Thank you—but I already have someone. The woman you took to be Amelie's nanny—Jenna,' he heard himself reply. Then cursed himself.

*Accidenti.* Why had he given anything away to the likes of Bianca Ingrani?

'Jenna?' Suspicion twisted in Bianca's voice at his casual use of her forename. 'You brought that girl to your *apartment*?'

And suddenly, impatiently, Evandro was fed up with it—with Bianca's persistence in trying to renew their affair. He wanted to get rid of her in the quickest way possible, even if it was none of her business.

'Yes,' he said tightly, 'Jenna is with me here.' He took a breath, urging her to get the message. 'Bianca, I'm sorry if you had hopes we might get back together again, but that isn't possible. I've moved on.' He made his voice conciliatory, complimentary, for courtesy's sake. 'Our time together was good, and I wish you all the very best—and a better man for you than me.'

He rang off, wanting only to be done with her. He turned back to Jenna, who was stirring the sauce again, but with jerky, mechanical motions. He set down his phone before winding his arms around her waist from behind, nuzzling her neck.

'Relax,' he said. 'I've given Bianca her marching orders.' He drew her close and felt her lean back against him, her muscles relaxing.

'She's so incredibly beautiful,' he heard her say, a little wistfully.

'Not to me—not any more,' he replied. 'And besides...' his voice hardened '...do you seriously imagine I would want to have anything to do with a woman who could speak as angrily as she did to Amelie at the *palazzo*? Upsetting her the way she did? No,' he finished decisively, 'Bianca is over and done with. She's nothing to me now.'

He turned Jenna around to him, not wanting her worrying a second longer about Bianca Ingrani, kissing her lightly at first, then more deeply, feeling passion build. But reluctantly he relinquished her. Now was not the moment—especially when Amelie's voice piped up from the doorway.

'Is dinner ready? Can I grate the cheese? Luisa and I were searching for unicorns—she found one and I found two!'

She babbled on happily, fetching parmesan from the huge fridge and sitting herself on one of the tall stools at the breakfast bar to start grating. Evandro reached for his half-consumed beer and fetched a bottle of chilled white wine from the wine fridge, pouring glasses for Jenna and himself as she put the fresh pasta on to cook.

An everyday, cosy, domestic scene…the three of them at dinner, convivial, affectionate and united.

*What I never had with Berenice.*

Once, at the start of his marriage, he had thought—hoped—that it might be so. Before those futile hopes had been destroyed.

His ex had destroyed everything—everything she had power over.

His eyes rested now on Amelie, busy with her grating, and then on Jenna, still at the stove. A chill plucked at him.

*What else will she seek to destroy, that woman who cursed my life?*

But he knew—he knew just what she would want to destroy next.

If she ever found out…

# CHAPTER ELEVEN

THE *PALAZZO* WAS warm and welcoming when they returned a fortnight later. Evandro had interspersed his
work with showing Jenna and Amelie the sights of the
region, from the rich Piedmontese countryside surrounding Turin to the splendours of the Alpine lakes and mountains beyond, making a second holiday of it.

Signora Farrafacci was welcoming, too, and all the
other staff.

Amelie ran upstairs with Loretta and Maria to show
them her holiday souvenirs and give them the presents
she'd bought for them—a carved wooden donkey each
from the seaside, and a stylish scarf from a very upmarket fashion house in Turin.

The scarves had not been the only items purchased
there—Evandro had indulged Amelie in some judiciously
selected frills and Jenna, too, had been the recipient of
his indulgence.

She had yielded to his insistence on enlarging her
wardrobe with clothes she could never have afforded on
her teacher's salary—even the generous one he was paying her—for two reasons only: to look her very best for
him, and to see his eyes light up when she wore the beautiful outfits he'd lavished on her.

A homecoming feast awaited them on their first night

back at the *palazzo*. And as she walked into the dining room with Amelie, her eyes went straight to Evandro, resplendent in a tuxedo for the occasion. Jenna felt a flush of pleasure go through her as his eyes swept over her, knowing that the beautiful evening gown she was wearing—dusky pink, cut on the bias—did things for her slender figure that were only and entirely for his benefit.

He kissed her hand with bowing gallantry. *'Bellissima,'* he murmured, his voice husky, his eyes speaking volumes. Then, tearing his gaze away, he dropped it to Amelie. 'And you, too, *carina*!' he exclaimed, and made a performance of kissing Amelie's hand as well, with smacking kisses which made her giggle.

Amelie's dress was pink, too, but pale as a rosebud, with a little bolero jacket.

'Which of us is prettier, Papà?' Amelie's voice piped up. 'You have to choose between us!'

Jenna glanced at Evandro, expecting him to make some jocular remark about the impossibility of his daughter's demand. But it did not come. Instead there was something in his face, just for a fleeting second, that made her suddenly go still.

It lasted only a moment, making her think she had imagined it, and then he was turning to fill their glasses with champagne and highly diluted Buck's Fizz for Amelie.

'To coming home!' he proclaimed.

The word *home*—so simple, so powerful—resonated in Jenna's head.

*Let this be home—oh, sweet heaven, let this be home.*

Home for ever, with the little girl she had come to love and the man she always would…

Longing filled her hope-filled heart. A heart that would surely break if she hoped in vain.

* * *

Evandro hung up the phone with satisfaction. He'd just booked Amelie into the summer holiday camp run by the convent school where she would be starting in the autumn. It would do her good to meet some of her future fellow pupils, as well as enjoy all the activities provided at the camp.

He had another motive for sending her too—a much more selfish motive. It would give him undivided access to Jenna. He would still have to pay attention to his work, of course—his responsibilities were too great to ignore—but other than that... He found himself wanting to take advantage of all the time he had left with her.

With sudden restlessness, he got to his feet. Though it was good—*very* good—to be back at the *palazzo*, he felt an impulse, powerful and compelling, to set off again. Somewhere far away, remote... Australia, New Zealand, the South Seas, even.

*Just the three of us—Amelie, Jenna and me. Somewhere far, far away, beyond the reach of—*

A light tap at the library door made him start. It was his housekeeper, coming in with his usual mid-morning coffee.

'Thank you.' He made himself smile, wanting his unwelcome thoughts banished.

He took the tray from her to deposit it on his desk and resumed his chair, but she did not leave.

'Is there something else, Signora Farrafacci?' he enquired courteously. There seemed to be an air of expectation about her, and her smile was fulsome.

'I just want to say,' she opened, 'how very much I—and all the staff—hope that for once all those pesky paparazzi are right. *We* would certainly welcome it!'

Evandro frowned. 'Paparazzi?' he said blankly.

'Normally, of course,' his housekeeper continued, 'I ignore all those rubbishy articles.' She gave a dismissive sniff. 'But in this case... Well...' her expression softened '...*such* a nice young lady, Signorina Jenna, and a *much* better choice to be the Signora Rocceforte you *deserve* after all you've been through—and poor little Amelie.' She drew breath, nodding. 'I've said quite enough for now—I'll leave you to your work.'

She sailed out, oblivious to the bomb she had just exploded in her employer's face.

As she closed the door behind her Evandro felt himself very slowly unfreeze. But it was an unfreezing that was like boiling oil being poured through his veins.

After his divorce he'd become inured to the prurient interest of the tabloids as he'd celebrated his newly single freedom. Bianca, he knew, had actively fed them stories about their affair, tipping the paparazzi off as to where he and she might be hitting the nightspots in Turin, Milan and Rome, angling things so that one day she might be described not coyly as his 'constant companion' but as his '*fidenzata*'—fiancée.

His mind raced urgently. He'd known the danger he was courting in claiming Jenna for himself right from the start—known the risks. But he'd overridden them, resolving—even after all his warnings to himself—that they were worth taking for what Jenna bestowed upon him. What he so wanted.

He'd done his best to minimise those risks. All the time he, Jenna and Amelie had been away he'd been scrupulous in keeping a deliberately low profile—choosing a family seaside resort that would hardly attract the attention of any paps wanting to snap the famous and fashionable and then, in Turin, deliberately not being seen out with Jenna—that single shopping expedition aside.

So, how the hell…?

He yanked his keyboard to him, urgently searching. In moments the offending article leapt on to the screen in front of him—along with photos.

He froze all over again.

*Bianca.* Had she vented her anger at his dismissal to her tame hack, who'd promptly scented a bigger story and gone digging for it?

The story claimed that Turin's most eligible *scapolo* had a new woman in his life whom he was treating with kid gloves—no louche nightspots and clubbing for them—and was already living with, having installed her in his apartment.

No way, the article purred in saccharine tones, could this unknown *signorina* be nothing more than his daughter's nanny… Not when the *vendeuse* at an exclusive fashion boutique had confirmed that he'd spent a fortune on couture clothes for her. Not when all three of them had been photographed leaving the shop, with Evandro Rocceforte's arm around the *signorina*'s shoulder, the two of them gazing at each other in *so* enamoured a fashion. Not when there were photos of the two *signorinas* going to the food market together, just like mother and daughter…

The article trilled on…

> *Can it be wedding bells in the offing, we wonder? Will it be second time lucky for newly divorced Evandro Rocceforte? A happy new family for his adorable little daughter—with a new mamma and a new love for our dashing Evandro?*
>
> *We hope so! How we adore a happy ending!*

Evandro stared at the screen, his blood turning to ice. Hell. Hell and damnation!

*I should have been more careful—more discreet. I should never have spoken to Bianca, never have taken Jenna to Turin...*

He threw himself back in his leather chair, staring ahead with bleak, impotent fury, his hands clenched over the arms of his chair, his mind filled with grim foreboding...

And in his head tolled the warning his lawyer had given him as he'd signed those papers the other man had so reluctantly put in front of him.

*'Do you realise the implications of what you are agreeing to?'*

And the words his lawyer had spoken next.

*'She can destroy your future.'*

The iron grip of his hands tightened. Would the inevitable letter come, fulfilling his lawyer's warning? Would the storm break over his head? Or would Berenice never find out about this damnable article?

He just did not know.

Face dark, jaw steeled, he knew all he could do now was wait.

And hope.

'Don't move.'

Evandro's voice was low and intense as Jenna's naked body was illuminated only by the full moon shining through the bedroom window.

'Don't move,' he said again. 'I want you exactly...*exactly*...like this.'

He knelt over her, his powerful legs caging her, and lifted her hands over her head, where her hair streamed across the pillow. A rasp broke from him as he straightened, one hand reaching down to shape her breast, and let his thumb play idly over her cresting nipple so that it peaked and strained against his palm.

She felt her back arch, heard a moan of pleasure sound in her throat. Her eyes clung to his and Evandro's eyes did not leave hers for an instant as he lowered his other hand to the secret vee between her thighs, easing into the delicate folds.

Her moan came again, more helpless yet, and her eyes fluttered shut as she gave herself over to the unbearably exquisite sensations he was drawing from her with his skilled stroking. She felt him lean forward slightly, making her aware of just how aroused he was, and she gloried in the knowledge. She ached for his possession, but he would not let her take him yet.

She felt her response mounting, the low, helpless moans in her throat coming faster and faster, and her lips parted, her head rolling back at how exquisitely, blissfully close she was as pleasure surmounted pleasure, growing and building, seeking the release she was now desperate for. The release that only he could give her.

She felt her spine arching in supplication... And then, just as she felt she could bear no more arousal, no more delay, his hands lifted from palming her straining breasts and the aching vee between her parted thighs. He was moving now, with a sudden, decisive, surging clenching of his taut-muscled thighs around her hips. He lifted her urgently, coming over her naked, hungry body with his hard and powerful one, and thrust into her, filling her body with his.

She gave a cry, her hands flying to his shoulders, clutching at their strength as he drove into her. Her legs netted his, and she cried out again as wave after wave of a bliss—a pleasure so intense she could not bear it— broke through her, consuming her.

She felt the molten fusion of their bodies uniting them, melding them each to the other, and she cried out his name and all but sobbed as she slowly, so very slowly, descended from the indescribable peak he had taken her to.

Her trembling body was still clinging to his as he gently relinquished her, drawing her back against him, his breath ragged on her shoulder. She could feel the pounding slug of his heartbeat, beating in time with her own.

Had it ever been that intense before? Had there been an urgency—almost a desperation—and a ravening hunger in his lovemaking tonight? As if the need to possess her had possessed him?

She lay in the strong circle of his arms, felt his embrace closer, tighter, than she had known it before, as he moulded her slender body against his as if he would never, never let her go.

Gladness filled her, and a sense of blessing so great that she felt her body relax now, her hectic heart and breathing easing along with his. She murmured his name, the syllables like a sweet caress, and folded her small hand over his much larger one.

How much she loved him. How very much...

The words blurred in her mind as consciousness was clouded with the soft, cocooning blanket of sweet slumber. Uniting them both in its somnolent embrace.

They were breakfasting, as usual, out on the terrace. Amelie was chattering away, enthusiastically telling them about all the fun things she was doing at summer camp. It was her second week there, and Jenna was so glad she was enjoying it. Not just for Amelie's sake, but also for her own. Darling though Amelie was, it was wonderful to have Evandro all to herself.

Her eyes went to him now. He was drinking his coffee, and there was a distracted air about him that had, she thought, been noticeable before from time to time, in the shuttering of his face or the veiling of his eyes.

Was he remembering Berenice, and his bitter unhappiness with her?

But he was free of her now. Free to find new happiness. Free to make his life anew.

*And, oh, please let it be with me.*

The familiar longing lodged so deep in her heart burned in her as ever, warring with the fear that she was longing for what could never be...

He looked up as Maria sallied forth onto the terrace, informing Amelie that the car was ready to drive her to summer camp. The little girl vaulted to her feet, grabbing her kitbag and bestowing a kiss upon Jenna's cheek and a quick hug upon her father, before gaily running off.

'For you, *signor*,' Maria said to Evandro, and deposited a clutch of mail beside his plate before taking herself off again.

As he did every morning when presented with the post, he started to leaf through it immediately, purposefully—presumably looking for work-related items, Jenna assumed. Halfway through the pile, he stilled. Then, abruptly, he extracted one of the letters and got to his feet. Not looking at her.

'Excuse me.'

His voice sounded terse, and tension was visible in his stance as he strode indoors. Jenna could only stare after him. Cold pooled inside her, and suddenly she did not want any more coffee.

*Something is wrong.*

And all the fears she had sought to dispel came rushing back.

\* \* \*

The heavily embossed paper lay on Evandro's desk, the ornate lettering of the name of the very expensive lawyers Berenice used leaping out at him, and the words they had written imprinted like red-hot metal on his brain.

So it had come.

The storm was breaking over him—he had not escaped it.

He took a heavy, ragged breath that seared his lungs.

Memory mocked him. Memories of that very first night at dinner, when he and Jenna had spoken of evil enchantresses and the malign spells they cast upon their victims.

*'All such spells can be broken,'* Jenna had told him.

*Not this one.*

A savage snarl broke from him and his fist crashed down upon the lawyer's letter—the letter that activated Berenice's final weapon against him. The weapon he was powerless to deflect. Powerless to defeat.

His defiance had been in vain. And now he could only do what must be done. He had no choice but to honour the vow he had made—no matter the cost.

And it *would* cost him. But not *just* him.

That was the bitterest part of all…

Jenna was in the schoolroom, sorting Amelie's schoolbooks. There were no lessons now that she was at summer camp all day, so Jenna was packing them away, putting aside the ones she herself had brought to Italy and putting the rest into a cupboard. Her mood was heavy, and that feeling that something was wrong still assailed her.

Mechanically, she went on, neatly putting Amelie's exercise books in subject order.

She heard Evandro's distinctive heavy tread out on the landing before he opened the door. And as he did, for a split second she had a flashback to the moment when Bianca and her friends had departed and he had come striding in, seizing her up, crushing her into his arms. Making her his own.

Then the memory was gone. He stood still inside the doorway, not coming forward. She paused in her actions and looked at him. His face was set, the deep lines scored around his mouth more pronounced than usual, and his expression was shuttered. Closed to her.

A sudden dread consumed her.

'Jenna.'

He said her name. Staccato, terse. He was forcing himself to say what he had to say—in the way that he must say it.

'I've heard...' he began, and the lie was forming in his head—the acceptable lie, the necessary lie. 'I've heard from my aunt. She is my father's older sister, and lives in Sorrento. She wants to meet Amelie—she's never yet had the opportunity, as she disliked Berenice and the dislike was mutual—and of course I would like Amelie to meet her great-aunt.'

He tried to make his voice sound reasonable, conversational.

But she was standing there motionless, frozen, the colour slowly leaching from her face.

*She knows. She knows what I am doing.*

Emotion twisted inside him, savage and cruel, sinking its fangs into his own flesh. But he forced himself on—there was no other way. No other way to do this.

'So, given that Amelie is now in summer camp, and when it finishes and before term starts I shall be taking her to Sorrento, this seems an opportune time for you to…' He stopped. Made himself shrug though his shoulders felt like lead, crushing his lungs. 'It's been good, this summer with you,' he said. 'And I shall remember it with appreciation. But—' He stopped again.

She was looking at him, but it was in the way she'd looked at him when he'd brought Bianca here, when Jenna had sat as white-faced as she was now. As if she was looking at him not just across the schoolroom, but across the space that parted them…the space that they could now never cross.

'You've moved on,' she said.

There was nothing in her voice—nothing at all. Nothing in her eyes or her face.

They were the words he'd said to get Bianca out of his life. He nodded. It took all his strength to do so.

Something changed in her face and she began to speak again. At first he did not hear her. Then he did.

'When would you like me to leave?'

He did not answer—could not. So she supplied the answer herself.

'Today would be best, I think,' she said. 'Only—' Her face suddenly constricted. 'Amelie… Amelie will be upset. She's become…become very fond of me…' She shut her eyes. 'And I of her,' she whispered.

She seemed to tremble, and it took all the strength he possessed to stay where he was.

'I'll make sure she understands,' he said. His voice sounded curt, even to himself.

He turned away. He could take no more of this. Not one fraction of a second more. He pulled open the schoolroom door again and was gone.

And in his head he heard Berenice's vicious, mocking laughter.

\* \* \*

Behind him, unseen by him, Jenna slowly, very slowly, finished putting the exercise books into the cupboard, closed the door. Then slowly, very slowly, she sank to the ground, her arms clenched around her knees, tears flowing from her eyes, agony slicing across her heart.

*How can he do this to me? So brutally—so callously? Have I been nothing to him, nothing at all?*

Her eyes lifted in stark anguish. She remembered how ruthlessly he'd despatched Bianca from his life.

*He was kinder to her than he was to me—wishing her well...*

She gave a choke, her face buckling, tears scalding. Pain searing like red-hot pincers was breaking her heart in two with the agony of Evandro's indifferent coldness— and the agony of her trampled love.

Amelie broke into a storm of weeping. Evandro had collected her at the end of summer camp and told her Jenna was leaving.

'But I don't want her to go! I don't want her to!' she sobbed wildly. 'I want her to stay here with us, Papà!'

Her tear-stained face pleaded with him, and little hands clutched at him desperately.

'Get her back, Papà! Please, please get her back!'

He pulled her to him, hugging her tightly. His heart wrung at her tearful grief.

'I can't, *mignonne*. I can't.'

*She can never come back.*

# CHAPTER TWELVE

JENNA LET HERSELF into her flat. It was airless and stuffy, so she went around opening the windows as mechanically as she'd sorted Amelie's books that morning. As mechanically as she'd closed the schoolroom cupboard door after Evandro had left the room and her useless, pointless tears had dried. And as mechanically as she'd gone up to her bedroom and packed her clothes.

Not the ones Evandro had bought her. They were not hers. They were for a woman she no longer was.

*The woman who longed for the heart's desire she could never have. Who longed for a family she could never have. Who longed for love from a man who would never love her.*

Agony had sliced across her heart again—an agony she'd been able to do nothing about. Because there had been nothing more for her to do except what she'd been doing. Nothing more for her to say except what she had said.

And one more thing. Something she could not leave undone.

Suitcase shut, passport and wallet in her handbag, she had gone through into Amelie's bedroom. Pain had twisted inside her—and pity for the child she was leaving, who would come home to find her gone.

An ancient memory had haunted the edges of her mind—being told that her mother had been killed in a road accident. Told that she would be going to live with her father now, an unknown stranger to her.

*But Amelie's father is not like mine. That is my comfort. She has a father who loves her dearly, as mine never did, who will always be there for her, always protect her, and for that she is blessed. And I was never her mother— only her teacher.*

So it was as her teacher that she had left her note for Amelie, saying how well she'd done in all her schoolwork, how she hoped the little girl would enjoy her new school in the autumn.

*I will always remember the lovely summer I spent here at this beautiful* palazzo, *with you and your* papà. *Be good, poppet, and look after your* papà, *for he loves you very, very much...*

She hadn't been able to write any more, with her eyes blurring, tears scalding again. Tears for the little girl she had come to love whom now she would never see again.

Nor would she see the man she loved either.

Because she was invisible to him once again.

Evandro's eyes went to Amelie, where she was playing with the dolls' house he'd bought her in Naples. She was pushing furniture around, rearranging rooms, but her manner was listless,

'She's unhappy,' his aunt said, following his line of gaze into her drawing room. They were sitting out on the balcony of her spacious apartment overlooking the Bay of Naples. Her eyes came back to her nephew, waiting for an answer. An explanation.

None came.

'You told me she'd adjusted very well to life here with you in Italy,' his aunt persisted. 'So, why is she unhappy?'

Evandro knew he must say something—but he also knew his aunt never minced her words. She certainly hadn't about his marriage, taking an instant dislike to his bride when she'd met her for the first time on Evandro's wedding day, and surveying with foreboding her young nephew's dazzled expression as he'd poured champagne for Berenice, who'd tilted her head at him coquettishly, eyes glittering with seductive promise, keeping him in hapless thrall...

'I repeat—why is the child unhappy?'

His aunt's sharp voice was insistent, breaking in on his grim reverie.

Evandro sought to make his voice offhand. 'She's missing her teacher—the one I hired for the summer to bring Amelie up to scratch for starting school this autumn. That's why I thought it a good idea to bring her here—to get to know you. I thought a change of scene might help.'

His words rang hollow, and his aunt looked at him shrewdly.

'There was an article,' she said, with a speculative edge in her voice, her eyes never leaving him, 'in one of those wretched tabloids you used to feature in so regularly once that witch of a wife was out of your hair, when you were always celebrating your freedom with some sultry piece or other! Except...' her voice changed '... this last article was different. And so was the female it mentioned.'

She looked at him, sipping her martini, waiting for his answer.

Again, it didn't come.

She eyed him straight on. 'It isn't just Amelie who misses her teacher, is it?'

He looked away, unable to meet his aunt's too-perceptive eyes, but not before he saw her expression change.

'You fool, Evandro! Oh, you fool!' she said softly.

But he did not need telling. He was fortune's fool—and had been since the moment he had married Berenice.

He was never to be free of her malignity.

*Never.*

Jenna was job-hunting, scrolling through the vacant teaching positions advertised online. She would move away—out of London. North, south, east, west… It didn't matter where.

Because there was only one place where she longed to be. A place that was barred to her for ever now. Barred to her by the one man she wanted to be with. And never could be again. The one place she'd wanted with all her heart, all her being, to be her home…a place to belong to…to be part of… And the one man she'd wanted with all her heart, all her being, to be hers. And she his.

She saw them, vivid in her mind, as real as if she were there. Saw the gracious *palazzo*, the sunlit terrace, the beautiful gardens, the shady woods above, the verdant valley below. Saw Loretta and Maria, bustling about, Signora Farrafacci sailing in her stately fashion through the beautiful rooms…and little Amelie running down the stairs, skipping along the terrace, riding her pink bicycle, handlebar ribbons flying, calling out in her piping voice, rushing up to hug her…

*And always Evandro—striding out to the terrace, lounging back in his dining chair at the head of the table, sweeping me into his arms, lowering his mouth to mine…*

She saw it all—but it was as if she were a ghost, drifting through the scene, seeing it but invisible to those in front of her. An outsider with no right to be there, no right to belong.

No right to love them all...

She gave a cry of anguish, pressing her hand to her mouth as if she could silence it. Silence all that clamoured within her—stifle and smother the searing agony of longing for what could never be again.

Evandro glanced at his watch. Amelie was staying on late at school today—something to do with choir practice, he recalled. He would fetch her later. Maybe take her out to supper. Something to cheer her up. Though she was settling down at the convent school, he still too often saw a doleful expression on her face.

But at least she was mentioning Jenna less. He was grateful for that—and not just for Amelie's sake.

No, he would not go there. Refused to go back there. To that very last moment when he'd stood in the schoolroom and told Jenna what he had. Brief and to the point.

*It had been the best way to end it.*

And she had gone. Packed her bag and left the *palazzo* as if she had never been there. Slipping away quietly, self-effacingly. Just...disappearing.

Invisible once more.

Now it was just he and Amelie making their home here in the *palazzo*.

He was doing his best to encourage Amelie to make new friends, exchange play dates, get involved with all the activities the school offered—like the choir practice she was at today.

As for himself, he was working from the *palazzo* as much as possible, although he still needed to be in Turin sometimes as well—still needed to allow for some essential business travel. But Amelie was fine here with his housekeeper and the staff to look after her when he was away, and he always spent time talking with her on the phone every evening, always brought her back a little present when he came home to the *palazzo.*

He was arranging his life around her, doing everything he could for her to ensure her happiness. Whatever had to be done.

*Everything that I have to. Everything. Whatever the cost.*

His mouth twisted, indenting the lines around it more deeply.

*A doting father indeed...*

With a jerking movement, he reached for the phone. He had business calls to make, and the afternoon was nearly over. What use was it to think of what it had cost him—of the price he had paid?

No use. It had cost, and he had paid. That was all there was to it.

Face shuttered, he started to key in the number he needed. But before he could connect there was a knock on the library door. Not the usual brief tap that presaged the entry of Signora Farrafacci with his coffee, but a sharper, heavier rap against the wood. And when she came in he could see at once that her usual calm demeanour was agitated.

'What is it?' he asked, frowning. He knew his housekeeper had been taken aback by Jenna's abrupt departure, but he had not encouraged any discussion of the matter and she knew better than to ask.

She came up to his desk now, definitely agitated. 'There's...there's someone arrived,' she said. Her voice was discernibly breathless, her bosom heaving. 'Demanding to see you.'

Evandro's frown deepened. 'Who?' he said. His first thought was Amelie—that something had happened to her. Alarm stabbed at him. And then a very, very different emotion.

Signora Farrafacci's bosom heaved again. 'It's...' She hesitated, then spat it out. 'Signora Rocceforte!'

Evandro froze.

Jenna stared out over the water. Its grey mass was smooth, giving no hint of the hidden turbulence beneath as the incoming tide met the outflowing current at this confluence of river and sea. On the far side of the wide estuary the low Kentish shore was almost indistinguishable from the level water.

She thrust her hands into the pockets of her jacket. Autumn was shortening the days, and the cool air already hinted at winter's incoming cold. This estuarine stretch of the Thames—in the Essex commuter town where she had found a temporary teaching position to cover an unexpected maternity leave—was not a landscape she knew, and its marshy reaches were bleak for all but the myriad seabirds that found refuge there.

*Was it a similar refuge to the one she sought? Refuge from pain...from memory. From what might have been but never was. Never could be.*

She made herself keep walking along the embankment, deserted except for dog walkers in the gathering dusk. An east wind, low but chill, keened over the water and she welcomed its scouring, as if it could scour out memory as well. And pain. And loss. And abject misery.

She quickened her pace. She must not wallow in her misery, must not endlessly bewail her loss.

*I have to make a new life—I have to. Have to accept that I filled my head with illusions, creating a false real-*

*ity for myself—false hopes and false longings. I wanted
to belong to Evandro—to be the woman he loved—but
I never did and eventually he rejected and ejected me.*

Deliberately she made herself replay the moment
of her dismissal. The brief brutality of it. Evandro just
standing there, telling her it was an 'opportune' moment
for her to go. Eliminating her from his life. His bed. Packing
her off with nothing more than a few brief words.

She felt her hands clench in her pockets, half with pain
and half with anger.

*I did not deserve such treatment! Such indifferent
brusqueness. Such a callous termination of what there
had been between us. Especially coming out of nowhere...*

She halted, frowning.

But had it?

The blow he'd inflicted in those brief, unbearable moments
had been so overwhelming she had not been able
to see out from under it. Now she forced herself to replay
the nightmare scene.

He had told her he had heard from his aunt, inviting
him and Amelie to visit her. Was that what that letter
had been about? The one that had been in the mail that
morning? The one that he had picked up before he got
to his feet, tersely excusing himself, striding indoors?

She remembered how she'd stared after him...how
she'd felt cold pooling inside her. Remembered the worry
spreading through her.

*Something is wrong*, she'd thought.

She heard the words again now, echoing in her memory.

*What could have been so wrong about a letter of invitation
from an aunt?*

She frowned again. But *had* that letter been from his
aunt? It hadn't looked like the kind of letter an aunt would

send... She screwed her eyes shut, trying to see it again in her mind. A large white envelope, businesslike, with the address printed, not handwritten, which surely an elderly aunt would have done, if she was writing to a family member? And the stamp...

Her eyes widened suddenly, as she dredged up subconscious memory.

*Not Italian—French.*

French?

*But he'd said his aunt lived in Sorrento.*

On sudden impulse she wheeled about, reversing her direction. It was as though a tide had turned within her, pushing back against the current sweeping her out into a drowning sea of loss and heartbreak. A new tide that brought new thoughts.

Protest rose in her like a litany.

*The Evandro who sent me packing like that, so callously and uncaringly, is not the Evandro that I know. Not the Evandro with sardonic deadpan humour...the Evandro who openly enjoyed my company, my conversation. Not the Evandro who took me into his arms, his bed... his life! Who kissed me, and embraced me, and laughed with me, and held me close...so close...*

The Evandro she knew was nothing like the blankfaced man who had looked across the schoolroom at her, terse and brusque, callous and uncaring, the lines around his mouth scored deeply, his eyes dark and shuttered. Sending her away as if there had been nothing between them—nothing at all. Sending her away as if compelled to do so...

*By what?*

And into her head came the words that had fallen from her lips that very first evening she had dined with him and Amelie.

*'Under a malign spell.'*

Her mind worked through it all. His marriage had been a disaster. She knew that—all the household knew that! But he was free of it and Amelie, his precious daughter, was with him now, safe and protected from her damaging, self-obsessed mother. There was nothing more that Berenice could do to harm him.

Or was there?

Jenna kept walking and picked up her pace, a sense of urgency filling her.

Evandro sat in the library, in the leather armchair set beside the unlit fireplace. The late October night was still mild, but it was unlit for another reason as well.

He had no wish to see flames of any kind, nor to catch the choking smell of smoke.

His grip on his brandy glass tightened and he took another mouthful. On the marble mantelpiece the steady ticking of the clock marked the seconds, the time that was passing so slowly. It was long past the midnight hour and silence had engulfed the house.

He finished his brandy, reached for the decanter, refilled his glass. He should stop drinking, but he was of no mind to do so.

He shut his eyes, resting his head back on the chair, face set. His jaw ached and he moved to touch his left cheek with his hand, then let it drop, not willing to feel the pain that still throbbed beneath the analgesic of alcohol. He took another mouthful of brandy instead, stretching out his legs stiffly, trying not to wince at the effort it took.

If he drank enough he might fall asleep here, in the chair. It would be better than going to bed. Better than lying there in its wide expanse. Alone except for memories. A savage self-mockery slashed across his mind. Those never left him alone.

Too many memories. Too bitter to bear. Too unbearable.

Memories of a woman he would never see again. Who was beyond him for ever.

*For ever.*

The damning words scythed across him, cutting deep into his core. His very being. All that was left of it…

Emotion seared him like flame across flesh already burnt and scorched. It was agonising.

In sudden, furious, unbearable desolation, he hurled his brandy glass into the fireplace. It shattered, but he did not hear the noise. Heard only a tearing, abject cry go up that was like the roar of a wounded beast, piercing the floor of heaven.

He only dimly realised that the noise had come from him.

Jenna jackknifed upright, eyes flaring open wide, heart pounding, instantly awake.

A dream—that was all it had been. A dream. But that cry, torn from a human soul…

*A dream—only a dream!*

But a dream so real, so vivid, that it was still there—and she was still in it. She tried to shake her head, to make herself wake out of it, but she could not. Her eyes were open, but it was not the bedroom she was seeing.

She heard her ragged breathing, felt her hands digging into the mattress, the headboard pressing into her spine. Her hectic heart rate did not ease, and it was still pounding as she got out of bed and went to the window, dragging back the curtains of her bedsit to stare out over the street, deserted now, with midnight long past, as though she might see out there what was in her head.

Then, numbly, she turned away.

A dream, she told herself again. That terrible broken cry was only a dream.

But what if it wasn't?

It was absurd to think so—irrational. And yet the dream she'd woken from had been so all-consuming that she needed to do something...anything...that might calm her.

Shakily, she reached for her laptop, hunkering down in her bed again and logging in, ignoring the late hour. She had to be at school tomorrow to teach, but sleep was beyond her now.

What she was searching for she did not know, but as if of their own accord she found her fingers typing the words 'Evandro Rocceforte' into the search engine. Halfway down the first page of results an article title leapt out at her.

Dread filled her as she clicked on the link and started to read. It was a press release from Rocceforte Industriale.

*It is with regret that we announce the resignation of chairman and chief executive Evandro Rocceforte, owing to ill health. In his place he has appointed...*

She read no more as icy, terrifying fear filled her.

# CHAPTER THIRTEEN

JENNA STOOD BY the side of the road where the local bus had deposited her. She had not been able to find a taxi in the town, and now the steep driveway up to the *palazzo* awaited her.

At least she had no luggage. That would have been an imposition—a presumption too far. A major part of her still told her that she was being insane to do what she had done—phoning the school to tell them that she would not be in today, then heading for Southend airport, taking the first flight out to Bergamo and then catching the train onwards.

But fear had driven her—and the searing memory of that terrible dream. And then the announcement she had read.

*What 'ill health'?*

She felt fear clutch at her again, overriding everything else. Overriding the impulsive insanity of what she was doing and driving her onwards with a terrifying question.

*What ill health would make him resign from the business that he was head of? He would never have done so lightly...*

She headed up the narrow drive, quickening her pace, her thoughts still as jumbled as they had been since last night.

*That letter he received...his swift and brutal dismissal of me...my feeling that something was wrong...and now this announcement of 'ill health'. Was it bad news about his health that was in that letter? Was that why he got rid of me?*

The questions tumbled through her brain, clashing with her fear and heightening it.

As she neared the sharp bend where the rocky outcrop forced the roadway around it, memory washed over her of that very first night—of running into the path of Evandro's speeding car to save him from danger.

It had been an impulse—instant and overriding. Just as this insanely executed journey was now.

She rounded the outcrop, striding onwards, ignoring the place where the drive continued on to the front of the *palazzo* and instead taking the shorter path cutting through the woods to the gardens behind. Just before she left the woods—before she allowed herself to look at the *palazzo*—she felt her eyes go to where the lightning-struck chestnut stood, cloven in two.

The branches that had trailed on the ground had been cleared, the burnt limbs severed, but the trunk of the tree remained, blackened and scorched. Dead and stricken and lifeless. And yet around the base... Her eyes rested there now, and emotion flooded her at the sight. New shoots were growing...

She let her gaze slip past it, down over the beautiful gardens to the *palazzo*'s façade.

It was as elegant, as perfectly proportioned as it always had been, with its symmetrical pediments and rows of sash windows catching the sunlight, the French doors opening up to the spacious terrace all along its length.

Exactly as she remembered it.

Exactly as she had dreamt it last night.

Exactly as it had always been.

Except—

Shock and horror jarred through her. The rear elevation of the *palazzo* was exactly as it always had been. And so was one room deep behind the enfilade of French doors. But beyond that—

Beyond that the entire frontage of the *palazzo* was a blackened shell, the marble-floored entrance hall half open to the sky. And in the air, acrid and dry, was the faint smell of smoke and ash and ruin.

Numb, disbelieving, she walked down through the gardens, feeling her heart pounding harder and faster with every step. As she gained the terrace a figure stepped out from the *palazzo*'s interior.

She gave a cry, her hand flying to her mouth.

Evandro stilled, turning his head.

That cry...

She was coming towards him, walking with a rapidity that was bringing her closer with every burning second. She blurred, going in and out of focus.

The last woman in the world he wanted to see him.

The only woman in the world he wanted to see.

And then she was there—in front of him. A woman who should not be there, who had no reason to be there... no cause. A woman who was looking at him with horror on her face.

'Dear God...' she said, breathing shallowly.

Her eyes, those clear pools as cool and as green as the shade under the canopy of trees where they'd held each other, were wide and fearful.

He felt his face twist. 'God,' he said, and his voice was harsh, 'had very little to do with it.'

He looked at her. His focus was poor, but forcibly

he made it work—such as it could now. A snap of pain flashed across his face—it felt like agony.

'Why have you come?'

That harshness was still in his voice, and he saw her flinch. But perhaps not on account of his voice alone.

She simply looked at him. 'I had to,' she said.

He saw her expression change as she tried to make sense of the sight in front of her.

'I heard you call out,' she said. 'In a dream.' Her words were disjointed. She stopped...went on again. 'Then I looked you up online. I found an article that said you had resigned from your company. Ill health, it said. But it didn't...it didn't say...'

She halted, and in her eyes were the things he would see in all eyes now. Must always see.

Pity—and horror.

'How...?' She swallowed, stopped.

He took a breath. 'Come inside, if you will,' he said. His voice was less harsh, now merely grating. 'I need to sit down,' he went on. 'Walking is still...difficult. As you can see.'

He indicated the cane in his right hand which could not stop him limping heavily, as he did now, heading indoors with a halting, painful gait. He went back into the library, sinking down with relief, loosening his hunched shoulders as he sank into the deep leather chair by the unlit hearth, indicating that she should take the chair opposite.

She did so, sitting down abruptly. He could still see the shock on her face—the pity and the horror.

'Tell me,' she said.

There was a plea in her voice. He did not need her to spell out what she wanted him to tell her.

He set his cane aside, leaning it carefully against the

mantel and stretching out his legs. The bones that had
been crushed by falling masonry, which were knitting
together again slowly and painfully, made the movement
difficult.

His voice was bleak as he answered her, hard and
terse. 'My wife came calling,' he said.

He saw Jenna stare.

His mouth twisted. 'My ex-wife,' he corrected.
'Though she never accepted that. She insisted on staying the night.' His voice was expressionless now. 'Ide-
ally with me.'

He heard Jenna gasp, but carried on, letting his eyes
rest on her, forcing them to focus by effort of will.

'When I...declined...her invitation, she retired, furious, to her room—one of the guest bedrooms at the front
had been made up for her—and proceeded to demand
dinner and bottles of vintage champagne, wine and li-
queurs, all of which she demolished.' His voice became
devoid of emotion. 'So that when she neglected to properly extinguish one of her cigarettes and it dropped to
the floor, it smouldered on the rug before working its
way along her discarded clothes to reach the curtains.'

He paused before going on.

'The smoke alarms went off, waking the household,
summoning the fire service. But the town is some way
off, as you know. And fire,' he said, 'spreads very swiftly
in old houses.'

He fell silent, his blurring gaze dropping to the fireplace, filling it, in his mind's eye, with the inferno that
burned in his head all the time now. The memory of the
roar of flames and the crack of burning timbers, the choking, suffocating smoke...

He lifted his gaze again, resting it on Jenna. She
looked bleak, unreadable.

'I tried to save her. Allow me that, if you will. I had wished her to hell—but not...' his voice twisted again '...not like that.'

He worked to find the right words.

'They say she died of smoke inhalation, and that because she had already passed out with so much alcohol in her system she would have known little of what was happening to her.' He paused again. 'She's been interred. The family plot in the churchyard. For decency's sake. For Amelie's sake—' he broke off.

'*Amelie*. Please tell me she didn't witness...' Fearful concern filled her voice.

'She was away,' he told her. 'The moment Berenice showed up I phoned the school to ask them to keep her with the boarders that night. Then, afterwards, it was impossible for her to come back until the place was made safe and I was out of hospital. But she's back here now, going to school every day—they thought it best for her to keep as much as possible to her normal routine. To minimise trauma.'

Jenna's clear-water eyes lifted to his. 'And you?' she asked quietly. 'Your trauma?'

'I'm alive,' he said. 'That is all that matters.' He stilled. 'For Amelie.'

Something flickered in her face. Something his damaged eyesight could not make out.

'Not just for Amelie,' she said.

And then, before his vision blurred again, he saw tears start to seep from the forest pools that were her eyes and flow silently down her cheeks.

She could not stop. The silent flow was impossible to halt. And why should she try and halt it? Why shouldn't she weep?

*He tried to save her—tried to save the woman who
had tormented him for so many years, who so recklessly
endangered not just herself but everyone here. In spite of
it all, he still tried to save her—risking his life for hers.
At such a cost.*

Through the tears she could not stop she beheld his
scarred and ravaged face. The left-hand side showed
emergency skin grafts, and the jagged slash across his
left eye was like a livid lightning bolt. The cane propped
beside him acted both as guide for his damaged vision
and support for his shattered leg.

Pity constricted in her—and so much more than pity.
Her heart overflowed with it.

He was holding out a handkerchief to her. It was large
and made of a fine cotton, with his initials in the corner.
There was a sardonic look in his eyes, a look so familiar
she thought time had slipped and the past had enveloped
her in its kindly embrace.

'Enough tears, Jenna,' he said. 'I'll survive. And you,
of all people, should not weep for me.' His voice was
harsh, but it was directed at himself, not her. 'Not after
what I did to you.'

She saw the lines surrounding his mouth that she had
once thought deep now scored like knife wounds, tightening to a whipped line.

'Not after that,' he said.

With a sudden movement Evandro got to his feet, unable
to bear sitting there any longer. He crossed to his desk,
not bothering to take his cane, his halting gait slowing
him, frustrating him. He yanked open the drawer of his
desk and took out the envelope that had sat there since
the day he'd sent Jenna packing.

He felt a pain stab him that had nothing to do with the still-healing bones in his injured thigh, but he made himself ignore it—as he ignored all the physical punishment his once-strong body had taken that hellish night.

He stared for a moment at the envelope he was holding, propping himself against the front edge of the desk so that it supported him, taking the weight off his half-crippled leg. He looked across at her, saw her expression change.

'That letter...' he heard her say faintly. 'The one that came... I thought, when I read the announcement of your resignation, that the letter had been bad news...about the ill health the article mentioned...'

She spoke disjointedly, sitting very still, knees drawn together, hands clenched in her lap.

'Not ill health,' he corrected, his voice empty. 'Ill will—'

He broke off, but knew he must say more.

He drew a harsh and heavy breath. Forced himself on. 'There was a reason, Jenna, why I did what I did to you—why I sent you packing the way I did.' He paused, still reluctant to speak.

*I never thought I would have to tell her. Never thought I would need to. Because I never thought I'd see her again—I thought that she was gone for ever from my life.*

After all, hadn't that been his intention? The very purpose that had driven him, that dark day, up to Amelie's schoolroom to do what he had? Sending her away, never to return?

Yet for reasons he could not fathom, dared not think about, she had returned to the *palazzo*. So he could not keep his silence while she sat there like that, with those useless, futile, wasted tears drying on her cheeks.

He took another breath, his tone changing. 'Jenna, understand this—ever since my divorce the tabloid press, the gossip columns, have made copy and head-lines out of me. They get a helping hand—from Bianca, for one. She liked to tip them off when I was going about with her. Partly because she enjoyed being in the lime-light and partly...' his eyes hardened '...because she hoped it might help in her goal of becoming the next Signora Rocceforte. She never had a chance, of course, but the hacks would have loved to break such a story. So when—'

He stopped. Then resumed resignedly. No point in starting this sorry tale only to bottle it now.

'There was a story, Jenna, published in one of the tabloid rags after we arrived back here from Turin—an article I never saw coming, which outlined how very dif-ferent you are from the likes of Bianca, and explained your presence in my life in a very different way. The re-porter attempted to paint you into the role Bianca never could attain—said that you were to me what she never had been nor ever could be. The consequence of which was...' he dropped the envelope on to his desk as if it were dangerous to touch '...this letter.'

He stared down at it now, heaviness crushing him. Then, like a switch, he snapped his eyes back to Jenna. She was sitting so still...so very, very still.

He made himself go on. Willing her to understand what he had done—why he had done it. Not so she would forgive him—never that—but so she would understand.

His damaged eyes rested on her. It hurt to see her. She was so close, yet so infinitely far away.

'Jenna, from the very first I knew it was...unwise... to be anything to you other than your employer and your pupil's father. Knew it was...unwise...to want anything more. Unwise to spend time with you, talk with you, laugh with you. Unwise to want you to shed your sad cloak of invisibility. Unwise to kiss you in the moonlight—'

His expression changed.

'That's why I put you from me—pushed you away. That's why I brought Bianca here with all her friends, wanting to banish my desire for you by flooding myself and my home with distraction. I thought it would help me to keep away from you. To undo what I had so unwisely begun.'

His eyes rested on her. She had not moved. Not one iota. She was as still as a statue made of living flesh.

He forced himself on. 'But I couldn't banish you from my thoughts, my longings. If anything, the whole endeavour only proved to me that it was *you* I wanted to be with, with every fibre of my being.'

His voice changed again. Dropped to a low intensity.

'You were everything that Berenice was not. You alone—of all the world—could draw from me the poison of my nightmare marriage. Your quiet ways and your quiet voice and your quiet loveliness... Your clear spring water eyes and your sylvan grace... And above all—oh, above all, Jenna, your honesty, your truthfulness, your kindness and your compassion. You were all that I craved—all I could not do without. You were the woman I wanted—needed—to make my life whole again.'

Into his head came the memory of standing out on the still-damp terrace after their first unforgettable night together, when he had made her his. Standing in the fresh morning sunshine after the storm that had devastated the chestnut tree, feeling the air that had been bright and clear and clean.

*'The world new-made,'* she had said.

He drew a breath, deep into his smoke-ravaged lungs. 'And so I cleared them all out—Bianca and her friends— and, heedless of the danger, came striding to claim you.' He shut his eyes. 'To make you mine.'

His eyes flashed open again.

'A dangerous word, Jenna...*mine*. And I knew the danger—God help me, I knew! Knew I should not claim you, knew I should be wise and never hold you in my arms, never kiss you, never sweep you into my bed, my life, my—'

He broke off. He shouldn't say any more. She had endured enough at his hands.

'I knew it,' he said instead, 'but I ignored it. Silenced it. Told myself I would take the risk even though I knew how real that risk would be, because of how very different from Bianca you were.'

He saw her expression change now. Saw a flickering that seemed to be a lightening and then a frown of puzzlement.

'Risk?' Her voice was strained and low. She was not understanding. 'What risk, Evandro? How?'

He tensed his jaw, sending pain shooting through the scars on his face. He was silent for a moment, his face grim. He did not want to tell her this—*por Dio*, he did not! But tell her he must.

'The risk,' he said, his voice like leaden stones, 'that I would have to choose.' He paused, looking at her, his eyes like weights upon her. 'Choose between you...and Amelie.'

Jenna heard the words but could not believe them.

'Evandro, I would never...never *dream* of...of—' She broke off, dismay at what he'd said vivid in her face. 'I would never, never make you do such a thing! How could you think it, Evandro? How could you think I would ever do anything to harm what you have with Amelie?'

She could hear the distress in her voice, along with the agitation and protest.

'How could you think, after everything I told you about how my own father chose my stepmother over me—rejecting me—that I would ever, *ever* want you to do that to Amelie? And why should I? Amelie is a darling! I love her as much as I love—' She broke off again, her face working. 'I would *never* make you choose.'

He held up a hand. 'Not you,' he said heavily. 'It would not be you making me choose—never you.'

Incomprehension furrowed her brow. 'But who?'

'Berenice,' he said flatly.

*'Berenice?'* Her incomprehension was total.

He pushed away from his desk, moved to sink down into the executive chair behind it,

'I have another sorry tale to tell you,' he opened, his voice still heavy. 'Ugly, but necessary.'

He seemed to hesitate, as if he had no wish to say what he must. Then, his expression steeling, he spoke, his voice harsh and grating.

'My father wanted to expand Rocceforte Industriale in a merger with a similar French company, Trans-Montane, which was in financial difficulties but which would have been a good match for us. Berenice had inherited a controlling interest in the company, so the obvious, easiest way for the merger to proceed was by...' he took a slicing breath '...by uniting our two families. To say I was in agreement would be an understatement.' There was scathing self-mockery in his voice now. 'I was happy to please my father—as I told you that day we had our tea party—and glad to do good for the company that had been in our family for over a hundred years, but I didn't marry for that reason alone.'

He paused again, and Jenna saw something in his face that stabbed at her. Heard a hollowing in his voice when he spoke next.

'I took one look at Berenice—and was lost.'

She saw him shift restlessly in his chair, heard the tension in his voice as he went on.

'I was twenty-five, full of romantic notions. My father was delighted. I would have a wife every man would envy me for, who would double our business overnight.' His voice changed, became etched with sadness now. 'And I would also bring him the joy of knowing that I was making a love match as wonderful as he had known—the match that had been taken from him by the death of my mother two years earlier. He wanted so much to see me happily married…to see me deeply in love—'

He broke off. Again Jenna saw something change in his face, becoming hard, twisting his mouth.

'As it happened, my wife wanted that too. She wanted me deeply in love with her. Besotted by her. She knew it would make me…malleable. Easy to manipulate. It was the same aim she had for all the hapless males she drew to her. But for me, her husband, it was even more important to keep me that love-struck, devoted fool who'd married her with stars in his eyes thinking he'd found his dream come true—his ravishing bride. She wanted me to be her faithful adoring husband, eagerly footing the bill for her every extravagance, lavishing everything she wanted upon her, doing anything for her—anything at all. Putting up with her capriciousness and her temper, her self-obsession and her narcissism, turning a blind and ever-forgiving eye to her constant affairs, indulging her in anything and everything she craved—and thinking myself privileged to be allowed to do so.'

His voice hardened even more.

'But although I'd thought the best of her when I'd married her, I came to see the worst of her. To see through her superficial allure, to see her for what she truly was—and she could not endure it. Was enraged by it. So she turned on all her powers to charm and seduce and beguile me, to draw me back into her manipulative clutches—determined not just to entrap me in her web again but to punish me for seeking to withdraw from her. Punish me,' he said grimly, 'by breaking my heart.'

He paused, his face emptying of all emotion.

'She could not do it,' he said. 'She could not make me stay love-struck for a woman who had no love for anyone, let alone her husband. She had lost her power over me. I stuck with her—tolerated her for Amelie's sake, even though I saw so little of her, and even for my father's sake. But after he died I knew I could endure it no longer. And when I divorced her it was the end of her power entirely. She was defeated. I was done with her.'

Jenna saw an expression form on his face that chilled her to the bone.

'But Berenice,' Evandro said, his words falling like stones, 'was not done with me.'

His eyes focused intently on hers as he went on, almost piercing her.

'And when I claimed custody of Amelie she struck.'

He looked away for a moment, as if seeing something far away that was out of reach to him. That always would be. Then his lasering gaze came back to her.

'My determination to wrest Amelie from her had shown her how much she could demand of me before she conceded custody—and it gave her a new power over me. Not just to force me to pay her a fortune for Amelie—over and above what I had already paid her for her divorce settlement—but to get something that would satisfy her even more. Would satisfy her lust for revenge on me for daring to reject her, escape her, divorce her. For denying her the pleasure of breaking my heart. *She* might not be able to break my heart herself—but she knew she could still break it using Amelie. It was the price,' he said, his voice empty of all emotion now, 'of finally conceding custody to me.'

She saw his darkened eyes flick to the letter he'd taken from the desk drawer and held up to her before discarding it on the desk's surface. Then his eyes came back to her.

'She demanded I sign a document that my lawyer was appalled by. He was horrified—and he warned me what she was intent on. "You are giving her the power to destroy your future," he told me. But I did not care. Could not. I knew it would give me Amelie and bring to an end the delays and prevarications and endless wrangling that Berenice was using to drag out the process. Amelie would come to me permanently. The custody battle would be over. Unless—'

Yet again, he broke off. Yet again, his gaze shifted away from her. And this time it did not come back to her as he continued to speak, as if his eyes were consciously avoiding her.

'She wanted to break my heart so she found a way. By making me choose…' and now his eyes lashed back to her '…choose between Amelie and any other woman who might come to mean something to me.' His face twisted. 'The likes of Bianca didn't bother her. She knew they were simply women for affairs—nothing more than that. But you—you, Jenna—were different. That damnable article in that tabloid, with its prurient speculation about who you were to me, reached her, and—just as I dreaded—she struck.'

His gaze dropped again to the letter lying on his desktop.

'It's from her lawyers,' he said. 'Relaunching the custody battle for Amelie—just as Berenice threatened she would. Unless—'

That word hung in the air again.

'Unless I did what I had agreed—what I'd promised in that document my lawyer was appalled by. And so I sent you packing.' He took a deep and weary breath. 'She forced me to choose. To choose between Amelie—and you.'

Emotion speared in Jenna as she heard his words, propelling her into speech just as it had before. 'That could never be a choice for you, Evandro! *Never.*'

Memory assailed her—not of that dreadful last day at the *palazzo*, but a memory much older than that. A memory of a father for whom that *had* been a choice. A father who had chosen very differently. Choosing his new wife and rejecting his daughter.

As Evandro never, never would.

As she would never want him to.

'No, it never could be.'

The words of this man, the father who had made a different choice from her own, echoed hers.

'It never could be. I could never hand Amelie back into Berenice's malign clutches—never betray the vow I made to protect her from her toxic mother always, no matter the cost. So I did what her lawyer's letter demanded,' he said, his voice emptying. 'I pushed you away. Despatched you back to England. Finished with you. End of—'

The staccato words fell away from him.

There was too much in Jenna's head—far too much.

Swirling like a maelstrom, her emotions were chaotic, and she felt entirely overwhelmed. But out of it all, one thing crystallised. One thing that made no sense. No sense at all after everything he'd told her. Something that furrowed her brow, made her get to her feet and go halfway towards his desk, then halt.

Her gaze dropped momentarily to the thick white envelope on the desk in front of him, with its typed address, its French stamp, its letter inside containing its cruel demand—Berenice's final vengeance on the man she had already wronged so much...her final threat to the child she had used as a weapon against her loving father. Then her eyes lifted to Evandro—to his ravaged face and the bleakness in his damaged eyes. She felt emotion move within her, but suppressed it. This was not the moment for it.

She felt her frown deepen, her troubled thoughts turn questioning. She took a breath, trying to make sense of something that made *no* sense. No sense at all. And when she spoke, her voice was filled with incomprehension.

'Everything you've told me about Berenice,' she began, picking her words carefully, 'everything Signora Farrafacci has let slip about her, everything that Amelie herself has said—and, even now, the way you described the horror of her death and how she brought it about by her irresponsible recklessness... Everything from Amelie's chaotic, unstable life with her—so absolutely unsuitable for a child—to her using Amelie as a bargaining chip in your divorce to extract a fortune from you, to her hedonism, extravagance, narcissism, selfishness and self-regard—her perpetual infidelities and her drinking... Everything points, surely, to her having had no chance at all at reversing the custody decision. So, how...' she took a laboured breath '...*how* could she ever have threatened you and Amelie in that way?'

Her voice was vehement.

'Evandro, what judge in the world—in any jurisdiction!—would hand Amelie back to such a mother? Would take her away from her father—'

He cut across her. His voice stark. 'But I'm not Amelie's father.'

# CHAPTER FOURTEEN

JENNA STILLED, eyes fixed on Evandro.

'I am not Amelie's father,' he said again.

Something seemed to pass across his face, then it was gone.

'Just who is will probably never be known. Not even to Berenice.' His voice held no emotion. 'As for DNA tests—well, the choice of candidates would be very broad. And international. Berenice had no interest in identifying him. She only threw the unedifying information my way when she saw me with the baby that up until then she had let me think was mine.' His expression was as harsh as his voice. 'The baby I'd hoped, so much, might mark a turning point for us. At that point my refusal to give up completely on the shambles of my marriage was being fed by my delusions that a child between us might salvage something decent and true. But when Berenice saw me cradling Amelie—a typical doting Italian father—it so enraged her to have me paying attention to anyone but herself that she threw at me, with sadistic mockery, the news that I was devoting myself to another man's bastard.'

His expression changed again.

'I knew that our marriage was over then. But the real cruelty of that moment was not in what she had thrown at me, but in the fact that there was now, in that unholy, toxic mess, a child… A child innocent of all the sordid circumstances of her conception and her birth, now trapped in the poisonous web of Berenice's jealousy, spite and self-obsession.'

Jenna saw him take another breath, ragged and harsh.

'The truth of Amelie's parentage became her ultimate weapon against me.'

He looked away, out over the terrace, as if he were watching Amelie playing out there, riding her pink bicycle up and down, golden hair streaming. The golden hair which she now knew came neither from Berenice nor Evandro. Jenna had finally got an answer to that question, it seemed.

'It was a weapon that would win her everything she wanted—the fact that I had no legal right to a child I loved, because she was not mine. Her rage at being usurped by another female in my life, her fury that I'd dared to see her for what she was, all found a weapon in Amelie's paternity. It was a gun perpetually pointed at me. And not just pointed at me—pointed at a victim far more vulnerable. At Amelie.'

He paused, his voice as tight as a garrotte.

'All she had to do was tell the court I was not Amelie's father and demand a DNA test to prove it. My claim for sole custody would crumble.' His voice tightened even more. 'Even if a judge had ruled her an unfit mother, Amelie would have been taken into care, lost in a system that, yes, might…*might*…have allowed me to adopt her—eventually—but after how much wrangling? How lengthy a process? But there was no certainty of that—none. Remember, I had never had more than minimal contact with Amelie—Berenice had seen to that, keeping perpetually on the move as she dragged the child around Europe and America, preventing me from forming a relationship with her. And even with Amelie in care, Berenice might have tried to regain custody of her. As I have bitter cause to know, she could be supremely manipulative and convincing—she would have done whatever it had taken to get Amelie back for the sole purpose of tormenting me, taunting me, knowing how desperately I wanted to save Amelie from her. How desperately responsible I felt for her.'

His voice emptied.

'I was Berenice's target—it was me she wanted to make suffer. But it would have been Amelie who'd be her victim. And I was responsible for that. If I hadn't shown Berenice how much I'd come to despise her, if I hadn't sought my freedom from the hell of our marriage, I might have been able to protect Amelie, or at least mitigate Berenice's damaging influence. But when she knew I was determined to break free from her, she wanted to use Amelie against me. And I could not allow that—could not abandon her to Berenice. I had to fight for her.'

Something moved in his eyes—a flash of emotion that pierced Jenna to the core. Emotion was rising in her like a tide she could not stop.

'I've tried...' he said, his voice low.

He was not looking at Jenna, but into himself, and Jenna could see his hands, as viciously scarred as his face, clench over the arms of his chair.

'I've tried to be the best father I could to Amelie— even though I'm not her father. To do the best I can for her. Because she deserves whatever even a non-father like me can do for her. Because she has no one else to protect her but me! I know I'm *not* her father, but—'

The emotion she could not stop—would not now have stopped for all the world itself—broke in Jenna.

She surged forward, carried on that unstoppable emotion, her hands slamming down on the desk.

Her eyes were blazing, her voice vehement. 'You *are* her father! You are her father in *every* way that counts. Do you think it takes DNA to make a father? My father gave me his DNA and nothing else. He never stood by me. He abandoned my mother, smashed our family to pieces by running off with another woman, and then treated me, when I was forced upon him, with coldness and resentment and rejection. He didn't care. He *never* cared about me. But *you* care. You care about Amelie and you love her—love her in every moment you spend with her, every hug you give her, every smile, each and every one. It is *love*, Evandro, *love* that makes you her father. *Love.*'

She had to make him believe it, accept what she was saying as true. Her voice was fierce with urging—with urgency.

'Love,' she said again, more quietly, but no less insistently, her eyes holding his, blazing still. 'Love and loyalty. The undying, unbreakable loyalty of a father  a true father, as you are, Evandro, and as you always will be—who places his child's happiness above and beyond everything else. You've stood by her through everything Berenice did or tried to do. You *are* Amelie's father, Evandro, in every vital meaning of the word—and no power in heaven or earth can say otherwise. None.'

She knew the blaze was still in her eyes, because she had to make him accept what she had said—it was the most important thing in the world to her. But it was a blaze that was becoming a glow—a glow to fill her heart. And not just hers.

She saw his eyes close, lashes splayed on his cheeks, and she could see the tension racking his shoulders begin to ease, see the veins standing out on the backs of his scarred hands relieved as his clenched grip loosened. He bowed his head for a moment, then lifted it again, opening his eyes.

Joltingly, he levered himself to his feet, coming around the desk to her. She turned towards him, but he remained a few feet away.

'Thank you,' he said, his voice low. 'And thank you for...for understanding.' The strain in his voice was audible. 'For knowing why...why I had to choose Amelie—'

He broke off, and looked away, as if he could not bear to look at her. She felt emotion turn and twist within her.

'I wish you had told me, Evandro. Told me what Berenice was threatening. I would have understood—I would have left at once. You would not have needed to tell me to go.'

*Let alone in the brutal, callous way you did.*

A silent cry sounded within her. She'd told herself, convinced herself while walking by the Thames, that the man who had severed her from his life so dismissively could not be the same man she had found such happiness with. That something was wrong. It had been a feeling so strong and overpowering that it had triggered that terrifying dream last night, compelling her to come here to discover this scene of devastation and destruction.

But to what purpose?

The question mocked her, pain stabbing again.

For herself—none, she realised with bitter pain.

*In my dream he was calling for me. But it was only in my dream—in my own longing. I was foolish to hope it could ever be real.*

Because for all that he had told her now, and for all the longing in her—seeing the terrible scars on his face, the pain from his mangled leg etched in his face—to take him into her arms, to shelter him from what he had endured with all the love she felt for him, he obviously didn't feel the same way.

*He has not swept me into his arms—taken me back.*

She forced the realisation into her head, cruel though it was.

He'd moved on from women like Bianca, who'd been necessary for him to regain his freedom after Berenice.

*Moved on to me—because I helped him build the relationship with Amelie he needed to make. Because I brought him comfort after all he'd been through—helped him put his tormented past behind him so that he could move on again—move on from me. He will never love me as I love him. Never want me as I want him.*

It hurt so much to think it, to know it, but she had to face it. Face it and accept it. Anguish filled her, an anguish that she knew she'd carry with her all her life... And then, dimly, she realised he had started to speak.

'But I *did* need to tell you to go, Jenna,' he said.

His voice was still harsh, and she wondered at it.

'I needed to tell you   and in the callous way that I did.'

She looked at him, not understanding.

'Because,' he told her, 'I needed to make you hate me.'

She stepped back. Expression blank. His words did not make sense.

'Jenna, I didn't tell you about Berenice's threat because I knew what you would say—that you would never dream of urging me to do anything but concede to it. You would leave me for Amelie's sake, never thinking to do otherwise. And there was nothing I could do. Except what I did.'

He took a scissoring breath, as if forcing himself to go on.

'It was the only way to make sure you left me feeling

relief. Relief at being shot of a man who could end his relationship with you in such a brutal manner.'

He looked away for a moment, as if reluctant to look at her, to see her standing there, hearing what he was telling her. Then his gaze snapped back to her.

'It was the best thing I could do for you, Jenna—make you hate me so that you would be free to find someone worthy of you.' He stopped, took another scissoring breath. 'And you will, Jenna. You *will* find someone worthy of you.'

His words pierced her, like arrows burying themselves in her twice-broken heart. The heart that had broken when he'd sent her away. The heart that had broken again, just now, when she'd realised that even though Berenice and the threat she posed were gone, he was still sending her away, willing her to meet another man—a man who was not him.

Cold, empty, bleak despair filled her. She should go—and now. That would be best. She had no place here—not any more. She was unwanted and unloved. Unnecessary to him. He'd made that clear. Was making it clearer still as she heard what he was saying now, his words less halting, more resolute, and her heart tore in two all over again, the grief of it overwhelming her.

'It was good that you returned to England when you did, Jenna. Back to your own life.'

He placed a hand down on the surface of the desk, as if he needed the support, and went on speaking, though his voice seemed to be coming from very far away. From a distant place that was beyond her reach and always would be.

'A life that is yours and yours alone. A life that, one day, you will share with someone you can give your heart to.'

He turned away abruptly, limping with painful strides

towards the doors to the terrace, one arm outstretched towards the door jamb to help take the weight off his damaged leg. He looked back towards her, his face strained, sunlight from the terrace throwing into stark relief the livid scarring from his burns, the puckered skin around his half-blind eye.

And there was something in the expression in his face now, as his eyes went to her, that was like a sudden vice around her broken heart. What was in his face was unbearable to see—and it was not because of his terrible scars.

'Berenice came here that day to gloat,' he said. 'To celebrate her victory over me—the fact that I had yielded to her threat. But if her death took that power from her it gave her another. Her final triumph.'

The bitterness in his voice lacerated Jenna.

'It made me the maimed and crippled wreck that I am now.'

Evandro turned away again, staring half blindly out over the unspoilt gardens of the *palazzo*, bathed in autumnal sunlight. At the garden's edge he could see the chestnut that had been struck by lightning the night he had presumed to make Jenna his own. The burnt and sagging limbs had been cut back, but the tree's blackened, divided trunk was still standing. Scorched and stricken.

*As I am.*

Bitterness assailed him again.

Even from the grave Berenice's malignity still reached him.

He released the door jamb, painfully turned to face into the room again. To face the woman he did not want to face. Whom he wished with all his being had never come here. Had never seen him like this.

He steeled his jaw. But it was good that she was seeing him like this—so she would know how Berenice had parted them from each other.

He let his eyes rest on her.

*One last time.*

In the silence he could hear the ticking of the clock on the mantel over the fire. He frowned. Amelie would be home from school soon—and she must not see Jenna. It was imperative that she did not.

'Jenna.' He spoke abruptly, limping towards her. He needed his damn cane, his leg was aching as he walked without it. 'You need to leave. Amelie will be back soon and I don't want her—' He stopped. 'I don't want her seeing you. It would…upset her.' He took a razoring breath. 'She would think you had come back. To stay.'

He saw her swallow, then nod. There seemed to be something wrong with her face. It must be the strain of looking at him, trying not to let her pity and revulsion show. He wanted to laugh—mocking the gods as they now mocked him. Or was it just Berenice mocking him?

His lawyer's warning sounded in his ears, as it had so many times.

*'You're giving her the power to destroy your future.'*

His mouth twisted.

*And she has—she has destroyed my future. Destroyed it from the grave.*

Jenna was speaking, her voice low, and as strained as the expression on her face. How slight she looked, how pale. Her face was as white as it had been the night she'd sat in the corner of the salon while Bianca and her friends had partied all around her.

*Looking as though her world had ended.*

'I'm sorry, Evandro,' she was saying now. 'So very, very sorry. Sorry for all…all this…' She stumbled on her words. 'I even wish I could feel sorry for Berenice,' he heard her say. 'But I can't. However dreadful her end—' She broke off, pressed her hand to her forehead. 'God must forgive her,' she whispered, 'for I can't. Not for what she caused to happen to you—not just through all the years of your marriage, but now—'

She broke off again, dipping her head, shutting her eyes.

Weariness pressed in on him. 'Jenna, go back to England. Go back and be thankful…' Something twisted in his voice—he could not stop it. 'Be thankful you are done with me. For your lucky escape.'

Her eyes flared open, her head lifting. 'Escape?'

There was something in her voice that had not been there before. What it was he didn't know, but it did not stop him saying what he must say now. Roughly. Brusquely.

'Yes—escape! Go, Jenna. Flee as fast as you can.'

He wanted her to go. He couldn't take this any longer. Couldn't endure seeing her standing there—so close and yet so infinitely far away.

But she was not moving. She was standing stock-still, and what it was that had filled her voice was now filling her face…

He saw her think for a moment before speaking again. There was still that difference in her voice that he could not make out. And something different in the way she was looking at him as well. Something he could not comprehend. Her gaze clung to him, the intensity of it piercing.

'Evandro, that day—that day you sent me away. Tell me one thing and one thing only…'

There was hesitation in her voice now, and again he could not make out why. He saw her take a breath, as if steeling herself, then she spoke again, her voice low, intense. Insistent.

'If Berenice had never threatened to reclaim Amelie would you have sent me away? Oh, perhaps not then, and not in the way you did, but when she started school...? Would you ever have sent me away?'

Her eyes, so clear, like spring water, were set on him. He could not escape them. Nor escape answering her.

A single word. All that he could say. All that was in him to say.

'No,' he said.

Jenna shut her eyes again. Weak with what she had done. Weak with the tumult of emotion pouring through her. So weak she could scarcely lift her eyelids to look at him again.

He had not moved, still standing by the open doorway, the sunlight still etching the dreadful scars across one side of his face.

But courage filled her, summoned into being by that single word he'd said. Courage and so much more.

*All the love I have for him.*

'So why,' she said, 'are you sending me away again?'

A savage look flashed across his ravaged face. 'Do you really think I would do anything else now?' he answered, his voice as low and savage as that look.

She filled her gaze with that same intensity and pinioned him. 'Now what?' she asked. Challenging him. 'Now that you have a limp and there are scars across your face?'

She walked towards him. He could send her away now and she would go—but for one reason and one only. The only reason that had any power at all.

*Because he does not love me the way I love him. That is the only reason I would leave him now.*

Emotion fuelled her.

She went on walking towards where he stood, dark against the sunlight beyond, tension in every line of his body.

'Don't do this, Jenna,' he said, his voice low. 'Don't waste yourself on me.'

She ignored him, halting a metre away from him. Never taking her eyes from him. She had something to say and he *would* hear her.

'Evandro, I will tell you this and you will hear me.' She made her voice clear—incontestable—as she said the words he had to hear. 'Of all that I know about you, I know this most of all: you show your love by protecting those you love—even at the cost of your own happiness. You showed it for Amelie, for the daughter you love so much—*your* daughter—by protecting her from Berenice, whatever it took. You protected me by sending me away, as harshly as you could, because you thought it would set me free to hate you. And now,' she said, and this was the final, most vital thing she had to say to him, 'you think this is another gift, don't you, Evandro? Freeing me from a man who thinks of himself as a "maimed and crippled wreck."'

She quoted his own cruel description of himself back at him and her expression changed as she put her final, vital question to him. The question on which depended all the happiness of her life.

'Do you really think, Evandro, that scars and a limp would stop me loving you?'

She heard her words resonate, heard the declaration that she could not, *would* not recall.

'I fell in love with you, Evandro. I fell in love with you

and I will stay in love with you for ever. And not one of the scars on your face, or anywhere else, for that matter, can make a jot of difference!'

She took his hand, feeling the damaged scar tissue against her fingers, and looked up at him. She could see nothing in his face, but that did not matter now. She had to make him understand. Had to declare it all. Dare all.

'I love you, Evandro. And I don't know whether you love me back or not, but right now all I know is this. *This!*'

He was still looking at her with an expression she could not read, as she softly, clearly, spoke words written so long ago that still rang true.

'"Love is not love which alters when it alteration finds... O no! It is an ever-fixed mark that looks on tempests and is never shaken..."'

She gazed up at him, pouring her heart into her words, her gaze and her hands on his.

'*Never*, Evandro.' She spoke with absolute certainty. 'Hear that word. Understand it. *Never.*'

She let his hand fall away from her. In her chest she could feel her heart beating fast as she waited for his reply.

'Send me away or not, Evandro,' she said quietly, resolutely. 'It will *never* stop me loving you.'

He met her eyes. Melded his gaze with hers. For one long, endless moment he did not speak. And then...

'What have I done,' he said finally, his voice low and slow, 'to deserve you?'

He took back her hands, both of them, cradling them in his, and she could feel the welts on them where burning shards had scorched his flesh as he'd tried to rescue the woman who had wrought such terrible destruction. The look on his face stopped the breath in her.

'From the very first you have been a gift past all deserving—'

He broke off. Then spoke again, his voice still low, but filled now with an intensity of emotion that reached into the deepest recesses of her heart.

'Pushing you away like that was more pain than I ever want to feel again. And last night...' his face shadowed, etched with remembered darkness '...last night as I sat here, in my wrecked body, my wrecked home, knowing I could never ask...beg...you to come back to me, maimed as I am, I cried out to heaven with my desolation. I believed that Berenice's vengeance had been more thorough than she could ever have dreamt of—'

She freed a hand, laying a finger on his lips, silencing him. Berenice had been denied her victory.

'She's gone, Evandro. She's gone. For ever. She can hurt and damage and harm none of us any more. And we have each other...' Joy was filling her, radiating outwards to embrace him, to embrace the whole world. *'For ever.'*

She let her fingers trace the ragged seams of his scars. Lifted her mouth to graze his softly, sweetly. Then drew back. In his eyes was all she had longed so much to see. All his love for her.

'My lovely, loving woodland sprite,' he said, his voice low and husky, 'whom I love so very much...'

Emotion was rich in his voice, and Jenna's overflowing heart swelled with radiant joy as she heard it.

He kissed her again, more deeply this time, and she felt tears dew on her lashes. But she would not shed them. This was not a time for tears...only for joy. Nothing but joy after so much heartache, and heartbreak, and tragedy, and pain. Now only joy—

*For us both...for ever!*

And for one more.

Footsteps sounded on the terrace, light and rapid.

'Papà! I'm home—are you in here?'

Amelie burst in through the open French doors, then halted dead in her tracks, dropping her school bag on the floor. Evandro lifted his mouth from Jenna's, but she felt his hand squeeze hers, not relinquishing it.

A cry of disbelieving delight and excitement broke from Amelie. 'You came! You came, you came, you came!'

She hurled herself at Jenna, and Jenna dropped down to hug her back, crushing Amelie to her, her heart overflowing all over again at seeing the little girl she had come to love so dearly.

'I wished and wished and prayed and prayed!' Amelie cried into Jenna's neck. 'And you came—you came!'

Jenna felt Evandro haltingly hunker down beside them. When he spoke his voice was warm and rich with love—for *both* of them, Jenna knew with another rush of joy.

'Yes, *carina*, she came—and we will never let her go again, will we?' His arm came around them, warm on Jenna's shoulder. 'Never.'

Her heart was singing and she was radiant with joy, rapturous with it. With a whole heavenly chorus of everlasting joy.

He straightened, and Jenna did likewise. She could see him wince at the pressure the movement put on his damaged leg.

'Poppet, your *papà* needs to sit down…'

Making a fuss of him, Amelie and Jenna helped Evandro to his leather armchair.

Evandro dropped a kiss on Amelie's head. '*Mignonne*, run and find Signora Farrafacci. Ask her for a bottle of champagne. For we are going to celebrate—now and for always! And do not hurry back *too* fast, because you see…' He bent his head and whispered something in a conspiratorial fashion to Amelie, whose face lit up before she hared off.

Evandro caught at Jenna's hand as she stood beside his chair. His slate-dark eyes glinted with gold and she felt her heart turn over, that heavenly chorus of joy inside her reaching a crescendo.

'I know that I should go down on one knee to say this,' he said, and there was a ruefulness in his voice as he spoke, 'but I might never be able to get back up again if I do, so instead—'

He drew her down to perch on the arm of the chair, taking her other hand as well, raising each to his lips in turn. His gaze was alight, pouring into hers, rich and lambent and full of love—oh, so full of love. And his voice, as he spoke, was deep and filled with all that she could ever want to hear.

'Will you, my beloved Jenna, be my own true love, all my life, and take my love for you all your life? You are my blessing and my joy, my heart's delight and my body's pleasure, the companion of my days…the passion of my nights. Be mine, as I am yours, for now and all eternity.'

She felt tears dew on her eyelashes again, and he kissed them away with soft kisses.

'Is that a yes?' he asked.

She could hear the humour in his voice—and so much more. A world of more…

'For now and all eternity,' she answered.

For one long, endless moment they gazed deep into each other's eyes, secure in the knowledge that all that had parted them had gone for ever. Then his mouth claimed hers again. She was his own true love—as she knew she always would be—and her heart soared higher yet with joy, and higher still. Time stopped and eternity began—love's creation and its gift.

And then, as their endless kiss sealed their love, their happiness, the library doors were flung open and Amelie burst in again, followed by Signora Farrafacci bearing champagne, and Loretta and Maria holding champagne flutes and a jug of orange juice for Amelie.

There was a cacophony of congratulations and laughter and excitement and happiness, and Amelie dancing around in joyful glee, and the pop of the champagne cork, and the fetching of more glasses for the housekeeper and the maids as well, and the brimming of flutes… And Jenna was embracing everyone, and glasses were raised in toasts and salutations and felicitations such that the noise must reach heaven itself.

Except that heaven was surely here right now…and always would be.

Jenna's joy-filled eyes swept the happy throng before coming back, as they always would, to her beloved Evandro…

*Mine, oh, mine at last. As I am his.*

And would be—always and for ever now.

# EPILOGUE

Amelie was messaging her friend.

Luisa, she's married him! I knew she would—I wished and wished, and prayed and prayed, and now she has! And I was bridesmaid. I wore a cream dress with lace on it and I will send you a photo, because it is lovely and I will keep it to wear again at special parties, my new mamma says.

It wasn't a big wedding, because poor Papà's bad leg is still not completely healed, and he has to have an operation on his eye so he can see properly again, and our home is still being repaired. It's very sad with it so much burnt down, and even sadder that my poor maman died, but Papà says she had a kind of illness inside her head, which is why I came to live here in Italy. I put flowers on her grave and the nuns pray for her, and so do I.

Reverend Mother says she is in heaven now, so she is not ill any more, or dead, because no one is ill or dead in heaven. And Reverend Mother says God has sent me a new mamma—not to take her place, but to be an extra mamma, one that's alive, and I can love her as well as Papà, which I do already.

And Papà asked would I like a baby brother or sister, like you already have, and I said yes, please, so he is going to ask Mamma to grow one especially for me.

And for them, too, as they would love to have a baby as well, my new mamma says. And I can help choose names when he or she is born.

It will take quite a long time for the baby to grow, so we shall have Christmas by ourselves, and then we shall go to Sorrento for New Year, and they will have fireworks at sea, and I can watch them from the balcony of my great-aunt's house. She is very old, but I like her, and she is looking after the dolls' house Papà bought me in the summer from Naples.

I am going to stop now, because my fingers are tired and it is time for dinner. I can wear whatever outfit I like, Mamma says, because it is the weekend, so I am going to wear the frou-frou skirt with the sequinned top which I love, even though Mamma doesn't, but she doesn't say so, and nor does Papà, but he doesn't say so either. But my maman in heaven bought it for me, so I think I should wear it for her.

She said as much to Jenna when she came downstairs, and Jenna kissed her gently and said that it was the right thing to do. It had been hard for Amelie to learn that Berenice was dead, but at least she knew that her father had nearly died himself, trying to save her.

'I did try, *mignonne*. I promise you with all my heart's love that I tried to save her,' he'd said, sad for the waste and tragedy of it all.

But Jenna's words echoed in him, helping him make what peace he could with Berenice's memory.

'No child is born bad. That's the first lesson a teacher must learn. Just as something made my father cold and unloving towards me, so something warped and twisted Berenice, even if we can't understand what it was. Maybe all we can say is that there was a sickness inside her—

and we can understand her better for that, Evandro. Feel compassion because she was never able to know happiness, as we are blessed enough to know it.'

Her eyes went to Amelie, lighting with the love she felt for the little girl.

'And she gave us both so great a gift, Evandro,' she said quietly. 'She gave us your daughter. For Amelie *is* your daughter, by every measure that counts.'

'And yours,' he said, taking her into his arms. 'Never, for an instant, think otherwise.'

'Ours.' She smiled.

And as they went into dinner, hand in hand, Jenna remembered how they'd stood, the three of them, out on the terrace at sunset, and how she'd longed so much for what they now—thankfully, truly—were.

Family.

Loving and united.

For all their days.

\* \* \* \* \*

# THE GREEK WEDDING SHE NEVER HAD

## CHANTELLE SHAW

For Oly, who will find his own solutions!

# PROLOGUE

A SHAFT OF evening sunlight slanting through the window struck the enormous diamond on Eleanor's finger. Set on a platinum band, the square diamond sparkled with fiery brilliance as she held her hand out in front of her to admire the ring. Earlier in the day she'd gasped when Jace had opened a small velvet box to reveal an engagement ring.

They had been walking beside the Seine in Paris when he'd halted and turned to her. 'Will you do me the honour of becoming my wife, *pouláki mou*?' he had asked her softly.

For a few seconds Eleanor had been too shocked to reply, wondering if she had misunderstood him. Jace Zagorakis was a gorgeous Greek god and it seemed impossible that he had proposed marriage to *her*—ordinary Eleanor Buchanan. It was the stuff of fairy tales.

'Do you really want to marry me?' she'd stammered.

'I do.' His sexy smile had sent her heart shooting towards the stratosphere.

'In that case, *yes*,' she'd said joyfully, blinking back tears of happiness as he slid the ring onto her finger. 'Oh, Jace, I love you so much,' she'd murmured when he drew her into his arms. 'Of course I'll marry you.'

'Good.' There had been satisfaction in his voice before he'd claimed her lips in a kiss that left her breath-less. 'I would prefer a small wedding as soon as it can be arranged. There is no reason to wait and I am impa-tient to make you my bride.'

Eleanor had felt as if she were walking on air when they'd spent the afternoon strolling through the Tuile-ries Garden before heading back to their hotel in sight of the Eiffel Tower. She had returned to her own room to change for dinner.

Now she used the key card Jace had given her and entered his suite. There was no sign of him, but she was early and perhaps he was still dressing, or in the shower. Heat spread over her face as her imagination ran riot, fuelled by memories of his powerfully muscu-lar physique when he had worn a pair of swim shorts on a yacht cruising around the northern Aegean islands two months ago.

Eleanor had been wildly attracted to him on the cruise and over the course of the following weeks, when he had flown to England from his home in Thessaloniki regularly to visit her, she had fallen in love with him. Incredibly, it seemed that Jace shared her feelings.

Crossing the lounge, she saw that the dining table was laid for an intimate dinner. There was a bottle of champagne on ice and a centrepiece of exquisite red roses. The flowers' heady perfume filled the air. Red roses for love. Eleanor's heart skipped a beat at the thought that Jace must have ordered the roses when he'd arranged for a celebration dinner to be served in his suite.

She placed the box of Greek pastries that she'd or-dered, knowing they were his favourite, on the table. This was her first visit to Paris. When they had arrived that morning, before taking her sightseeing Jace had led her to a Greek café where they had been served tiny cups of strong black coffee and honey cakes. Eleanor had been amused to discover that ultra-sophisticated and frankly enigmatic business tycoon Jace Zagorakis had a weakness for sweet pastries.There were many more things she had yet to learn about her future husband, she mused. No doubt her grandfather would have advised against rushing into marriage after a whirlwind romance. But Kostas had died six months ago and, although Eleanor missed him, she felt a sense of freedom that she had not experienced while Pappoús had been the head of the family. Not that there were many members of her family left. Just her brother and sister, who resented that Kostas had named her his heir to the hotel business, Gilpin Leisure.

With a faint sigh, Eleanor dismissed thoughts of her problematic siblings. Today was the most wonderful day of her life and she was cocooned in a bubble of happiness. Glancing across the room, she saw through an open door a bedroom with a four-poster bed. Her heart gave a lurch of nervous anticipation. Tonight she planned to sleep with Jace, but it would be her first sexual experience. He was unaware that she was a virgin and she hoped he would not be disappointed.

When he kissed her the passion between them was electrifying, she reminded herself. Jace had awoken her desires, but he had been patient and not rushed her into sex. Now, though, she was eager to give herself to him and show her love for him with her body as well as her heart.

The prospect of losing her virginity did not worry Eleanor, but her old insecurities surfaced at the idea of being naked in front of Jace. He was bound to notice the scar on her back. It ran from the base of her neck all the way down her spine, the result of an operation when she was thirteen to correct a curvature of her spine. The condition, called scoliosis, had required surgery, where two titanium rods and numerous screws had been inserted in her back.

The surgery had been successful but she'd struggled with body image issues, especially when she had started dating, and a boyfriend had reacted with horror to her scar. Self-consciousness about her body was one reason why she had avoided serious relationships. Jace had broken through her reserve, but on the boat in Greece she'd worn a high-neck swimsuit or covered up with a sarong.

Her pulse leapt when she heard his gravelly, accented voice. The voile curtain across the open glass doors moved in the breeze and she glimpsed his tall figure standing on the suite's private balcony. He was holding his phone in front of him and Eleanor realised that he was on a video call.

'Takis, did you receive my message?'

'I certainly did,' replied a disembodied male voice. 'I assume the announcement that you are engaged is a joke, seeing how you have always maintained that you are a die-hard bachelor with an aversion to marriage.'

'The situation is not as it seems,' Jace drawled.

Eleanor had started to walk back across the room, intending to wait out in the corridor until Jace had finished his conversation. But she hesitated, puzzled by his cynical tone. The two men were talking in Greek, which she spoke fluently, having been taught it by her grandfather.

'So, you are actually engaged to Eleanor Buchanan.' The man on the phone, Takis, sounded shocked. 'Even though she is the granddaughter of Kostas Pangalos, who you despised when he was alive.'

'My hatred of Kostas has not lessened since his death,' Jace said in a harsh voice that Eleanor had never heard from him before.

She felt a sensation like an ice cube sliding down her spine. Her conscience urged her to leave. Jace wasn't expecting her to arrive for another ten minutes and she should respect his privacy. But her feet were welded to the floor when Takis spoke again.

'For years you've told me how Kostas swindled your father out of his share of their hotel, and Dimitri was financially ruined. So why on earth would you marry your enemy's granddaughter?' Takis sounded incredulous.

'You know I tried to buy the Pangalos, before Kostas died, but he rejected my offer. When I heard that he'd left Eleanor in charge of Gilpin Leisure, I did not know if she was aware of the feud that had existed between my father and her grandfather,' Jace said in a grim tone. 'That's why I asked you to approach her and try to persuade her to sell the Pangalos hotel.'

'Having met Eleanor, I'll admit I'm surprised by your choice of bride,' Takis murmured. 'I mean she is charming and pretty in an understated way, but she's not the sex bomb type you usually go for. Her party-loving sister, on the other hand, is stunning, from photos I've seen of her in the media.'

Jace laughed, but it wasn't his warm, sensual laugh that had attracted Eleanor to him when she'd first met him in Greece. He sounded cold and cynical.

'It's true that Eleanor is not an eye-catching peacock like her showy sister. She is more of an unremarkable sparrow. But my engagement to her is not a love-match.'

Eleanor gave a choked cry. She felt numb with shock and it was as if her lungs were being crushed in a vice, making it agony to breathe. Jace often called her *poul-láki mou,* which in English meant 'my little bird'. She had believed that his pet name for her was a sign of his affection. But he had compared her to a boring brown sparrow! As if that wasn't hurtful enough, he evidently thought her sister Lissa was attractive.

The pain in Eleanor's chest felt as though an arrow had pierced her heart. Jace *loved* her, she assured herself frantically. Why else would he have asked her to marry him?

But he hadn't actually said how he felt about her.

Doubt slid like a poisonous serpent into her head as she acknowledged that he had never uttered the three little words she longed to hear. When she had told him that she loved him, Jace had responded by drawing her into his arms and kissing her until she'd trembled with desire. But she had just heard him say that she was un-remarkable.

She stared at her reflection in the full-length mirror on the wall and the scales fell from her eyes. Her new dress that she'd rushed out and bought when Jace had invited her to spend the weekend with him was a roman-tic froth of pink tulle, but it wasn't glamorous. She had tied her long hair back with a matching pink ribbon. The dress's sweetheart neckline was more daring than her usual restrained style, and before coming to meet Jace she had lost her nerve and covered up with a cardigan.

Compared to the elegant Parisian women Eleanor had noticed shopping on the Champs-Elysées, and who had no doubt caught Jace's eye, she was neither sophis-ticated nor sexy. In truth, she had wondered why he was attracted to her. It turned out that he'd been lying to her all along. Nausea churned in the pit of Eleanor's stomach. She had taken extra care putting on her make-up, but now tears spilled from her eyes and two black tracks of mascara ran down her cheeks.

She recalled that a few weeks after her grandfather had suffered a fatal heart attack, a man had come to Francine's—the hotel in Oxford owned by Gilpin Leisure—and introduced himself as Takis Samaras, CEO of a Greek luxury hotel chain, Perseus. He had been very keen to buy the Pangalos, but she'd told him she had no intention of selling any of Gilpin Leisure's assets.

Now she knew that Jace wanted the hotel and he did not care about her. She was devastated to discover what he really thought of her and she wanted to run away and hide like a wounded animal, but she forced herself to remain where she stood when he spoke again.

'Marriage to Eleanor is the only way I can claim back the hotel that her grandfather took from my father. I have discovered that a clause in Kostas's will stipulates that the Pangalos must remain within the family's ownership.' Jace swore. 'The wily old fox must have gloated, believing he had prevented me from getting my hands on the hotel that by rights should be half mine. But I met his granddaughter and it was easy to make Eleanor fall in love with me.'

Jace pocketed his phone and strode across the balcony. He'd heard a faint sound from inside his suite and through the voile curtain he glimpsed a shadowy figure. There was the faint click of a door closing and when he stepped into the room there was no one there.

His frown cleared when he saw on the table a cake box with the name of a Greek bakery on the lid, and he guessed that one of the hotel's staff had delivered it to his suite. He opened the box and smiled, certain that Eleanor was responsible for ordering the selection of sweet treats: *baklava*, *loukoumades* and his particular favourite, *kataifi*—little pastries drenched in almond syrup.

Jace drank alcohol in moderation and he had never taken drugs, but he had confessed to Eleanor that he had a sweet tooth. It was typical of her to have remembered and arranged the thoughtful gift. He ran his hand over the stubble on his jaw and swore beneath his breath as he thought of his diffident fiancée.

Two months ago, Jace had decided on a whim to visit the Pangalos Beach Resort on Sithonia, a peninsular in the region of Halkidiki in northern Greece. It was the first time he had returned to the hotel since he was eleven years old, and he'd been swamped by bitter memories of how he and his parents had been forcibly evicted from the building by Kostas's security staff.

The Pangalos had been extensively refurbished, and inside it was almost unrecognisable. But when Jace had stepped into the lobby he'd pictured his mother and father standing arm in arm, waiting to greet guests. It was the personal touches that made families return year after year, Jace's father had insisted. Guests who stayed at the Pangorakis hotel, which had been its name back then, were made to feel as though they were part of a big, happy family.

But Kostas had been determined to attract a different class of clientele: the super-rich, who wanted five-star luxury and were prepared to pay for it. Arguments about the future direction of the hotel had led to a breakdown in the two men's friendship, and Kostas, backed by money from his wealthy English wife and aided by influential Greek friends, had seized control of the Pangorakis, later changing its name to the Pangalos.

Six months ago Kostas had died suddenly and, to everyone's surprise, he had left his granddaughter Eleanor in charge of Gilpin Leisure. The company owned an upmarket boutique hotel, Francine's, in Oxford, and the Pangalos Beach Resort in Greece. By all accounts, Eleanor's older brother, Mark Buchanan, had been furious at being overlooked by his grandfather. Eleanor had appointed him as General Manager of the Pangalos, but Jace had heard rumours that Mark was more interested in playing blackjack in the casino than managing the hotel.

When Jace had strolled across the pool terrace he'd taken scant notice of a young woman sitting on a sun lounger, her head bowed over a book. But he'd overheard a waiter who had brought her a drink saying, 'Will that be all, Miss Buchanan?'

The name had caught Jace's attention and he'd recognised Eleanor from a newspaper photo when her grandfather's death had been announced. Nondescript was his first opinion of her. Dark blonde hair pulled back from an unprepossessing face. Pale skin, turning pink on her shoulders from the sun. Good legs, he'd noted, before skimming his eyes over her shapely figure.

She was wearing a one-piece swimsuit that covered her body from neck to thigh but nevertheless did not disguise the gentle curves of her hips and the firm swell of her breasts. Oddly, Jace had found her modest costume more alluring than the skimpy bikinis worn by other women sunbathing by the pool. In his opinion, the unknown was intriguing, rather like a birthday present that was still wrapped.

There had been no plan in his head when he'd sat

down on a vacant sun lounger next to Eleanor. He had flirted with women since he was a teenager and discovered that his dark good looks and muscular physique commanded female attention. With consummate skill he had drawn Eleanor into conversation. He'd watched her closely when he had introduced himself, but she had shown no reaction to his name.

To his surprise, Kostas's granddaughter was charming, if a little too serious. Eliciting one of her rare smiles became a challenge, and the upward curve of her wide mouth had an unexpected effect on Jace's libido. He had decided that it might be useful to get to know her better, but marriage had not been in his mind when he'd joined her on a cruise around the islands of Thasos and Lemnos.

During the trip, Eleanor had confided that she felt overwhelmed by the responsibility that had been thrust on her by her grandfather. 'I want to fulfil Pappoús's expectations, and I hope he would be proud of me,' she'd told Jace. 'He established the Pangalos hotel and made it a success without help from anyone.'

Jace had gritted his teeth at hearing how Kostas had rewritten the hotel's history without crediting the hard work and sacrifice his father had made. But it was clear that Eleanor had loved her grandfather, and Jace had held back from telling her the truth—that Kostas had ruthlessly conned Dimitri out of his share of the business that the two men had started together.

Jace had been fifteen when he'd found his father's body at the bottom of a cliff. Incredibly, Dimitri had still been alive and with his last breaths he had entreated Jace to take back the family's share of the hotel on Sithonia for his mother's sake. For twenty years Jace had been driven by his hatred of Kostas and his determination to honour his father's dying plea. Eleanor was his chance, he'd realised. Marriage to her would allow him to claim part-ownership of the Pangalos hotel, and there was the added satisfaction of knowing that Kostas would turn in his grave.

The plan was perfect and yet so simple, Jace thought now as he walked over to the bar and poured a generous measure of single malt whisky into a glass. He checked his watch. Two minutes to seven. Eleanor would be here soon. In fact, he was surprised that she hadn't arrived early for their celebratory dinner. Her infatuation with him had made it easy for him to seduce her.

He frowned as he recalled the look of stunned joy in Eleanor's hazel eyes when he'd asked her to marry him. Obviously, he had not told her the real reason why he had asked her to be his wife. His ultimate goal was to seize absolute ownership of the Pangalos. Kostas had ruined his father, and so he would ruin Kostas's legacy. Marriage was the price he was prepared to pay to get his hands on the hotel.

Jace sipped his whisky and brooded that marriage was a fool's game. Several of his friends had been stung with expensive divorce settlements. He was thankful that Katerina had turned him down years ago. Hell, it had hurt at the time, and for a while he'd nursed a broken heart. But her rejection had emphasised the life lesson he'd learned from Kostas's betrayal of his father. Loyalty counted for nothing and money was everything. Except that in this instance, even though Jace was a self-made multi-millionaire, he was prevented from buying the Pangalos by a clause in Kostas's will.

So he would marry Eleanor Buchanan and it would be a sweet victory to finally avenge his father's destruction. The only pity was that Kostas would never know he had lost. As for his blushing bride, Jace's body tightened in anticipation of taking Eleanor to bed later tonight. He knew she wanted him. Her ardent response when he kissed her had been a pleasant surprise. Rather more surprising was his urgency to make love to her. He sensed that her reserved nature hid a sensuality which he was looking forward to awakening.

As Takis had pointed out, Eleanor was not in the league of the sexually confident women Jace usually chose for his lovers. He kept his life free from emotional entanglements and he planned to do the same when he married. When Eleanor was his wife he would provide her with a luxurious lifestyle for the duration of their marriage, and he would give her a generous divorce settlement. He dismissed a twinge of guilt that he was involving her in a feud which she was unaware of.

Deeply satisfied with the way things had worked out, he drank the rest of his whisky and checked his watch again. One of the things he liked about his fiancée was her punctuality. He had left nothing to chance, and had wooed Eleanor diligently for the past couple of months, flying over to England most weekends to see her. Every time he'd collected her to take her out to dinner she had been waiting on the doorstep and hadn't disguised her pleasure at seeing him. Thinking of Eleanor's eagerness evoked another pang of guilt as Jace acknowledged that he would never love her.

There was a knock on the door and Jace went to open it, wondering why Eleanor had not used the key card he'd given her.

'Monsieur Zagorakis.' The concierge stood in the corridor. 'I have a package for you from Mademoiselle Buchanan.'

'*Merci.*' Jace frowned as he took the sealed envelope

from the man. He closed the door and ripped open the envelope. The diamond engagement ring that he had placed on Eleanor's finger earlier in the day fell into his palm. What the hell?

The accompanying note was brief.

*I know what you did and I don't want to marry you.*

Jace's jaw clenched. His mind flew back to when he had been a young man and he recalled Katerina's mocking rejection of his marriage proposal. He'd saved his wages from his job as a labourer on a building site for months so that he could buy her an engagement ring, but she had looked scathingly at the tiny diamond he'd proudly offered her.

'*Of course I'm not going to marry you! I want a husband with money and career prospects,*' Katerina told him. '*Not someone who spent time in prison and has a criminal record. You're a sexy stud, Jace, but you are not good enough for me.*'

Soon after, he'd heard that Katerina had married a wealthy shipping tycoon who was old enough to be her father. Jace reread Eleanor's note and something black and ugly coiled through him when he realised that she must have found out about his past.

He'd seen no reason to tell her. It had happened a long time ago and he'd paid his debt to society. The stakes had been too high. He hadn't explained that he'd been to prison, fearing she might refuse to marry him. No marriage meant no hotel, and no possibility of honouring the promise he had made to his father.

Jace stared at the diamond ring glittering in his palm and swore. He picked up the phone and pressed the number for Eleanor's room. She did not answer, and her mobile went straight to voicemail. Cursing, he put a call through to the reception desk and learned that Mademoiselle Buchanan had checked out five minutes ago.

*Theos.* Anger ran like molten lava through Jace's veins as his plan to reclaim the Pangalos unravelled. It had always been about the hotel, but there was an inexplicable heaviness in his chest when he thought of Eleanor. She had seemed besotted with him, yet she'd left without a word. Why hadn't she given him a chance to explain what had really happened when he'd been given a prison sentence?

The answer was obvious to him. Despite his wealth and his meteoric rise to success, he could not escape from his past. He had clawed his way out of the gutter, but Eleanor must have decided that he was not good enough to be her husband, Jace thought bitterly.

# CHAPTER ONE

*One year later*

ELEANOR LOVED THE peace and tranquillity of flying in a hot-air balloon. The balloon floated on the breeze, creating a magical sensation of stillness and silence. She could taste the crisp morning air and feel the sun on her face.

After gaining her private pilot's licence six months ago, she and another pilot, Nigel, had clubbed together to buy a balloon and they took it in turns to fly whenever the weather was suitable. The conditions were perfect this morning. She had met Nigel and the ground crew in a field before dawn, and they had helped her to inflate the balloon and heat the air inside the canopy with the burner. Eleanor had climbed into the basket, the ropes were untied and the balloon rose gently into the sky.

The mist had cleared with the sunrise and the view over the Oxfordshire countryside from two thousand feet up was breathtaking. In the distance she could see the graceful spires of the university buildings, while below, the River Thames was a ribbon of silvery blue curling through the green fields. As the balloon drifted serenely over a park, she heard dogs barking and recognised the sweet song of a skylark.

Her first experience of ballooning had been as a child when she'd been diagnosed with scoliosis and had to wear a back brace to prevent the curve in her spine from getting worse. She had hated being trapped in a rigid plastic jacket that fitted underneath her arms and went down to her hips. Her condition had prevented her from doing many physical activities, but her parents had continued to take her brother and sister on adventure holidays and skiing trips. Eleanor had stayed with her grandparents and she'd put on a brave face and assured everyone that she did not mind missing out on family events. But inside she'd felt hurt. Scoliosis made her different, a problem for her parents, and, she was convinced, less loveable than Mark and Lissa.

Her grandfather had been the only person who'd seemed to understand how Eleanor felt. One time when her parents and siblings were away, Pappoús had arranged for her to have a flight in a hot-air balloon. It had been an amazing experience and while in the air she had forgotten about her back pain and lack of mobility.

Since her surgery she had been able to lead a normal life, but she'd continued to suffer from a lack of self-confidence. Hearing Jace describe her as unremarkable had spurred Eleanor on to prove to herself that he was wrong, and she had fulfilled her dream of becoming a balloon pilot.

Flying required her to stay focused and in the moment, and today more than ever she was glad of the distraction to stop herself from remembering that a year ago Jace had proposed to her. *No*, she would not think about him, she ordered herself. And she definitely wouldn't cry. She'd wasted enough tears on Jace Zagorakis.

Down on the ground, something glittered brightly

and caught her attention. It was probably caused by the sun on a window, but the sparkle evoked memories of the diamond engagement ring Jace had placed on her finger. Eleanor screwed up her eyes to hold back her tears that brimmed despite her best effort to banish them, along with memories of the lying Greek who had shattered her heart. She had not told anyone about her engagement, which was probably the shortest on record, she thought bitterly.

She'd had a lucky escape, she reminded herself. If she hadn't overheard Jace's phone conversation she would have slept with him in Paris. And she would have married him, unaware that he did not love her. All he'd wanted was the hotel on Sithonia. Eleanor brushed away a tear. A year ago she'd listened to her heart and ignored her common sense, which had warned that sexy, charismatic Jace was out of her league.

She forced her mind from the past, frustrated that she had allowed memories of Jace to infiltrate her aerial sanctuary. Flying the balloon gave her a sense of identity and pride that she had completed the extensive training and passed the exams to earn her pilot's licence. After an hour she looked for a suitable field where she could land and contacted the ground crew on the two-way radio to tell them where to meet her. Bringing the balloon down required all her piloting skills as she controlled the rate of descent. When she was safely down on the ground and the balloon had been packed away, she congratulated herself for not thinking about Jace for a whole hour.

Balloons could only fly early in the morning or in the evening when the air was cooler and more stable. By ten a.m. Eleanor was driving through the centre of Oxford on her way back to Francine's. The hotel had been named after her English grandmother, whose family had bought the historic property and turned it into the finest hotel in the county.

For the past year Eleanor had thrown herself into work. Before her grandfather had died, he'd talked about updating the Oxford hotel's rather dated interior. When Eleanor had inherited the company, she'd pushed ahead with plans for Francine's to undergo an extensive refurbishment. It had meant closing the hotel for three months while the work was carried out, and the loss of revenue, combined with escalating building costs had led to a dramatic dip in Gilpin Leisure's profits.

Fortunately, the Pangalos was doing well, so her brother had assured her. She had put Mark in charge of the beach resort to make up for him being snubbed by their grandfather. Since she'd broken off her engagement, she had distanced herself from the place where she'd first met Jace. There was no reason why she would have to meet the lying toad ever again, but to be on the safe side Eleanor did not plan on going to Greece any time soon.

An expensive-looking black saloon car was parked at the front of Francine's when Eleanor drove onto the forecourt. Business had been slow to pick up since the hotel had reopened, but the marketing department had run a promotional campaign to attract new bookings. With any luck, whoever owned the luxury car would decide to stay in the most expensive suite for a month, she thought as she drove round to the back of the hotel.

A private wing adjoining the main building had been Eleanor's home since her parents had died in an accident when she was twelve, and she and her brother and sister had been brought up by their grandparents. She had a meeting with the hotel's event's manager scheduled for eleven o'clock and ran up to her room to change her clothes before heading into the kitchen to grab a coffee.

She was surprised to find that her sister was up and dressed before midday. Lissa lived in London and only came back to Oxford occasionally, usually when she wanted money. Pappoús's decision to put Eleanor in control of her sister's trust fund until Lissa was twenty-five had put a further strain on their relationship.

'Where have you been?' Lissa yawned and sounded uninterested. She did not wait for Eleanor to reply. 'There's a guy here to see you. He didn't give his name, but he said that he's involved with a hotel chain in Greece called Poseidon…or Perseus. Something like that.'

Eleanor's heart had stopped when Lissa mentioned Greece. 'I've heard of Perseus Hotels,' she said flatly. Fifteen months ago Takis Samaras had been very keen to buy the Pangalos, but now she knew that he had been sent by Jace. 'Did Mary give any more details about this man?' She was surprised that her secretary hadn't asked the visitor to make an appointment.

Lissa shook her head and her platinum blonde bob swirled around her face. 'He didn't go into the hotel. He came to the house.' She grimaced. 'The doorbell woke me up. He insisted that he has something important to discuss with you and he's waiting in the sitting room.'

Eleanor shrugged. 'I have an idea what he wants, but he's wasting his time. It was Pappoús's wish that the Pangalos remains in the family's ownership.'

'And of course you would never go against his wishes,' Lissa mocked. 'Even when we were children you were always boringly well-behaved. I guess that's why Pappoús made you his heir.'

'I take my responsibility for Gilpin Leisure seriously,

but it doesn't mean that I'm boring,' Eleanor muttered, stung by her sister's comment.

Lissa's brows rose. 'You dress like a nun, you hardly ever go out, and you haven't had a serious relationship in living memory.'

Eleanor bit her lip. For the brief time she'd been dating Jace, her sister had been in California, trying to launch an acting career. Lissa's dig about her clothes was unfair. She glanced down at her black pencil skirt, white blouse and black cardigan, teamed with low-heeled black court shoes. 'I have to dress smartly for work,' she defended herself.

'Take my advice and ditch the cardigan,' Lissa told her. 'The Greek guy is a hunk and he's not likely to take an interest in you when you're dressed like his mother.'

'I don't want him to take an interest in me.' God forbid, Eleanor thought with a shudder. One devious Greek was enough. Jace had broken her heart and she would never be idiotic enough to trust a man ever again.

She finished her coffee and walked down the hallway, but hesitated outside the sitting room. A year ago she had felt utterly humiliated when she'd overheard Jace state the real reason he had asked her to marry him. If he had sent his friend to Oxford for a second time to try to persuade her to sell the Pangalos, she would let Takis know that he'd had a wasted journey.

Eleanor opened the sitting room door and her eyes flew to the tall, imposing figure standing facing the window, silhouetted against the brightness outside. He had haunted her dreams too often, and she instantly recognised the breadth of his shoulders and the arrogant tilt of his head.

'*You?*' Her breath was squeezed out of her lungs and she clung to the door handle as her legs turned to jelly.

Jace Zagorakis turned around and Eleanor's heart stopped beating as she stared at his chiselled features that were imprinted on her psyche. He was still sinfully beautiful, but his face seemed harder, the high cheekbones sharper, giving him a predatory look that made her heart slam against her ribcage.

From across the room his eyes appeared to be black, but she knew that they were the colour of bittersweet chocolate and fringed by impossibly long black lashes. His thick, dark brown hair was stylishly groomed but curled rebelliously over his collar, and his facial stubble did not disguise the uncompromising set of his square jaw.

Eleanor's gaze was drawn to his mouth that curved in a sardonic smile as if he were amused by her startled reaction to him. What had he expected? she wondered. Had he thought that she would be pleased to see him?

For months after she'd fled from his hotel suite in Paris, she had hoped he would come after her and explain that it had all been a misunderstanding, and he was really in love with her. But he hadn't contacted her in a year and her misery had turned to anger and disillusionment. She was tempted to run away from the man who had treated her with such callous disregard. But Eleanor Buchanan was not a coward and she uncurled her fingers from the door handle and lifted her chin as she walked further into the room.

'This is a surprise, Jace. Although I can't say it's a pleasant one.' She was pleased that she sounded composed even though her heart was thumping.

He strolled towards her, but to her relief he halted several feet away. An amused smile still played on his lips, but his eyes resting on her face were watchful.

'I recall a time when you were pleased to see me, Eleanor,' he drawled. His gravelly voice with its discernible Greek accent was deliciously sexy and Eleanor could not control a quiver of response to his raw masculinity.

She flushed, remembering that when they had been dating and Jace had come to Oxford to visit her, she had run into his arms, eager for his kiss. She had been like an exuberant puppy wagging its tail for its master's attention, she thought with embarrassment.

'Why are you here?' she demanded.

His brows rose at her abrupt tone. 'I want to talk to you.'

'I'm busy. If you have something important to discuss, I suggest you speak to my secretary to arrange an appointment.' She glared at him, her anger mounting. How dare he walk back into her life as if nothing had happened? 'You lost the right to want anything from me after what you did.'

Jace's dark eyes flashed, but Eleanor sensed the effort he made to control his temper. 'What did I do?' he asked mildly.

'Don't pretend you don't know. I *heard* you.' Her voice shook with emotions she was desperate to hide from him. 'I came to your hotel room in Paris and overheard you talking on your phone to Takis Samaras. You told him that you planned to marry me because you wanted my grandfather's hotel.'

'So it was you who left a box of pastries,' Jace murmured. His eyes searched her face intently, as if he were trying to read her thoughts. 'And you listened in on my private conversation. Was that the reason you ran out on me without telling me you were leaving? You switched off your phone and I had no way of knowing if you were safe.'

'Like you cared,' she mocked. 'Of course it's why I

left. Do you think I would have stayed and pretended that everything was all right between us after I'd discovered that you didn't...that you don't...?' She broke off and bit down hard on her lip so that she tasted blood.

'I don't what?' he prompted.

Eleanor closed her eyes and when she opened them again he was still there in front of her, not a figment of her imagination but a living, breathing, impossibly handsome man who had never given a damn about her.

'You don't love me,' she said flatly. 'Do you?'

His silence extinguished the tiny flame of hope that had burned valiantly inside her. What a fool she was to have wondered if his visit was because he had realised that he had feelings for her after all. Bitterness filled the void where her heart had been until Jace had ripped it out.

'I don't suppose it was a coincidence that you went to the Pangalos last spring,' she said dully. 'You must have known I was staying there, and you made a point of introducing yourself. But you only pretended to be interested in me.'

He frowned. 'That's not true. I went to the hotel by chance and recognised you.'

'I told you I was leaving the next day for a cruise around the islands. Was it a coincidence that you joined the yacht just before it was about to sail? I don't think so,' she answered for him. 'I think you deliberately set out to seduce me, and you plotted to seize control of the Pangalos because of an alleged feud between your father and my grandfather.'

'The feud was real,' Jace said harshly. 'My father and Kostas were best friends until your grandfather got greedy. He and his clever lawyers conned my father out of his half-share of the hotel. But it wasn't only that my father was bankrupt and he and my mother lost everything they had worked for, including our home.' Jace's jaw hardened. 'My father was devastated that his friend, who he had trusted and loved, showed him no loyalty. Kostas destroyed my father and broke his heart.'

'And so you decided to break mine. Is that why you did it?' Eleanor's voice cracked. 'You wanted revenge for a crime that frankly I don't even believe happened. My grandfather was a good man and he would not have behaved in a way that was illegal or immoral. But what *you* did was unforgivable.'

She dashed her hand over her face and was mortified to find her cheeks were wet. 'I was a sexual innocent and I didn't stand a chance against you—an experienced playboy.'

The air between them crackled with tension. Eleanor wondered when Jace had stepped nearer to her without her being aware of him moving. He loomed over her, six-feet-plus of physical perfection and so close that her senses were assailed by the spicy scent of his aftershave.

'Are you saying you were a virgin when we met?' he asked curtly. 'You spoke in the past tense, so does that mean you are no longer one?'

She clenched her hands by her sides and fought the temptation to slap his arrogantly beautiful face. 'It's none of your damned business.'

Jace did not know why he had probed Eleanor about her private life. Even more inexplicable was the surge of jealousy he felt at the idea of her in another man's bed. It wasn't as if they had been lovers and, even if they had, he'd never had a problem moving on at the end of a relationship. Admittedly, he hadn't wanted their engagement to be over, but that was only because he had needed to marry Eleanor to acquire the Pangalos hotel.

Jace could have sworn that he did not have a possessive bone in his body, but he felt an overwhelming urge to pull Eleanor into his arms and kiss the sulky line of her mouth until her lips softened beneath his. A year ago he had enjoyed her eager response to his caresses more than he'd cared to admit. When she'd walked into the room a few minutes ago, his heart had banged against his ribs.

He remembered on the yacht in Greece she had worn a one-piece swimsuit that moulded her gorgeous curves. From the start he had been attracted to Eleanor's understated sensuality and his fingers itched to unbutton her prim blouse and cradle her full breasts in his hands. Chemistry still existed between them, simmering beneath the surface. Desire heated Jace's blood and his body tightened. He hadn't felt this alive for the past year, and he was confident that if he kissed Eleanor her resistance would melt.

'You must have laughed at me behind my back,' she said with a catch in her voice. 'I fell in love with you, but it was all just a game to you, wasn't it?'

He did not know how to answer her, and guilt was an uncomfortable weight in the pit of his stomach. He wished he could wipe away the tear that slid down her cheek, but he knew he'd lost the right to comfort her after he'd callously used her. Eleanor had simply been a means to an end. He had seen an opportunity to reclaim the hotel that his father had been cheated out of by her grandfather and he'd seized it without considering the impact his behaviour might have on her.

In his mind, Jace saw his father's battered and bloodied body. Dimitri had died from his injuries without revealing if he had walked too close to the edge of the cliff and fallen by accident, or if he'd jumped. The inquest had been inconclusive, but if Dimitri had chosen to end his life then Kostas Pangalos had blood on his hands, Jace thought grimly.

'It was never a game,' he told Eleanor. 'It was about reclaiming my father's share of the Pangalos and you were collateral damage.'

She inhaled sharply. 'God, you bastard.'

His jaw clenched. 'Believe what you like, but if you had married me I would have endeavoured to be a good husband. I hated your grandfather, but I would have treated you well.'

'*Treated me well?*' Her hazel eyes turned almost green when she was angry, Jace noticed. 'I'm not a puppy you could train to sit up and beg for scraps of your attention.'

'I never thought of you in that way. I liked that you did not hold anything back in your response to me.' His eyes narrowed on the betraying pink stain that spread over her face. 'And I think you still want me.' He could read the signs. Her pupils were huge, dark orbs and she was breathing fast so that her breasts rose and fell jerkily. 'If I kissed you now, would you push me away?'

She recoiled as if he were the devil. 'I hate you. The thought of your touch revolts me.'

'*Theos!*' Jace raked his hand through his hair when Eleanor spun away from him and retreated to stand behind the sofa. He did not know why he had challenged her, or why he had wanted to provoke her into admitting that desire was still a potent force between them.

'I'd like you to leave,' she said stiffly. 'Whatever you came here for, I'm not interested.'

'I guarantee you will be after you've heard what I'm

about to tell you concerning the Pangalos.' He walked across the room and lowered himself into an armchair.

'You're wasting your time. A stipulation in my grandfather's will prevents me from selling the hotel.' Eleanor's eyes flashed. 'Even if it were possible, I wouldn't sell it to you if my life depended on it.'

'I wonder what you would be prepared to do to keep your brother out of prison.'

'I don't know what you are up to, Jace. But I won't fall for your lies again.'

His jaw tightened. He hadn't expected Eleanor to welcome him with open arms, but her contemptuous tone riled him. 'I never lied to you.'

'You let me think that you were in love with me.'

'Did I actually say so?'

She stared at him and he sensed the effort it took her to control her emotions. 'No,' she muttered at last. 'I thought you were a prince. But I discovered that you are just a man, and not a nice one.'

'What you felt was infatuation based on sexual attraction,' he growled, trying to ignore the tug of remorse he felt when she brushed her hand across her eyes. 'If you had married me, the Pangalos hotel would not be in its current dire financial situation.'

Eleanor shook her head. 'I don't believe you. If there was a problem my brother would have told me.'

'Your brother *is* the problem.' Jace's patience evaporated. 'Sit down, Eleanor, and listen to me. The Pangalos has huge debts and could be forced into insolvency.'

He had her attention now. She walked around the sofa and sat down on the end furthest away from him. 'You're lying. I spoke to Mark a few days ago and he told me that the hotel is fully booked for the rest of the summer.'

'Most of the bookings are package deals bought through holiday companies, but you know as well as I do that the hotel won't receive money for the rooms it lets out for several months. In the meantime the staff need to be paid and there are the running costs of the hotel. There is also an outstanding tax bill owed to the Greek government that your brother failed to pay. If the Pangalos is forced to declare bankruptcy, then you, as the director of Gilpin Leisure, will be legally required to close down the hotel and sell off its assets to pay back the creditors.'

Eleanor had paled while Jace spoke. She leapt to her feet. 'What you have told me is a pack of lies. You can't possibly know confidential financial details about the Pangalos.'

'It would appear that I know more than you,' Jace said drily. 'I have a reliable source of information and I understand that when you inherited Gilpin Leisure you gave control of the Pangalos to your brother.'

'Mark was devastated that my grandfather made me his successor. My brother is the oldest grandchild and it was assumed that he would inherit the company.' She sighed. 'I don't know why Pappoús chose me. His decision caused a lot of resentment from my brother and sister towards me.'

'Kostas wouldn't have cared about that. He was first and foremost a ruthless businessman, and it's my guess that he put you at the head of the company because you are more sensible than either of your siblings.'

'By sensible I suppose you mean boring.'

'I did not find you boring during our relationship, *poulóki mou.*' His body stirred as he remembered the softness of her lips when he'd kissed her and how she had opened her mouth to the gentle pressure of his to allow his tongue access to her moist interior.

'You likened me to a drab sparrow,' she said flatly. 'We didn't have a relationship, but you fooled me into thinking that we did.'

Jace stood up and studied Eleanor's shuttered expression. The woman he'd met fifteen months ago had been shy with him at first, but she had gradually opened up. There was a vulnerability about her now that smote his conscience. He had not intentionally set out to hurt her, and he regretted that it had happened. But he would not be swayed from his determination to take back the Pangalos hotel.

'I suggest you contact your brother and ask him to explain the state of affairs. The only way you can save the Pangalos is if you find someone who will be willing to put money into the business. But it won't be easy to persuade an investor to take on the hotel's enormous debts. That's why you need me. I am prepared to rescue the Pangalos in return for you giving me fifty per cent ownership of the hotel.'

Eleanor's eyes flashed with anger. 'You must be joking. I wouldn't give you the time of day. Even if there is some truth in what you have told me, which I seriously doubt, I won't allow your grubby hands anywhere near the hotel that meant so much to my grandfather.'

Jace controlled his temper with difficulty. 'All I am asking is that you give back what should be mine. Your grandfather stole my father's share of the Pangalos, and it is only fair that you should return it to me.'

'Life isn't fair. If it was, I wouldn't have met you,' Eleanor said coldly.

Her jibe stung. 'You don't mean that,' Jace murmured. He watched Eleanor's eyes widen when he stepped closer to her. The pulse at the base of her throat was beating erratically. 'You can tell yourself that you hate me, but a year ago the passion was real for both of us.'

He wanted to kiss her one more time and taste her sweet breath in his mouth. When he lowered his face towards hers, he heard her catch her breath. For a split second Jace was tempted to forget about the feud between their families, which had nothing to do with him and Eleanor.

An image flashed into his mind of his father's body sprawled at the bottom of the cliff. His sanity returned and he jerked his mouth away from the temptation of Eleanor's lips.

'Pappoús entrusted the Pangalos to me and I will never share it with you,' she said tautly.

'Never say never,' Jace drawled. Eleanor would discover that she needed his help. But he had waited more than twenty years to avenge his father's death, and he could wait a little longer. He took a business card from his wallet and held it out to her. She did not take it and he dropped it down on the coffee table. 'When you call me and beg for my help, you had better hope that I will treat you more fairly than Kostas treated my father.'

# CHAPTER TWO

'MARK! THANK GOD!' Relief poured through Eleanor when her brother answered his phone. 'Where are you? I've been so worried. You disappeared two days ago, and your phone was switched off.' She took a deep breath. 'I'm at the Pangalos. The auditors have found discrepancies with the accounts.'

'I know where you are. Lissa warned me that you left Oxford in a hurry to go to Greece. The truth is that I couldn't face you, El.'

'You spoke to Lissa but not to me?' Eleanor tried to ignore a stab of jealousy that her brother and sister shared a bond which she was excluded from. It had been the same when they were growing up. She had been the awkward middle child—not bold and daring like Mark, and lacking Lissa's precocious prettiness. Her scoliosis had set her further apart from her siblings and glamorous parents, and she had become more introverted and found solace in books.

'I don't understand what has been happening.' She had felt guilty for sending the auditors to check over the Pangalos's accounts after Jace had accused her brother of financial irregularities. Mark would be able to explain why money was missing, she assured herself. 'It has been discovered that you transferred money out of the Pangalos's account into your private bank account. The hotel owes money to many of its suppliers. There is an unpaid final tax demand and the staff haven't been paid their salaries this month.'

'It's a mess, I know,' her brother groaned. 'I only needed one big win and I could have replaced all the money.'

Eleanor's heart plummeted. 'You promised that you had stopped gambling. I put you in charge of the Pangalos because you gave me an assurance that you had sorted your life out and were ready to take on the responsibility of managing the hotel.'

'I swear I tried to give up. But the adrenalin rush is like a drug. I placed a few bets online and to start with I won back all I'd gambled and more. But then my losses started to mount up and I borrowed money from the hotel, intending to pay it back with my next big win.'

'But, surprise, surprise, you didn't win.' Eleanor bit her lip. She knew that gambling could be an addiction as serious as alcoholism or drugs. Her brother needed help, not criticism. 'Why didn't you tell me?'

'I was sure my luck would change. I didn't want to admit that I had mucked up again,' Mark said in a low voice. 'Grandfather was right when he made you his successor instead of me. I thought I had got lucky a few months ago when I was introduced to a Greek entrepreneur at a party. I'd had a fair bit to drink, to be honest, and when I mentioned that I had a cash flow problem, Jace was really understanding.'

'Jace?' Eleanor said sharply.

'Jace Zagorakis. He owns a property development company, Zagorakis Estates, and has a stake in a luxury hotel chain called Perseus. He's a well-known figure in Greece. Have you heard of him?'

'Vaguely,' Eleanor said through gritted teeth.

'Well, he offered to lend me money so that I could replace what I'd taken from the Pangalos.' Mark spoke quickly, stumbling over his words. 'But I didn't replace it. I gambled with it because the odds were in my favour. I was due a big win. It was my turn and I was certain I would hit the jackpot.'

'How much did you lose?' Eleanor felt sick when her brother told her. 'So there is no money to pay the Pangalos's bills.'

'It's worse than that. Zagorakis has demanded full repayment of the money I owe him, and he's threatened to take me to court if I don't pay up. As a named director of the Pangalos, I can be held personally liable for its debts. The hotel could be forced into insolvency and there is a good chance I would be sent to prison for tax evasion.'

Mark fell silent again and when he next spoke Eleanor was chilled by the darkness in his voice. 'I'll be honest, El. I've seriously thought about ending it all so that I can be with Mum and Dad.'

She inhaled sharply. 'Don't say that.'

'I still miss them.'

'I know,' she said gently. 'I miss them too.'

When her parents had died, Lissa, the baby of the family, had received the most attention from other relatives while Eleanor had retreated further inside herself. Grief had made Mark an angry and difficult teenager. But at night Eleanor had often heard him crying in his bedroom. She had wanted to go in and comfort him, but she'd felt unsure that he would welcome her, and she'd crept back to her own room.

'I'll find a way to sort out the problems at the Pangalos,' she told her brother. How, she did not know, but she was desperate to reassure him. 'Mark, please look after yourself. Where are you?'

'Ireland. It was the last holiday we had with Mum and Dad. Do you remember we stayed at a riding stables and took the horses out every day?'

'I didn't go with you. It was before my back surgery and I couldn't ride because I had to wear the body brace.'

Eleanor had overheard her parents discussing the difficulties of taking her on a horse-riding holiday because of her spinal condition. Their relief when she had offered to stay with her grandparents had been obvious, and she had tried not to feel hurt. After the holiday, her brother and sister had returned to England and her parents had flown to Sri Lanka, where they had died in an accident without her ever seeing them again.

Scoliosis had affected her childhood and her relationship with her family, she acknowledged sadly. But now Mark needed her help and she would do everything she possibly could to save him and the Pangalos hotel.

Eleanor ended the call after eliciting a promise from her brother that he would seek professional help for his problems. With mounting despair she studied the columns of figures in front of her, which added up to the staggering debt that Mark had accrued. Ordinarily, she would have been able to transfer money between Francine's and the Pangalos to cover the unpaid bills, but the Oxford hotel had not made a profit for three months while it was being refurbished. Eleanor had taken out a business loan to pay for the work, and her application to the bank for more credit had been turned down.

Fortunately, Gilpin Leisure had reserves which she could use to pay the staff's wages and cover most of the Pangalos's running costs. But there was still the huge tax bill that Mark had omitted to pay, as well as the six-figure debt he owed to Jace Zagorakis.

Damn the man! Eleanor did not believe it had been a coincidence that Jace had met her brother at a party. He had used his charisma to gain Mark's trust, like he had gained hers. But Jace's ulterior motive was to take ownership of the Pangalos, which he insisted her grandfather had stolen from his father. When she had taken a look through the hotel's records, she had not found any evidence to confirm Jace's story. Dimitri Zagorakis had sold his share of the hotel to Kostas and the transaction had been overseen by lawyers.

She tried to quell a rising sense of panic as she faced the seriousness of the situation. It was stuffy in Mark's office, where she had been holed up for much of the past two days. She needed air, and she stood up and walked over to open the window. The office was on the top floor of the hotel and overlooked the resort's exclusive bungalows and the private beach that was one of the best on Sithonia. A long stretch of white sand ran down to a turquoise sea that was ideal for swimming, although most of the affluent guests preferred to sit on sun loungers, sipping cocktails.

Pappoús had been proud of the five-star holiday complex he had created but, unless Eleanor could find a solution to the Pangalos's financial crisis, she would be unable to save the hotel from bankruptcy. Guiltily, she accepted that she should have kept a closer eye on her brother. She'd put her faith in Mark and made him a director of the hotel because she had wanted her brother to like her, Eleanor acknowledged with painful honesty.

She walked back to the desk and her gaze fell on Jace's business card. He had been arrogantly confident that she would call him. Fury bubbled up inside her, but she could see no other option than to plead with him for more time to try to raise the money Mark owed him.

Her heart was thumping when she called the number on the card. A woman's voice spoke and said that she was Jace's PA. Jace was unlikely to have answered his office phone, Eleanor silently berated herself, feeling foolish because her mouth had dried at the prospect of speaking to him.

The PA listened to her request for a meeting with Jace before putting her on hold while she checked his diary. 'Mr Zagorakis can fit you in tomorrow at five p.m., Miss Buchanan,' she said when she came back on the line. 'He says he has been expecting to hear from you.'

Eleanor pictured a self-satisfied smirk on Jace's diabolically handsome face, and her temper sizzled. Feeling too restless to remain in the office, she took the lift down to the ground floor and walked through the magnificent marble-tiled lobby. When she'd visited the Pangalos as a child, she had thought it was a palace. Her grandfather had entrusted his beloved hotel to her, but she had allowed herself to be ruled by her emotions when she'd put her brother in charge.

As she walked past the hotel's boutique, she caught sight of herself in the glass shopfront and her steps slowed. Was the drab-looking woman with her hair scraped off her face really her? Her skirt was unfashionably long, and her cardigan that she'd pulled around her shoulders because the air-conditioning was chilly added years to her. Lissa had criticised her clothes for being frumpy. Far worse had been when she'd overheard Jace's opinion of her.

*Unremarkable.*

It still hurt, and tears pricked her eyes. But as Eleanor stared at her reflection she acknowledged that Jace had been right. She was old before her time and weighed down with the responsibility of running Gilpin Leisure. Long hours in the office back in Oxford meant that she never had time to shop for clothes or visit a hair salon, and her social life was non-existent.

Seeing Jace again had reinforced how jaw-droppingly handsome he was. How could she have believed that he had been attracted to *her* a year ago? Her beautiful sister was much more Jace's type. Eleanor bit her lip. During her childhood, she'd often felt lonely. When she'd met Jace it had felt like a fairy tale and she'd been flattered by his attention.

The truth was that she'd been desperate to be loved. But he hadn't loved her. He had made a fool of her and now she hated him. *Hated him!* But Jace was pulling all the strings and tomorrow she would have to throw herself on his mercy.

Pride stiffened Eleanor's backbone as much as the metal rods supporting her spine. She turned her gaze from her reflection in the shop window to the mannequin displaying a figure-hugging scarlet dress. Jace had likened her to a timid sparrow, but tomorrow he was going to get the shock of his life when he discovered that she would not give up a share of the Pangalos without a fight. And before she went into battle, Eleanor decided, stepping into the boutique, she needed some armour.

'Do you remember the parties in the ballroom, Jace?'

'I do.' Jace smiled at his mother. 'Every week you and Bampás hosted a party for the guests who were about to return home at the end of their holiday.'

The food and drink had been provided free of charge by his parents. It was a way of thanking the guests for choosing to stay at the Pangorakis hotel and to encourage them to return the following year, his father had said.

'The children had so much fun. I used to love seeing their happy faces.' Iliana sighed softly. 'They were good times, before we lost the hotel. Your poor father never came to terms with what happened.' Her voice faded and she closed her eyes, the lashes making dark fans against her sallow skin. 'I wish...'

Jace leaned closer to the daybed in the orangery at his house in Thessaloniki where his mother spent much of her time these days. 'What do you wish, Mamá?'

'To go back just once more before... I leave this world.'

'The specialist thinks you could live for a year or more. He is confident the drugs will slow the spread of the cancer.'

Jace's throat felt constricted and he swallowed hard. He picked up his mother's hand and raised it to his lips to kiss her bony fingers. Her hands had scrubbed floors and done all sorts of menial work so that she could earn money to feed them both after his father had died.

Hatred of Kostas Pangalos festered like poison inside him. But he was close now to avenging his father and reclaiming the hotel. When he remembered how greatly his mother had suffered in the years since his father's death, Jace assured himself that his ultimate goal to seize complete control of the Pangalos so that it would no longer be Kostas's legacy was justified.

'Very soon I will take you back to the Pangalos and we will rename it the Zagorakis. Will that make you happy, Mamá?'

'How can you do that? Kostas...'

'Is dead. Today I intend to secure a deal which will see the hotel returned to us.'

Jace frowned when he thought of Eleanor. He had backed her into a corner, and he knew she had no choice but to give him a fifty per cent share of the Pangalos to save her brother's neck. She would only have turned to him as a last resort, which meant she had failed to raise enough money to pay off Mark Buchanan's debts.

Taking back the hotel had been his driving force for the whole of his adult life, but Jace did not feel as satisfied as he'd expected. Eleanor had made it clear that she despised him. When he'd asked her to marry him a year ago, he had deliberately not spoken of love. But guilt tugged uncomfortably in his gut when he remembered how unworldly Eleanor had been. She had made an unexpected impression on him and he'd found himself thinking about her often since she had broken off their engagement.

He forced his mind away from the memory of Eleanor's tears when he'd sprung a visit on her in England a week ago, and realised that his mother was speaking.

'You are a good son, Jace. When you were sent to prison I cried every night because I could not afford lawyers to fight your case. It was a travesty of justice.'

Jace's jaw clenched. Prison had been hell, and he still felt bitter that he'd been found guilty of a crime because of a rich man's lies. There were parallels between what had happened to him and how Kostas had employed corrupt lawyers to seize control of the Pangalos from his father. A few years ago, Jace had bought out the company owned by the man who had been responsible for him going to prison and immediately fired him. Now he was poised to reclaim the Pangalos, but in another twist of fate his mother was terminally ill.

'I take my own justice,' he murmured. There was steel beneath his soft voice. 'My business interests have made me very wealthy and you do not have to worry about me, Mamá.'

'I do worry about you though. When I am gone, you will be alone. I wish I could live long enough to see you married and settled with a woman who you love as much as your father and I loved each other.'

'None of us knows what the future holds,' Jace said diplomatically. There was no point upsetting his mother by telling her there was zero chance of him marrying for romantic reasons. He had believed he was in love once, but Katerina had proved that real love, the self-less, unconditional kind that his parents had shared, was a rarity.

An odd thought came into his mind. If his engagement to Eleanor has lasted for longer than a day, he was certain his mother would have liked her and approved of her as his future wife. But he could not turn the clock back.

Before he left for his office he had a quiet word with Anna, his mother's nurse. 'Try to persuade her to eat something. She needs to build up her strength.'

'I'll do my best,' the nurse promised, 'but she has a poor appetite.'

The day dragged. Jace told himself that the hours passed slowly because he was impatient to finalise the deal to reclaim the Pangalos that had been his goal since he was fifteen. It definitely had nothing to do with the prospect of seeing Eleanor again. His edgy mood was exacerbated by the oppressive atmosphere. A storm had been forecast, and outside his office window sullen grey clouds were mustering in the sky.

Just before five o'clock, the nurse phoned his private mobile number and explained that his mother had tripped over in the garden. 'She is not injured other than some bruising, but she is upset and would like to speak to you,' the nurse said.

While Jace was talking to his mother, his PA put her head round the door and informed him that Miss Buchanan had arrived. He glanced at his watch and noted that Eleanor was as punctual as ever. 'Tell her that I will see her shortly,' he mouthed to Rena.

His mother was sobbing on the phone. 'I am a silly old woman, and a burden to you.'

'Of course you are not a burden.'

'I won't be for much longer,' his mother choked. 'We both know the truth, Jace. I am dying. It breaks my heart that I'll never meet the woman you eventually marry. If I could only be sure that you will be in a happy relationship it would not hurt so much to leave you.'

Consoling his mother took some time and when he finally said goodbye to her Jace sighed heavily. It occurred to him that if his original plan to marry Eleanor a year ago had happened, his mother would have had peace of mind in her last months. It was a shame he couldn't change things. Before Eleanor had discovered the truth behind his marriage proposal, she had been eager to be his wife. But what if he *could* turn the clock back to a year ago?

He pulled his mind from his thoughts when he noticed the time and realised that over half an hour had passed since Eleanor had arrived for their appointment. He stepped out of his office and met his PA in the corridor.

'Miss Buchanan left a few minutes ago. I explained that you were unavoidably detained, but she said that she refused to play mind games,' Rena said, giving him a puzzled look.

Cursing beneath his breath, Jace took the lift down

to the ground floor. He was incensed that Eleanor had walked out on him *again*! He'd been gutted when she had left him in Paris. Her abrupt departure then had stirred memories of the sense of abandonment he'd felt after his father had died, leaving the unanswered question of whether Dimitri had chosen to end his life. Jace had learned valuable lessons in the past. Good things never lasted, the people you cared about left and happiness was ephemeral.

His heart sank when he strode through the lobby, which was empty apart from the receptionist sitting behind a desk. Eleanor had gone. *Theos*, he had banked on her needing his help. Did she have a rich lover who she had persuaded to pay off her brother's debts? Why the hell did the idea of her in another man's arms make his blood boil?

Ahead of him, a woman emerged from the cloakroom and walked quickly towards the revolving glass doors. Her stiletto heels clipped against the marble floor. Jace's eyes travelled up her shapely legs to the hem of her short red dress that stopped several inches above her knees. Her dark blonde hair had streaks of paler gold and fell in sexy layers to just below her shoulders. Something about the sway of her hips as she walked seemed familiar. But it couldn't be...

She was almost at the exit. '*Wait.*' Jace increased his pace and caught up with her. He put his hand on her arm and felt her stiffen when he spun her round to face him. '*Eleanor?*' He stared at her, stunned by her transformation from the demure woman who had briefly been his fiancée to this dangerously beautiful, scarlet-clad siren.

'You have no right to manhandle me,' she snapped. Her hazel eyes turned green and flashed with fury.

Jace dropped his hand down to his side, but his body

refused to obey his brain and move away from her. His nostrils flared as he breathed in her perfume—a sultry, sensual fragrance that sent a rush of heat to his groin. A year ago he had been attracted to Eleanor's understated prettiness, but this new and exciting version of the woman he had once planned to marry was intriguing and *hot*!

His jaw hardened when he saw her glance towards the door. Jace knew he must ignore his libido and focus on his goal. 'Are you really prepared to risk losing the Pangalos and your brother's freedom?' he asked her silkily.

The scathing look she gave him would have shrivelled another man. 'My brother is sick. His gambling addiction is out of control. What kind of terrible person are you to lend him money, knowing it would fall through his fingers? You might as well have given him a spade so that he could dig his own grave.'

Jace felt his gut clench when he saw a betraying shimmer of moisture in her eyes. 'I was not aware when I lent Mark money that he is a compulsive gambler. I simply thought he maintained an expensive lifestyle and lived beyond his means. If you knew he had a problem, why did you put him in charge of the Pangalos?'

'He told me he had stopped gambling.' She bit her lip. 'I hadn't realised how serious his problem is. My brother needs help, not a threat of prosecution.'

Jace shrugged. 'If you are serious about wanting to save him, come up to my office so that we can continue this discussion in private.'

He roamed his eyes over her flushed face and lingered on her scarlet-glossed lips. An idea of how he could fulfil his dying mother's wish—as well as his father's final plea—seeded in his mind and took root.

'I am confident we can strike a deal that will give us both what we want,' he told Eleanor.

*'Will you walk into my parlour?' said the Spider to the Fly.*

The line from the poem Eleanor had loved as a child popped into her head as Jace ushered her into his office. His secretary had been unable to disguise her curiosity when he had given instruction that he did not want to be disturbed for the rest of the afternoon. The snick of his office door closing made the butterflies in Eleanor's stomach flutter harder.

He held out a chair and she sank down onto it, relieved she hadn't stumbled in her four-inch heels that she was still getting used to. She grimaced when her skirt rode further up her thighs and tried to tug it down until she realised that Jace was watching her.

'You have had a change of style,' he murmured as he walked around his desk and lowered his long frame into the leather chair. 'I approve of your new look.'

Eleanor felt herself blush and silently cursed her fair skin and lack of sophistication. If only Jace wasn't so mesmerisingly sexy. His sculpted features were a work of art and the dark stubble shading his jaw accentuated his raw masculinity. A helpless longing swept through her as her gaze lingered on his mouth and she remembered the firm pressure of his lips on hers.

Although they had not had sex in the few months they had been dating, they'd indulged in heavy petting. Jace's kisses had driven her wild with desire and her breasts had ached when he'd bared them and rubbed his thumbs over her swollen nipples. A tingling sensation in that area now made Eleanor glance down, and she was mortified to see the hard points of her nipples jutting beneath her dress.

She looked up again, and as her eyes met his across the desk the predatory gleam in the dark depths of his evoked a throb of response deep in her pelvis.

'I'm sure you don't want to waste your *valuable* time discussing my appearance,' she said curtly, thinking of how he had kept her waiting. No doubt his intention had been to demonstrate that he had power over her, but she refused to be intimidated.

He leaned back in his chair and appraised her from between his narrowed gaze. 'I assume the reason for your visit is to ask for more time to try to raise the money your brother owes me. My answer is no.'

'I need three months to restructure the company's finances, and I should be able to pay back at least part of Mark's debt,' she said urgently. 'Surely you can wait three months?'

Jacc's eyes glittered. 'I have waited for twenty years to take back what Kostas stole from my family.'

Eleanor stared at his hard-boned face and wondered how she had missed the ruthlessness beneath his charm a year ago. Love had blinded her, she acknowledged bitterly. Defeat tasted rancid in her mouth. 'You want fifty per cent of the Pangalos,' she muttered.

He nodded. 'But the hotel is not all I want. I've raised the stakes.'

'What else can you possibly want from me?'

'Marriage.' He met her stunned expression with a smile that bared his white teeth and reminded Eleanor of a wolf. 'I want you to marry me.'

# CHAPTER THREE

'I MUST SAY that I preferred your first proposal,' Eleanor said after she had stopped laughing. Because she was sure Jace was joking. Her stupid heart had leapt when he'd mentioned marriage, but she wasn't the gullible idiot she'd been a year ago. 'Paris was much more romantic,' she mocked. 'You even gave me a sparkly ring.'

Amusement and something like admiration gleamed in his dark eyes. 'You can wear your engagement ring again once we have finalised the details of our marriage.'

The joke had gone far enough. Eleanor looked away from him, desperate to hide how much he had hurt her. 'I wouldn't marry you if the continuation of the human race depended on it.'

'In that case you had better hope your brother likes prison food.'

'Don't threaten me.' She curled her hands into fists in her lap as a mixture of fear and fury swept through her.

'Face facts, Eleanor,' he drawled. 'I have the power to ruin Mark and force the Pangalos to be declared insolvent, meaning that lawyers will take charge of the hotel and sell off its assets to pay its creditors. I will be able to buy up the assets and I could end up owning a one hundred per cent share of the Pangalos.'

Eleanor had a business degree and knew the laws

concerning a company going into liquidation. She felt sick. 'Why didn't you do that a year ago instead of going through the charade of asking me to marry you?'

He shrugged, drawing her attention to his broad shoulders sheathed in a superbly tailored charcoal-grey suit. Jace had once told her that he had started his working life as a labourer on a building site, and Eleanor guessed it was where he had developed his powerfully muscular physique.

'Your brother hadn't racked up huge debts for himself or the hotel a year ago,' he drawled. 'If we marry, the hotel will be deemed a marital asset and I will gain the fifty per cent share that my father originally owned before Kostas betrayed their friendship.'

'Are you really so cold that you would marry for such a cynical reason?' Eleanor muttered.

'I certainly wouldn't marry out of a misplaced sense of sentimentality.' Jace grimaced. 'However, my mother is a born romantic and she is desperate to see me happily married before she dies.'

Eleanor's attention was caught by the undercurrent of emotion in his voice. 'Is that likely to be soon?'

'Doctors have given her six months to a year to live.'

'I'm sorry.' She bit her lip. 'But why would us marrying make your mother happy? We don't love each other.'

'You accepted my proposal a year ago because you were in love with me,' he reminded her.

She flushed, thinking of how easily she had been taken in by his calculated seduction. 'I'm not in love with you any more, that's for sure.'

'Good,' he said coolly. 'It will make things much less complicated if we keep emotions out of our marriage.'

'I'm not going to marry you, Jace.' She stood up and looked frantically over to the door, keen to escape from this man who, even though she knew she would never mean anything to him, made her weak with longing to feel his lips on hers.

It was just her body's physical response to his magnetism, Eleanor assured herself. Jace had uncovered a sensual side to her that she'd been unaware of. In the past year she'd tried to forget how he had aroused her desire. She hadn't been remotely tempted to try to replicate the feeling with any other man. But five minutes in Jace's company had turned her into a mass of molten need.

'Why not?' he demanded in that slightly cynical, slightly amused tone of voice that made her grind her teeth.

'How can you ask that? There are a million reasons why I refuse to be your wife.'

'I can think of two very good reasons why you should consider it. Your brother's freedom and the Pangalos hotel,' he listed, his brows lifting when she shook her head.

'I'll find the money to pay back Mark's debts some other way that doesn't involve a loveless marriage to a man I despise.'

'We both know I am your brother's only hope of salvation. Sit down, Eleanor, and hear me out.'

She sat, compelled by the intensity of his gaze and his sheer force of will.

'What I am offering is a straightforward deal. Marry me and your brother's slate is wiped clean, plus I will pay all the Pangalos's outstanding bills. A prenuptial agreement will make us joint owners of the hotel and, after my mother dies, we will divorce and each receive a fifty per cent share of the business.'

'It's a crazy idea,' Eleanor muttered. She'd be even crazier to contemplate agreeing to Jace's suggestion.

'There is one other thing. My mother must not find out that you are Kostas's granddaughter. She knows nothing about you. Your mother took your English father's name on their marriage and there is no reason why you would be associated with the name Pangalos.'

Eleanor frowned. 'Are you saying you would want your mother to think we had married for conventional reasons? I'm sure you could convince her that you are in love. After all, you fooled me,' she reminded him curtly. 'But I loathe you, and I'll never be able to pretend that you are the man of my dreams.'

She jumped up again and walked quickly towards the door. But Jace moved with the deadly speed of a panther and clamped his hand over hers on the door handle.

'Is there a man in your life who is responsible for the change in your appearance? Do you dress to please a lover?' His cool voice belied the blistering intensity in his gaze as he stared down at her from the advantage of his superior height.

'I dress to please myself,' she snapped. Her breath snagged in her throat as she breathed in his seductive male scent: spicy cologne mixed with something indefinable and uniquely Jace. 'My private life is my own affair but if, for argument's sake, I said that I have a boyfriend, you would presumably drop the idea of us marrying.'

'Not necessarily. I foresee that we would both have a certain amount of freedom within the marriage, but I'd expect you to be discreet, as I will be.'

Tears stung Eleanor's eyes, but she willed herself not to cry in front of Jace. She'd thought that he could not hurt her more than he'd already done, but she had been wrong. His detachment was a painful reminder that he had only pretended to desire her a year ago. But, in a strange way, knowing what he really thought of her would make her even more determined to ignore her sexual attraction to him—*if* she agreed to his outrageous marriage demand.

'So I would be your wife in name only?' she clarified.

'The extent of our relationship will be up to you, and I will abide by your decision.'

In other words he could take her or leave her. She was mortified by the thought that if she indicated she wanted their marriage to include sex, Jace might force himself to make love to her.

'I imagine your boyfriend was public school educated and has a job in the City, or perhaps he is a historian studying for a doctorate at one of Oxford University's illustrious colleges,' Jace drawled. 'But a *boy* will not satisfy your passionate nature, *omorfiá mou.*'

'You really are a jerk,' she spat, scarlet-faced. 'If you remember, I speak Greek and I know you don't think much of my looks. Save your false flattery for someone who is foolish enough to believe a word that comes out of your mouth.'

She hated him with every fibre of her being, but her treacherous body hadn't got the message. Eleanor could not prevent her gaze from focusing on his mouth, which he had used with such exquisite effect when he'd kissed her.

And not just on her lips. She remembered his mouth on her breasts, his wicked tongue teasing her nipples before he closed his lips around one turgid peak and then the other, making her tremble with needs that only Jace had ever aroused. Now she understood that his caresses had been part of his campaign to trick her into marriage, but even knowing the extent of his duplicity did not douse the fire inside her.

Jace's eyes glittered with anger and something else that made Eleanor's pulse accelerate when he released his grip on her fingers curled around the door handle and slid his hand beneath her chin.

'Do you think I am pretending now?' he growled. His free hand captured hers and held it against his chest so that she felt the hard thud of his heart.

The warmth of his body through his shirt evoked a flood of heat between her thighs. Her bra felt too tight, her nipples scraping against the lace cups. But she couldn't—*wouldn't*—surrender to his expert seduction again.

'It was all a game to you,' she choked.

'This was real.' His stark voice sent a shiver through her. She watched his head descend and knew she should move away from him. But another instinct as old as the story of Eve kept her standing there, waiting, willing him to close the gap between them and claim her mouth with his.

Her lips unconsciously parted and she heard his breathing quicken. The air was heavy with sexual tension. But could she believe the hunger in Jace's eyes, or was it a continuation of the cruel game he'd started a year ago?

From outside, a clap of thunder shook the windows and shattered the fraught silence in the room. Eleanor blinked and realised that it was almost dark in Jace's office. A sudden white flash of lightning momentarily illuminated his tall figure, but his expression was hidden from her and he was a stranger.

With a low cry, she snatched her hand from his silk shirt stretched across his chest. 'I won't marry you. *I won't.* You can have fifty per cent of the Pangalos, and

I'll appoint a new manager to take Mark's place so that I never have to see you again.'

This time when she grabbed the handle and opened the door, he did not try to stop her from leaving. She fought the urge to run along the corridor to the lift. When she stepped inside, before the doors closed, she looked back towards Jace's office and felt no surprise that he had not followed her. All he wanted was part ownership of the Pangalos, but she would not sign over the deeds until she had it in black and white that he would cancel her brother's debts.

To avoid the complicated one-way traffic system in Thessaloniki, Eleanor had parked her car a few streets away from Zagorakis Estates' office building. Thunder rumbled overhead as she hurried along the pavement where café owners were scrambling to carry chairs and tables inside before the furniture was blown over by the ferocious wind. Towering dark clouds obliterated the sun and the sky had turned a strange sulphur-yellow colour.

The rain started with the suddenness of a tap being turned on, and within minutes she was soaked to the skin. Cursing her high heels, she kicked off her shoes and carried them in her hand as she ran along the street. A sleek silver sports car drew up alongside her and the window slid down. Eleanor glanced at Jace behind the wheel and ran faster.

'Eleanor, get in the car.' He swore and drove on past her, stopping at a junction directly in her path. He leaned across and opened the passenger door.

'Go away!' Eleanor shouted at him over the howl of the wind.

'*Theos!* Get in the damned car!'

Hailstones mixed with the rain lashed her skin. She saw Jace's thunderous expression and decided that it was safer to obey him.

'Put your seatbelt on,' he growled when she had shut the door. Shivering, Eleanor complied, and Jace drove off. The smell of rain from her clothes and dripping-wet hair permeated the car and, looking down, she saw that her dress was clinging to her breasts. Conscious of Jace glancing at her, she folded her arms in front of her to hide her jutting nipples. He muttered something beneath his breath and switched on the car's heater.

'My car is not far from here,' she told him stiffly.

'There are reports of flash flooding on the highway, and you can't make the two-hour journey back to Sithonia in wet clothes. I'll take you to my house so that you can dry off.' Without giving her a chance to argue, he continued, 'Why did you run off like that when the storm was about to break?'

Eleanor wondered if he was referring to the weather phenomenon or the tempest that had brewed between them in his office. 'I can't marry you,' she muttered.

'Is that because you have a romantic ideal of what marriage should be?'

Stung by his cynicism, she said defensively, 'I believe in marrying for love. My grandparents were married for fifty years before Nanna Francine died. My parents were happily married, and the only thing that made their deaths more bearable was knowing they were together at the end.'

She was aware of Jace's brooding gaze on her before he turned his attention back to the road. The driving conditions were terrible, and the windscreen wipers could hardly cope with the heavy rain.

'I remember you mentioned that your parents died in an accident when you were a child.'

'They were on a second honeymoon to celebrate their twentieth wedding anniversary. Someone noticed my mother get into difficulties while she was swimming in the sea. Dad went to help her, and they were both swept away by the strong current. Their bodies were found washed up on a beach two days later.'

'It was tough to lose one parent when I was a teenager and I can only imagine how devastating it must have been when you were orphaned.' The gruff sympathy in Jace's voice curled around Eleanor's heart.

'Mark struggled the most to come to terms with what happened. He didn't get on with my grandfather.'

'But you did, presumably, and that's why Kostas made you his heir.'

Eleanor sighed. 'He was quite controlling, and my brother and sister were argumentative, so there were clashes. I think Pappoús liked me because I tended to agree with him to keep the peace.'

She had spent much of her childhood feeling that she was a disappointment to her parents because of her scoliosis. After they had died, she'd realised that she could win her grandfather's approval and affection by being obedient and amenable.

Sometimes it felt as if she had spent her whole life trying to please people, Eleanor thought. It had not been her choice to be made her grandfather's heir and have the responsibility of Gilpin Leisure thrust upon her. And now, to save the Pangalos and her brother, Jace had demanded that she must marry him. But it would be a fake marriage, just as their romance a year ago had been fake, on his side at least.

She was jolted from her thoughts when Jace drove

through a set of cobalt-blue iron gates and stopped in front of a whitewashed villa, built in the Cycladic style synonymous with the architecture of the Aegean islands. Through the torrential rain, Eleanor saw that the house resembled a series of cubes with flat roofs and arched windows framed by shutters of brilliant blue.

'The back of the house overlooks the sea, and on a clear day you can see the peninsular of Kassandra and beyond it, across the bay, Mount Olympus. But not today,' Jace said with a grimace. He slipped off his jacket and draped it around Eleanor's shoulders before he climbed out of the car and strode round to open the passenger door. Eleanor gasped as the wind whipped her breath away and drove stinging rain into her face. Jace caught hold of her hand and they ran towards the house.

When they were inside and Jace closed the front door the sound of the storm was muffled by the thick walls. Eleanor looked around the vast entrance hall with a white marble floor. Through an open door she could see a living room where a frail-looking woman was lying on a sofa.

'Jace, thank goodness you are back,' the woman spoke in Greek. 'There are news reports that power lines and trees have been brought down by the gale.' She noticed Eleanor. 'Oh, you have brought a guest home.'

'Stay where you are,' Jace commanded as the woman attempted to stand up. He put his hand beneath Eleanor's elbow and drew her forwards. 'This is my mother, Iliana. Mamá, I'd like you to meet Eleanor Buchanan. She is English but she speaks Greek fluently.'

Eleanor felt self-conscious that she was still wearing Jace's jacket around her shoulders, but at least it covered her dress, which was sticking to her body like a second skin. Jace's shirt had taken the brunt of the rain and it clung to his torso so that his black chest hairs were visible through the damp silk.

She tore her gaze from him and stepped closer to the sofa. '*Kalispera*,' she murmured as she shook hands with his mother. Iliana was painfully thin and the skin on her bony hand felt papery. The signs of illness were on her tired face, but her dark eyes gleamed with warmth and curiosity as she studied Eleanor.

'You have a beautiful name.'

'Thank you. My grandfather chose it.' Eleanor froze and dared not glance at Jace, who had tensed when she'd unthinkingly mentioned her grandfather. There was no reason why she shouldn't speak of Kostas Pangalos just because Jace had warned her not to, she told herself. She had only heard his version of an alleged feud between his father and her grandfather. But if there *was* any truth in the story she did not wish to upset Jace's fragile-looking mother.

Eleanor shivered, feeling chilled to the bone in her wet dress. Iliana immediately looked concerned. 'You must go and get dry. Will you stay to dinner?'

'Eleanor will have to spend the night here,' Jace answered before she could speak, flashing the phone he held. 'News reports say the storm is set to last until the morning.' He placed his hand in the small of her back and steered her towards the door. 'Come with me and I'll find you something to wear.'

How had she ended up in the enemy's camp? Eleanor wondered ruefully as she followed Jace up the grand staircase. He strode along the landing on the second floor and opened a door into a charming guest bedroom decorated in the same simple style as the rest of the house, with white walls and blue shutters at the windows.

'The bathroom is through here.' He opened another door into an en suite bathroom. 'A shower will warm you up. I'll take your clothes to be laundered.'

Eleanor was so cold that her teeth chattered. 'Do you need me to help you undress?' Jace asked.

'Pigs will fly before I'll allow you to take my clothes off.'

His sexy grin stole her breath. She hated how her heart performed a somersault just because when Jace smiled he reminded her of the charismatic, irresistible man she had fallen in love with a year ago.

'Keep telling yourself that, *pouláki mou,*' he drawled.

'Don't call me that,' she muttered. 'I heard you say to Takis Samaras that my sister is a beautiful peacock, but you think I am an unremarkable sparrow. If Lissa had inherited the Pangalos, no doubt you would have been keen to marry *her.*'

Jace gave her a thoughtful look. 'Your sister is attractive, and she seems to have made a career out of dating rich male celebrities. I have met dozens of Lissas, but I've never met anyone as unique or as beautiful as you.'

Eleanor shook her head. 'You don't have to try to win me over with pretty lies any more,' she told him with quiet dignity before she walked into the bathroom and locked the door behind her.

When she emerged from the shower ten minutes later and wrapped a towel tightly around her body before cautiously stepping into the bedroom, she discovered that Jace had left one of his shirts for her to wear. Her layered hairstyle took minutes to dry with a hairdryer. The shorter length was sexier than when she'd worn her hair in a schoolgirlish plait, Eleanor decided. Had that unconsciously been her aim when she'd decided on a makeover of her hair and clothes? she wondered. Had she hoped to make Jace sit up and notice her?

She studied her reflection in the mirror. The borrowed shirt came down to her mid-thigh and was just about presentable to wear to dinner. She grimaced at the hectic flush on her cheeks and her dilated pupils that were evidence of the effect Jace had on her. A knock on the door made her heart skip a beat, but she was greeted by a maid who had come to show her the way to the dining room.

Although it was early in the evening the storm had turned the sky as dark as night, and lamps had been switched on in the house. When Eleanor entered the dining room her gaze was immediately drawn to Jace. He had changed out of his wet clothes and looked divine in black jeans hugging his lean hips and a fine-knit black sweater that moulded the defined ridges of his abdominal muscles.

She forced herself to walk further into the room, conscious of his gaze roaming over her legs all the way down to her red stiletto heel shoes before moving up to the rest of her body. Could he tell that she was braless? She had draped her underwear over the heated towel rail while she showered, but only her knickers had dried enough to wear.

'Like I said, uniquely beautiful,' Jace murmured as he strolled towards her.

Eleanor opened her mouth to tell him to *stop*. How could he lie so glibly? Did he not possess an iota of compunction? But her angry words died before she uttered them when she recognised stark hunger in his eyes.

Desire. For her. A nerve flickered in his jaw and her heart pounded as she realised with a jolt of shock that he wasn't pretending. Jace wanted her with the same

CHANTELLE SHAW                           65

fierce need that she felt for him. The knowledge restored
a little of her pride. The glittering intensity in his gaze
put them on an equal footing, and she could not restrain
a shiver of reaction.

'Do please come and sit down, Eleanor,' Jace's
mother invited.

Belatedly, Eleanor realised that she and Jace were
not alone. Snatching oxygen into her lungs, she whirled
away from him at the same time as he stepped back
from her and raked his fingers through his hair.

A maid arrived with a trolley and proceeded to serve
dinner. Jace held out a chair for Eleanor and when she
was seated he took his place at the head of the table.
There were two bottles of wine on the table, a red and a
white. He half filled his mother's glass with white wine
and poured Eleanor a glass of Pinot Noir. Her eyes met
his, and she told herself not to read anything into the
fact that he had remembered she did not like white wine.

Across the table his mother gave her a curious look.
'Have you known my son long?'

'Um...'

'Eleanor and I met more than a year ago,' Jace murmured when she hesitated.

'A year! Well, I am delighted to finally be introduced
to you.' Iliana gave a rueful smile when Eleanor's eyes
rested on a large purple bruise on her face. 'I tripped
over in the garden while I was trying to prune the bougainvillea,' she explained. 'Unfortunately, I'm not as
agile as I used to be.'

'I employ a gardener so that you can sit and enjoy the
garden,' Jace admonished his mother gently.

'I like to do what I can. But I am embarrassed to
admit that I called Jace at his office this afternoon and
cried like a baby,' Iliana told Eleanor.

She darted a look at Jace. Had he been unable to keep her appointment time because he'd been comforting his mother after her accident? His closed expression gave nothing away. She looked down at her plate of moussaka. The food was delicious but she barely noticed what she was eating, feeling guilty when she remembered how she had stormed out of his office, convinced that he'd been toying with her like a cat with a mouse.

'I saw on the news programme that the storm caused a tidal surge and many properties on the coast have been damaged,' Iliana commented.

Eleanor's heart sank. The last thing she needed was a pile more bills if the hotel had suffered damage.

'I hope your accommodation hasn't been affected. Are you staying in Thessaloniki?'

'No, on Sithonia, at the...um... Pangalos Beach Resort.' Eleanor dared not look at Jace after she had spoken unthinkingly again.

Iliana's expression was wistful. 'I have not been there for many years, but I've heard that the facilities are excellent. My husband used to partly own the hotel, and we lived there until Dimitri's business partner cheated us out of our livelihood.'

'Goodness, what happened?' Eleanor feigned surprise and ignored Jace's warning stare.

'Dimitri's partner, Kostas Pangalos, wanted to sell the Pangorakis,' Iliana explained. 'My husband could just about afford to buy the other fifty per cent, but Kostas claimed that he had done more to make the hotel successful. In court, his lawyers persuaded the judge to award Kostas two-thirds of the business and Dimitri was only given one third.'

Iliana sighed. 'The decision gave control of the hotel to Kostas and he bought my husband out. It was heart-breaking to have to leave our home and the hotel that we loved and where Jace had lived his whole life. We opened another hotel, but Dimitri's heart was not in it. He was deeply upset that the man he had considered to be his best friend had turned on him. But I was not so surprised. I always thought that beneath Kostas's charming manner he was utterly ruthless.'

'I suppose it's necessary to be fairly ruthless to be successful in business,' Eleanor murmured. She felt sick at hearing what her grandfather had done, but she had no reason to disbelieve Jace's mother.

'Kostas destroyed my husband,' Iliana said flatly. 'Our second hotel did not do well and, in desperation, Dimitri asked his old friend for a loan. Kostas could afford it. His wife had inherited a top hotel in England and the Pangalos, as he renamed our hotel, was making a fortune. But he turned Dimitri's request down and we were declared bankrupt. Soon after, my husband took his own life.'

'We don't know that for sure, Mamá,' Jace said softly. 'The inquest was inconclusive, and it could have been an accident.'

Iliana shook her head. 'Your father did not stumble and fall off the cliff. His heart was broken, and Kostas Pangalos was responsible for his death as much as if he had pushed Dimitri over the edge.'

# CHAPTER FOUR

JACE STOOD IN the orangery and watched the rain lash against the glass. He had not switched on the lamps and the room was illuminated sporadically when the moon appeared from behind clouds scudding across the night sky.

He sipped his whisky. Listening to his mother's account of how Kostas had destroyed his father had reinforced Jace's determination to claim his family's rightful share of the Pangalos. But he had taken no pleasure in Eleanor's obvious shock. She had managed to hide her distress from his mother, but not from him. He'd heard a tremor in her voice when immediately after dinner she'd made an excuse that she had a headache before going to her room.

Lying did not come naturally to Eleanor, Jace brooded. She was the most guileless and honest person he had ever met. He remembered her shy smile a year ago when she'd confessed that she had fallen in love with him. Instead of feeling triumphant that his plan to claim the hotel was coming to fruition, he had admired her bravery and felt uncomfortable with himself.

But when he'd kissed her and passion had exploded between them he had told himself that Eleanor had mistaken lust for a deeper emotion. Now he believed her when she said she hated him. It was an inescapable fact that if she had not discovered his motive for proposing to her in Paris he would have married her for the Pangalos.

A faint sound from behind him made Jace turn his head and he watched Eleanor walk barefoot into the orangery. She did not notice him standing in the shadows as she crossed to the window and stared out at the dark garden. His gaze lingered on her delectable curves, which he could make out beneath his borrowed shirt, and his body clenched hard as desire ran like wildfire through his veins. Where once her sensual allure had been muted, her transformation into a sexy siren evoked a throb of need that centred in his groin.

'Headache gone?' he murmured.

She spun round and he heard her swiftly indrawn breath. 'I didn't see you there.'

'I guessed as much,' Jace said wryly. 'You made it clear when you disappeared after dinner that you would rather spend time with the devil than with me.'

'I couldn't sleep.' She turned away from him and hugged her arms around her body. 'I'm sorry for what my grandfather did to your family.' Her voice sounded raw, as if she had swallowed broken glass. 'Pappoús...' She swallowed audibly. 'When I was growing up, I thought he was firm but fair and... I loved him. But now I wonder if I ever knew him. The man who treated me kindly was the same man who cheated your father.' She drew in a ragged breath. 'I understand now why you must hate me.'

'I don't hate you,' Jace growled. 'I hated Kostas and I want my father's rightful share of the Pangalos, but I wish you hadn't been caught up in an old feud between our families that had nothing to do with you.'

'Why didn't you tell me when we first met?' Eleanor jerked her head in his direction and her eyes flashed in the darkness.

'I couldn't risk it. Kostas had chosen you as his heir, but I knew nothing about you. You might have been as ruthless as your grandfather and refused to hand over my father's share of the hotel.'

'So you deliberately set out to make me fall in love with you.' She bit her lip. 'Your treatment of me was as cruel as anything Pappoús did.'

'Kostas destroyed my family,' Jace growled angrily. His blissful childhood with his parents had ended abruptly when they were forced to leave the hotel and they had been homeless and without hope. Life had been different after that, as his father struggled with depression and his mother had scrubbed floors for a pittance. Jace had spent years plotting and planning to destroy Kostas, but now the old man was dead and he had left his granddaughter to succeed him.

A year ago Jace had been prepared to destroy Eleanor, but his conscience pricked that she had not deserved what he had done to her. Only now did he acknowledge how cruelly he had betrayed her. Without conscious thought, he strode across the room and halted in front of her. The seductive fragrance of her perfume assailed his senses and his gut clenched.

'You ripped my heart out and made a fool of me, and I will never forgive you,' she whispered.

He swore when he glimpsed the shimmer of tears in her eyes. In the near darkness, with the storm still raging outside, he sensed that her emotions were heightened, as were his. Jace was strongly tempted to kiss the stubborn line of Eleanor's mouth until her lips softened.

But giving in to his clamouring libido would complicate the situation even more, he reminded himself.

'I don't need your forgiveness,' he told her curtly. 'All I want is your signature on a marriage certificate.'

'You can't be serious about wanting to marry me when there is so much animosity between us. You could have any woman you want.' Eleanor blushed when Jace raised his brows. 'Don't be coy,' she muttered. 'You know you're a catch.'

'Money tends to do that,' he said drily.

'I'm sure you are well aware of the effect you have on the female sex.'

'I'm interested to know what effect I have on you.'

She met his gaze steadily and Jace experienced the unfamiliar sensation of being judged and found wanting. 'I think you are beautiful but flawed,' Eleanor told him. 'I've seen inside your soul and there's nothing there but an empty void.'

He shrugged. But he was stung by her evaluation of him. 'That is why you will be my perfect temporary wife, *omorfiá mou*. You won't harbour hopes that I will fall in love with you.'

'No, I won't make that mistake again, Jace.' Eleanor's voice was as dry as a desert. She sighed. 'During dinner, when you went to your study to take a business call, your mother told me how hard life was for both of you after your father died. She said you had to leave school early and get a job.' Eleanor hesitated. 'Your mother also mentioned that you deserved to be lucky after something terrible happened to you.'

Jace stiffened. This was an opportunity to tell Eleanor that he had served a prison sentence. But he balked at trying to explain that his conviction for assault had been unjust and he had acted in self-defence. A judge hadn't believed his version of what had happened, so why would Eleanor? Grimly, he acknowledged that he had done nothing to earn her trust.

'Ah,' he murmured, as if he'd just realised what his mother had meant. 'I believed I was in love once, but my girlfriend dumped me for a richer man. I suppose it seemed terrible at the time, but I had the last laugh when I won a million euros on a lottery game.'

Eleanor looked startled. 'Did you try to persuade your girlfriend back with your winnings?'

'No, I used the money to establish a property development business. It was a safer bet than Katerina, who had shown that she was a gold-digger,' Jace said sardonically. 'It was the first ticket I'd ever bought and, unlike your brother, I knew that the odds of another big win if I gambled again were minuscule. The money gave me the opportunity to do something with my life. I worked hard, and within five years my business portfolio was worth twenty times my original win.'

He had clawed his way to the top. Kostas's betrayal of his father had taught him never to trust anyone, Jace brooded. He was proud of everything he had achieved.

'Now you are reputed to be one of the wealthiest men in Greece,' Eleanor murmured. 'But I have the one thing you want but cannot buy.'

She released a shaky breath. 'Your mother told me that she would be overjoyed to see you married before she dies. My brother talked of ending his life because he is worried about his debts. So I'll marry you, and you will gain fifty per cent of the Pangalos. More importantly, we will be able to help the people we care about. But our marriage will be a business arrangement, as you suggested. For your mother's sake I will pretend to be your loving wife in public, but in private we will lead separate lives. Discreetly, of course,' she added coolly.

It was exactly what Jace had wanted. A marriage that would make his mother happy in the last months of her life and secure him half-ownership of the Pangalos. He should feel exultant, but he was infuriated to hear Eleanor state in a prim voice, so at odds with her sex siren looks, that she wanted an open marriage.

Did she have some guy in the background? Jace wondered furiously. He gritted his teeth at the idea that once Eleanor was his wife she might plan to slip out of the marital home to spend nights or maybe weekends with a lover. Yes, such an arrangement could work in his favour too. But he had not slept with a woman since before he'd met Eleanor fifteen months ago. The realisation made him frown. He did not want a mistress. He wanted his eager bride of a year ago.

Jace remembered how his body had been taut with anticipation at the prospect of taking Eleanor to bed in Paris. He had been turned on by her beguiling mix of innocence and sensuality. The way she was looking at him now, with a hungry desire that turned her hazel eyes green, shook his resolve to keep his hands off her.

'You can forget about us having an open marriage,' he told her bluntly. 'I won't stand for you flaunting your affairs with other men while you are my wife.'

She looked confused and then angry. 'It was your idea. You said we would both have freedom within the marriage.'

Jace was irritated that she quoted him, and he tried to recall what other crass things he might have said. 'I am a well-known figure in Greece, and the media take excessive interest in my personal life. It would be deeply upsetting for my mother if she heard rumours that we were not committed to our marriage.'

He stared down at Eleanor and felt a curious tug in his chest as he roamed his gaze over the delicate contours of her face. It amazed him that he had overlooked her English rose beauty initially. Her eyes darkened, the pupils dilating so they were fathomless black pools ringed by irises that had turned as green as a stormy sea. He knew she felt the simmering awareness between them, and when her tongue darted across her bottom lip it took all Jace's willpower not to sweep her into his arms and crush her mouth beneath his.

'You have a reputation as a playboy. Do you expect me to believe that you will remain celibate during our marriage?' Her hair swirled in a fragrant cloud around her shoulders when she shook her head. She gave him a belligerent look as she placed her hands on her hips.

The action drew Jace's attention to her breasts rising and falling quickly beneath the shirt he'd lent her. The outline of her nipples through the thin cotton answered the question that had plagued him throughout dinner. She wasn't wearing a bra and he felt his body respond to the invitation she was throwing out.

'I have no intention of living like a monk,' he drawled. Her indignant expression brought a mocking smile to his lips. 'Don't go there, *omorfiá mou*,' he warned softly. 'I certainly won't force you to have sex with me, if that was the accusation you were about to make. But I guarantee that at some point our marriage will include a sexual relationship.'

She took a deep breath that made her breasts swell so that the buttons down the front of the shirt appeared to be in danger of pinging open. 'You are *so* arrogant.'

'And you are a pretty little liar if you deny that you

want this,' Jace said roughly. He could no longer fight his desire for Eleanor that pumped powerfully through his veins. When he slipped his hand beneath her chin and tilted her face to his he saw the same urgent excitement in her eyes that consumed him. But he forced himself to hold back.

'I am not restraining you in any way,' he murmured. 'You are free to leave. But if you don't move in the next ten seconds, I give you fair warning that I am going to kiss you.'

'Go on then.'

The words slipped out of Eleanor's mouth before she could stop them. She felt herself blush, but she stared at Jace's heartbreakingly handsome face as he lowered his head towards her and her feet refused to budge. There was no chance she would fall in love with him again, she assured herself. He was a lying toad and she hated him, but she craved his kiss.

Who was she kidding? She wanted more than his kisses. She had been startled by his accusation that she might want affairs with other men. Jace was the only man she wanted. A year ago he had given her a glimpse of her own sensuality and her body felt cheated that she had not experienced the sexual fulfilment his caresses had promised.

He moved his hand up and cupped her cheek, brushing his thumb lightly over her sensitised skin. The oddly tender gesture caused her heart to slam headlong into her ribcage. She snatched a breath seconds before he grazed his mouth across hers. The effect was electrifying. Every cell in her body quivered with acute awareness of him and with a need she did not fully understand but it made her tremble and shift closer to him.

Jace groaned and lashed his arm around her waist, pulling her against the muscled hardness of his thighs. And Eleanor melted. Any lingering thoughts of resistance disappeared as she responded to Jace's demands with a helplessness that would have appalled her if she had been capable of rational logic. There would be time for self-recrimination later. Now there was simply fire and flame as Jace licked his way into her mouth and tangled his tongue with hers.

He tasted of smoky whisky and Eleanor felt as if she had come home. His mouth fitted hers perfectly and his fierce passion eased a little the hurt he had inflicted on her heart a year ago. He slid his hand into her hair and angled her head while he deepened the kiss and it became an erotic feast.

With a soft moan, Eleanor wound her arms around his neck and pressed herself against his whipcord body. This was what she had dreamed of night after night since she had fled from him in Paris. Jace was her master and she became alive beneath his magician's touch.

Compelled by feminine instinct and a desperation to be even closer to him, she slipped her hands beneath the hem of his sweater and discovered the tantalising warmth of his bare skin. Her fingertips explored the ridges of his abdominal muscles before moving up to skim across the whorls of hair that grew on his chest.

Touching him wasn't enough. She wanted to see him. She must have spoken her thoughts aloud because he gave a rough laugh and yanked his sweater over his head with clumsy haste rather than his usual grace.

Outside, the storm had cleared, leaving a white moon to cast a pearlescent gleam into the orangery and over Jace's half-naked body. He could have been a sculpture by Michelangelo but, unlike cold marble, his skin felt warm to Eleanor's lips when she kissed the place above where his heart thudded unevenly.

He growled something unintelligible and seized her in his arms once more, bringing his mouth down on hers and kissing her with untrammelled passion. His fingers deftly unfastened the buttons on her shirt and Eleanor felt a tiny stab of jealousy at the evidence of his expertise at undressing women. But when he parted the edges of the shirt and bared her breasts, setting her away from him so that he could look at her, his husky groan evoked a throb of desire between her legs.

'*Eísai ómorfi,*' Jace said in a strained voice. He repeated in English, 'You are beautiful.'

The hot gleam of desire in his eyes made Eleanor *feel* beautiful. Whatever had happened in the past, *this* now was real. The slight unsteadiness of Jace's hand when he reached out and cupped her breast told her that it was not a calculated seduction. The chemistry smouldering between them was too strong for either of them to resist.

She caught her breath when he stroked his thumb across her nipple and brought it to a tingling, hard peak. With a soft sigh, she arched towards him and he claimed her lips once more in a shockingly sensual kiss that plundered her soul. Eleanor was conscious only of Jace, his mouth wreaking havoc and his caresses increasingly bold as he trailed his fingertips over her stomach, down to her knickers, where the lacy panel between her legs was damp with her arousal. Nothing mattered but that he should assuage the insistent ache there.

A sudden, shocking bright light replaced the pale gleam of the moon. Eleanor stiffened as Jace tore his lips from hers and cursed beneath his breath. He narrowed his eyes against the glare of the overhead light.

'Is something wrong, Mamá? Do you feel ill?'

Iliana was standing in the doorway and looked embarrassed. But Eleanor was even more mortified and hastily tugged the shirt over her breasts.

'*Sygnómi,*' his mother apologised. 'I thought I had left my reading glasses in here and I did not want to disturb Anna. But I have disturbed you.'

'You may as well hear our news, Mamá,' Jace said softly. 'We were going to tell you in the morning.' He draped his arm around Eleanor's shoulders and smiled down at her. The warning glint in his eyes jolted her back to reality and reminded her that once again he was only pretending to be in love with her. But this time she was part of the pretence and she gave him a saccharine-sweet smile.

He stared at her intently as if he were trying to read her mind. Let him try, she thought. A year ago she had worn her heart on her sleeve, but now she was wary and determined that he would not hurt her again.

'Eleanor has agreed to be my wife,' Jace told his mother. 'We are going to be married. Not only that, but earlier today I finalised a deal which will return my father's share of the Pangalos hotel to the Zagorakis family.'

Iliana looked stunned for a moment before her lined face broke into a joyous smile. 'My prayers have been answered. Everything I hoped for has come true, and when I take my last breath I will be at peace.' She clasped Eleanor's hand. 'I see tenderness in the way my son looks at you. And you love him, don't you?'

Eleanor hesitated and her gaze flew to Jace's inscrutable expression. She had a better understanding of why he had cold-heartedly seduced her a year ago. He had loved his father and now he wanted to make his mother happy before she died. Jace wasn't completely heartless. Before they had been interrupted, his desire for her had been real. She'd felt the hard proof of his arousal against her hip. But he would never fall in love with Kostas Pangalos's granddaughter and she must not forget it.

'Jace knows how I feel about him,' she murmured, and wondered why he frowned.

Bright sunshine on an English summer's day poured through Eleanor's office window at Francine's hotel and set the enormous diamond on her finger ablaze.

'That's quite a rock.' Her sister sounded envious.

Eleanor sighed. Her engagement ring was certainly eye-catching and must be worth a fortune. When Jace had returned the ring to her before she'd left Greece two weeks ago its sparkling brilliance had been a mocking reminder that the diamond solitaire held no emotional significance. The truth was that she would have preferred a less showy ring. Perhaps she was more like a brown sparrow than a peacock, as Jace had once described her, she thought ruefully.

'You are a dark horse,' Lissa said. 'How did you manage to persuade one of the richest and sexiest men in Europe to marry you? I wasn't aware that you knew Jace Zagorakis until I read the announcement of your engagement in the newspaper. You might have told me first.'

To Eleanor's surprise her sister sounded hurt. 'There wasn't time,' she explained hurriedly. 'Jace wants us to marry as soon as possible because his mother is ill. He made the press announcement on the same day that notice of our marriage was published in a local Greek newspaper, which is the rule before we could apply for a wedding licence.'

She looked back at her computer screen, frowning when she thought of the amount of work she still had to do. Jace had tried to persuade her to stay at his house in Thessaloniki for the month leading up to their wedding, but she'd insisted on returning to Oxford. She had things to sort out, she'd told him. But the real reason was that she hadn't trusted herself to live in close proximity to Jace. Their separation was a chance for her to build her defences against his charisma but, annoyingly, he invaded her dreams every night.

As well as a lack of sleep, Eleanor had been dealing with numerous issues at the Oxford hotel. A serious leak in one of the upstairs bathrooms had flooded two of the newly refurbished suites, which had incurred more expense. She'd had no time to prepare for her move to Greece, and hadn't even bought a wedding dress yet.

'I can't believe that Craig has decided to relocate to Canada,' she groaned. 'I had intended to promote him to General Manager of Francine's. I'll keep my position as Vice President of Operations, but I will be living in Halkidiki and involved with running the Pangalos. I want to feel confident that I'm leaving Francine's in good hands, but none of the applicants I've interviewed for the GM role have been right.'

'You could give the position to me.' Lissa grimaced when Eleanor stared at her. 'I know you think that I spend my life going to parties but, as a matter of fact, I went to college in London and studied for a diploma in hotel management. For the last six months I've worked in a management role at the Bainbridge Hotel in Mayfair. It was only a junior position, but I'm capable of running Francine's if you would give me the chance.'

'But you were never interested in the hotel.'

'I was always interested, but when I asked Pappoús if

he would give me a trial job so that I could prove I was prepared to work hard, he refused. You were the chosen one,' Lissa said bitterly. 'Pappoús didn't think much of me and Mark. It was always Eleanor with her business degree. Eleanor who never disagreed with him. You were his favourite because you reminded him of Mum.'

Eleanor thought of her beautiful, elegant mother. 'I'm not a bit like her.'

Lissa nodded. 'You have the same serene air that Mum had. And now that you've ditched those awful granny cardigans and got a new hairstyle you look amazing.' She grinned at Eleanor's shocked expression. 'You look like a woman in love.'

Eleanor was tempted to confide to her sister the real reason why she was marrying Jace. She certainly wasn't in love with him, she assured herself. But during his nightly phone calls he was charming and amusing and seemed genuinely interested in what she had to say. She had found herself relaxing and opening up to him as she'd done when he had courted her fifteen months ago.

Memories of his passionate kisses in Greece on the night of the storm were rarely out of her mind. Jace had made it clear that he would not force her into his bed. If they had not been interrupted she would have made love with him because she couldn't resist him, Eleanor thought ruefully. Why shouldn't she take what Jace was offering? whispered a voice of temptation in her head. She wanted to have sex with him, but she would not confuse lust for love, and she was strong enough to walk away from him when the fire between them died.

'Please give me a chance.' Lissa's voice pulled Eleanor back to the present.

She frowned, remembering how Mark had said the same thing. But her little sister had grown up and was a stronger character than their brother. Eleanor was shocked that Lissa had been jealous of her relationship with their grandfather. 'I thought you wanted to be an actress,' she murmured.

'I realised in California that I don't have enough talent. And I refused to sleep with the film director who invited me to dinner to discuss a possible role in his film.' Lissa gave her a pleading look. 'I won't let you down.'

'Well… Craig doesn't go to Canada for two months. You could shadow him and…'

'Oh, thanks, El.' Lissa beamed. 'You won't regret it. Now you can stop worrying about Francine's and get on with preparations for your wedding.' She picked up a bridal magazine from Eleanor's desk. 'Have you chosen a wedding dress?'

'Not yet. What do you think of the one on the front cover?'

Her sister shook her head. 'It will make you look like a meringue. She flicked through the pages and showed Eleanor an overtly sexy fitted gown with a plunging neckline and a fishtail skirt. 'This would suit you. If you wear a dress like this on your wedding day, your hunky fiancé will be impatient to rip it off you.'

Eleanor could not restrain a little shiver as she imagined Jace's hands caressing her body on their wedding night. 'Will you come shopping with me?' she asked Lissa. 'I need to buy a trousseau and I'd appreciate your advice.'

## CHAPTER FIVE

FOLLOWING THE SATNAV'S instructions, Jace drove along a narrow lane on the outskirts of Oxford and through a gate into a field. Although it was early in the morning, a crowd of people were milling about. Not for the first time he asked himself why he had interrupted his flight back to Greece from New York, where he'd had a series of business meetings, and instructed his pilot to make a stopover in England.

On the passenger seat of his car was a bouquet of pink roses that he had impulsively bought at the airport for Eleanor. Jace never did anything by impulse. He planned every aspect of his life with calculated detachment, and in the past when he'd given flowers to a lover his PA had ordered them from a florist.

He frowned as he recalled his conversation with Eleanor's sister when he'd arrived at Francine's hotel. Lissa had looked at him curiously. 'Eleanor has gone to a balloon event with her friend Nigel and she left me in charge of the hotel for the weekend. I'm going to be the General Manager of Francine's after my sister marries you and moves to Greece,' Lissa had said with pride in her voice.

Perhaps Lissa Buchanan wasn't as superficial as his first opinion of her, Jace had mused before he'd dismissed Eleanor's sister from his mind. He hadn't understood what Lissa had meant by a balloon event, but as he drove across the field he saw that people were grouped around hot-air balloons which were being inflated. He had no idea why Eleanor had got up at the crack of dawn to watch balloons. More to the point, what was the exact nature of her relationship with 'her friend' who she planned to spend the weekend with? Jace wondered as he parked the car and strolled over to some people.

'Sure, Eleanor is here with Nigel. They never miss a club event,' someone told Jace, pointing to a blue and white balloon.

He headed across the field in the direction of the group standing around a wicker basket attached to a striped balloon. His steps slowed when he spotted Eleanor and he felt an inexplicable tug in his chest as he studied her. She was delectable in tight-fitting jeans and a bubble-gum-pink tee shirt that moulded her high, firm breasts. Her hair was caught in a loose knot on top of her head and she looked natural and wholesome, and at the same time achingly desirable.

Jace's attention had been riveted on Eleanor, but he shifted his gaze to the lanky guy with hair flopping into his eyes who she was with. Eleanor was smiling as she chatted animatedly to the guy. Suddenly she threw her arms around his neck and the two of them hugged.

Jace was unprepared for the sensation of an iron band wrapping around his chest and squeezing the air out of his lungs. A lead weight dropped into his stomach and there was a bitter taste in his mouth. He might have suspected that what he was feeling was jealousy if the idea wasn't laughable. Since Katerina had shown her true colours many years ago, he hadn't allowed himself to get close to any woman on an emotional level and he kept his affairs purely physical.

Eleanor had been different. Their courtship had been gentle but with simmering chemistry below the surface. Jace acknowledged that it was not surprising if she had replaced him in her affections with a new boyfriend. But seeing her wrapped around Mr Floppy-Hair infuriated him. She had agreed to marry *him,* and part of the deal was that neither of them would stray outside of the marriage.

Jace dismissed as irrelevant the fact that Eleanor was not his wife yet. Their wedding was in a week's time. He had put a diamond the size of a rock on her finger, and he had every right to demand to know what the hell was going on.

He strode across the dew-damp grass, frowning as he watched Eleanor climb into the basket, above which the balloon was now inflated. The guy she had been hugging climbed into the basket with her.

'Jace!' Her eyes widened when she saw him. 'What are you doing here? I wasn't expecting you to come to Oxford.'

'Evidently not,' he drawled, looking pointedly from Eleanor to her companion.

'This is Nigel.' She looked puzzled when Jace hooked his leg over the side of the wicker basket. 'You can't come in. There is only room for two people.'

'In that case one of us will have to get out.' He glowered at the other man.

'I'll leave you to it,' Nigel said hurriedly and climbed out of the basket.

Jace decided that if looks could kill, the glare Eleanor directed at him would make him a dead man.

'What was that about?' she demanded frostily.

His eyes narrowed on her flushed cheeks and his body reacted predictably to the sight of her breasts rising and falling swiftly beneath her tight tee shirt. 'Is Mr Floppy your lover?'

'Mr Flop…? Oh, you mean Nigel. He's a friend, nothing more.'

'You were plastered all over him.'

Her breath hissed between her teeth. 'He had just told me that his wife is expecting their first baby after several years of trying to get pregnant. I'm really happy for Nigel and Clare. How *dare* you behave like a possessive jerk?'

Jace was intrigued by Eleanor's outburst of temper. A year ago she had kept her passionate nature hidden from him, or maybe he had not taken the time to discover the real woman behind her rather bland shell. There was nothing bland about her now, he brooded, his eyes fixed on her moist lips as her tongue darted over them.

'Eleanor, are you ready to launch?' Nigel called out.

'Ready,' Eleanor shouted above the noise of the burner that was shooting flames into the mouth of the canopy.

Jace tensed when he realised that the balloon was rising into the air and the crew had let go of the ropes which had secured the basket to the ground. 'Do you actually mean to go up in this thing?' He watched Eleanor fiddling with the burner equipment. 'Surely we need someone with us who knows what they're doing?'

'I *do* know what I'm doing. I'm a qualified balloon pilot.'

'*You?*'

'Why are you so shocked?'

He blew out a breath. 'I didn't know you were a fan of dangerous sports.'

'Ballooning isn't dangerous when it's done properly.' She held his gaze and Jace looked away first when she said drily, 'You never really knew me.'

After a moment, Eleanor said, 'I gained my balloon pilot's licence a while ago. The weather is unpredictable in England, so I went to a flight training school in Turkey and did a crash course.'

The ground was a long way down. Jace took a deep breath. 'That's not funny.'

'What? Oh, sorry, no pun intended.' She stared at him. 'Are you okay?'

'I'm not a fan of heights,' he gritted, his jaw clenched.

'But you own your own jet and regularly fly across the world for business.'

'I trust my pilot.'

'Well, like it or not, you'll have to trust me. I'm going to turn the burner off now that we have reached the right altitude.'

The silence that enveloped them was like nothing Jace had ever experienced before. 'Look at the view,' Eleanor urged him. 'Isn't it incredible?'

The Oxfordshire countryside was spread beneath them, a patchwork of fields criss-crossed with green hedges and the silver glint of the river. But Jace still felt ill at ease. 'Where are we going?'

'Wherever the wind takes us. There is no way of steering the balloon. The only control the pilot has is altitude. We'll go higher if I turn the burner on to heat the air inside the canopy, and when we land I'll open a vent to allow the air to escape from the balloon so that I can control the rate of descent.'

Jace was captivated by Eleanor's enthusiasm. 'I love ballooning because every flight is an adventure,' she told him. 'One day I hope to fly over the African plains.

I've heard that the views of the wildlife on the Seren-geti from a balloon are amazing.'

'And for an adrenalin junkie there is the added risk of landing next to an irate lion,' Jace said sardonically. When he'd met Eleanor fifteen months ago he had thought she was sweet and charming, but adventurous was not an adjective he would have used to describe her. 'What made you decide to train as a balloon pilot?'

'You did,' she said quietly.

He frowned. 'How so?'

'You made me feel like I was worthless. I needed to prove to myself that I deserved better than to be a pawn in your revenge.'

Jace swore. 'I never thought you were worthless.'

Eleanor turned away from him and curled her hands over the edges of the basket. 'Pappoús introduced me to ballooning. He had a friend who was a pilot and used to take me for flights.' Her voice cracked. 'I loved my grandfather and I foolishly fell in love with you. But you are as ruthless as you have told me Pappoús was.'

'*Theos!* I am nothing like Kostas.' Jace's nostrils flared as he sought to control his anger. But guilt curdled in his belly when he forced himself to scrutinise his behaviour. He had betrayed Eleanor's trust. Even worse, he had justified his actions by telling himself that in a war there were always innocent casualties. Hurting Eleanor's feelings had been the price he'd been prepared to pay to seize control of the Pangalos and destroy Kostas's legacy. Grimacing, Jace acknowledged that he could not change what he had done in the past. But he owed Eleanor his honesty before she married him.

The soundless flight of the balloon was surreal,

and the air smelled crisp and clean when Jace inhaled deeply. There was something magical about drifting across the endless blue sky.

Freedom.

He remembered what it had felt like to be denied his freedom. Sometimes in his dreams he heard the sound of the warders' keys when the prisoners had been locked in the cells every evening. Each morning had begun with the cells being unlocked, surly men shuffling out into the corridors, the stench of sweat and the clang of metal doors.

'When I was younger, I spent two years in prison,' he said abruptly.

Eleanor stared at him. 'What did you do?'

'I was found guilty of grievous assault.' Jace waited for her to make a comment, but her silence gave no clue to her thoughts. He continued tensely, 'It's true that I punched someone. But I acted to defend Takis when I saw that his assailant had a knife.'

'Was the Takis you tried to protect the same Takis Samaras who you sent to persuade me to sell the Pangalos?'

Jace nodded. 'We go back a long way, and we're as close as brothers.' He rubbed his hand around the back of his neck to ease the knot of tension. He did not know how he had expected Eleanor to react. She was clearly curious, and he wanted to unburden himself of the secret he had kept from her.

'When my father died, he left debts which my mother had to pay off. Although she had helped him run the hotel, she lacked any formal qualifications and could only get low paid work. I quit school to get a job so I could help to support us.'

'Iliana told me that you pretended to be older than

your age so that foremen would take you on as a labourer,' Eleanor murmured.

'I met Takis on a building site. He was young like me, and had left home to escape his abusive father. We went out one night and were set on by a group of youths. Running away seemed our best option as we were outnumbered, but Takis tripped over. I went back for him and saw the knife, so I punched the guy who was about to use it.'

'I don't understand why you were sent to prison for trying to protect your friend.'

'The assailant fell backwards when I punched him and hit his head on the pavement. He was knocked unconscious and slipped into a coma.' Jace grimaced. 'I felt really bad about what I'd done. I hadn't meant to cause serious injury. But the young thug who had attacked Takis came from a wealthy family and his father paid witnesses to say that I had started the fight.'

'What about the knife? Surely it was evidence that you had acted in defence?'

'According to the witnesses' statements there was no knife. It was mine and Takis's word against theirs, and in court no one believed us.'

'So you went to prison.'

'Takis took care of my mother while I served my sentence, and some time later I heard that the guy I'd punched had made a full recovery. I shared my cell with a British man who was serving time for embezzlement. He taught me to speak English, so at least the two years were not completely wasted,' Jace said wryly. 'When I was released from prison I got a job with a building firm and fell for the boss's daughter.' He gave a cynical laugh. 'Katerina refused to marry me after I told her I'd been to prison.'

'Oh, Jace,' Eleanor said softly.

His eyes narrowed as he tried to gauge what was going on behind her serene face. Was she judging him? 'I have no way of proving that my version of what happened is the truth. Takis will back me up, of course, but I realise you might not believe me.'

'I believe you.' She shrugged. 'There's no reason for you to lie. You don't care what I think of you. Even if you had committed a crime and deserved to go to prison, it would not change my decision. I have no choice but to marry you to clear my brother's debts. What made you tell me?'

'Our wedding is likely to be of public interest in Greece, and it's possible a journalist might dig up the story. I wanted you to hear it from me first.'

Jace exhaled heavily. 'I admit that I withheld my real reason for asking you to marry me a year ago,' he said gruffly. Remorse tugged in his chest as he accepted that he had hurt her. She had wanted Prince Charming, but Jace knew he was just an ordinary man with flaws. He could never have lived up to Eleanor's expectations of a fairy tale romance, but now at least she understood that they both had something to gain from marrying.

'Let's agree to be honest with each other for the duration of our marriage,' he murmured. The woman he had met a year ago had been uncomplicated and he could not believe that Eleanor had secrets. Although finding out that she was a balloon pilot had been unexpected. Jace acknowledged that he had jumped to conclusions about her friend Nigel. 'Is there anything you want to tell me?'

'Like what?' She sounded oddly defensive and turned around to activate the burner so that their conversation could not continue over the noise of the flames.

When it was quiet again Jace said casually, 'Do you have any other extreme hobbies—cage diving with sharks, perhaps?' Was it his imagination, or did she relax when she realised that he was teasing her?

'No, nothing like that. I don't have any secrets.' Eleanor's gaze slid away from him and he was certain she had lied.

At Jace's house in Thessaloniki, Eleanor was preparing for her wedding. 'There, that's the last one.' Her sister huffed out a breath. 'Your husband is going to curse when he has to undo all the tiny buttons down the back of your dress.' Lissa stepped to one side, leaving Eleanor's reflection in the mirror. 'I hate to say I told you so, but I knew you would look stunning in a dress that shows off your sexy figure.'

Eleanor forced a smile. She had to admit that the wedding dress her sister had picked out suited her curvy shape. Made of white silk overlaid with lace, the dress's low-cut neckline pushed her breasts high and emphasised her narrow waist and the contours of her hips before the skirt flared down to the floor. Intricate lace detailing on the back of the bodice hid her scar, and a row of pearl buttons ran from the base of her neck all the way down the dress.

In the rush to choose a dress and shoes, as well as pack up her life to move to Greece, she hadn't considered the problem of unfastening the buttons so that she could take the wedding gown off. Her sister's assumption that Jace would undress her made Eleanor feel sick with nerves.

She had denied she had any secrets, but if they spent their wedding night together he would discover her physical imperfection. Jace might be so appalled when he saw the scar on her back that perhaps he wouldn't stick around to find out she was a virgin. Memories of her first boyfriend's horrified reaction to her scar twisted the knot of tension in the pit of Eleanor's stomach even tighter.

'Hey, where have you gone?' Lissa asked softly. 'You're not supposed to look sad on the most romantic day of your life.'

'I...' Eleanor broke off. Part of her wanted to confide in her sister and explain that romance wasn't on the cards in her marriage. She had become much closer to Lissa recently, but the memory of the conversation she'd overheard when Jace had likened her sister to a beautiful peacock and *her* to a dull sparrow still rankled.

'You must wish that Mum and Dad were here,' Lissa murmured. 'It's a pity that Mark couldn't make it to the wedding, but hopefully he will get the help he needs at the rehabilitation clinic in Ireland.' She squeezed Eleanor's hand. 'I'm glad we've got each other.'

'So am I.' Eleanor blinked back tears, hating herself for her silly jealousy of her sister. 'You look lovely.' Lissa's bridesmaid's dress was cornflower-blue, the same colour as her eyes, and her pale blonde bob framed her striking features.

Lissa grinned. 'I hope the best man thinks so.'

'He is Jace's best friend, Takis Samaras.'

'Takis...what a hunk. I'm going to flirt shamelessly with him at the reception.' Lissa walked over to the dressing table and opened a box from which she carefully lifted out a bouquet of palest pink roses. 'From your fiancé,' she said as she gave the bouquet to Eleanor. 'We had better go. The car is waiting.'

The rosebuds were beginning to unfurl and release their exquisite perfume. Eleanor swallowed the lump in her throat and reminded herself that Jace had sent her the bouquet for no other reason than he wanted to convince the guests, especially his mother, that their wedding was a love match.

But she must not forget that their marriage was a business deal. The previous day she had signed a pre-nuptial agreement which specified that the Pangalos Beach Resort would become a shared marital asset. In the event of a divorce, both parties would receive a fifty per cent share of the hotel. A second document stated that the entirety of Mark Buchanan's debt to Jace would be cancelled when Eleanor became Mrs Zagorakis.

Everyone was happy, or so it would appear. If the bride's heart felt as if it were breaking when she walked into the Town Hall where the groom was waiting, none of the guests who saw Eleanor's serene smile would have guessed.

Jace was standing with the mayor, who was to con-duct the wedding ceremony. But Eleanor only saw the enigmatic man she was about to marry, and her pulse quickened when she recognised the gleam of desire in his eyes as he watched her approach him. Jace looked impossibly handsome in a navy-blue suit that screamed designer. The superbly tailored jacket emphasised the width of his shoulders and Eleanor's breath left her in a rush as she pictured his naked, muscular chest beneath his white silk shirt.

Trying to ignore the voice in her head that whispered, *If only this was real*, she stood beside Jace while the mayor spoke the words of the civil ceremony, which was much shorter than a traditional Greek church wed-ding. Before she could blink, it seemed, the mayor pro-nounced them husband and wife.

Eleanor stared down at the gold band Jace had

slipped onto her finger and tensed at the realisation of what the wedding ring represented. She was legally bound to him for the next few months. She glanced over at his mother, who seemed to grow frailer every day. Iliana was smiling and clearly delighted to see her son finally married.

But then Jace lowered his head and every thought flew from Eleanor's mind when he brushed his lips across hers. There had barely been any physical contact between them since he'd kissed her on the night of the storm, more than a month ago. A few times his arm had brushed against hers when they had been walking next to each other and once, when she had been chatting to his mother, Jace had sat down on the sofa beside her and casually looped his arm around her shoulders. She had been excruciatingly aware of the hardness of his thigh pressed up against her.

Now Eleanor's heart pounded as he dipped his tongue into her mouth and the kiss became intensely sensual. Her senses went haywire when she smelled his spicy cologne and heard his low groan as her lips parted beneath his passionate onslaught. She clutched his jacket and felt the warmth of his body through the material. The taste of him lingered on her lips when he eventually lifted his head, and the predatory gleam in his dark eyes sent a quiver of longing through her.

But then he stepped away from her and she snatched her hand from his chest, her cheeks reddening when Jace said softly, 'I'm looking forward to being alone with you later, *omorfiá mou,* but first we have to get through the reception.'

A marquee in the garden at his house provided seating for the fifty guests, most of whom Eleanor had not met before. A few were business colleagues. Many of

Jace's friends were entrepreneurs like him, successful men who worked and played hard. Some had glamorous wives and others, like Takis Samaras, were lone wolves who had no desire to settle down.

Jace had been the leader of the wolf pack, Eleanor surmised. During the wedding dinner she was aware that several women sent him overt or even quite blatant glances. The idea that the sophisticated socialites were his ex-mistresses, or they were candidates for the position, evoked a corrosive burn in the pit of her stomach which she assured herself was not jealousy. She discovered that drinking a glass of champagne made her feel less tense, and by her third, or possibly her fourth glass, she really didn't care if Jace had a different mistress for every day of the week.

When dusk fell the garden was illuminated by hundreds of fairy lights that danced in the faint breeze like golden fireflies. The air was filled with the scents of jasmine and orange blossom and fragrant roses that had been twined around the supporting pillars of the marquee.

The wedding was everything Eleanor had dreamed of when she had been in love with Jace, but it was all fake and she was suddenly tired of trying to keep up the pretence. Her jaw ached from smiling, she had a thumping headache and she was desperately thirsty. But when she beckoned to a waiter and reached for another glass of champagne from the tray, darkly tanned fingers closed around her wrist and pulled her hand down.

'I think you have had enough alcohol.' Jace's gravelly voice made Eleanor's stomach muscles tighten. He sent the waiter to bring her a glass of water. When they were alone she glared at him.

'Have you been keeping tabs on how much champagne I've drunk?'

'No, but I noticed you didn't eat much at dinner, and it's never a good idea to drink on an empty stomach.'

'You're not my keeper.' She hugged her arms around her, fighting an urge to wrap them around his waist and rest her head on his big chest. Guests were starting to leave at the end of the reception and soon she and Jace would be alone. She felt vulnerable and out of her depth.

'I am your husband.' The possessiveness in his voice made her temper flare.

'That doesn't mean you can tell me how to live my life. Or were you planning to keep me barefoot and pregnant during our temporary marriage?' she asked sarcastically.

His eyes narrowed. 'If you *were* to conceive my baby, our marriage would not be temporary. I believe strongly that a child deserves to grow up with both its parents.'

Eleanor was startled by the intensity in his voice. 'Fortunately, there's not a chance that I'll fall pregnant by you,' she muttered, glad of the darkness that hid her hot cheeks as she thought of the contraceptive pills she'd been prescribed by her GP before she'd left Oxford. It wasn't that she planned to sleep with Jace, but it was better to be safe than sorry.

Eleanor heard her sister calling her name and was thankful for the excuse to hurry away from Jace. In truth, she did feel a bit light-headed and it was probably a good thing she hadn't drunk another glass of champagne, but she resented him treating her like a child. Inexplicably, tears stung her eyes. Her wedding day was over, and she was on her way up to bed on her own. She would have to ask Lissa to unbutton her dress with the excuse that she wanted to change into the sexy night-gown her sister had persuaded her to buy.

'I just wanted to say goodbye and good luck,' Lissa said when Eleanor met her on the terrace. 'I've managed to persuade Takis to give me a lift to the Pangalos. It turns out that he is staying at the hotel too.' She glanced over at the devilishly attractive man with jet-black hair and an unsmiling face. 'So far, he hasn't reacted to my subtle hints that I fancy him, but it's a two-hour drive to Sithonia and, fingers crossed, he'll stop playing hard to get.' She hugged Eleanor. 'I've got to go.'

'Just a minute...' Eleanor began, then sighed as she watched her sister scoot after Takis. She continued into the house and at the top of the stairs she walked along the corridor to the room she had been given when she'd arrived from England. It was connected to the master bedroom but the door between the rooms could be bolted from her side. Jace had said that for their marriage to be believable they must appear to sleep together.

Ten minutes later, her arms aching from reaching behind her back to try and undo the fiddly buttons on her dress, Eleanor conceded defeat. She spun round when the connecting door opened and Jace lounged in the doorway.

'I thought the door was locked,' she said in a breathless voice quite unlike her own. 'I usually check it, but I forgot tonight.'

'Perhaps one of the staff unlocked it. Or perhaps you left it unlocked on purpose,' he drawled.

'I assure you I didn't.'

He strolled further into her room. 'So you say, but your body is sending out a different message, *pouláki mou*.'

'*Don't* call me that. It's unflattering.'

'It's not meant to be.'

'You think I am a drab sparrow.' She took a step backwards and banged her hip on the corner of the dressing table.

Jace shook his head as he came closer. He had discarded his jacket and tie and the sleeves of his shirt were pushed up to his elbows. Wiry black chest hairs and an expanse of olive-tanned skin were visible where the top of his shirt was open. Eleanor hated how her heart leapt when his mouth curved upwards in a meltingly sexy smile.

'I think you are beautiful. When I saw you in your wedding dress you blew my mind,' he said gruffly.

'Stop right there.' Eleanor held out her hand to ward him off. She had been down this path once before, and she was determined not to fall for his husky voice and the seductive gleam in his dark eyes. 'You said you wouldn't force me to sleep with you.'

'*Theé mou!*' he exploded. 'Of course not. Do you really think that of me?' His jaw clenched. 'No, don't answer. I have a feeling I won't like your reply.'

He raked his hand through his hair. 'I wanted to thank you for marrying me and making my mother the happiest I can remember seeing her. She learned a few days ago that the treatment for her cancer has been unsuccessful, and there are no more options. It's simply a matter of time now.'

'I'm so sorry to hear that.' Eleanor bit her lip. 'But I feel terrible for lying to your mother, and my sister, and everyone who came to our wedding and wished us well, unaware that our marriage is a…a farce.'

'Is it?' Jace murmured. Somehow, he had moved without her realising and he was too close and yet not close enough.

'What else can it be?' she asked helplessly, mesmerised by his potent masculinity.

'Whatever we want it to be.' He slipped his hand beneath her chin and tilted her face. She felt as if she were drowning in his liquid gaze and her lips parted of their own volition when he brushed his mouth over hers in a featherlight caress. He kissed her again, taking little sips of her lips, tantalising, teasing. Not enough.

'This is not a lie. Our desire for each other is real and we are both enslaved by it,' he growled, his warm breath grazing her cheek before he kissed his way down her neck to the edge of her wedding dress.

# CHAPTER SIX

JACE TURNED HER in his arms so that he was standing behind her and pushed her hair aside to gently nip her earlobe with his teeth, sending starbursts of sensation shooting through her. His chest rumbled as he made a sound somewhere between a laugh and a groan. 'That's a lot of buttons. I'll try to be patient while I undo them.'

His words chilled Eleanor's blood. If he unfastened her dress he would see her scar. His hands moved from her shoulders and she felt him release the top button. 'No.' She was galvanised to action and jerked away from him. 'I don't want you...'

He stared at her and sounded puzzled rather than frustrated by her apparent change of heart. 'I would never do anything you did not want. But I know you want me, Eleanor.' His Greek accent was thick when he spoke her name.

She shook her head and the room whirled alarmingly. 'I don't... I don't feel very well.' Her stomach churned, and she gasped and fled into the en suite bathroom, just managing to turn the key in the lock before she leaned over the basin and was horribly sick.

When she'd finished and had brushed her teeth, Eleanor grimaced at her reflection in the mirror. Her face was as white as her wedding dress and her mascara was smudged, making her look like a panda. But she couldn't stay in the bathroom all night. As she stepped into the bedroom Jace came towards her carrying a glass of water and a plate.

'I had one of the staff bring you a sandwich.' He frowned when she shuddered. 'You need to eat something. How many glasses of champagne *did* you drink today?'

'I lost count,' she admitted. 'I didn't notice its effect while I was talking to the guests, but now I feel terrible.'

'I should have realised,' Jace said shortly. 'You are my wife and I am responsible for your welfare.'

His words sparked Eleanor's temper. 'I don't want to be a responsibility. I'm not a child.'

'You act like one sometimes. Why did you run away in Paris instead of talking to me and having an adult discussion about what you had overheard me say on the phone?'

'You told Takis that your engagement to me was not a love match. What was there to discuss?' Hurt throbbed in her voice. She lifted her hand to her pounding head. 'Why is the room spinning?'

'You feel dizzy because too much alcohol in your blood can affect your balance. The best thing will be to go to bed, but you can't sleep in your dress. If you don't want me to take it off, I'll call a maid to come and help you.'

Eleanor was tempted to take the coward's way out. To delay the inevitable. She was sure that when Jace saw her scar his desire for her would cool rapidly from fiery hot to cold ashes. But perhaps it was better this way. He had said she was beautiful, but he would discover the truth and then they could continue with their marriage as planned—a business arrangement, nothing more.

'Let's get this over with,' she muttered, turning around so that she was facing the dressing table.

'I've had more encouraging invitations,' he said drily.

'I don't doubt it.' She remembered a stunning brunette at the wedding who had introduced herself as a member of Jace's finance team. Angeliki had made it clear she hoped for a more personal role in his life.

'Hold your hair up.' Jace's breath felt warm on her neck when she obeyed. She felt his fingers at the top of her dress as he worked on the buttons. Lower and lower he went, and now she was aware of the two sides of the bodice separating to reveal...

His breath hissed between his teeth. He did not say a word, but she saw his shocked expression in the mirror. Tears welled in Eleanor's eyes, but she forced herself to stand unmoving while he continued to open her dress down to her waist.

'Now you know,' she choked. 'I'm hideous.'

'No...'

'*Yes!*' She jerked away from him. 'You don't have to pretend that you're not horrified by my scar. I saw your face in the mirror. You think I'm repulsive.' Tears streamed down her face and her shoulders shook with the force of her sobs. This was the moment she had dreaded. Jace's shocked silence *hurt*.

'You can have any woman you want. Beautiful, perfect women with unblemished bodies. Why on earth would you want me?' She gulped air into her lungs. Her close-fitting wedding dress was constricting, and its beauty mocked her. 'Go away, Jace,' she whispered brokenly.

'I'm not going anywhere, *matia mou*.' Jace kept his voice unemotional, recognising that Eleanor's emotions were on a knife-edge. He could not deny he'd been shocked when he had uncovered her scar. But repulsed? Never. His insides twisted as he remembered the pain in her voice when she'd insisted that her scar made her ugly.

He had been rendered breathless by her loveliness at his first sight of her wearing her bridal gown. In the run up to the wedding he had been constantly aware of her. She had obviously followed his advice that she would need a new wardrobe for when they were married, although she'd refused to allow him to pay for her clothes. But seeing her in sexy outfits which showed off her fantastic figure had ratcheted up his desire.

The nights had been worse, knowing that she was in bed in the room adjoining his. Knowing too that the desire that made his body ache was mutual. Chemistry had simmered between them and his libido had been eagerly anticipating their wedding night.

Jace hadn't realised that Eleanor had drunk way too much champagne at the reception, and he guessed she was unused to drinking a lot of alcohol. He felt a tug in his chest as he stared at her tear-stained face. 'You can barely stand upright,' he said softly. 'Let's get you into bed. Where do you keep your nightwear?'

She pointed to a drawer and he opened it and pulled out a wisp of black silk. Colour stormed into her face when he held up the seductive negligee. 'Not that one, obviously,' she muttered.

'Why obviously?'

'A sexy nightdress won't change what I am.'

'And what do you think you are?'

'Disfigured. That's what a boyfriend called me when he saw my back.' She rubbed her hand across her face. 'Tony was in the sixth form at school. I'd fancied him for ages, and I couldn't believe it when he asked me out. We went on a couple of dates and he seemed to really like me.'

Her voice dropped so low that Jace had to strain to hear her. 'We went to a pool party at another friend's house. I felt nervous about wearing a bikini, but everyone was having fun in the pool...so I took my shirt off. When Tony saw my scar, he said it...it was disgusting. In front of all my friends he told me to put my shirt back on because my scar was repulsive.'

Jace swore. 'The guy was a crass idiot. I assume you broke off your relationship after he was so insensitive?'

'He dumped me right there at the party,' she said flatly. 'I felt so embarrassed. But he was right. My scar is an ugly disfigurement, which is why I keep it covered up.'

A red mist obliterated every thought in Jace's head as rage pumped through him and he clenched his fists. The one and only time he'd resorted to physical violence to defend his best friend had resulted in him being sent to prison. But he would willingly serve a life sentence if he could spend five minutes with the young punk who had cruelly destroyed Eleanor's self-confidence. Jace was taken aback by a feeling of protectiveness that he had never experienced before.

'You wore a high-neck swimming costume on the cruise around the northern islands.' He remembered she had looked wistfully at some colourful bikinis in a street market on Lemnos, but she'd refused his offer to buy one for her.

She nodded. 'I was flattered by your attention. You made me feel attractive, but I was afraid you would be put off by my scar.'

It was little wonder that Eleanor had fled from his hotel room in Paris after she'd overheard him tell Takis why he had asked her to be his wife, Jace acknowledged grimly. She had already suffered with low self-esteem and his behaviour must have felt like a betrayal. Guilt left a bitter taste in his mouth. He looked away from her vulnerable expression and took an oversized tee shirt out of the drawer.

She held out her hand for the shirt. 'Will you please turn around?'

Jace forbore from mentioning that he had seen her naked breasts before. He crossed the room and drew back the bedcovers, ready for Eleanor to climb into bed. She groaned as she lay back against the pillows.

He turned the lamp's dimmer switch to its lowest setting and pulled a chair closer to the bed before he sat down and stretched his long legs out in front of him. 'How did you get your scar—some kind of accident?' he asked gently.

She let out her breath slowly. 'I had a medical condition called scoliosis. Basically it's a twist in the spine which causes the back and shoulders to be misaligned. I was eight when it was first noticed that I was standing awkwardly. Mum was always telling me not to slouch. The GP sent me for an X-ray which showed that my spine was curved, and for the next five years I wore a back brace for twenty-three hours a day.

'That sounds grim. It must have affected your childhood.'

'I couldn't do many of the activities that my brother and sister were able to do.' Eleanor sighed. 'My parents struggled to cope with my condition. Dad was a famous show jumper and Mum had been a junior gymnast champion before she became a model. They had a glamorous lifestyle and I guess they were unprepared for having a child with a disability. When I was thirteen I had surgery to straighten my spine. The operation happened a few months after my parents died and they never knew that I was finally free of the body brace.'

The sadness in her voice twisted Jace's insides. Eleanor's childhood had been as tough as his own, albeit for different reasons. He had blamed Kostas for destroying his family, and still blamed him, Jace reminded himself.

The feud between his father and Kostas Pangalos had happened a long time ago. Of course he wanted to avenge his father's death, but he regretted hurting Eleanor. He wished he could turn the clock back, and that the situation between them was different. Jace frowned. What was he thinking? He had shunned long-term relationships and commitment for most of his adult life. Oh, he'd soon got over Katerina. But he had decided that love—the lasting kind—wasn't for him.

Eleanor's breathing slowed as she fell asleep and her long lashes fanned on her cheeks. How had he thought she was uncomplicated? Jace thought ruefully. She was compassionate, courageous, irritatingly independent, and she fascinated him more than any woman ever had.

The truth was that he should ignore his hunger for her and keep their marriage to a business arrangement as he had originally planned. Except that his plan had been hijacked by his sexy wife. She rolled onto her side and tucked her hand beneath her cheek. Her lips were slightly parted, and he longed to kiss her. But he was not her prince, he reminded himself. He could not offer her the happy ever after he suspected she wanted. Eleanor was a beguiling mix of innocence and sensuality and Jace had no idea what he was going to do about her.

Eleanor leaned back in the plush leather seat on Jace's private jet as the plane accelerated down the runway and lifted off the ground. She noticed that his fingers gripped the armrests at the moment of take-off.

'Are you feeling any better?' he asked her a few minutes later.

'I feel fine, thank you.'

'You're a terrible liar.' He sounded amused, almost indulgent, and she steeled her heart against his charisma. She winced when he removed the enormous pair of sunglasses that she'd worn to hide the evidence of her first, and she vowed last, hangover.

'The stewardess will bring some food, and after you have eaten you can sleep off your headache.' His smile did strange things to her insides. 'Aren't you curious to know where we are going for our honeymoon?'

'I don't care,' she said stubbornly. 'The only reason you sprung a honeymoon on me is to make your mother believe that our marriage is real.' She snatched her sunglasses back and shoved them on her nose. 'Anyway, I expect you would prefer to be jetting off with your attractive financial advisor. At the wedding reception, Angeliki dropped hints that you are interested in more than her numeracy skills.'

His soft laughter was like golden honey sliding over her, and for some reason Eleanor felt the ache of tears behind her eyelids. 'There's no need to be jealous, *pouláki mou*,' he drawled. 'It's a rule of mine not to mix business with pleasure and I am never tempted to cross the line between employer and staff.'

'I'm not jealous,' Eleanor snapped, thinking that Jace had not actually denied he was attracted to Angeliki. But, before she could press him further, the stewardess arrived and handed her a glass of orange juice. She drank it thirstily and managed to eat a couple of mouthfuls of croissant to satisfy Jace. She settled back in the

seat, but her eyes flew open when a pair of strong arms
scooped her up and held her against his chest.

'You will be more comfortable in bed,' Jace assured
her, carrying her as if she weighed no more than a doll.
He strode into the bedroom at the back of the plane.
'We'll be in the air for approximately eight hours. Perhaps you will be in a better mood when you wake up.'

'Why did you spend last night in my room?' She had
been shocked to find him sprawled on the chair beside
her bed in the morning.

'I stayed in case you were sick again, or needed anything. I don't think you have been drunk very often.'

'It was my first time.' She flushed, thinking of the
other first time that she'd thought might happen on her
wedding night. Maybe she was destined to remain a
virgin for ever.

Jace sat on the edge of the bed and smoothed her hair
back from her face. Apart from the thicker stubble on
his jaw where his beard needed a trim, he was his usual
urbane self and devastatingly sexy in pale jeans, cream
polo shirt and a casual mid-blue blazer.

'Would you like me to stay with you now?' he murmured.

Her eyes locked with his and it would be so easy to
melt in the heat of his gaze. The mysterious alchemy
that was always there between them sizzled and she
was intensely aware of him, and of her body's reaction to him. Her nipples felt hot and tight beneath her
bra, and molten heat pooled between her legs when she
imagined him stretching out on the bed and lifting her
skirt up to her thighs so that he could slip his hand inside her knickers.

Eleanor swallowed audibly and Jace's eyes glittered
when her tongue darted across her lower lip. It would

be so easy to become spellbound by his magic. But afterwards what would become of her?

'No, that won't be necessary,' she said stiffly and shut her eyes before she succumbed to the temptation that was always and only Jace. She heard him sigh softly and seconds later the click of the door closing. Only then did she allow her tears to slide silently down her face.

It was dark when they landed and immediately transferred to a four-by-four that whisked them away to an unknown destination. Eleanor's headache had developed into a migraine and she barely noticed her surroundings. She was vaguely aware of Jace carrying her and laying her down on a soft bed.

'These are painkillers.' He gave her two tablets and held a glass of water to her lips. 'You must eat something, *matia mou*.' His voice was soft and low as if he knew that her head felt as if it might explode. 'Take a bite of this,' he urged.

She bit into a banana, swallowed and took another bite before she sank back on the pillows and into oblivion.

When she opened her eyes she had no idea how long she had been asleep, or where she was. Feeling disorientated, she cautiously sat up and was relieved that she no longer felt as if someone was drilling into her skull. In the shadowy half-light she made out the time on her watch. Five-thirty a.m. Her stomach growled. Wherever she was, she hoped they served breakfast early. She wondered where Jace was sleeping.

The silence was profound, but gradually she began to hear noises. Birdsong, but no birds that she recognised, and other unfamiliar sounds. And then it came.

A deep growl that reverberated in the air and through her body. Primitive, awe-inspiring.

A door opened and Jace stepped into the room. 'Good, you're awake.'

'Th-that was a *lion*,' Eleanor stammered. 'Where *are* we?'

'Africa. Tanzania, to be precise, in the Serengeti National Park. How is your headache?'

'Gone.' She stared at him. He looked more gorgeous than ever in khaki chinos and a collarless white shirt. She was conscious that her hair was a tangled mess. 'Jace…?'

'You've got ten minutes to shower and get dressed before breakfast. We need to make an early start.'

'Where are we going?'

'You'll see.' His grin sent her heart into a tailspin. This was the Jace she had fallen in love with—which made him dangerous.

Half an hour later they were in the four-by-four, driving across the open plains. The sky had lightened to indigo and the sun was a band of gold on the horizon, against which broad acacia trees were silhouetted. Eleanor caught her breath when she saw a hot-air balloon being inflated by a couple of ground crew.

'There's our transport,' Jace said as he helped her out of the vehicle. The gossamer curtain of an early morning mist was beginning to clear and the dawn was almost upon them.

'This isn't real, is it?' Eleanor whispered. 'I'm going to wake up and find it's a dream.'

He gave an odd crooked smile, as if he felt pleased by her reaction. 'We have a pilot who is also a guide to tell us about the wildlife we'll hopefully see today. But another time you will be able to fly the balloon yourself, once the balloon company have checked that your pilot's licence is valid.'

Eleanor climbed into the basket and watched Jace do the same. 'But you dislike heights. You don't have to come on the flight if you would rather not.'

'I'm not letting you go up without me, *pouláki mou*.'

She told herself not to read anything into the possessiveness in his voice. Jace was a typical Greek male, she thought ruefully. She swallowed, trying, and failing, to control her emotions. 'Why did you arrange such a wonderful surprise?'

He exhaled deeply. 'I suppose I am trying to make amends.' At her puzzled look, he continued. 'From the age of fifteen my life was dominated by my hatred of your grandfather and everything Kostas represented, including his family.'

'Me, in other words,' Eleanor said flatly.

His jaw clenched. 'I wanted revenge for my father's death, and I was determined to claim my family's share of the Pangalos. I didn't care who I damaged along the way to achieving my goal.'

'I understand. I do,' she insisted when he frowned. It didn't make it hurt any less, but she accepted that Jace had not acted with deliberate cruelty a year ago. 'You didn't think of me as a person. I was simply a pawn in your desire for vengeance.'

'That's not true.' He raked his hand through his hair. 'Even though you were the granddaughter of the man I despised, I found myself liking you. The connection between us was not part of some elaborate plan. And the attraction still exists now. You feel it the same as I do.'

She coloured. 'That's just sex.'

'I'd like it to be,' he said softly.

Eleanor was aware of her heart thudding painfully

hard beneath her thin cotton shirt. 'What are you saying, Jace?'

He captured her hand in his strong fingers and
rubbed his thumb over the pulse beating frantically in
her wrist. 'I'd like to call a truce in our marriage for
as long as it lasts. It would be pointless to deny that I
want to make love to you when I'm turned on simply
by looking at you,' he said huskily. 'I think you want
me too, *ómorfi gynaíka mou.*'

The warmth blazing in Jace's eyes when he called
her his beautiful wife evoked a spurt of happiness inside Eleanor, and her heart refused to listen to the words
of caution in her head. Her gaze locked with his dark
eyes as he lifted her hand up to his mouth and pressed
his lips against the new wedding band on her finger.

'You're not wearing your engagement ring,' he commented.

'I'm scared I'll lose it. A diamond that size must be
extremely valuable.'

'But you don't value things by their financial worth,'
he said musingly.

Their conversation could not continue over the roar
of the burner as the pilot prepared for take-off. The
ground crew let go of the tether ropes and the balloon
rose gracefully into the air. Eleanor saw Jace's knuckles
whiten as he gripped the edge of the basket. He caught
her gaze and his sheepish grin caused the bubble of
happiness inside her to expand.

'Ballooning is recognised as the safest form of avia-
tion,' she told him.

He gave her a sardonic look. 'We are standing in a
picnic basket suspended beneath an oversized table-
cloth, and the balloon is powered by a glorified Bunsen
burner. What part of that is safe?'

'But look at the views.' She caught her breath. 'Look, down there…giraffes…do you see them? Oh, my goodness, there's a baby one.'

Their pilot and guide, Yaro, smiled. 'Plenty more animals for you to see. I'll fly low over the watering hole where there will be zebra and elephants. And we should spot some lions. The National Park has the biggest population of lions in Africa.'

Eleanor leaned back against Jace's chest when he slid his arms around her waist and drew her close. The air was cool in the early morning before the sun had properly risen, and she revelled in the warmth of his body and the hardness of his thighs pressed against her bottom.

Beneath them the majestic panorama of the Serengeti stretched as far as the eye could see. 'I think this must be the most beautiful sight on earth,' she whispered.

'I agree.' Jace's voice was very deep. Eleanor was unaware that he was looking at her when he spoke.

It had been a truly magical day, Eleanor thought later in the evening. After the balloon flight, their guide had driven them to a camp beside a lake and they'd eaten lunch while they watched a huge flock of flamingos wading through the shallows. The birds' bright pink feathers made a stunning contrast to the blue lake. In the afternoon they'd climbed into an open-roof truck and headed out across the plains, where they saw majestic elephants and dainty impala and, incredibly, a rare black rhino. Tears had filled Eleanor's eyes when they'd spotted a lioness with three cubs.

'Africa is everything I had imagined and so much more,' she'd whispered to Jace.

'I'm glad, *pouláki mou*.' His expression had been

hidden behind his sunglasses but the warmth in his voice had curled around her heart. She had told herself not to read too much into the easy companionship she felt with him. He had suggested a truce but in the same breath he'd reminded her that their marriage was temporary.

Now they were back at their luxury lodge. Eleanor had washed off the dust from the day with a relaxing bubble bath while she'd watched the short but dramatic sunset through the window. The sky had turned into an artist's palette of purple, pink and gold as the huge orange sun sank below the horizon.

Dinner had been prepared and served in the lodge by friendly staff. She and Jace had sat on the terrace, eating delicious food and listening to the night-time sounds of the Serengeti—the trumpeting of elephants, hyenas howling and the repetitive chirring of the nightjars in competition with the frantic chirping of cicadas.

When the staff left and they were alone, Eleanor stood by the balcony rail and looked up at the inky-black sky, scattered with a million stars.

'The full moon looks close enough to touch,' she murmured when Jace strolled over to join her. Throughout the day she had been intensely aware of him when he'd sat beside her in the truck with his arm casually draped across her shoulders, or lightly touched her face to draw her attention to a herd of wildebeest in the distance.

She inhaled the spicy scent of his cologne mixed with something earthier and profoundly masculine, uniquely Jace. He had changed for dinner and his black trousers and matching shirt emphasised his tall, muscular physique. Liquid warmth pooled between her thighs, and she felt the sharp pinch of her nipples and did not need to look down to know that their outline was visible beneath her amber silk wrap dress. The material felt sensual against her breasts and the glitter in Jace's eyes during dinner had told her that he knew she wasn't wearing a bra.

Eleanor took a deep breath before she turned to face him. 'I've been thinking about what you said earlier, and... I agree.'

One black brow quirked. 'You agree with what, exactly?'

Her thoughts had gone round in circles all day and returned to the one thing she was certain of. She was attracted to Jace—fiercely, overwhelmingly attracted in a way she had never been with any other man. He had said he wanted to have sex with her, but he'd made no attempt to sell her a romantic ideal. Jace had been honest with her, and she was tired of playing games. But admitting in words what she wanted was daunting.

'This,' she murmured. She placed her hand on his chest and felt the uneven thud of his heart beneath her fingertips. Moving her hand higher, her fingers gripped the collar of his shirt and she lifted up on her toes and pressed her lips against his mouth.

His immediate response banished her fear that she might have read the situation wrong. With a low growl that sounded as predatory as the lions who roamed the plain, Jace seized her in his arms and pulled her against his whipcord body. For a few seconds he allowed her to take the lead, and she kissed him lingeringly, flicking her tongue out to explore the sensual shape of his lips.

He made a rough sound and took control, sliding one hand into her hair to clasp the back of her head as he deepened the kiss and it became spine-tinglingly erotic. He tasted of whisky and desire. She opened her mouth

to the demanding pressure of his and traded kiss for
kiss as their passion grew hotter, wilder, a conflagra-
tion that blazed out of control.

Jace lifted his head and stared down at her, and the
stark hunger glinting from his narrowed gaze stoked
Eleanor's excitement. But when he caught hold of her
hand and drew her inside the lodge and into the master
bedroom she halted in the doorway and looked at the
enormous bed beneath a canopy.

'Wait.'

He released his breath slowly. 'Of course you can
change your mind, *omorfiá mou*,' he said in a strained
voice.

'I haven't, but *you* might when I tell you that I haven't
done this before.' She watched his face as comprehension dawned and he frowned when she whispered, 'You
will be my first.'

# CHAPTER SEVEN

'WHY ME?' JACE refused to acknowledge the inexplicable euphoria that swept through him following Eleanor's admission. It had crossed his mind once or twice that she might be a virgin, but he hadn't really believed it. If he had not known that she couldn't tell a lie convincingly to save her life, he would find it hard to believe her now.

He was a red-blooded male and she was all of his fantasies rolled into one in a silky dress that clung to her sweet curves. During dinner, he had been too distracted by picturing her naked breasts beneath her dress to do justice to the food. The outline of her pebble-hard nipples jutting through the silky material had kept him in a permanent state of arousal. But there were bigger issues at play here than his out of control libido.

'If you have chosen me to be your first lover because of a misguided belief that my emotions will be involved, I have to tell you that you'll be disappointed,' he said tautly.

'Why?' She threw his question back at him. 'Don't you believe in love?'

He shrugged. 'I believe it exists for some people, but more often it comes with unrealistic expectations.' Somewhere deep inside Jace was the teenage boy who had discovered his father's body. He was haunted by the unanswered question of whether Dimitri had chosen death and deliberately abandoned his family. Jace associated love with pain and loss. Who needed love? Not him.

Eleanor met his gaze steadily. 'If you are worried that I'll fall in love with you, don't be. I gave you my heart once and you trampled all over it. I won't offer it again.' She shrugged. 'But you are very attractive, and I've fancied you for ages. I'd like my first sexual experience to be with a man who knows what he is doing.'

Jace told himself he was relieved by her assurance, but he was stung by her cool tone. 'How come you are a virgin at twenty-five?'

The slight tremor of her lower lip betrayed her vulnerability and stirred his protective instincts. 'Tony, the boy from school, was my first boyfriend. His reaction to my scar knocked my confidence and I retreated from the dating scene and focused on getting good grades in my exams.'

Eleanor sighed. 'Pappoús was so proud when I was accepted into Oxford University. He made it clear that he did not want me to be distracted from my studies, so I didn't get involved much in student life because I wanted his approval. As a child with scoliosis I was sure that my parents couldn't love me as much as they loved my brother and sister, but when they died I was my grandfather's favourite. I realise now that he was controlling,' she said ruefully. 'He groomed me from when I was quite young to be his successor as head of Gilpin Leisure.'

Eleanor said earnestly, 'I'm not ruthless like Pappoús, and I regret that he cheated your father out of his share of the Pangalos.'

The protective feeling that Jace could not ignore tugged in his chest when he saw the sparkle of tears on her lashes. 'I knew within minutes of meeting you that you are not morally reprehensible like your grandfather,' he told her gruffly. He ran his finger lightly down her cheek, tracing the path of a single tear, and then walked across the room and switched on the music system.

'Dance with me,' he murmured when he returned to her and drew her into his arms.

'You want to *dance*?'

She was stiff with tension, her eyes huge and full of uncertainty. Her defencelessness made his gut twist because he knew he must accept some of the blame for her wariness. But there was awareness in her gaze too. Desire that he easily recognised because it burned in him with the same fierce intensity.

'Humour me, hmm?' He urged her to move with him to the slow tempo of the seductive jazz number, sliding his hand down to her bottom to pull her closer so that her pelvis was flush with his. He heard her soft gasp when she felt the hardness of his arousal. And he ached. *Theos,* how he ached to carry her over to the bed, shove her dress up to her waist and thrust his swollen shaft between her soft thighs.

But Jace knew he must curb his impatience. His beautiful virginal wife needed careful handling. His wife! Odd how possessive he felt, and in a far recess of his mind an alarm bell sounded. He ignored it and continued to dance with her, hip to hip, her soft breasts crushed against the hard wall of his chest. The sultry fragrance of her perfume filled his senses when he pressed his lips to her throat and kissed his way up to nuzzle the tender place behind her ear.

Gradually he felt her relax as their bodies swayed

with the music. Eleanor rubbed her pelvis sinuously against him. *Don't rush her*, Jace warned himself, but he had never known desire like this, so hot and urgent. She entranced him more than any woman ever had, and he exhaled a ragged breath when he untied the front of her dress and pushed the two sides apart.

Her breasts were perfect round peaches, the creamy skin softly flushed with pink and tipped with darker nipples that swelled to hard peaks when he stroked his thumb pads over them. He pushed her dress off her shoulders so that she was naked apart from a pair of tiny panties. When he slipped his hand between her legs he felt the wetness of her arousal that drenched her silky underwear.

'Jace...' Eleanor's sweet breath filled his mouth and he felt a quiver run through her as he eased the panel of her knickers aside and rubbed his finger over her moist opening until, like a rosebud unfurling, her soft folds parted to allow him to push the tip of his finger into her.

*For her—all for her.* He fought to bring his rampant libido under control, but his resolve to take things slowly was tested when she undid his shirt buttons and skimmed her hands over his bare chest. With a muttered curse, he scooped her up in his arms and strode over to the bed. He laid her on the mattress and rolled her onto her stomach.

She instantly tensed and tried to turn over, but he gently held her there with a hand on her shoulder and traced his other hand lightly along her spine, following the path of the thin white scar that snaked all the way down from her neck to the small of her back. She flinched, and he instantly stopped.

'Does your scar hurt when I touch it?'

'No. But how can you bear to touch it?' she choked. 'It's grotesque.'

Jace frowned. 'Do you often take a look at your back?'

'I never look at it. The nurse in the hospital held up a mirror so that I could see my scar after she had removed the dressing. I was so shocked.' There was a catch in Eleanor's voice. 'The nurse warned me that there was still a lot of bruising, which would fade, but the scar looked like I had been sliced in half. It's an ugly, raised purple wound.' She pushed up from the mattress. 'Please don't look at it. I hate it. I hate…my body.'

'Eleanor, *mou*,' Jace said deeply. His lungs felt oddly constricted when she hung her head and refused to look at him. A tear dripped from her face onto the black satin bedsheet and was joined by another damp spot and another. He stood up and held out his hand to her. 'Come with me.'

'It's all right,' she whispered. 'I don't need you to escort me to my bedroom.'

She swung her legs off the bed, and he caught hold of her hand and led her over to the long mirror on the wall. 'Stand there.'

'Why? What are you doing?'

Instead of replying, Jace picked up the free-standing mirror from the dressing table and positioned himself behind her, holding the mirror at an angle so that Eleanor could see the reflection of her back. 'Your scar is not as you have pictured it in your mind,' he said softly. 'It's more than ten years since you had the surgery, and perhaps immediately afterwards the scar was more obvious. As you can see, it has faded. But, even if it hadn't, a scar would not detract from your beauty.'

He saw her throat work as she swallowed. 'It…it's

not as bad as I thought,' she said slowly. 'Not as red and lumpy as it was in the hospital.' Her eyes met Jace's in the mirror. 'But I am scarred. My body will never be perfect.'

'Your body would not be *your* body without your scar,' he said intently. 'You are perfect. There is a quote by a philosopher, Matshona Dhliwayo: "*Scars are a warrior's beauty marks.*" You are a warrior, Eleanor.' Jace turned her to face him and wiped away her tears with his thumb pads. 'You are not defined by your scar, but your strength and great compassion are a result of everything you have been through.'

Eleanor was drowning in Jace's dark gaze. She did not feel like a warrior and her stomach gave a nervous flip when he moved his hand to the zip on his trousers. She watched him undress and caught her breath when he lowered his boxer shorts to reveal the jutting, hard length of his manhood. Naked, he was a Greek god: powerfully muscular, his bronzed skin gleaming like satin in the lamplight.

'If you keep looking at me like that, this is going to be over embarrassingly quickly,' he growled. 'I want to make your first time good for you.'

She bit her lip and dragged her gaze from his impressively large erection up to his face. 'I've never touched a man…there,' she admitted.

'*Theos!* You're going to kill me.' He took her hand and placed it on his body, where the dark hairs grew thickly at his groin. Eleanor was fascinated by his masculine form as she ran her fingers lightly along his shaft and he shuddered. He felt like steel wrapped in velvet and the prospect of taking him inside her made her hesitate.

'Are you sure you want to go ahead with this?' Jace asked thickly. 'I would not try to force you in any way.'

Eleanor remembered the accusation she had made on their wedding night and felt ashamed. 'I know you wouldn't,' she quickly assured him. 'But... I don't want you to have sex with me out of pity.'

'*Opa!*' Jace looked stunned for a moment. 'The only person I pity is me. I've been tied up in knots for weeks, months, wanting you.' A dull flush ran along his cheekbones. 'The truth is that I haven't had sex with anyone since before I met you at the Pangalos well over a year ago, and celibacy is not a state I particularly enjoy.'

She stared at him. 'But in Paris you didn't...'

'Make no mistake, I was looking forward to making love to you. After you left, having sent back your ring, I assumed I would forget about you. But you were on my mind a lot,' he muttered.

'I couldn't forget you either,' Eleanor whispered. The wound he had inflicted on her heart healed a little, knowing that he had desired her in Paris. Perhaps even the deepest scars faded in time. She curled her fingers around his erection and heard his swiftly indrawn breath. 'I know this isn't for ever, but right now I want to have sex with you.' She knew she was blushing, but she ploughed on. 'You said that you want to make love to me...so what are you waiting for?'

From across the Serengeti plains came the thunder roar of a lion. The primitive sound reverberated around the room. A male preparing to mate. Jace clamped his hand over Eleanor's. 'Touch me like this,' he commanded softly, sliding her hand up and down his penis in a rhythmic action.

'Like this?' She felt a thrill of feminine pleasure when he groaned.

'Exactly like that, *pouláki mou*.' His eyes glittered as he hooked his fingers into her knickers and tugged them down her legs. 'Allow me to return the pleasure.' He slipped his hand between her legs and rubbed his thumb pad across the tight nub of her clitoris, sending starbursts of exquisite sensation through her.

This time when he lifted her into his arms and carried her over to the bed, he laid her on her back and straddled her, his knees on either side of her hips. And then he leaned forwards and claimed her mouth in an intensely sensual kiss that plundered her soul. Time ceased to exist, and Eleanor was conscious only of Jace's lips trailing a path down her throat and lower.

Sitting back on his haunches, he cradled her breasts in his palms and his clever fingers played with her nipples before he bent his head and took one taut peak into his mouth. The feeling of him sucking, hard, drew a moan from her and she clutched his hair and held him to his task. He moved across to her other nipple and drew wet circles around it with his tongue, teasing her until she made a husky plea and he closed his lips around the sensitive tip.

When her whimpers told him that she could not take any more of the sweet torment he was inflicting on her breasts, he shifted so that he was stretched out beside her and feathered his hand over her skin, exploring the indent of her waist and her flat stomach. His fingers traced lazy patterns in the cluster of dark gold curls between her thighs before he pushed her legs apart and stroked her inner thigh.

She moved restlessly, wanting him to… Her breath left her in a rush when he slid a finger into her wet heat and stretched her a little so that he could insert a second finger.

'Jace…' She gasped his name and arched her hips towards his hand as sensation built when he swirled his fingers inside her. Ripples deep in her pelvis warned that she was close to climaxing. It was tempting to go with the insistent drumbeat in her veins, but instinctively she knew that the pleasure would be even greater when he possessed her fully. She pushed his hand away. 'I want…'

'I know, *matia mou*.' His voice was like rich velvet wrapping around her. He rolled away and opened the bedside drawer.

'I'm protected,' Eleanor whispered shyly when she saw the packet of condoms in his hand.

'Well, then.' His sexy smile stole her breath. But when he positioned himself over her and pushed her legs wider apart, the predatory gleam in his eyes caused her heart to miss a beat. Excitement mixed with faint apprehension made her tense as he lowered himself onto her so that his steel-hard erection pressed into her belly. 'Try to relax,' he murmured against her lips before he kissed her slowly, his breath filling her mouth, the evocative male scent of him swamping her senses so that there was only Jace.

She felt the tip of his manhood against her opening and her feminine instincts kicked in, dispelling any lingering doubts, and making her impatient to feel his hard length inside her. He slid his hands beneath her bottom and lifted her so that her pelvis was flush with his, and then he eased forwards and carefully thrust into her, claiming her inch by inch.

Sweat beaded his brow and Eleanor sensed the restraint he was imposing on himself. She had expected discomfort but there was none, just a glorious feeling of fullness as he drove deeper, withdrew, thrust again and withdrew until she caught his rhythm.

'Ah, Eleanor, *mou.*' He spoke to her in Greek, soft words telling her how beautiful she was, and how much he desired her. She felt the thunder of his heart and heard the hoarse sound of his breaths as he increased his pace. His face above her had an intent expression that warned her he was losing control.

Faster, harder, she followed his lead in an age-old dance, and could not tell where she ended and he began. They moved as one, soaring ever higher, and suddenly she was there. He held her at the edge for timeless seconds, and then he moved again, thrusting deep and sending her spinning into the vortex of an orgasm that drove the air from her lungs in a shuddering, sobbing breath.

He wasn't done, and drove into her with an urgency that clutched at her heart. This Jace was strong yet vulnerable—her man, her master. When he let out a savage groan and collapsed on top of her while his big body shuddered with the force of his release, Eleanor simply held him and pressed her mouth against his rough jaw, trailing her lips up to meet his in a lingering kiss.

A long time later he rolled off her and she felt the coolness of the air circulated by the fan above the bed, and a coolness emanating from him that she knew she did not imagine.

'That was incredible, *omorfiá mou.*' Jace propped himself up against the pillows and folded his arms behind his head. His sultry smile was that of a satisfied lover, but his eyes were guarded. 'The next few months promise to be an amazing ride.'

It was a test, Eleanor realised, and one she had no intention of failing. She slid across the mattress and stood up. He had reassured her that he found her beautiful despite her scar, but she did not quite have the confidence to turn her back on him while she was naked. She picked up his shirt from the floor and slipped it on.

Jace's eyes narrowed when she sauntered over to the door. 'Going somewhere?'

'I'll spend the rest of the night in my room. I'm a restless sleeper,' she explained, not entirely untruthfully when she remembered the nights she had tossed and turned in bed, missing him.

'I have a feeling that I'm going to be restless tonight too,' he said drily. 'It makes sense to be restless together, *pouláki mou*.' His killer smile almost cracked her resolve to be as cool as him.

She shrugged. 'You know where to find me if you get lonely in the night. By the way, sex with you exceeded my expectations.'

Restless wasn't the word. Eleanor was too wired to sleep and when she reached her room she continued into the en suite bathroom, discarded Jace's shirt and stepped into the shower cubicle. Memories of his powerful body pumping into her stirred her desire once more so that she lowered her hand to between her legs and touched herself the way he had done.

'I know a better way to satisfy your urges,' a familiar voice drawled.

Her eyes flew open and she felt her face burn when she discovered that Jace had entered the shower and was watching her pleasure herself. She hastily snatched her hand away, and his throaty laugh was rough with sexual hunger.

'Don't stop on my account. It's pretty evident how much you turn me on,' he muttered as her eyes widened at the sight of his jutting erection. 'You drive me crazy.' He pulled her up close to his naked body. Rivulets of water from the shower spray ran down him, plastering the whorls of black chest hairs against his torso. 'Just when I think I've figured you out, you surprise me again.'

She hadn't imagined that he had deliberately created an emotional distance between them, and perhaps it was not surprising after the rapture of their lovemaking, Eleanor thought. Jace was worried that she might overstep the boundaries he had put in place.

'You're gorgeous, but you are not irresistible,' she told him lightly. 'I won't lose my head or my heart over you.'

His eyes narrowed and she sensed he was frustrated because he could not read her thoughts. 'But you did lose your virginity to me,' he reminded her softly. 'I'm honoured, Eleanor.'

Why was she playing this game when what she really wanted was to be in his arms and in his bed? she asked herself as Jace lowered his head and covered her mouth with his in an achingly tender kiss that became increasingly erotic. He trailed kisses down her neck and over her breasts, paying homage to each nipple until she squirmed and rubbed her hips sinuously against his burgeoning arousal.

'Let me finish what you started,' he murmured, pushing her back against the shower wall and dropping to his knees in front of her. She made a choked sound, half protest, half plea when he clasped her hips with his big hands and pressed his face between her thighs.

He used his tongue with an artist's skill and licked his way inside her while she writhed against his mouth, her shock at his intimate caresses forgotten as pleasure swiftly built to a crescendo. It was too much to bear and her orgasm was sharp and intense, making her cry out as aftershocks ripped through her trembling body.

When Jace stood and lifted her into his arms, Eleanor felt boneless and her head lolled on his shoulder as he strode down the corridor to his bedroom. The closeness she felt with him, the connection she had always sensed between them was just sex, she told herself firmly. She was not going to fall in love with Jace again because it would end in heartache. He had reminded her that their marriage had a time limit and, when all was said and done, he'd married her to claim his family's share of the Pangalos hotel.

Eleanor was so incredibly responsive, was Jace's first thought in the hazy moments before he was fully awake. The previous night he had carried her out of the shower and, in his urgency to make love to her, they hadn't had time to grab towels and dry themselves. He had taken her back to his bed and tumbled them both down on the black satin sheets.

She had been as eager as him for sex. If he had not felt the fragile barrier of her womanhood the first time that he'd made love to her, he would find it hard to believe she had been a virgin. The shy young woman he had wooed in Oxford, a lifetime ago it seemed now, had turned into a siren and he could not resist her lure.

But he'd long suspected that Eleanor had suppressed her sensuality. Last night had been a revelation. She had been uninhibited when he'd lifted her on top of him and she'd straddled him, supporting her weight with her hands on his chest as she'd lowered herself onto his swollen length. He had played with her breasts while she rode him, shaking her dark blonde hair over her shoulders and leaning forwards so that he could take one pebble-hard nipple and then the other into his mouth.

He had come hard and fast and his groan of satiation had mingled with her cries of pleasure as they'd climaxed simultaneously. Jace had found himself oddly reluctant to withdraw from her. When he had finally rolled her off him she was already asleep, and he had succumbed not long after her.

Now he stretched and felt the delicious heaviness of muscles that had not been used for too long. He had a healthy enjoyment of sex but, on the few occasions that he'd invited a woman to dinner in the past year, his libido had been worryingly non-existent and he'd made an excuse and dropped his date home at the end of the evening.

Jace frowned when he discovered that he was alone, and wondered if Eleanor had returned to her room during the night. *Theos*, she could be infuriatingly independent. Obviously, he was relieved that she understood the rules of their marriage. He had been concerned that she might hope for more from their relationship than he was prepared to give.

He was sure his fascination with her would fade in a few months. When they divorced, Eleanor would be able to search for a man who would love her as she deserved to be loved. Of course, there was no danger that she would fall in love with *him,* after he had emotionally blackmailed her into marriage.

Guilt twisted in his gut as he thought of his original intention to seize complete control of the Pangalos from her. Just before the wedding, he had changed his mind and asked his lawyer to draw up a new prenuptial agreement, which Eleanor had signed. There was no way she would find out that he had planned to betray her a second time, he assured himself.

Unsettled by the heaviness that dropped like a lead weight into the pit of his stomach, he rolled onto his side just as she pushed the voile curtain aside and stepped into the room from the balcony. Jace's breath snagged in his throat and he had no explanation for the sensation of his heart being squeezed in a vice as he studied her lovely face. Her wide hazel eyes sparkled with excitement.

'Oh, good, you're awake. You have to come and see the most spectacular sight.'

'The sight I'm looking at right now is spectacular, *omorfiá mou*.' Hell, he sounded corny, Jace thought ruefully, but his beautiful wife blew him away.

Eleanor blushed. 'You are just trying to persuade me back into bed.'

'Guilty as charged. If I throw back the sheet, you'll understand why I want you to take off my shirt and get your naked little derrière over here pronto.'

She gave a husky laugh. 'I will. But first come outside; there's something I want to show you.'

With a deep sigh, he grabbed his robe and padded after her. The lodge overlooked a watering hole where a herd of elephants were gathered. Jace counted at least twelve adults and several babies. In the early morning sunshine, the close-up sight of the magnificent creatures was awe-inspiring.

'Aren't they wonderful?' Eleanor whispered. 'Our honeymoon in Africa is the most incredible experience.'

He loved her enthusiasm and her joy for life. Her smile did strange things to his heart rate. When their eyes met, he was aware of a connection that he did not understand and refused to acknowledge as anything more than white-hot sex.

'I can promise you another incredible experience,' he murmured as he tugged her by her hand back inside. There he removed his shirt from her delectable body and shrugged off his robe. He kissed her lips, her breasts, pushed her down on the bed and spread her legs so that he could put his mouth on her and taste her feminine sweetness. Her husky moans made him harder, hungrier, and he hooked her legs around his waist and entered her with a powerful thrust, over and over again, until she tensed beneath him and his control shattered and they tumbled together into the abyss.

# CHAPTER EIGHT

'HOW DOES IT feel to be back at the Pangalos?' Jace asked his mother. 'It has taken a long time, but finally our rightful share of the hotel has been returned to us.'

'It has changed a lot since Dimitri co-owned it with Kostas. The refurbished hotel is almost unrecognisable, and the clientele are very glamorous.' Iliana sighed. 'Kostas was the visionary in the business. Your father was happy to keep it as a small hotel for families, but the truth is that it did not make much profit. Now the Pangalos Beach Resort is regarded as the best five-star resort in northern Greece.'

'I am sure the hotel's reputation would have grown just as well if Bampás had remained in charge,' Jace said loyally. It was not the first time his mother had hinted that Dimitri had lacked the flair to run a successful business. His father had been a kindly man, but he'd been no match for Kostas's ruthlessness.

Jace exhaled heavily. He'd felt on edge since he and Eleanor had returned to Greece two days ago from their honeymoon in Africa that he had arranged at the last minute. It had been unlike him to act impulsively, but her vulnerability on their wedding night had made him feel guilty that he'd forced her into marrying him.

Could he say that he was any better than her grandfather? he asked himself grimly. His ultimate goal had been to take full control of the hotel. It had seemed so simple. Kostas had destroyed his father, and so he would destroy Kostas's legacy. But Jace had come to realise that he did not want to hurt Eleanor more than he already had. She had innocently been caught up in the feud between their families, but now they both owned fifty per cent of the Pangalos and it was time to forget about the past.

He frowned, thinking of how Eleanor had insisted that she wanted to live at the Pangalos resort rather than at his house in Thessaloniki.

'It makes sense for the manager of the hotel to live on the resort so that I can deal with any problems that arise immediately,' she'd argued. 'It's a couple of hour's drive to your office in Thessaloniki. I'm sure you will want to focus your attention mainly on Zagorakis Estates, so why don't you base yourself in the city during the week and spend the weekends at the Pangalos?'

'You are my wife,' he'd reminded her tersely. 'Our marriage will not seem convincing if we live apart most of the time.'

Jace told himself it was a good sign that Eleanor did not expect the honeymoon to continue now they were back in the real world. The two weeks they had spent in Africa had been great if he was honest. It was the first time since he had started his property development company a decade ago that his life had not been dominated by work. Sure, he'd allowed himself time to socialise, but every successful entrepreneur knew that more business deals were made through networking at parties than in the boardroom. He'd had mistresses, but he had never spent time with them away from the bedroom.

Eleanor had been a virgin until their marriage, but she'd proved to be a delightfully willing pupil and sex with her had left him feeling satisfied in a way he had never felt with his previous lovers. He'd assumed she enjoyed their lovemaking as much as he did, and he was rattled that she'd suggested they live apart. He was glad that she wasn't a clinging vine, but the Eleanor he had wooed sixteen months ago had been eager to please him, unlike now, when she was irritatingly independent and stubborn. But he had not really known her the first time he'd asked her to be his wife, Jace acknowledged. And having hurt her deeply once, he could not blame her for putting up barriers.

Jace was becoming familiar with the uncomfortable stab of his conscience where his wife was concerned. He forced his mind back to the present. 'Are you sure you don't want to come and live in the apartment here in the hotel which used to be our home?' he asked his mother.

She shook her head. 'I was happy living here with your father, but since he died there are too many sad memories.'

Through the window Jace could see the cliff that he had scrambled down when he'd heard his father's faint cry from far below. He'd cut his hands on the jagged rocks in his haste to reach the bottom of the cliff. The sight that had met him would be etched on his memory for ever. His father's body twisted at an unnatural angle, blood pouring from a wound on his head. Instinctively, Jace had known there was no time to get help. Dimitri's breaths had been laboured and he'd been barely conscious. But he had roused himself when Jace had knelt beside him.

*'Promise me you will destroy Kostas as he destroyed*

*our family. Take back the hotel any way you can for your mother's sake. It is too late...for me...'*

'Jace?' His mother's voice pulled him from the dark place in his mind. 'Will you and Eleanor live in the apartment?'

'No,' he said abruptly. 'We have moved into one of the private villas by the beach. I thought that if you lived here, I would be nearby to take care of you.'

'Anna is a good nurse. And you will want to spend as much time as possible with your beautiful wife.' Iliana's eyes twinkled. 'Perhaps there will be good news before long. A baby,' she said when Jace looked puzzled.

'Ah! We are not planning anything like that at the moment,' he muttered, relieved that he had started to push his mother's wheelchair and she could not see his face.

'Don't leave trying for a family too long. I can't tell you how happy I am that you have settled down. Eleanor is the perfect wife for you.'

Jace pictured his wife when he'd left her asleep at the villa where they were now living. They had enjoyed each other twice last night, and he'd woken before dawn to find her pert derrière pressed up against his hip. The invitation had been irresistible, and he'd eased his erection between her thighs while he'd slid his hands around her to play with her breasts. The sex had been leisurely at first and then urgent as passion built to a crescendo and he'd climaxed seconds after her.

Give it a few weeks and his fascination with Eleanor would turn to boredom, Jace assured himself. No woman had ever held his interest for long. He helped his mother into the car and felt a pang when she leaned back against the seat and closed her eyes. The signs of her illness were evident on her lined face. He wished he had been able to bring her back to the hotel sooner. It was ironic that his mother seemed more pleased about his marriage than the fact that his name was now included on the deeds of the Pangalos.

The car drove away, taking Iliana and her nurse back to Thessaloniki. Jace hesitated on the steps of the hotel, tempted to return to the villa and Eleanor. When they were together he forgot about why he had married her. But that was a dangerous path to take. There was no future to their marriage, and he did not want there to be. He had decided a long time ago that he was better off alone.

He walked across the opulent lobby and opened the door into the office he had decided would be his. And stopped dead. Eleanor was sitting behind the desk—*his* desk. His eyes roamed over her scarlet jacket, which was buttoned low down and revealed a tantalising glimpse of the deep vee between her breasts. She seemed to have forgotten to wear a blouse, Jace noted furiously. It was something that Takis Samaras appeared to be well aware of, from the way he was staring at Eleanor's cleavage as he leaned over her, resting his hip against the desk.

His wife and his closest friend were laughing, their heads bent towards each other as they shared a private joke. Jace felt a sensation like corrosive acid fizzing in the pit of his stomach. He had never experienced jealousy before, but the sight of *his wife* smiling flirtatiously at another man made him want to rip Takis's head off.

Eleanor glanced over at him and Jace convinced himself it was a guilty blush that spread across her face. 'We have a visitor,' she said unnecessarily. 'Takis was telling me such a funny story.'

Jace gritted his teeth, aware that his friend could lay on the charm when he chose to. 'Was he?' he said curtly.

Takis straightened up and strolled across the room. Amusement gleamed in his eyes as he murmured, 'Good to see you, Jace. I thought I'd come and check out your new acquisition. The Pangalos,' he added drily when Jace's gaze flew to Eleanor. 'So, you finally took control of the hotel, as you always planned to do.'

After Takis had walked out of the office, saying that he wanted to take a look at the pool and spa, Eleanor glared at Jace. 'What's got into you? You've got an expression like you've been sucking on a lemon. I thought you would be pleased to see Takis.'

'Evidently you were pleased,' he said curtly. He raked a hand through his hair, perplexed by the wild emotions storming through him. He did not do emotions. But the possessiveness he felt for Eleanor made a mockery of his belief that he would find it easy to walk away from her when their marriage ended. The likelihood was that they would be able to divorce in a matter of months. His mother's health was failing, and when she was no longer here there would be no reason for him to continue with his fake marriage. Except that it had not felt fake when they had been on their honeymoon. He had enjoyed being with Eleanor, and not only in bed.

He forced his mind away from his confused thoughts when he realised that she was speaking.

'What did Takis mean when he congratulated you on taking control of the Pangalos? I agreed to give you a fifty per cent share. All decisions about the hotel will be made by both of us.'

Jace shrugged. 'I guess Takis made a slip of the tongue.' He watched Eleanor stand up and walk around the desk. His body clenched with desire as he ran his eyes over her slender legs beneath her short scarlet skirt. Her stiletto heel shoes made her legs seem even longer.

'I did not expect you to come to work today,' he murmured. 'Why don't you take a few days off to recover from jet-lag after the flight from Africa?' He stepped closer to her and slid his arm around her waist, drawing her up against him so that they were hip to hip. He knew she must feel the hard proof of his arousal. The pulse at the base of her throat was beating erratically. 'I have a few things to see to here and then I'll join you at the villa for a siesta.'

Eleanor pulled out of his arms. 'It's a tempting idea, but I have far too much to do. As you are aware, my brother left a lot of problems at the Pangalos that I need to sort out.' She resumed her seat behind the desk. 'I doubt I'll finish here until late this evening. Maybe we can order take-out for dinner—unless you want to cook tonight?'

In the past Jace had frequently cancelled a date when work had demanded his time. But he did not enjoy it when Eleanor made it clear that she was prepared to prioritise business over spending time with him. Once again, he reminded himself that this was exactly the kind of relationship he wanted. Eleanor knew her own mind and did not assume he would drop everything for her. The flip side was that she would not change her schedule because he'd asked her to.

What had happened to the lovestruck woman who had been waiting eagerly on the doorstep when he'd arrived to take her out to dinner in Oxford? Jace brooded. The answer struck him with a thud in his chest. Eleanor had fallen out of love with him, and there was no reason at all why the realisation made him feel empty inside.

She glanced up from her computer screen. 'I put your

briefcase in the smaller office next door. No doubt you'll spread your time between the hotel and your business in Thessaloniki, so I might as well have the bigger office. There is one other thing I want to discuss with you.'

'Go on,' Jace drawled.

'Elias, who is head of marketing, told me that you had spoken to him about changing the name of the hotel to the Zagorakis. I disagree.'

'For what reason?'

'Changing the name will incur a lot of unnecessary expense at a time when the hotel's finances are unstable.'

'Due to your brother's mismanagement,' Jace said sardonically.

Eleanor flushed. 'True, and I accept some of the responsibility because I trusted Mark. But, whatever you think of my grandfather, he made the Pangalos what it is today, and you can't simply ignore the fact that it is his legacy. You are not the sole owner of the hotel. We own it jointly, and I won't accept changing the Pangalos to your name, Zagorakis.'

Jace's gaze narrowed on Eleanor's determined face. Did she have any idea how sexy she looked with her hair swept up in an elegant chignon and her full lips coated in a scarlet gloss that tempted him to walk around the desk and haul her into his arms? On one level he was annoyed that she was prepared to argue with him. He was used to getting his own way. But he found himself enjoying their verbal sparring. It was refreshing to have her challenge him and he admired her strong will, which matched his own. Being married to her would never be boring.

'Zagorakis is your name too,' he reminded her. 'My suggestion is to name the hotel after both of its owners.'

'Our marriage is a temporary arrangement,' she said coolly. 'I won't be Zagorakis after we divorce, and I'll revert to my maiden name.'

'Fine, we'll leave the idea of changing the name for now.' Jace did not accept defeat but he realised he would have to use different tactics to persuade Eleanor. His body tightened as he imagined employing various erotic methods of persuasion.

'Did the marketing director mention my other idea, to host a party here? Every year, Zagorakis Estates organises a charity fundraising ball which attracts interest from businesses and celebrities around the world. The invitations went out a few months ago, but we can notify guests of the change of venue. Apart from raising a lot of money for good causes, it will be good advertising for the hotel.'

'I think it is an excellent idea.' Eleanor's smile lit up her lovely face. Jace had no explanation for the way his heart seemed to expand to fill his chest.

Disconcerted by feelings that were new and frankly terrifying, he turned away from her and strode towards the door, growling, 'At least we agree on something.'

Butterflies swooped in Eleanor's stomach. At the last minute she was plagued with self-doubt. Why had she agreed to wear the dress to what was being labelled by the media as *the* party of the year? The charity fundraising ball had a guest list that read like the *Who's Who* of Europe's social elite, and a top magazine had donated a huge sum of money to the charitable fund established by Zagorakis Estates for excusive photograph rights of the party.

Eleanor's dress had been loaned to her by a famous design house. Made of ruby red silk overlaid with lace, the dramatic front of the bodice was eye-catching, but at the back the material skimmed her shoulders before falling away in a deep cowl to her waist and then fell in soft folds to the floor. It meant that her back was bare, and when she angled the dressing table mirror she could see that her scar was clearly visible.

She could not go through with it and wear the dress tonight, she decided frantically. The idea of making herself so vulnerable when people saw and perhaps commented on her scar made her feel sick.

Footsteps sounded on the marble floor outside in the hallway, and she whirled away from the mirror just in time as Jace opened the door and walked into the bedroom. He stopped in his tracks and stared at her, his expression unreadable as it so often was, but she noticed a nerve jump in his jaw.

'You look incredible,' he said in a rough voice that caused the tiny hairs on her body to stand on end. She reminded herself that he could not see her back. Jace had insisted that her scar did not make her unattractive, and when they were alone she almost believed him. But she wondered how he would react to the idea of her wearing a dress that drew attention to her naked back in public.

Her heartrate quickened when he prowled towards her. The feral gleam in his eyes evoked a wild hunger inside her and she felt her nipples harden.

'So do you.' She flushed when she realised that she had spoken her thoughts aloud. But it was the truth. He was breathtaking in a tuxedo that clung to his powerfully muscular body. This was only the second time she'd seen him in the past two weeks, and she'd missed him so much. Too much, a voice in her head warned. Since they had returned to Greece after their honeymoon, Jace had spent most of the time in Thessaloniki, while she had remained at the villa on the Pangalos resort.

He had told her that a problem had arisen at his property development company and he'd needed to be at Zagorakis Estates' offices in the city. There was no reason why he would lie, but she sensed that he had been deliberately avoiding her. The close bond she had felt with him in Africa had disappeared. Perhaps she'd imagined it had existed.

On their first day working at the Pangalos together, Jace had been different. Maybe he had thought she would hand the running of the hotel over to him. It would be easy to be overwhelmed by his commanding personality, but Eleanor had refused to allow him to dominate her. They owned the hotel jointly and she was determined to be involved in every policy decision.

'The guests will start to arrive soon, and as we are the hosts of the party we should be in the ballroom to greet them,' he murmured. 'Are you ready?'

She bit her lip. 'Give me a few minutes to change my dress.'

'Why on earth do you want to change it?' He reached into his jacket and withdrew a slim velvet box. 'The other day I asked you the colour of the dress you would be wearing so that I could select jewellery to match,' he said as he lifted up a stunning ruby and diamond necklace. 'Turn around and I'll put it on you.'

Eleanor hesitated and then spun round. She heard Jace draw a sharp breath and knew he could see what she had seen in the mirror. Her scar was even more noticeable now she had gained a light suntan, and it was a stark white line running down her spine.

'The designer asked me to wear the dress because

the huge press coverage of the party will be a promotional opportunity for the fashion house,' she explained, her voice a shaky whisper in the silence, which
stretched her nerves to breaking point. 'I… I agreed
if they would donate money to the Scoliosis Support
charity. It's a fantastic chance to bring public attention
to the charity.' She swallowed. 'But now I'm not sure
I can go through with it.'

Jace was so close behind her that she felt his warm
breath stir the tendrils of hair that had escaped from
her chignon and curled at her nape.

'I think it is a wonderful thing for you to do, *pouláki mou*.'

The gentleness in his voice brought tears to Eleanor's eyes. 'You are the only person who has ever seen
my scar, other than my first boyfriend when I was a
teenager. What if other people have the same reaction
as he did?'

'In that case they would not be worthy to breathe
the same air as you,' Jace said fiercely. He sounded so
protective, and her heart gave a jolt when she looked at
their reflections in the mirror and saw admiration and
something hotly possessive in his expression. This was
the Jace who had made love to her on their honeymoon
with a tender passion that had made her think he cared
for her a little.

She gasped as he bent his head and pressed his mouth
to her neck. He trailed his lips lower, following the
line of her scar and restoring her confidence with each
gentle kiss.

Lower and lower. Jace dropped onto his knees and
continued his featherlight kisses down to where the scar
ended at the base of her spine. With each kiss, the hurt
and shame that Eleanor had felt at her first boyfriend's

reaction to her scar eased. She felt healed inside, just as her skin had healed on the outside and was not the raised, angry scar that had so appalled her when she had been a teenager. Now the scar was a thin white line. It was not pretty but, thanks to Jace, she felt proud that she bore the mark of a survivor.

His hands were on her hips and heat bloomed inside. Desire for him, only and always him. When he stood up, she leaned back against his chest while he nuzzled the sensitive place behind her ear.

'You are beautiful, Eleanor, *mou*.' He sounded very Greek and his gravelly voice rumbled through her. 'But your beauty is not only skin-deep. You are beautiful in here—' he rested his hand just beneath her breast '—in your heart. At the party I will be proud that you are my wife.'

He eased away from her and fastened the ruby necklace around her throat. The stones felt cool against her heated skin. She met his eyes in the mirror and saw the hunger she felt for him reflected in his glittering gaze.

'Tonight I will make love to you while you are wearing the necklace and nothing else,' he promised. His sexy smile stole her breath. 'Hold that thought, *omorfiá mou*.'

Jace searched the crowded ballroom for Eleanor. One of the advantages of being so tall was that he could see above most people's heads. He spotted her standing by a pillar, talking to her sister. Anticipation ran as hot as wildfire through him. The party would end at midnight. He checked his watch. Twenty minutes to go. Somehow, he would have to curb his impatience to take his wife home to bed for a little while longer.

She had been amazing tonight, and no one but him

would have guessed that she'd felt nervous about wearing a dress that revealed her scoliosis scar. It had been Eleanor's idea to pose for a photographer who had taken pictures of the backless dress. She had spoken honestly about the spinal condition she'd suffered from as a child, and the surgery to insert a titanium rod into her back, which had straightened her spine but left her with a forty-centimetre scar.

'I hope that by telling my story and showing my scar, I can encourage other people who have suffered the trauma of major surgery to feel proud of their scars,' Eleanor had told a journalist. She had looked at Jace and they'd shared a conspiratorial smile when she'd said, 'Scars are the badges of a warrior.'

Emotions that he could no longer deny swirled inside Jace. He had kept away from Eleanor since they had returned from Africa, believing that her impact on him would fade if he did not see her or have sex with her. Work issues at Zagorakis Estates had given him a convenient excuse to remain in Thessaloniki, but he had found himself thinking about her all the time, and many nights he'd almost given into the temptation to leap into his car and drive to the villa at the Pangalos resort to claim his wife.

Their separation had not lessened his desire for her, and this weekend he'd moved back to the villa permanently, or at least until his marriage ended, Jace reminded himself, aware of an odd hollow feeling in his gut.

'May I have the pleasure of this dance, Mrs Zagorakis?' he murmured when he strode over to Eleanor and slipped his arm around her waist.

Her smile was like sunshine on a rainy day, and when he led her onto the dance floor and drew her close she fitted against him as if her body had been designed exclusively for his. Jace wondered if she could feel the urgent thud of his heart beneath her ear when she rested her head on his chest. The light from the glittering chandeliers above them brought out the myriad golden shades of her hair. *Theos*, he would write a sonnet next, he thought sardonically. But as they swayed together in time with the music, nothing existed but him and Eleanor, and Jace found himself wishing for things he'd told himself he would never want.

'How is your sister?' he murmured, more to break the dangerous spell that Eleanor was casting over him than any real interest in Lissa. 'I don't know.' A tiny frown wrinkled Eleanor's brow. 'She asked if Takis had been invited to the party and looked disappointed when I explained that he'd had to cancel at the last minute. And come to think of it, Takis said he couldn't make it after I mentioned that Lissa was going to be here. But he is here. I'm sure I saw him standing by the bar. Do you think something is going on between them?'

Jace shrugged. 'Takis told me his plans changed suddenly and he was able to come tonight. But as to a romance between him and your sister, I'm not so sure. Takis is a lone wolf.'

'Like you?' Eleanor suggested softly.

'Mmm, but I'm not planning to spend tonight alone.' His wife's scarlet-glossed mouth was an irresistible temptation and he bent his head and kissed her, uncaring that they were in public.

Eleanor was tying him in knots, but Jace could not forget that her grandfather had ruined his father. Guilt twisted like a serpent inside him. His unexpected feelings for his wife felt like a terrible betrayal of his father and the suffering his parents had endured after Kostas had seized control of the Pangalos.

There had been a time when Jace had planned to avenge Dimitri's death by taking the hotel from Eleanor. But he was shocked to realise that he did not care about the hotel or the feud. All he cared about was his wife's uninhibited response when he kissed her, and the gut-wrenching tenderness of her touch when she cupped his cheek in her hand and looked into his eyes with her clear and gentle gaze, as if she understood the confusion in his heart.

# CHAPTER NINE

BRIGHT SUNSHINE REFLECTED off the white walls of the master bedroom in the private villa at the Pangalos Beach Resort. Beyond the open bi-fold doors, the azure infinity pool seemed to merge with the cerulean sea and the cloudless blue sky, while the vivid pink bougainvillea climbing over the trellis on the balcony was a sight to behold.

Eleanor sat up in bed and linked her arms around her knees. She loved early mornings before the hotel complex stirred, when the stretch of golden sand beyond the villa was empty of people and sun loungers. Summer was drawing to an end, but the weather was still warm and settled and the hotel was fully booked.

She and Jace lived partly at his house in Thessaloniki to be near his mother, and partly at the villa on Sithonia. Eleanor had fallen in love with Greece. Who was she kidding? She would be happy living anywhere with Jace, she thought ruefully when he strolled out of the shower room that he had made his own, while she preferred the en suite bathroom, which had a luxurious free-standing bath.

She had realised lately that she could very easily fall in love with her husband, who this morning looked mouth-watering in an impeccably tailored grey suit, crisp white shirt and navy-blue silk tie. It was little things that made inroads on her heart. Like how Jace always woke first in the mornings and brought her a cup of her favourite English tea. Sometimes, when she was in a rush to get to work, she would skip breakfast, but at her office she would find that he'd arranged for yoghurt, fruit and freshly baked rolls to be delivered from the hotel's kitchen.

He often bought her flowers and other little gifts: a book he knew she wanted to read, her favourite perfume, inexpensive jewellery when they wandered hand in hand around the market and she admired a necklace made of shells, or some pretty silver earrings. He gifted her with expensive jewellery too, and smiled ruefully when she preferred to wear a thin gold chain with an olive branch pendant that he had bought for her when they'd taken a boat trip to the island of Lemnos.

The trip had reminded Eleanor of when she had fallen in love with Jace on the island cruise, and she had warned herself not to rush headlong into repeating the mistakes of the past. But the olive branch necklace seemed like a symbol of hope. She returned the kind gestures Jace showed her by cooking meals that she knew he liked, and she made sure there was always a bottle of the single malt whisky he favoured in the cupboard.

Their relationship was not the sterile marriage deal that Jace had offered her, a lifetime ago, it seemed. He took care of her, and Eleanor could not deny that it felt wonderful knowing she could rely on him after she had spent so many years feeling alone and rather abandoned by her parents, who had not known how to cope when she was diagnosed with scoliosis.

As for her scar, she barely gave it any thought now,

and she felt confident wearing a bikini or dresses with a low-cut back. On the night of the charity ball, Jace had told her she was beautiful and he had made her believe in herself. Never again would she allow herself to be defined by her scar. She was a warrior, and she would always be grateful to Jace for showing her how strong she was.

But dare she offer him her heart again? She knew him better now, and the truth was that she *liked* him. He was an honourable man who had been trapped by the promise he had made his father when he was a teenager to seek revenge after Kostas had destroyed his family.

Eleanor sighed. What she felt for Jace was not the infatuation she'd felt when he had swept her off her feet last year. With hindsight, she understood that he had been a fantasy figure—Prince Charming to her Cinderella. She had wanted him to rescue her from her dull life and her insecurities. But his betrayal had made her take a good look at herself.

She had realised that she'd been in awe of her grandfather when she was growing up, and always anxious to please him. And she had been in awe of Jace the first time he had asked her to marry him. She'd put him on a pedestal, but her expectations had been unrealistic. Now she knew he was a man with great strengths but also flaws that made him endearingly human and offered the tantalising idea that maybe he was not as emotionless as he wanted her to believe.

From outside the villa came the sound of a helicopter. Eleanor met Jace's dark gaze and something intangible and ephemeral hovered in the air between them before he gave a slight shake of his head, as if he found his thoughts puzzling. 'There's Sotiri to take me to the airport,' he murmured. 'I can't say I'm looking forward to the long-haul flight to Perth.'

'I know you said that the distance is too far for your private jet to make without refuelling, but travelling first class on a commercial plane means you will have a bed and you can sleep during the flight.'

'Mmm, I should get more sleep than I do sharing a bed with you.'

'Whose fault is that?' She pretended to pout.

He grinned. 'Yours, but I'm not complaining. I love your uninhibited response when we have sex.'

*Love*. Eleanor looked away from his impossibly handsome face, hoping he could not tell that her heart had leapt when he'd casually dropped the word into the conversation. How was she here again? she wondered. What had happened to her confident belief that she understood the difference between lust and love?

Was she a fool to think that perhaps there was no difference? When Jace made love to her it felt like more than just sex, although she did not have the experience to know if there was a difference, she acknowledged ruefully. Jace was the only man she had ever wanted, and a little voice in her head whispered that he was the only man she would ever want.

He had hurt her badly in the past, and the idea of laying herself open to being hurt again was terrifying. But sometimes in life you had to take risks. She was different from the person she had been when she had first met him. She was stronger and more confident, but was she brave enough to risk Jace's rejection a second time?

'Hey, where have you gone, *pouláki mou*?' The mattress dipped as he sat on the bed and slid his hand beneath her chin, tilting her face up to his. 'You have looked pale for a few days.' His voice was concerned when he brushed his fingers lightly against her cheeks. 'There are shadows beneath your eyes. Perhaps you are unwell. I'll call my doctor and ask him to visit you for a consultation.'

There were times like now, when Jace treated her with such tenderness, that made her think he might care for her a little. But she was afraid to hope in case the castle of dreams she had built came tumbling down.

She smiled. 'I don't need to see a doctor. You're not the only one who needs to catch up on sleep.'

He did not look convinced. 'Don't do too much while I'm away. I wish you had agreed to come to Australia with me. We could have had a few days holiday after I'd wrapped up my business meetings.'

'I thought I should stay behind so that I can visit Iliana while you are away.' Jace's mother had recently moved into a hospice. The doctors had said that she was unlikely to live to see Christmas, but mercifully she was not in pain and kept in remarkably good spirits.

Jace stood up, but he remained standing by the bed and stared down at Eleanor. His expression was hidden beneath his hooded eyelids. 'I'll insist that you come along on my next business trip.'

She nodded, but inside she felt sick at the thought that she might not be his wife for much longer. He had secured his half-share of the Pangalos, and when his mother was no longer here there would be no reason for their marriage to continue.

He leaned down and claimed her mouth in a lingering kiss that tempted her to pull him down onto the bed so that they could make love one last time before he left for his trip to the other side of the world. But she resisted because she did not want him to think she was needy.

'Bye then,' she said airily.

His gaze narrowed. 'Will you miss me?'

'I doubt I'll have time while I'm busy running the hotel.'

'Speaking of which, my lawyer has some paperwork for you to sign. It's to do with the planning application for the new villas we are hoping to build on the holiday complex.'

Jace picked up his briefcase and walked out of the bedroom without a backward glance. Minutes later Eleanor heard the helicopter take off. She dashed her hand over her eyes, angry with herself because she missed him already. It was the first time they had been apart since he had moved back to the villa, but she had better start getting used to living without him, she thought.

She had a job to do, managing the hotel, but when she got out of bed she was overcome by a wave of dizziness. It was not the first time it had happened and, although she had assured Jace that she wasn't ill, she did not feel right. There was nothing she could put her finger on but maybe she was slightly anaemic, which might explain why her period was a few days late.

In the bathroom she searched through the cupboard for the packet of multi-vitamins she'd bought the previous winter in England. It wouldn't hurt to start taking them again. Another box containing a popular herbal supplement that she'd used until recently fell onto the floor. She picked it up and happened to glance at the label.

*Do not take if pregnant or taking the birth control Pill.*

Frowning, she read the leaflet inside the box and discovered that the tablets could decrease the effectiveness of hormonal contraceptives. She hadn't mentioned to her GP when he'd prescribed the Pill that she used the over-the-counter herbal remedy which was reputed to help with mood swings. With a sense of dread she checked the calendar on her phone and realised that her period was ten days late.

She had been so absorbed in her life with Jace that she'd lost track of time. But she couldn't be pregnant, Eleanor reassured herself. Medications and even herbal remedies always came with a long list of contraindications, and the likelihood that the Pill hadn't worked properly was probably minuscule.

Over the next few days she tried to put the idea of pregnancy out of her mind, telling herself that she was worrying needlessly and her period was bound to start soon. But it didn't, and on the fifth day after Jace had gone to Australia, Eleanor drove to a village further along the coast to buy a test from a pharmacy. Few people at the Pangalos Beach Resort or the local area on Sithonia knew she was Kostas Pangalos's granddaughter, but everyone recognised her as Kyriá Zagorakis, wife of the wealthy new owner of the Pangalos. She did not want unfounded rumours that she was pregnant to circulate.

Early the next morning she stared disbelievingly at the blue line on the pregnancy test and checked the instructions again. *Positive*. Feeling numb, she sat on the edge of the bath, aware of her heart beating frantically in her chest like a trapped bird. Needless to say, this was not what she or Jace had planned to happen.

Jace! How would he react to the news? She was quite sure he did not want a baby. He did not want her to be his wife for any longer than was necessary to convince his mother that he had settled down to a life of domestic bliss.

He phoned mid-morning while she was at the office trying to concentrate on a financial report. It was some time in the evening in Perth, and he was about to go out to dinner with a business client. Jace sounded a million miles away and for once Eleanor was glad when he rang off at the end of their stilted conversation. She had decided not to give him her momentous news until he returned to Greece, although it was tempting to take the coward's way out and tell him over the phone rather than face to face. Her secret burned inside her, and she must have sounded odd because twice Jace asked how she was feeling.

Later that afternoon her secretary informed her that the lawyer had arrived. However, the man who entered the room was not the elderly lawyer Vangelis Stavridis, who Eleanor had met when she had signed a prenuptial agreement before her marriage. The young man who shook her hand introduced himself as Orestis Barkas, a junior member of Jace's legal team.

'There are a lot of documents regarding the planning application that require your signature,' he said, putting a large file on the desk. He rolled his eyes. 'Greek bureaucracy! Your husband has already checked the paperwork and signed it. I can see that you are busy and there is no need for you to read it all; just sign at the bottom of each page.'

Eleanor grimaced at the pile of papers, but her grandfather had taught her to read every detail before she signed her name and she picked up the first document. Some while later she was only halfway through the pile and heartily bored of the intricacies of building permits and energy performance regulations. The young lawyer was becoming fidgety.

'Seriously, you only need to skim through the pages. Jace is happy with everything.'

'I'm sure he is.' She had the odd sensation of hearing her blood thundering in her ears as she reread the typed paragraphs which stated that in the event of her divorce from Jace he would become the sole owner of the Pangalos Beach Resort. Eleanor would be unable to contest the agreement or change her mind once she had signed the document.

Somehow, she managed to hide her distress from the lawyer. 'Why don't you leave the paperwork with me and I'll have the documents couriered over to you when I've signed them?' she suggested.

'Are you feeling unwell?' her secretary asked when Eleanor stumbled through the door into the outer office a few minutes after Orestis Barkas had left.

'Actually, I'm not feeling too good.' It was the truth. There was a sharp pain beneath her breastbone where her heart had shattered and a dull ache in the pit of her stomach. 'I'll go back to the villa and try to sleep it off.'

She didn't cry. Couldn't. She was frozen inside and wandered aimlessly from room to room in the villa, ending up in the bedroom that she had shared with Jace for the past months. She pictured him sprawled on the bed, the sheet draped low over his hips and the bulge of his arousal a tantalising invitation. God, she loved the way he made love to her. He never made any secret of his desire for her and the possessive gleam in his eyes when he thrust his hard shaft deep inside her had given her hope that love could take root in even the stoniest heart.

But Jace's heart was a lump of granite. The damning

document she'd found slipped in among the planning application paperwork was proof that he only wanted the hotel. Sure, he enjoyed taking her to bed, but he was unlikely to be pleased about the consequences of their passion.

Eleanor realised that she had not given any thought to the baby she was carrying. Her pregnancy seemed unreal, but in a little less than nine months she would have the responsibility of bringing up a child on her own.

Jace's name flashed on her phone and with a heavy heart she read his text.

It's midnight here and I'm about to go to bed. I wish you were with me, pouláki mou. When I come home we need to talk.

Indeed they did. She stepped outside onto the terrace and looked up at the stars that were starting to appear as dusk deepened to night. Tears blurred her vision and the starlight fractured as if she were looking into a kaleidoscope. Her phone pinged with another message from Jace, but she did not read it.

She had trusted him. Worse than that, she had fallen in love with him. There was no point denying it to herself any more. He had dismantled her barriers one by one and she had been powerless to resist him.

*Fool.* She had dared to hope that this time things would be different. But for Jace it had always been about the Pangalos and revenge. Fury swept white-hot through her and she lifted her arm and hurled the phone into the pool, watching it sink to the bottom before she collapsed onto the cold marble tiles and let her tears fall.

Eventually, when she was cried out, she knew she must go to bed and try to sleep for the baby's sake. But in the bathroom she discovered that there was no baby after all. The dull ache low in her stomach had intensified to a painful cramping and she was bleeding. An Internet search on her laptop revealed that early miscarriages were fairly common, and there was no need for her to call a doctor unless she bled heavily.

Eleanor felt bereft. It was no good telling herself that it was probably for the best. A baby would have been a link with Jace. She felt as if she were on an emotional rollercoaster. Jace's second betrayal was even more devastating than the first time he'd tried to trick her out of the Pangalos. The positive pregnancy test had been a shock. But now there was no baby and she had nothing.

Jace's business trip to Perth had been frenetic, and the long flight home had seemed endless. But he felt energised by the prospect of a shower, a stiff whisky and Eleanor beneath him. He reversed the order in his mind and smiled to himself as the helicopter prepared to land in the grounds of the villa.

He'd managed to cram a week's worth of meetings into six days so that he could catch an earlier flight back to Greece. The trip had been successful, and he'd finalised a number of deals that would ensure Zagorakis Estates' expansion into Australasia. But his mind was not on business as he pictured Eleanor's delight when he arrived home unexpectedly.

She never held anything back in her response to him, and his body tightened as he imagined kissing her soft mouth and cradling her gorgeous, pert breasts in his hands. Sometimes he wondered if he would ever have enough of her delectable body. But it wasn't just sex that he'd missed while they had been apart, he acknowledged. In the middle of important business meetings he'd found himself remembering how Eleanor's eyes lit up when she smiled, and the tender way she stroked the back of his neck when he lay lax on top of her in those mindless moments of utter relaxation after they'd made love.

Jace had also missed Eleanor's business acumen. They had become a team running the Pangalos, and more and more he respected her quick brain and her management skills, to the point that he was considering offering her a place on the board of his property development company. She had inherited her grandfather's instinct for recognising a brilliant deal and it was easy to see why Kostas Pangalos had made Eleanor his successor.

Jace frowned, unsettled by his train of thoughts. How had he allowed his relationship with his temporary wife to develop into friendship, a partnership and a closeness that had nothing to do with sex? Guilt snaked through him as he wondered what his father would have made of his marriage to Kostas's granddaughter. The two men had been bitter enemies and Jace had grown up hating Kostas. But he did not hate Eleanor. Far from it. He raked his hand through his hair and refused to examine in depth how he felt about her. She was his wife, and right now things were good between them, so why complicate the situation?

Dusk had fallen and Jace was surprised that there were no lights on in the villa. It occurred to him that Eleanor might be working late in her office at the hotel. But when he strode down the hall and saw a thin gleam beneath the bedroom door his heart gave a jolt which mocked his belief that he was in control of his emotions.

'Hey...' His voice trailed off. The spurt of pleasure he felt when he saw Eleanor quickly turned to confusion as he watched her walk from the wardrobe over to the bed and dump a pile of clothes into a suitcase.

She froze at the sound of his voice and gave him a startled glance before she turned her back on him. At the end of their honeymoon in Africa he had been amused watching her pack with military preciseness, but now she threw shoes and clothes randomly into the case.

'What do you think you're doing?' Jace asked her softly. He was aware of his heart beating painfully hard, and he felt the same sense of dread that he remembered feeling when he'd clambered down the cliff, following a trail of blood, and had seen his father's body lying in a twisted heap on the ground below.

'I'm leaving you.' Eleanor did not look at him, but Jace noticed that her hands shook as she rolled a silk blouse into a ball and shoved it into the suitcase. With an effort he dampened down his temper, sensing that her emotions were balanced on a knife-edge.

'Care to tell me why?'

'*Well, I wonder, Jace.*' She whirled round to face him, all semblance of cool gone, her eyes darkening from hazel to the sullen green of a stormy sea. 'Perhaps it has something to do with this.'

She snatched up a piece of paper from the bed and held it out to him. He took it from her, and his brows snapped together when he skimmed his eyes down the page. 'How did you get this?'

'It was tucked away amongst the paperwork you sent your lawyer to get me to sign. Don't fake innocence,' she hissed when he shook his head. 'You are a lying, cheating bastard.' Her voice shook. 'Unluckily for you, Pappoús taught me never to trust anyone, even lawyers—especially lawyers.'

'Funny that, when it was Kostas's own corrupt lawyers who paved the way for him to cheat my father out of his rightful share of the Pangalos.' Jace exhaled heavily, remorse tugging on his conscience when Eleanor paled. 'I did not instruct Vangelis to ask you to sign this document.'

She gave him a disbelieving look. 'It wasn't Vangelis who came to see me. It was a younger man, Orestis… I've forgotten his other name.'

'Barkas. He recently joined my legal team, but after a mistake like this he can start looking for another job.'

'Don't shoot the messenger,' she said wryly. 'Whether or not the junior lawyer was meant to show me the document, the fact is that it exists, and you must have had it drawn up so that you could seize total ownership of the Pangalos.'

Eleanor shook her head. 'I was such a fool to trust you for a second time. You keep telling me how terribly my grandfather behaved towards your father, but look in the mirror, Jace. You are no better than Kostas.'

His jaw clenched. But Jace could not refute Eleanor's accusation. 'I admit that immediately after you agreed to marry me in return for my promise to clear your brother's debts, I asked my lawyer to set out terms of our divorce which would give me one hundred per cent of the Pangalos. But by the time of the wedding I had got to know you better, and I instructed Vangelis to write a different prenuptial agreement giving both of us fifty per cent. That was what you signed before we married, and this—' he threw the document onto the bed '—should have been destroyed.'

Jace took a step towards her and cursed beneath his breath when she shrank away from him. '*Pouláki mou,*

I am telling you the truth. I swear I did not attempt to cheat you out of your share of the Pangalos.'

She turned away from him and shoved more clothes into the suitcase. 'It doesn't matter. I don't care,' she said dully. 'This morning I did a pregnancy test. I'd been feeling weird for a while, and my period was late. The test was positive.'

There was a buzzing sound in Jace's ears. He heard Eleanor speak but the words that came out of her mouth did not make any sense. His shock rapidly turned to comprehension. No wonder she was behaving oddly, and her body was so tense that she looked as if she might snap. A million thoughts zoomed around in his head, but the question of how it had happened after she'd assured him that she was protected against pregnancy was not important.

'I told you on our wedding day that if you became pregnant our marriage would no longer be a temporary arrangement,' he said. 'A child needs and deserves to grow up with both its parents if possible.' Something fiercely possessive swept through Jace when he stared at his beautiful wife, and the mother of his child.

'Are you saying you would want to stay married to me if I had your baby?' Eleanor was clearly shocked. But the more Jace thought about it, the more he found himself liking the idea of making their relationship permanent.

'Absolutely. Divorce is now out of the question.'

'There isn't a baby,' she burst out. 'After the lawyer's visit I discovered that I was bleeding, and I'd miscarried.'

*'Theé mou!'* The tightness in Jace's chest felt as though his lungs were being crushed. 'Did it happen because you were upset after reading the original pre-nuptial agreement?'

'No, I don't believe so.' She released a shaky breath. 'I'd had backache all morning and if I hadn't done the pregnancy test I would just have assumed that my period had started late.'

Jace raked his fingers through his hair. His logical brain told him he should feel relieved that Eleanor was not pregnant, but he was thrown off-guard by her latest revelation. Why had he been so eager to seize the excuse of a baby to alter the terms of their marriage? Was it because he *wanted* to remain married to Eleanor?

Rocked by this astounding thought, he stared at her lovely face and felt his heart contract when he saw tears in her eyes. He wanted to take her in his arms and hold her, comfort her, but he instinctively knew she did not want that from him. The damning document that he'd forgotten about these past months had driven a chasm between them and he did not know how to bridge it.

'How do you feel about...?' He balked at saying *the failed pregnancy* or *the baby*, when there was no baby, and settled for, 'The situation?'

'I didn't believe I could be pregnant. The test result was a big shock,' she said in a choked voice. 'I hadn't got my head around the idea of having a baby, but then I wasn't.'

Jace watched her close the zip on the suitcase. She lifted the case off the bed, and he put his hand on her arm. 'I realise that you are upset,' he said carefully. 'But don't be too hasty to dismiss what we have, *matia mou*.'

She shook her head so that her dark blonde hair swirled around her shoulders in a fragrant cloud and Jace's body clenched.

'We don't have anything. Sure, the sex is great—' she stalled him before he could argue '—but it's not enough for me. My very brief pregnancy made me realise that I was wrong to marry you. I was desperate to save my brother from prison, but the truth is that Mark has to seek professional help for his gambling addiction, and save himself. I love him, but I'm not responsible for him.'

Jace was startled by Eleanor's serious tone and dropped his hand, allowing her to move away from him. 'You said that our marriage is not enough for you, so what do you want?' he asked gruffly.

'Love.' She met his frown with a rueful smile. 'The one thing you will never feel for me because I am Kostas Pangalos's granddaughter. But I deserve to be loved for *me*,' she said with fierce pride. 'Not held to account for a feud that happened when I was a child. I want to fall in love with a man who truly loves me. I want to stand in a church with him and proclaim our love in front of family and friends. And one day I hope that a positive result on a pregnancy test will fill me with joy rather than dread.'

'You're upset about losing the baby?'

She nodded. 'But it wouldn't have worked, both of us stuck in an unhappy marriage for the sake of our child.'

Jace watched her walk across the room and felt sick in the pit of his stomach when he realised that she actually meant it, and she was leaving him. Did she think he would chase after her, or beg her not to go? His jaw hardened. He did not need her. He had never needed any woman.

'Where will you go?' he demanded. Call her bluff, he thought grimly, and see how quickly she backtracked.

'I've arranged to stay at an apartment in Thessaloniki. It's near to the hospice so that I can go with you to visit your mother. I suggest we don't tell her that we have broken up. She was so happy at the wedding and there is no need to upset her for the time she has left.'

'Clearly you have thought this out,' he drawled, glad of the white heat of his temper. But inside he felt icy-cold. 'What about your responsibilities managing the hotel?'

'I've asked the deputy manager to stand in for me. Ultimately, I expect you will want to appoint a manager to work alongside you, as…as we used to do' Her voice shook, but she quickly recovered. She halted next to the dressing table and took a pen out of her handbag, scrawled something on a piece of paper and held it out to him.

Jace took it and his heart crashed into his ribs as he stared at Eleanor's signature on the original prenuptial agreement which gave him one hundred per cent ownership of the Pangalos. 'What are you doing?'

'I'm giving you the only thing you really want.' Her sad smile wrecked him. 'You've won, Jace.'

# CHAPTER TEN

'*TI KANEIS,* MAMÁ?' Jace murmured as he leaned over the bed and kissed his mother's cheek. Every day he asked her how she was, but every day she looked thinner and frailer and his eyes told him that her life was fading.

Iliana's eyes fluttered open and she smiled. 'I wasn't expecting you. Eleanor said that you were working late.'

'I came here straight from the office.' He did not admit that he put off returning to his empty house until as late as possible every evening. He had left the villa at the Pangalos resort the day after Eleanor had called time on their marriage. In Thessaloniki he was closer to the hospice where his mother was being cared for by the excellent staff.

On previous days Eleanor had met him in the hospice's car park, and they had visited his mother together. Somehow, they had put on a show of being lovestruck newlyweds, but he'd felt Eleanor's fingers tremble when he held her hand like lovers did, and when she had leaned close to him and rested her head on his shoulder he'd been unable to control his pounding heart.

Jace had assured himself that if he gave her space she would see sense and want to resume their marriage. He'd had several erotic fantasies in which Eleanor tried to persuade him to take her back. Invariably this had involved her taking her clothes off and begging him to make love to her, and of course he had relented and taken her to bed because sex with her was the best he'd ever had.

He bent his head towards his mother to catch what she was saying. 'You just missed your wife. She told me she was going home to cook your favourite dinner.'

Jace appreciated Eleanor's tactful lie. Memories swamped his mind of when they had prepared evening meals together at the villa on Sithonia. His culinary skills stopped at omelettes, but Eleanor enjoyed cooking and she had pottered about the kitchen, stirring ingredients in various saucepans, or stepped into the garden to pick fresh herbs for a salad dressing while he sat on a stool, drinking a glass of good red wine and slicing up tomatoes or zucchini when required.

And they had talked—about issues at the hotel, ideas for his property development business, a film they'd watched the previous night. He missed the easy companionship they'd shared. Hell, he missed *her*.

'Eleanor is a lovely girl with a kind heart,' his mother murmured. 'Kostas's granddaughter does not take after him.'

Jace stiffened. His mother's voice was weak, and he wondered if he had heard her correctly. 'How did you find out?'

She gave him a gentle smile. 'I recognised her on that first evening when you brought her to the house during the storm. There was a photograph of Kostas's family in the newspaper when he died. I believe it was a surprise that he had put Eleanor in charge of his hotel business.'

Jace let out his breath slowly. 'I didn't tell you who Eleanor was because I thought you might be upset that

I had married the granddaughter of the man responsible for my father's death.'

'Eleanor cannot be held responsible for Kostas's actions.' Iliana closed her eyes and Jace thought she had fallen asleep, but then she said softly, 'I have been thinking about what happened to Dimitri.'

'Don't upset yourself,' Jace urged. 'Nothing can change the past.'

'But my perception of events has changed. Your father loved me, and he adored you. We tried for many years to have a child, and when you were born Dimitri wept tears of joy as he held his son in his arms.'

Iliana's eyes flew open and she said in a stronger voice, 'Your father would not have chosen to leave you, Jace. It is true that he was devastated when his best friend betrayed him. For a long time I blamed Kostas. But I believe in my heart that Dimitri fell to his death by accident. His eyesight was poor, and many times I warned him against walking on the clifftop.'

Jace felt a lump in his throat when he saw a tear trickle down his mother's sallow cheek. She held out her bony hand and he carefully clasped her fingers. Her breathing was shallow. Her gaze held his, and her tender smile was weary. 'Your father loved you,' she whispered. 'Dimitri was the love of my life and he would be as glad as I am that you have found your for ever love with Eleanor.'

'Thank you for coming,' Jace said brusquely to Eleanor when the last of the mourners who had attended his mother's funeral departed. He had organised a small gathering of close friends at the house after the service to commemorate Iliana's life. It had struck him that he was the last Zagorakis. Neither he nor his parents had

had siblings, and the only distant relative of his father
had died a few months ago.

'I was glad to come,' she said quietly. 'I was fond of
your mother.' She hesitated. 'It's a sad day and I didn't
want you to go through it alone.' She turned away from
him, murmuring that she had left her jacket in the orangery.

Jace watched her walk away from him and his jaw
clenched. *Alone.* The truth was that he could be in a
roomful of friends and feel alone. A yawning chasm
had opened up inside him in the two weeks since he'd
stood by and allowed Eleanor to walk out of the villa.
He told himself that he could not have prevented her
from leaving. He couldn't give her the fairy tale she
longed for. But the idea that she might be looking for
love, and maybe she'd already met Mr Right, kept Jace
awake at night. He had put his inability to sleep, eat or
function in any meaningful way down to grief for his
mother. Or it could simply be sexual frustration, he
thought with grim self-derision.

Today was the first time he had seen Eleanor since
his mother had died peacefully in her sleep a week ago.
She looked elegant and stunningly beautiful in a silk
shift dress that couldn't make up its mind if it were
green or hazel—the same as her eyes. In front of the
guests they had continued with the pretence of being
happily married. Except that it hadn't been pretence,
Jace brooded. He had felt the happiest he had ever been
when Eleanor had shared his life. And he was fairly
sure that she had been happy too. Why hadn't it been
enough for her? Why did women always want more?

Why was he running away from the best thing that
had ever happened to him? Jace's heart slammed into
his ribs as he was finally honest with himself. Eleanor

had signed the Pangalos over to him, and before he had met her last year he would have sworn that the hotel was everything he desired. But he could not laugh with a hotel, or talk to a hotel. He had been driven to claim the Pangalos by a desire for vengeance. Now all he cared about was claiming the only person who understood him—his wife.

She must be out of her mind, Eleanor thought as she stepped into the master bedroom. What she was doing defied common sense, but her heart ached as she remembered Jace's sombre expression when his mother's coffin had been lowered into the grave. He was hurting. Oh, he hid it well, and at the reception after the funeral he had been his urbane and charming self. But she knew it had been an act. Jace Zagorakis, self-made multimillionaire with a playboy reputation and more friends than there were stars in the sky, had looked utterly alone.

No doubt he would say it was how he liked to live his life. A lone wolf without emotional commitments, without emotions. But Eleanor was not fooled. He had loved his parents, who were now both dead. He cared deeply for his close friend Takis, who had been at the funeral, looking grimmer and more unsmiling than ever.

Jace had the capacity to love and it broke her heart that he would never love her. But he needed her tonight. Her fingers shook as she ran the zip on her dress down and the silk shift slithered to the floor. After a second's hesitation, she unclipped her bra, tugged off her knickers and slipped beneath the sheets. The shutters at the window were open, and the moonlight cast a pearly glow into the room and over the bed.

The bedroom door swung open and she heard Jace expel a ragged breath. He lounged in the doorway, as

tall as a giant, his muscular body silhouetted against
the light in the hallway.

'Well, well…' he drawled.

'I don't want to talk,' she said fiercely.

He gave a rough laugh as he walked into the room
and closed the door behind him. 'Talking is not at the
top of my list either.' His hand moved to his belt as he
approached the bed. Eleanor's gaze locked with his, and
the chemistry that had always simmered between them
blazed. She shifted position so that she was kneeling on
the mattress and slowly lowered the sheet.

The air felt cool on her naked breasts and her nipples
hardened and jutted provocatively forwards. Jace made
a low growl when she cupped her breasts in her palms
before skimming her hands lower to the vee of tight
curls at the junction of her thighs. It was empowering to
play the temptress, and the feral gleam in his eyes as he
halted next to the bed evoked a flood of sticky warmth
between her legs. With a sultry smile, she slid her finger into her feminine heat and saw his eyes darken as
he watched her pleasure herself.

'Witch,' he said thickly. 'Are you sure…?'

'I said no talking.' He would never say the words
she longed to hear, and she could not tell him how she
felt about him. But tonight she would show him with
her body the secret she held in her heart. Tonight she
would make sure that he never forgot her.

She undid the buttons on his shirt and pushed it off
his shoulders, running her hands over his bunched bi-
ceps before moving to his chest and exploring the defined ridges of his muscular physique. His skin was
warm satin beneath her fingertips, the whorls of black
chest hair slightly abrasive against her palms. She followed the arrowing of hair down to the waistband of

his trousers and unzipped him, deliberately brushing her hand over the bulge of his arousal.

He bent his head and pressed his mouth to her neck, trailed hot kisses along her collarbone and moved down to her breasts, laving each pebble-hard nipple in turn until she trembled with need. Eleanor cupped her hands around his face and dragged his mouth up to hers. The kiss exploded between them, wild yet sweet, a sensual feast as their tongues tangled.

Jace stripped off the rest of his clothes and she pulled him down on top of her, spreading her legs so that his hard shaft pressed against her opening.

'I want you now. I can't wait,' she told him urgently. He made a harsh sound in his throat and lowered himself onto her, easing his erection deep inside her. It was bliss after two weeks without him and Eleanor moaned softly when he drew back and thrust slowly into her again, filling her, completing her. She speared her fingers into his hair and pressed her face against his throat, licking the slight saltiness of his skin before she nipped him with her teeth.

His primal groan of desire sent a shiver of feminine triumph through her. She pushed him off her, and when he rolled onto his back she straddled him and took his thick length inside her.

'You are incredible, *omorfiá mou,*' he rasped as she rolled her hips to meet his powerful thrusts and the rhythm became faster, harder until they soared together to a place of exquisite pleasure that was uniquely theirs.

For a long time afterwards, Eleanor did not move while she stored every detail, every sensation of Jace's lovemaking in her mind. The steady rise and fall of his chest told her that he had fallen asleep. Moonlight highlighted the sharp edges of his cheekbones and the sensual curve of his mouth. His eyelashes made dark crescents on his skin. In sleep he looked younger and she glimpsed the boy beneath the man.

'Goodbye,' she whispered against his lips. 'I will always love you.'

Jace woke to the pale light of dawn and for a moment he wondered if he had dreamed, as he so often did, of Eleanor. The languorous ache in his muscles told him that she had been real and not a figment of his imagination. She had seduced him and made love to him with an unguarded passion and he felt disappointed, but not surprised, that she had gone.

He reached for his phone and called the security team he'd tasked to ensure her safety. Not because he wanted to stifle her independence, but for his peace of mind, needing to know that no harm would come to her. After a brief conversation he ascertained that Eleanor had arrived back at her apartment late the previous night, and she had left again in her car half an hour ago. Jace had a good idea where she was heading, and he strode into the bathroom to shower, determined that he would not let her go again.

Unless she wanted her freedom. He felt the sensation of a lead weight dropping into the pit of his stomach, knowing that he had no right to keep her in a marriage that he'd insisted on for all the wrong reasons. Guilt cramped in his gut. And something else. Fear. What if he was too late to finally recognise the true reason why he had wanted Eleanor to be his wife?

He stared at his face in the mirror and grimaced as he ran his hand over the stubble on his jaw. His eyes looking back at him were dull, their bleak expression reflecting how he felt when he imagined a future without Eleanor. It would be nothing more than he deserved, he acknowledged. But he was hanging onto hope. It was all he had. A whispered promise against his lips that he might have dreamt, but perhaps had been real. There was only one way to find out.

The sliding glass doors in the bedroom at the villa on the Pangalos resort were open. The view of the turquoise pool and the sea beyond it was spectacular, but Jace's gaze was fixed on Eleanor. She was sitting at the top of the pool's stone steps and had her back to him.

He felt a tug in his chest as he paused and drank in the sight of her in a skimpy bikini, remembering how she used to cover up her body because she'd felt self-conscious about her scoliosis scar. When he walked noiselessly across the terrace he noticed a new mark on her back, close to her scar, and saw that it was a delicately inscribed tattoo. Just one word: *Warrior*.

She heard his footsteps and jerked her head in his direction, a wealth of emotion in her eyes before her lashes swept down, and Jace sensed that she was hastily erecting her defences.

'Did you know I would be here?'

'Of course I knew. I know everything about you, *matia mou*,' Jace said softly. 'You have no secrets from me.'

A blush spread over her face and she looked away from him. 'Why did you come after me?'

'Did you imagine I wouldn't, after what we shared last night?'

'We had sex.'

He was tempted to argue that it had been so much more, but he let it go for now. 'I like this,' he murmured, tracing his finger over her tattoo.

She gave a faint sigh. 'You taught me to be unafraid and to accept myself.'

His heart contracted. 'You were a warrior long before we met,' he said gruffly. 'Will you come inside? There are things we need to discuss.'

'Like what? I won't contest the divorce, and I've given you the Pangalos. What else is there to talk about?'

'Please.'

'Fine,' she muttered, ignoring his hand that he held out to help her to her feet. She jumped up and marched into the villa through the French windows that led into the sitting room. Arms folded defensively in front of her chest, she stared at him mutinously. 'Well?'

Eleanor wished that Jace would stop staring at her with an intent expression in his eyes that made her foolish heart tremble. Why didn't he just give her the divorce paperwork to sign, which was the reason she assumed he was here? She had managed to hold herself together driving from Thessaloniki to Sithonia, but tears were perilously near the surface.

She hadn't expected to see him again after she'd left him asleep last night, and this was pure torture. Typically, he looked amazing in faded jeans and a cream shirt with the sleeves rolled up to his elbows, revealing his tanned forearms thickly covered with black hair. Arms that would never hold her again.

He moved to the coffee table and took some papers out of his briefcase.

'Give me a pen and I'll sign the divorce application,' she said curtly. But when she skimmed her eyes over the documents she discovered that they were the two versions of the prenuptial agreement, one of which she had signed before she'd married Jace. The other was the original agreement that she had been unaware of until she'd signed it two weeks ago and forfeited her share of the hotel.

Jace took both documents from her and ripped them into tiny pieces, which fluttered to the floor in a mockery of the confetti that had been thrown at their wedding.

'I don't understand,' she said shakily.

'I hope this will explain.' He handed her another document and Eleanor caught her breath when she read it.

'Is this a joke? It says that you rescind all rights to the Pangalos Beach Resort, and I have sole ownership.'

He nodded. 'To make things absolutely clear, I have suggested calling the hotel by a new name.'

*'Eleanor's Hotel.'* She read the new name out. 'But… you married me for the hotel. My grandfather cheated your father out of his share.' Eleanor bit her lip. 'I don't want a hotel that is tainted by so much bitterness.' She thrust the new document at Jace. 'Keep it. I know how much the Pangalos means to you.'

'It means nothing to me,' he said savagely. 'There is only one thing—one person I care about.' Raw emotion thickened his voice. 'And that is you, *pouláki mou.*'

'Don't.' It was too cruel to offer her a dream when she was certain he would tear it down again.

He gave a wry smile. 'Are you asking me not to call you my little bird, or not to care about you?'

She shook her head, determined not to drown in his liquid gaze. 'Don't tell me any more lies. That's all I ask.'

'That's it, though. You have never asked for anything. Even the money you needed from me was to help your brother. I took advantage of your generous heart,' Jace said seriously, no smile on his lips now and an expression of uncertainty in his eyes that shook Eleanor. Jace Zagorakis—*uncertain*. It wasn't possible; he was the most self-assured man she had ever met. But a nerve flickered in his jaw and his tension was tangible when he picked up a box from the table and gave it to her. 'Open it.'

Mystified, she opened the lid and lifted out a little wooden carving of a sparrow. It was exquisite, and had been carved with such detail that each individual feather was perfect. 'Oh! How beautiful!' she murmured.

'Yes.' Jace was looking at her, not the carving, and Eleanor's heart missed a beat. 'Do you remember in Africa, we visited the Maasai tribe and one of the elders had carved various animals and birds? I asked him to make the carving. The elder said that the little sparrow does not seek attention like many of its colourful cousins, but a wise man knows that it is the bravest and most beautiful of all the birds.'

Jace's mouth twisted. 'I am not wise; I'm a fool. I ignored what my heart was telling me since before we went to Paris.'

She stiffened and placed the carving on the table. 'I was the fool to believe that you felt the same way about me as I did for you. In my defence, you were a very convincing fiancé and I was totally taken in by you. But in the back of my mind I wondered why you never mentioned love.' She shrugged. 'It became clear when I overheard your phone call with Takis, telling him that you were not in love with me.'

'That's what I told myself.' Jace raked his hand through his hair and took a jerky step towards her. 'I've never told you that I found my father at the bottom of the cliff. His injuries were horrific, but he was still alive—just.'

'Jace, don't,' Eleanor pleaded. The pain he clearly felt as he relived the terrible memory tore at her heart.

He closed his eyes briefly. 'I need to explain why I treated you so badly. My father made me promise that I would take care of my mother and reclaim the hotel for her. I was fifteen and I swore as I held my father's broken body that I would take vengeance on Kostas Pangalos.'

'Jace…' she pressed her knuckles against her mouth to hold back a sob '…it's over. The Pangalos is yours.'

'I don't want it.' He cupped her cheek in his hand, a hand that was as unsteady as the erratic thud of Eleanor's pulse. 'I want you to be my wife till death do us part, as we promised each other when we married.'

She stared at him, unable to believe what she was hearing. He stared back at her and she was afraid to trust what his night-dark eyes seemed to be telling her.

'*Why*, Jace? We made your mother happy before she died, and you have honoured the promise you made to your father. There is no reason for us to stay married.'

'There's this,' he said raggedly before he pulled her into his arms and lowered his head, claiming her mouth in a devastating kiss that sent her defences tumbling. He kissed her with fierce passion and such aching tenderness that she could not resist him. She felt the thunder of his heart when she laid her hand on his chest. Gone was the coolly controlled Jace who, even in the wildest moments of passion, had kept something back from her.

Now he kissed her as if he were a starving man and she was a feast. His big body shook as he crushed her to him, and his lips moved from her mouth, over her cheeks, the tip of her nose and claimed her lips again with a desperation that made her tremble.

At last he lifted his head and her breath snagged in

her throat when she saw that his eyelashes were wet.
'I love you.'

Eleanor swallowed. 'Before...' she meant when he
had courted her in England '... I would have given the
earth to hear you say those words to me.'

'Does that mean you no longer want me to tell you
that my heart is yours for as long as I live?' he said
tautly.

'Only say it if it's true.'

His throat worked. 'I deserve your mistrust, but
please believe me, *agapi mou*. I love you more than I
knew it was possible to love. I fell in love with you that
first week we spent together on the boat cruising around
the islands. It's true,' he said deeply when she looked
doubtful. 'But I couldn't admit how I felt. It seemed like
a betrayal of the promise I had made to my father if I
fell in love with Kostas's granddaughter.'

'That's just it,' Eleanor choked. 'I can't change who I
am, and the bitterness you feel for my grandfather will
always come between us.'

Jace brought his other hand up to cradle her cheek.
'I don't want to change anything about you, my angel.
I love you because you are *you*. Beautiful and courageous, and with a depth of compassion that humbles
me.'

He sighed. 'I used guilt as an excuse not to tell you
how I felt about you. The truth is that I was devastated
when my father died, and I saw that my mother was
heartbroken. I never wanted to fall in love and risk the
pain of loss.'

He smoothed her hair back from her face. 'Prison
was hell, and soon after I was released I met Katerina
and fell hard for her. When she made it clear that I
wasn't good enough for her, I resolved never to put my

heart on the line again. But then I met you, and you fell in love with me. You gave your love freely and bravely, even though you had suffered loss when your parents died. But I was a coward, and scared to admit to myself that I loved you beyond reason.'

Jace hesitated. 'Did I dream that last night you made love to me with love in your heart?'

Slowly she shook her head, trying to summon the courage to take a leap of faith. 'You didn't dream it.'

His gentle smile stole her breath. 'It was *never* just sex. Every time we made love, I told you with my body what my stubborn brain refused to accept. You are my world, Eleanor, and I have discovered these past weeks that the world is a dark and lonely place without you.'

He stared at her with eyes that were suddenly bleak when she did not respond. 'Will you give me another chance, *pouláki mou*, and allow me to try to win your love again? I swear I will prove that I truly love you with all my heart and soul, with everything that I am. Yours for eternity.'

Finally, Eleanor believed him, and happiness exploded inside her. 'I never stopped loving you,' she said softly. 'Even when I told myself that I hated you, I was hopelessly in love with you. Why else do you think I agreed to a marriage of convenience? It was my chance to try and win your love. But when I thought you had betrayed me again it felt that all hope had gone, especially as I had lost the baby who would have been a link between us.'

Jace groaned. 'I'm sorry I hurt you.'

She pressed her finger against his lips. 'Let's make a pact to leave the past behind and look to the future.'

He drew her close, and she curled her arms around his neck and laid her head on his chest, entranced by the urgent thud of his heart that echoed her own. For timeless moments they simply stood there, wrapped in each other's arms while love enfolded them. And then Jace kissed her, and it felt new and wonderful because now Eleanor knew there was love in his tender caresses. He claimed her lips with sensual passion and the fire that was always between them blazed.

'*Se agapó, kardiá mou,*' he said thickly as he carried her into the bedroom and tumbled them down on the bed. Her bikini, his clothes, were hurriedly removed, and their naked limbs entwined. 'You do realise that I plan to spend the foreseeable future making love to you?' Jace murmured as he positioned himself over her.

Eleanor gave him a joyous smile. 'I can't wait for our future together to begin.'

'It begins now, my love.'

# EPILOGUE

THE HOT-AIR BALLOON rose gently into the blue sky. Below was the breathtaking scenery of the Meteora, a landscape dotted with huge monoliths and towering rock formations, on top of which several Greek monasteries clung perilously. The distant mountains were capped with snow that glinted in the golden sunrise.

Eleanor shut off the burner and turned to Jace. 'Isn't this amazing? I'm glad you came. You seem more relaxed in the balloon now.'

He grinned. 'I trust my pilot.'

She thought her heart might burst with happiness. 'I trust my co-pilot,' she said softly.

'I will never give you cause to doubt me.' He moved closer to her in the balloon basket and dropped down onto one knee. Eleanor's eyes widened when Jace took a square box out of his pocket and opened it. Inside was an exquisite engagement ring: a light blue sapphire surrounded by small diamonds that sparkled as brightly as the snow on the mountains. The delicate beauty of the ring brought a lump to her throat.

'You already gave me an engagement ring,' she murmured, feeling guilty that she was not wearing the huge diamond solitaire.

'I thought you would be impressed if I gave you a

flashy, expensive ring, but I should have known that you do not value something by how much it cost. This suits you much better,' Jace said as he slid the pretty ring onto her finger, next to her wedding band. The sapphire was the clear blue of the sky.

'The ring is perfect, thank you.' Eleanor hesitated. 'Would you mind if I donated the diamond solitaire to the Scoliosis Support charity? They are holding an auction to raise money which will be used to give children with scoliosis some fun experiences, like I had when I was introduced to ballooning.'

Jace stood up and kissed the tip of her nose. 'I think it's a great idea. And, speaking of ideas, what do you think of having a ceremony to renew our wedding vows? I want to stand with you in front of family and friends and proclaim our love for each other.' He smiled, seeing that she remembered what she had said to him before she'd walked out of their marriage.

She nodded eagerly. 'I'm sure my brother would come, and bring his new fiancée. It will be lovely to meet Joanne. Mark seems to have put his problems behind him now that he's busy working with the horses on her family's stud farm in Ireland.' With a faint frown, she said, 'I might also get a chance to find out what's wrong with my sister. Lissa has seemed unhappy lately. When I told her that I've arranged with the bank for her to have full access to her trust fund, she burst into tears. Will you invite Takis?'

Jace nodded. 'I have already mentioned to him that we might want to hold the ceremony and reception at Eleanor's Hotel.'

'I think I would prefer to have it somewhere else. Even though the hotel's name has changed, I'll always think of it as the Pangalos, with its history of the feud between our families. I'm glad we sold the hotel to Takis. It's a fresh start for us.'

'You haven't told me yet if you are going to accept a position at Zagorakis Estates. We work well together.'

Eleanor took a deep breath. 'I would like to work alongside you in the future. I think we should renew our vows soon, while I can still fit into my wedding dress.' She gave Jace a tremulous smile. 'I've been feeling a bit nauseous recently. I didn't mention it because I didn't want you to worry,' she said quickly when he frowned. 'Anyway, the doctor sent me for an ultrasound scan, and… I'm still pregnant.'

Jace stared at her. '*Still* pregnant?'

'The doctor said it's likely that I conceived twins three months ago, and miscarried one of them. But the other baby is absolutely fine. I…we…are expecting a little girl.'

'*Theos!*' Jace looked stunned.

'You are pleased, aren't you?'

The expression of pride and pleasure in his eyes convinced her. 'My angel. How could you doubt it? Of course I'm pleased. I'm over the moon,' Jace assured her huskily. 'I'm the luckiest man in the world.'

Five and a half months later Eleanor gave birth to a healthy daughter. Jace was with her throughout her labour and his eyes glistened when he cradled the infant in his arms.

He sat on the edge of the hospital bed and kissed Eleanor tenderly. 'I love you. And I love our baby girl. Now we are a family.'

She gave him a tired but joyful smile. 'I love you too. Family sounds nice. But our baby needs a name.'

'Your middle name is Rose, and my mother's middle name was Acacia. What do you think of calling her Acacia Rose?'

'I think it's perfect.'

Jace looked down at the baby's tiny face, peeping out from the shawl she was swaddled in. He marvelled at her exquisite features. 'Our daughter is as beautiful as her mother,' he said softly. His heart was full. Love, family and a future that looked shining bright. 'Everything is perfect.'

\* \* \* \* \*

# MILLS & BOON

## Coming next month

### CINDERELLA'S NIGHT IN VENICE
Clare Connelly

As the car slowed to go over a speed hump, his fingers briefly fell to her shoulder. An accident of transit, nothing intentional about it. The reason didn't matter though; the spark of electricity was the same regardless. She gasped and quickly turned her face away, looking beyond the window.

It was then that she realized they had driven through the gates of City Airport.

Bea turned back to face Ares, a question in her eyes.

'There's a ball at the airport?'

'No.'

'Then why…?' Comprehension was a blinding light. 'We're flying somewhere.'

'To the ball.'

'But…you didn't say…'

'I thought you were good at reading between the lines?'

She pouted her lips. 'Yes, you're right.' She clicked her fingers in the air. 'I should have miraculously intuited that when you invited me to a ball you meant for us to fly there. Where, exactly?'

'Venice.'

'Venice?' She stared at him, aghast. 'I don't have a passport.'

'I had your assistant arrange it.'

'You—what? When?'

'When I left this morning.'

'My assistant just handed over my passport?'

'You have a problem with that?'

'Well, gee, let me think about that a moment,' she said, tapping a finger to the side of her lip. 'You're a man I'd never clapped eyes on until yesterday and now you have in your possession a document that's of reasonably significant personal importance. You could say I find that a little invasive, yes.'

He dropped his hand from the back of the seat, inadvertently brushing her arm as he moved, lifting a familiar burgundy document from his pocket. 'Now you have it in your possession. It was no conspiracy to kidnap you, Beatrice, simply a means to an end.'

Clutching the passport in her hand, she stared down at it. No longer bothered by the fact he'd managed to convince her assistant to commandeer a document of such personal importance from her top drawer, she was knocked off-kilter by his use of her full name. Nobody called her Beatrice any more. She'd been Bea for as long as she could remember. But her full name on his lips momentarily shoved the air from her lungs.

'Why didn't you just tell me?'

He lifted his shoulders. 'I thought you might say no.'

It was an important clue as to how he operated. This was a man who would do what he needed to achieve whatever he wanted. He'd chosen to invite her to this event, and so he'd done what he deemed necessary to have her there.

'Your business is too important to our company, remember?' She was grateful for the opportunity to remind them both of the reason she'd agreed to this. It had nothing to do with the fact she found him attractive, and everything to do with how much she loved her friends and wanted the company to continue to succeed.

'And that's the only reason you agreed to this,' he said in a deep voice, perfectly calling her bluff. Was she that obvious? Undoubtedly.

*Continue reading*
**CINDERELLA'S NIGHT IN VENICE**
Clare Connelly

*Available next month*
www.millsandboon.co.uk

# COMING SOON!

We really hope you enjoyed reading this book.
If you're looking for more romance, be sure to
head to the shops when new books are
available on

## Thursday 15th April

To see which titles are coming soon, please visit
**millsandboon.co.uk/nextmonth**

# MILLS & BOON

## THE HEART OF ROMANCE

## A ROMANCE FOR EVERY READER

**MODERN**

Prepare to be swept off your feet by sophisticated, sexy and seductive heroes, in some of the world's most glamourous and romantic locations, where power and passion collide.

**HISTORICAL**

Escape with historical heroes from time gone by. Whether your passion is for wicked Regency Rakes, muscled Vikings or rugged Highlanders, awaken the romance of the past.

**MEDICAL**

Set your pulse racing with dedicated, delectable doctors in the high-pressure world of medicine, where emotions run high and passion, comfort and love are the best medicine.

**True Love**

Celebrate true love with tender stories of heartfelt romance, from the rush of falling in love to the joy a new baby can bring, and a focus on the emotional heart of a relationship.

**Desire**

Indulge in secrets and scandal, intense drama and plenty of sizzling hot action with powerful and passionate heroes who have it all: wealth, status, good looks…everything but the right woman.

**HEROES**

Experience all the excitement of a gripping thriller, with an intense romance at its heart. Resourceful, true-to-life women and strong, fearless men face danger and desire - a killer combination!

To see which titles are coming soon, please visit

**millsandboon.co.uk/nextmonth**

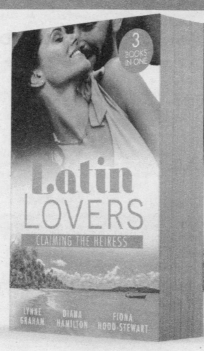

# MILLS & BOON
## *Desire*

Indulge in secrets and scandal, intense drama and plenty of sizzling hot action with powerful and passionate heroes who have it all: wealth, status, good looks... everything but the right woman.

*t might just be true love...*

# MILLS & BOON

## HEROES

*At Your Service*

Experience all the excitement of a gripping thriller, with an intense romance at its heart. Resourceful, true-to-life women and strong, fearless men face danger and desire - a killer combination!